DRAGON'S TEETH I.

In tragic times like these, an el derly
au thor has noth ing to give but words.
This col lec tion of words is ded i cated
to the men and women in many parts
of the world who are giving their
lives in the cause of free dom and hu -
man de cency.   - Upton Sinclair

Au tumn 1941

World's End	1913 - 1919
Be tween Two Worlds	1919 - 1929
Drangon's Teeth	1929 - 1934
Wide is the Gate	1934 - 1937
Presidential Agent	1937 - 1938
Dragon Harvest	1938 - 1940
A World to Win	1940 - 1942
Presidential Mission	1942 - 1943
One Clear Call	1943 - 1944
O Shep herd, Speak!	1943 - 1946
The Return of Lanny Budd	1946 - 1949

Each vol ume is pub lished in two parts: I and II.

DRAGON'S TEETH I.

Upton Sinclair

LCCN: 67058718

ISBN: 1-931313-03-2

Dis trib uted by Ingram Book Com pany

Printed by Light ning Source Inc., LaVergne, TN

Pub lished by Si mon Pub li ca tions, P.O. Box 321 Safety Har bor, FL

When I say "his to rian," I have a mean ing of my own. I por tray world events in story form, because that form is the one I have been trained in. I have sup ported my self by writ ing fic tion since the age of six teen, which means for forty-nine years.

… Now I re al ize that this one was the one job for which I had been born: to put the pe riod of world wars and rev o lu tions into a great long novel. …

I can not say when it will end, be cause I don't know ex actly what the char - acters will do. They lead a semi-independent life, being more real to me than any of the people I know, with the single exception of my wife. … Some of my char ac ters are peo ple who lived, and whom I had op por tu nity to know and watch. Oth ers are imag i nary—or rather, they are com plexes of many people whom I have known and watched. Lanny Budd and his mother and fa ther and their var i ous rel a tives and friends have come in the course of the past four years to be my daily and nightly com pan ions. I have come to know them so in ti mately that I need only to ask them what they would do in a given set of cir cum stances and they start to en act their roles. … I chose what seems to me the most re veal ing of them and of their world.

How long will this go on? I can not tell. It de pends in great part upon two pub lic fig ures, Hit ler and Mus so lini. What are they go ing to do to man kind and what is man kind will do to them? It seems to me hardly likely that ei - ther will die a peace ful death. I am hop ing to out live them; and what ever happens Lanny Budd will be some where in the neigh bor hood, he will be "in at the death," ac cord ing to the fox-hunting phrase.

These two foxes are my quarry, and I hope to hang their brushes over my mantel.

In the course of this novel a num ber of well-known per sons make their ap - pearance, some of them living, some dead; they appear under their own names, and what is said about them is fac tu ally cor rect.

There are other char ac ters which are fic ti tious, and in these cases the au thor has gone out of his way to avoid seem ing to point at real per sons. He has given them un likely names, and hopes that no per son bear ing such names ex ist. But it is im pos si ble to make sure; there fore the writer states that, if any such co in - cidence occurs, it is accidental. This is not the customary "hedge clause" which the author of a *ro man à clef* pub lishes for le gal pro tec tion; it means what it says and it is in tended to be so taken.

Various European concerns engaged in the man u fac ture of mu ni tions have been named in the story, and what has been said about them is also ac cord ing to the re cords. There is one Amer i can firm, and that, with all its af fairs, is imag i nary. The writer has done his best to avoid seem ing to in di cate any ac - tual Amer i can firm or fam ily.

...Of course there will be slips, as I know from ex pe ri ence; but *World's End* is meant to be a his tory as well as fic tion, and I am sure there are no mis takes of im por tance. I have my own point of view, but I have tried to play fair in this book. There is a var ied cast of char ac ters and they say as they think. ...

The Peace Con fer ence of Paris [*for example*], which is the scene of the last third of *World's End*, is of course one of the greatest events of all time. A friend on mine asked an au thor ity on mod ern fic tion a ques tion: "Has any - body ever used the Peace Con fer ence in a novel?" And the re ply was: "Could any body?" Well, I thought some body could, and now I think some body has. The reader will ask, and I state ex plic itly that so far as con cerns his toric char - ac ters and events my pic ture is cor rect in all de tails. This part of the manu - script, 374 pages, was read and checked by eight or ten gen tle men who were on the Amer i can staff at the Con fer ence. Sev eral of these hold im por tant po si - tions in the world of troubled international affairs; others are college presi - dents and professors, and I promised them all that their letters will be con fi den tial. Suf fice it to say that the er rors they pointed out were cor rected, and where they dis agreed, both sides have a word in the book.

Contents:

BOOK ONE

The Morning
Opes Her Golden Gates

1

The Old Beginning

I

LANNY BUDD was the only occupant of a small-sized reception-room. He was seated in a well-padded armchair, and had every reason to be comfortable, but did not appear so. He fidgeted a good deal, and found occasions for looking at his watch; then he would examine his fingernails, which needed no attention; he would look for specks of lint on his tropical worsted trousers, from which he had removed the last speck some time ago. He would look out of the window, which gave on one of the fashionable avenues of the city of Cannes; but he had already become familiar with the view, and it did not change. He had a popular novel on his knee, and every now and then would find that he could not interest himself in the conversation of a set of smart society people.

Now and then one of several white-clad nurses would pass through the room. Lanny had asked them so many questions that he was ashamed to speak again. He knew that all husbands behave irrationally at this time; he had seen a group of them in a stage play, slightly *risqué* but harmless. They all fidgeted and consulted their watches; they all got up and walked about needlessly; they all bored the nurses with futile questions. The nurses had stereotyped replies, which, except for the language, were the same all over the world. "*Oui, oui, monsieur. . . . Tout va bien. . . . Il faut laisser faire. . . . Il faut du temps. . . . C'est la nature.*"

Many times Lanny had heard that last statement in the Midi; it was a formula which excused many things. He had heard it more than once that afternoon, but it failed to satisfy him. He was in rebellion against nature and her ways. He hadn't had much suf-

3

fering in his own life, and didn't want other people to suffer; he thought that if he had been consulted he could have suggested many improvements in the ways of this fantastic universe. The business of having people grow old and pass off the scene, and new ones having to be supplied! He knew persons who had carefully trained and perfected themselves; they were beautiful to look at, or possessed knowledge and skills, yet they had to die before long—and, knowing that fact, must provide a new lot to take their places.

Lanny Budd belonged to the leisure classes. You could tell it by a single glance at his smiling unlined face, his tanned skin with signs of well-nourished blood in it, his precise little mustache, his brown hair neatly trimmed and brushed, his suit properly tailored and freshly pressed, his shirt and tie, shoes and socks, harmonizing in color and of costly materials. It had been some time since he had seen any bloodshed or experienced personal discomfort. His life had been arranged to that end, and the same was true of his wife. But now this damnable messy business, this long-drawn-out strain and suffering—good God, what were doctors and scientists for if they couldn't devise something to take the place of this! It was like a volcanic eruption in a well-ordered and peaceful community; not much better because you could foresee the event, going in advance to an immaculate *hospice de la maternité* and engaging a room at so much per week, an *accoucheur* at so much for the job.

A surgeon! A fellow with a lot of shiny steel instruments, prepared to assist nature in opening a woman up and getting a live and kicking infant out of her! It had seemed incredible to Lanny the first time he had heard about it, a youngster playing with the fisherboys of this Mediterranean coast, helping them pull strange creatures out of the sea and hearing them talk about the "facts of life." It seemed exactly as incredible to him at this moment, when he knew that it was going on in a room not far away, the victim his beautiful young playmate whom he had come to love so deeply. His too vivid imagination was occupied with the bloody details, and he would clench his hands until the knuckles were white. His protest against nature mounted to a clamor. He thought: "Any way but this! Anything that's decent and sensible!" He addressed his ancient mother, asking why she hadn't stuck to the method of the egg, which seemed to work so well with birds and snakes and lizards and fishes? But these so-called "warm-blooded creatures," that had so much blood and spilled it so easily!

II

Lanny knew that Irma didn't share these feelings. Irma was a "sensible woman," not troubled with excess of imagination. She had said many times: "Don't worry. I'll be all right. It doesn't last forever." Everybody agreed that this young Juno was made for motherhood; she had ridden horseback, swum, played tennis, and had a vigorous body. She hadn't turned pale when she crossed the threshold of this hospital, or even when she heard the cries of another woman. Things always went all right with Irma Barnes, and she had told Lanny to go home and play the piano and forget her; but here he sat, and thought about the details which he had read in an encyclopedia article entitled "Obstetrics." From boyhood he had had the habit of looking up things in that dependable work; but, damn it all, the article gave an undue proportion of space to "breech presentations" and other variations from the normal, and Lanny might just as well have been in the delivery-room. He would have liked to go there, but that would have been considered an extreme variation from the normal in this land of rigid conventions.

So he sat in the little reception-room, and now and then the perspiration would start on his forehead, even though it was a cool spring day on the Riviera. He was glad that he had the room to himself; at times, when somebody came through, he would lower his eyes to his book and pretend to be absorbed. But if it was one of the nurses, he couldn't keep from stealing a glance, hoping that it was *the* nurse and *the* moment. The woman would smile; the conventions permitted her to smile at a handsome young gentleman, but did not permit her to go into obstetrical details. "*Tout va bien, monsieur. Soyez tranquille.*" In such places the wheel of life revolves on schedule; those who tend the machinery acquire a professional attitude, their phrases become standardized, and you have mass production of politeness as well as of babies.

III

Lanny Budd was summoned to the telephone. It was Pietro Corsatti, Italian-born American who represented a New York newspaper in Rome and was having a vacation on the Riviera. He had once done Lanny a favor, and now had been promised one in return. "Pete" was to have the news the moment it happened; but it refused to happen, and maybe wasn't going to happen. "I know how you feel," said the correspondent, sympathetically. "I've been through it."

"It's been four hours!" exclaimed the outraged young husband.

"It may be four more, and it may be twenty-four. Don't take it too hard. It's happened a lot of times." The well-known cynicism of the journalist.

Lanny returned to his seat, thinking about an Italian-American with a strong Brooklyn accent who had pushed his way to an important newspaper position, and had so many funny stories to tell about the *regime fascista* and its leaders, whom, oddly enough, he called "wops." One of his best stories was about how he had become the guide, philosopher, and friend of a New York "glamour girl" who had got herself engaged to a fascinating aristocrat in Rome and had then made the discovery that he was living with the ballerina of the opera and had no idea of giving her up. The American girl had broken down and wept in Pete's presence, asking him what to do, and he had told her: "Take a plane and fly straight to Lanny Budd, and ask him to marry you in spite of the fact that you are too rich!"

It is tough luck when a journalist cannot publish his best story. Pete hadn't been asked not to, but, all the same, he hadn't, so now Lanny was his friend for life, and would go out of his way to give him a break whenever he could. They talked as pals, and Lanny didn't mind telling what only a few of his friends knew, that Irma had done exactly what Pete had said, and she and Lanny had been married on the day she had found him in London. As the Brooklyn dialect had it, they had "gone right to it," and here was the result nine months later: Lanny sitting in a reception-room of an *hospice de la maternité*, awaiting the arrival of Sir Stork, the blessed event, the little bundle from heaven—he knew the phrases, because he and Irma had been in New York and had read the "tabs" and listened to "radio reporters" shooting out gossip and slang with the rapid-fire effect of a Budd machine gun.

Lanny had promised Pete a scoop; something not so difficult, because French newspapermen were not particularly active in the pursuit of the knightly stork; the story might be cabled back to Paris for the English language papers there. Lanny had hobnobbed with the correspondents so much that he could guess what Pete would send in his "cablese" and how it would appear dressed up by the re-write man in the sweet land of liberty. Doubtless Pete had already sent a "flash," and readers of that morning's newspapers were learning that Mrs. Lanny Budd, who was Irma Barnes, the glamour girl of last season, was in a private hospital in Cannes awaiting the blessed event.

The papers would supply the apposite details: that Irma was the only daughter of J. Paramount Barnes, recently deceased utilities magnate, who had left her the net sum of twenty-three million dollars; that her mother was one of the New York Vandringhams, and her uncle was Horace Vandringham, Wall Street manipulator cleaned out in the recent market collapse; that Irma's own fortune was said to have been cut in half, but she still owned a palatial estate on Long Island, to which she was expected to return. The papers would add that the expectant father was the son of Robert Budd of Budd Gunmakers Corporation of Newcastle, Connecticut; that his mother was the famous international beauty, widow of Marcel Detaze, the French painter whose work had created a sensation in New York last fall. Such details were eagerly read by a public which lived upon the doings of the rich, as the ancient Greeks had lived upon the affairs of the immortals who dwelt upon the snowy top of Mount Olympus.

I V

Lanny would have preferred that his child should be born outside
the limelight, but he knew it wasn't possible; this stream of elec-
trons, or waves, or whatever it was, would follow Irma on her
travels—so long as she had the other half of her fortune. As a matter of fact the fortune wasn't really diminished, for everybody else
had lost half of his or hers, so the proportions remained the same.
Irma Barnes still enjoyed the status of royalty, and so did the fortunate young man whom she had chosen for her prince consort.
In the days of the *ancien régime*, when a child was born to the queen
of France it had been the long-established right of noblemen and
ladies to satisfy themselves that it was a real heir to the throne and
no fraud; no stork stories were accepted, but they witnessed with
their own eyes the physical emergence of the infant dauphin. Into
the chamber of Marie Antoinette they crowded in such swarms that
the queen cried out that she was suffocating, and the king opened
a window with his own hands. It wasn't quite that bad now with
the queen of the Barnes estate, but it was a fact that the newspaper-
reading and radio-listening public would have welcomed hourly
bulletins as to what was going on in this *hospice de la maternité*.

But, damn it, even Lanny himself didn't know what was going
on! What was the use of planning what to say to newspaper reporters about the heir or heiress apparent to the Barnes fortune,
when it refused so persistently to make itself apparent, and for all
the prince consort knew the surgeon might be engaged in a desperate struggle with a "cross-birth," or perhaps having to cut the
infant to pieces, or perform a Caesarean section to save its life!
Lanny dug his fingernails into the palms of his hands, and got up
and began to pace the floor. Every time he turned toward the bell-
button in the reception-room he had an impulse to press it. He was
paying for service, and wasn't receiving it, and he was getting up
steam to demand it. But just at that juncture a nurse came through
the room, cast one of her conventional smiles upon him, and remarked: "*Soyez tranquille, monsieur. Tout va bien.*"

V

Lanny called his mother on the telephone. Beauty Budd had been through this adventure two and a half times—so she said—and spoke as one having authority. There wasn't a thing he could do, so why not come home and have something to eat, instead of worrying himself and getting in other people's way? This was the woman's job, and nobody in all creation was so superfluous as the husband. Lanny answered that he wasn't hungry, and he wasn't being allowed to bother anybody.

He went back to his seat in the reception-room, and thought about ladies. They were, as a rule, a highly individualistic lot; each on her own, and sharply aware of the faults of the others. He thought of those who made up his mother's set, and therefore had played a large part in his own life; he recalled the sly little digs he had heard them give one another, the lack of solidarity he had seen them display. They had been polite to Irma, but he was certain that behind her back, and behind his, they found it difficult to forgive her for being so favored of fortune. However, as her pregnancy had moved to its climax they had seemed to gather about her and become tender and considerate; they would have come and helped to fetch and carry, to hold her hands and pull against them in her spasms of pain, had it not been for the fact that there were professional women trained for these services.

Lanny thought about his mother, and her role in this drama, the stage entrance of another soul. Beauty had been an ideal mother-in-law so far. She had worked hard to make this marriage, for she believed in money; there was in her mind no smallest doubt of money's rightness, or of money's right to have its way. Had not her judgment been vindicated by the events of a dreadful Wall Street panic? Where would they all have been, what would have become of them, if it hadn't been for Irma's fortune? Who was there among Irma's friends who hadn't wanted help? Go ahead and pretend to be contemptuous of money if you pleased; indulge yourself in Pink talk, as Lanny did—but sooner or later it was proved that it is money which makes the mare go, and which feeds the mare, takes care of her shiny coat, and provides her with a warm and well-bedded stall.

Beauty Budd was going to become a grandmother. She pretended to be distressed at the idea; she made a *moue*, exclaiming that it would set the seal of doom upon her social career. Other handicaps you might evade by one device or another. You might fib about the number of your years, and have your face lifted, and fill your crow's-feet with skin enamel; but when you were a grandmother, when anyone could bring that charge publicly and you had to keep silent, that was the end of you as a charmer, a butterfly, a professional beauty.

But that was all mere spoofing. In reality Beauty was delighted at the idea of there being a little one to inherit the Barnes fortune and to be trained to make proper use of the prestige and power it conferred. That meant to be dignified and splendid, to be admired and courted, to be the prince or princess of that new kind of empire which the strong men of these days had created. Beauty's head was buzzing with romantic notions derived from the fairytales she had read as a child. She had brought these imaginings with her to Paris and merged them with the realities of splendid equipages, costly furs and jewels, titles and honors—and then the figure of a young Prince Charming, the son of a munitions manufacturer from her homeland. Beauty Budd's had been a Cinderella story, and it was now being carried further than the fairytales usually go. Grandma Cinderella!

VI

Lanny couldn't stand any more of this suspense, this premonition of impending calamity. He rang the bell and demanded to see the head nurse; yes, even he, the superfluous husband, had some rights in a crisis like this! The functionary made her appearance; grave, stiff with starch and authority, forbidding behind pincenez. In response to Lanny's demand she consented to depart from the established formula, that all was going well and that he should be tranquil. With professional exactitude she explained that in the female organism there are tissues which have to be stretched, passages which

have to be widened—the head nurse made a gesture of the hands—
and there is no way for this to be accomplished save the way of
nature, the efforts of the woman in labor. The *accoucheur* would
pay a visit in the course of the next hour or so, and he perhaps
would be able to put monsieur's mind at rest.

Lanny was disturbed because this personage was not in attendance
upon Irma now. The husband had assumed that when he agreed
to the large fee requested, he was entitled to have the man sit by
Irma's bedside and watch her, or at any rate be in the building, prepared for emergencies. But here the fellow had gone about other
duties, or perhaps pleasures. He was an·Englishman, and was probably having a round or two of golf; then he would have his shower,
and his indispensable tea and conversation; after which he expected
to stroll blandly in and look at Irma—and meanwhile whatever dreadful thing was happening might have gone so far as to be irremedi-
able!

Lanny resumed his seat in the well-cushioned chair, and tried to read
the popular novel, and wished he had brought something more constructive. The conversation of these fashionable characters was too
much like that which was now going on in the casinos and tea-
rooms and drawing-rooms of this playground of Europe. The financial collapse overseas hadn't sobered these people; they were still
gossiping and chattering; and Lanny Budd was in rebellion against
them, but didn't know what to do about it. Surely in the face of
the awful thing that was happening in this *hospice*—knowing it to
be their own fate through the ages—the women ought to be having
some serious concern about life, and doing something to make it
easier for others! They ought to be feeling for one another some of
the pity which Lanny was feeling for Irma!

VII

The door to the street opened, and there entered a tall, vigorous-
appearing American of thirty-five or so, having red hair and a cheerful smile: Lanny's one-time tutor and dependable friend, Jerry Pendleton from the state of Kansas, now proprietor of a tourist bureau

in Cannes. Beauty had phoned to him: "Do go over there and stop his worrying." Jerry was the fellow for the job, because he had been through this himself, and had three sturdy youngsters and a cheerful little French wife as evidence that *la nature* wasn't altogether out of her wits. Jerry knew exactly how to kid his friend along and make him take it; he seated himself in the next chair and commanded: "Cheer up! This isn't the Meuse-Argonne!"

Yes, ex-Lieutenant Jerry Pendleton, who had enlisted and begun as a machine-gun expert, knew plenty about blood and suffering. Mostly he didn't talk about it; but once on a long motor ride, and again sitting out in the boat when the fish didn't happen to be biting, he had opened up and told a little of what he had seen. The worst of it was that the men who had suffered and died hadn't accomplished anything, so far as a survivor could see; France had been saved, but wasn't making much use of her victory, nor was any other nation. This battle that Irma was fighting in the other room was of a more profitable kind; she'd have a little something for her pains, and Lanny for his—so said the former doughboy, with a grin.

More than once Lanny had been glad to lean on this sturdy fellow. That dreadful time when Marcel Detaze had leaped from a stationary balloon in flames it had been Jerry who had driven Lanny and his mother up to the war zone and helped to bring the broken man home and nurse him back to life. So now when he chuckled and said: "You ain't seen nothin' yet," Lanny recognized the old doughboy spirit.

The tourist agent had troubles of his own at present. He mentioned how fast business was falling off, how many Americans hadn't come to the Riviera that season. Apparently the hard times were going to spread to Europe. Did Lanny think so? Lanny said he surely did, and told how he had argued the matter with his father. Maybe the money values which had been wiped out in Wall Street were just paper, as so many declared; but it was paper that you had been able to spend for anything you wanted, including steamship tickets and traveler's checks. Now you didn't have it, so you didn't spend it. Lanny and his wife could have named a score of people who had braved the snow and sleet of New York the past winter and were glad if they had the price of meal tickets.

Jerry said he'd been hard up more than once, and could stand it again. He'd have to let his office force go, and he and Cerise would do the work. Fortunately they had their meal tickets, for they still lived in the Pension Flavin, owned and run by the wife's mother and aunt. "You'll have to take me fishing some more and let me carry home the fish," said the ex-tutor; and Lanny replied: "Just as soon as I know Irma's all right, we'll make a date." The moment he said this his heart gave a jump. Was he ever going to know that Irma was all right? Suppose her heart was failing at this moment, and the nurses were frantically trying to restore it!

VIII

The surgeon arrived at last: a middle-aged Englishman, smooth-shaven, alert, and precise; his cheeks were rosy from a "workout" in the sunshine followed by a showerbath. He had talked with the head nurse over the telephone; everything was going excellently. Lanny could understand that a surgeon has to take his job serenely; he cannot suffer with all his patients; whatever others may do, he has to accept *la nature* and her ways. He said he would see Mrs. Budd and report.

Lanny and his friend resumed their discussion of depressions and their cause. Lanny had a head full of theories, derived from the Red and Pink papers he took. Jerry's reading was confined mostly to the *Saturday Evening Post* and the Paris edition of the New York *Tribune;* therefore he was puzzled, and couldn't figure out what had become of all the money that people had had early in October 1929, and where it had gone by the end of that month. Lanny explained the credit structure: one of those toy balloons, shining brightly in the sunshine, dancing merrily in the breeze, until someone sticks a pin into it. Jerry said: "By heck, I ought to study up on those things!"

The surgeon reappeared, as offensively cheerful as ever. Mrs.

Budd was a patient to be proud of; she was just the way a young woman ought to keep herself. The "bearing-down pains," as they were called, might continue for some little time yet. Meanwhile there was nothing to be done. Lanny was dismayed, but knew there was no use exhibiting his feelings; he too must maintain the professional manner. "I'll be within call," said the surgeon. "You might as well get it off your mind for a while." Lanny thanked him.

After the surgeon had gone, Jerry said: "When do we eat?" Lanny wanted to say that he couldn't eat, but he knew that Jerry was there for the purpose of making him change his mind. It was dinner-hour at the Pension Flavin, and Jerry recited a jingle to the effect that he knew a boarding-house not far away where they had ham and eggs three times a day. "Oh, how those boarders yell when they hear the dinner-bell!"—and so on. This was the sporting way to deal with the fact that your mother-in-law runs a medium-priced pension in the most fashionable of Riviera towns. Lanny knew also that he hadn't visited the Pendleton family for some time, and that, having won the biggest matrimonial sweepstakes, it was up to him to show that he didn't mean to "high-hat" his poor friends.

"All right," he said; "but I'll be glum company."

"The boarders know all about it," responded Jerry.

Indeed they did! Wherever the boarders came from and whatever they were, they knew about the Budd family and felt themselves members of it. For sixteen years Jerry Pendleton had been going fishing with Lanny Budd, and the boarders had eaten the fish. At the outset Jerry had been a boarder like themselves, but after he had driven the Boches out of France he had married the daughter of the pension. And then had come the time when another of the boarders had married Lanny's mother; from that time on, the boarders had all regarded themselves as Budds, and entitled to every scrap of gossip concerning the family.

IX

Driving back to the hospital, Lanny took the precaution to stop and purchase several magazines, French, English, and American.

He would equip himself for a siege, and if one subject failed to hold his attention he would try others. Arriving at the reception-room, he found that he was no longer alone; in one of the chairs sat a French gentleman, stoutish and prosperous, betraying in aspect and manner those symptoms which Lanny recognized.

The stranger's misery loved company, and he introduced himself as an *avocat* from a near-by town. It was his wife's first *accouchement*, and he was in a terrible state of fidgets and could hardly keep his seat; he wanted to bother the nurses with questions every time one entered the room. He seemed to Lanny absurdly naïve; he actually didn't know about the "bearing-down pains," that they were according to the arrangements of *la nature*, and that women didn't very often die of them. Speaking as a veteran of some ten hours, Lanny explained about the stretching of tissues, and comforted the stranger as best he could. Later on, seeing that his advice was without effect, Lanny became bored, and buried himself in the latest issue of the *New Statesman*.

He would have liked very much to inquire whether there had been any change in the status of his wife; but the egregious emotionalism of Monsieur Fouchard reminded him that the Budds were stern Anglo-Saxons and should behave accordingly. He resolutely fixed his attention upon an article dealing with the final reparations settlement of the World War, now more than eleven years in the past, and the probable effects of that settlement upon the various nations involved. This was a subject of interest to a young man who had been born in Switzerland of American parents and had lived chunks of his life in France, Germany, England, and "the States." His many friends in these countries belonged to the ruling classes and took political and economic developments as their personal affairs.

The surgeon was a long time in returning, and Lanny began once more to feel himself a defrauded client. He forgot that there are telephones, whereby an obstetrician can keep informed as to his patient while reading the latest medical journal at home or playing a game of billiards at his club. When the Englishman at last appeared, he informed the anxious husband that the time for action was approaching, and that Mrs. Budd would soon be taken to the delivery-room. After that Lanny found it impossible to interest himself in what *L'Illustration* had to report about the prospects for the spring Salons—important though this subject was to one who earned his living by buying or selling works of art on commission.

There was no use trying to be Anglo-Saxon any longer. Better give up and admit the hegemony of mother nature. Lanny put down his magazine and watched Monsieur Fouchard pacing the floor of the reception-room, and when Monsieur Fouchard sat down and lighted a cigarette, Lanny got up and did the pacing. Meanwhile they talked. The Frenchman told about his wife; she was only nineteen, her charms were extraordinary, and Monsieur Fouchard spared no details in describing them. He wanted to tell the whole story of their courtship and marriage, and was grateful to a stranger for listening.

Lanny didn't tell so much; nor was it necessary. Monsieur Fouchard had heard the surgeon call him by name, and was aware who this elegant young American must be. He had read about Irma Barnes, and began to talk as if he were an old friend of the family, indeed as if he were about to take charge of Irma's convalescence and the nursing of her infant. Lanny, who had grown up in France, knew that it wasn't worth while to take offense; much better to be human. They would set up a sort of temporary association, a League of Husbands in Labor. Others might be joining them before the night was over.

X

The *accoucheuse* of Madame Fouchard arrived, a Frenchwoman; she succeeded in persuading the husband that it would be a long time before the blessed event could take place, so that gentleman bade his fellow league-member a sentimental farewell. Lanny answered a call from his mother and reported on the situation; after pacing the floor some more, he sat down and tried to put his mind upon an account of a visit to the hanging monasteries of Greece. He had seen them as a boy, but now wouldn't have cared if all the monks had been hanged along with the monasteries. He simply couldn't believe that a normal delivery could take so long a time. He rang the bell and had a session with the night head nurse, only to find that she had learned the formulas. *"Tout va bien, monsieur. Soyez tranquille."*

Lanny was really glad when the door opened and a lady was escorted in, obviously in that condition in which ladies enter such places. With her came a French gentleman with a dark brown silky beard; Lanny recognized him as a piano-teacher well known in Cannes. The lady was turned over to the nurse's care, and the gentleman became at once a member of Lanny's league. Inasmuch as Lanny was a pianist himself, and had a brother-in-law who was a violin-virtuoso, the two might have talked a lot of shop; but no, they preferred to tell each other how long they had been married, and how old their wives were, and how they felt and how their wives felt. This confrontation with nature in the raw had reduced them to the lowest common denominator of humanity. Art, science, and culture no longer existed; only bodies, blood, and babies.

Lanny would listen for a while, and then he would cease to hear what the bearded Frenchman was saying. Lanny was walking up and down the floor of the reception-room, with beads of perspiration standing out upon his forehead. Oh, God, this surely couldn't be right! Something dreadful must be happening in that delivery-room, some of those things which the encyclopedia told about: a failure of the mother's heart, the breaking of the "waters," or one of those irregular presentations which occur in varying percentages of cases. Manifestly, if the *accoucheur* had encountered trouble, he wouldn't come running out to tell the expectant father; he'd be busy, and so would the nurses. Only when it was all over would anyone break the tragic news; and then Lanny would never be able to forgive himself.

A serious defect in the practical arrangements of this *hospice de la misère!* There ought to be some system, a telephone in the delivery-room, a bulletin board, a set of signals! It is a problem which calls for collective solution; the opening of a paternity hospital, a place for expectant fathers, where they may receive proper care! Nurses will have some time for them. Attendants will consider their feelings, and give them information—perhaps lectures on the subject of obstetrics, especially prepared for sensitive minds, with the abnormalities omitted or played down. There will be soft music, perhaps motion pictures; above all there will be news, plenty of it, prompt and dependable. Perhaps a place like a broker's office, where a "Translux" gives the market figures on a screen.

Every time Lanny came near the wall with the bell-button he wanted to press it and demand exact information as to the condition of his beloved wife. Every time the French music-teacher asked him a question it was harder to conceal the fact that he wasn't listening. A damnable thing! Put the blame wherever you chose, on nature or on human incompetence, the fact remained that this wife whom he loved so tenderly, with so much pity, must be in agony, she must be completely exhausted. Something ought to be done! Here it was getting on toward midnight—Lanny looked at his wristwatch and saw that three minutes had passed since he had looked the last time; it was only twenty-two minutes to eleven— but that was bad enough—some thirteen hours since the labor pains had begun, and they had told him it was time to leave her to her fate. Damn it——

XI

A door of the room opened, and there was a nurse. Lanny took one glance, and saw that she was different from any nurse he had seen thus far. She was smiling, yes, actually beaming with smiles. "*Oh, monsieur!*" she exclaimed. "*C'est une fille! Une très belle fille! Si charmante!*" She made a gesture, indicating the size of a female prodigy. Lanny found himself going suddenly dizzy, and reached for a chair.

"*Et madame?*" he cried.

"*Madame est si brave! Elle est magnifique! Tout va bien.*" The formula again. Lanny poured out questions, and satisfied himself that Irma was going to survive. She was exhausted, but that was to be expected. There were details to be attended to; in half an hour or so it should be possible for monsieur to see both mother and daughter. *"Tout de suite! Soyez tranquille!"*

The teacher of piano had Lanny Budd by the hand and was shaking it vigorously. For some time after the American had resumed his seat the other was still pouring out congratulations. *"Merci, merci,"* Lanny said mechanically, meanwhile thinking: "A girl! Beauty will be disappointed." But he himself had no complaint. He had been a ladies' man from childhood, seeing his father only at long intervals, cared for by his mother and by women servants. There had been his mother's women friends, then his half-sister and his stepmother in New England, then a new half-sister at Bienvenu, then a succession of his sweethearts, and last of all his wife. He had got something from them all, and would find a daughter no end of fun. It was all right.

Lanny got up, excused himself from the French gentleman, and went to the telephone. He called his mother and told her the news. Yes, he said, he was delighted, or would be when he got over being woozy. No, he wouldn't forget the various cablegrams: one to his father in Connecticut, one to Irma's mother on Long Island, one to his half-sister Bess in Berlin. Beauty would do the telephoning to various friends in the neighborhood—trust her not to miss those thrills! Lanny would include his friend Rick in England and his friend Kurt in Germany; he had the messages written, save for filling in the word "girl."

He carried out his promise to Pietro Corsatti. It was still early in New York; the story would make the night edition of the morning papers, that which was read by café society, whose darling Irma Barnes had been. After receiving Pete's congratulations, Lanny went back for others which the French gentleman had thought up. Astonishing how suddenly the black clouds had lifted from the sky of a young husband's life, how less murderous the ways of mother nature appeared! It became possible to chat with a piano-teacher about the technique he employed; to tell one's own experiences with the Leschetizsky method, and later with the Breithaupt; to explain the forearm rotary motion, and illustrate it on the arm of one's chair. Lanny found himself tapping out the opening theme of

Liszt's symphonic poem, *From the Cradle to the Grave*. But he stopped with the first part.

XII

The cheerful nurse came again, and escorted the successful father down a passage to a large expanse of plate-glass looking into a room with tiny white metal cribs. Visitors were not permitted inside, but a nurse with a white mask over her mouth and nose brought to the other side of the glass a bundle in a blanket and laid back the folds, exposing to Lanny's gaze a brick-red object which might have been a great bloated crinkled caterpillar, only it had appendages, and a large round ball at the top with a face which would have been human if it hadn't been elfish. There was a mouth with lips busily sucking on nothing, and a pair of large eyes which didn't move; however, the nurse at Lanny's side assured him that they had been tested with a light, and they worked. He was assured that this was his baby; to prove it there was a tiny necklace with a metal tag; monsieur and madame might rest assured that they would not carry home the baby of an *avocat*, nor yet that of a teacher of piano technique.

The bloated red caterpillar was folded up in the blanket again, and Lanny was escorted to Irma's room. She lay in a white hospital bed, her head sunk back in a pillow, her eyes closed. How pale she looked, how different from the rich brunette beauty he had left that morning! Now her dark hair was disordered—apparently they hadn't wished to disturb her even that much. Lanny tiptoed into the room, and she opened her eyes slowly, as if with an effort; when she recognized him she gave him a feeble smile.

"How are you, Irma?"

"I'll be all right," she whispered. "Tired, awfully tired."

The nurse had told him not to talk to her. He said: "It's a lovely baby."

"I'm glad. Don't worry. I'll rest, and get better."

Lanny felt a choking in his throat; it was pitiful, the price that women had to pay! But he knew he musn't trouble her with his superfluous emotions. A nurse came with a little wine, which she took through a tube. There was a sedative in it, and she would sleep. He took her hand, which lay limp upon the coverlet, and kissed it gently. "Thank you, dear. I love you." That was enough.

Outside in the passage was the surgeon, all cleaned up and ready for the outside world. His professional manner was second nature. Everything was as it should be; never a better patient, a more perfect delivery. A few hours' sleep, a little nourishment, and Mr. Budd would be surprised by the change in his wife. A lovely sturdy infant, well over nine pounds—that had caused the delay. "Sorry you had such a long wait; no help for that. Do you read the Bible, Mr. Budd? 'A woman when she is in travail hath sorrow, because her hour is come: but as soon as she is delivered of the child, she remembereth no more the anguish, for joy that a man is born into the world.' In this case it's a woman, but we're no longer in ancient Judea, and the women are bossing the show. In my country and yours they have the vote, and they own more than half the property, I'm told; it's their world, and what they are going to do with it we men have to wait and find out. Good night, Mr. Budd."

"Good night," said Lanny. He owed the man thirty thousand francs, which sounded like a thumping price, but the franc was low. Lanny didn't begrudge it. He thought: "I'd have offered a hundred thousand an hour ago!"

2

Those Friends Thou Hast

I

THE house on the Bienvenu estate in which Irma and Lanny were living was called the Cottage, but was nearly as large as the villa and uniform in style, built around a central patio, or court; the walls were of pink stucco with window shutters of pale blue, and a red-tiled roof over its single story. It looked out over the ever-changing Golfe Juan, and beyond to the mountains behind which the sun went down. The house was only three years old, but already the banana plants in the patio were up to the eaves, and the bougain-villaea vines were crawling over the tiles. Early April was the love-liest time of the year, and the patio was a little paradise, with blos-soms of every hue exulting in the floods of sunshine. The young mother might lie on a chaise-longue in sun or shade, and read in a New York paper about March weather, with icy gales wrecking the seashore cottages and piling small boats up on beaches.

In the most exquisite of silk-lined bassinets lay the most precious of female infants, with a veil to protect her from over-curious insects. Near by sat a trained nurse, a mature and conscientious Church of England woman. She had two nursemaids under her orders, which were based on the latest discoveries in the physiology and psychology of infants. There was to be no coddling, no kissing, no rocking to sleep of this mite of royalty; there was to be no guesswork and no blundering in its care; no hostile germs were to steal past the barricades which surrounded it, and anyone who showed the least trace of a cold was banished from the premises. Guests and even relatives had to obey the orders of the all-knowing Miss Severne; she was armed with authority to defy even grandmothers. As for Irma, she had agreed to make the supreme sacrifice; every four hours the precious bundle was to be brought for her nursing, and she was to be on hand, no matter what temptations the world of fashion might put in her way. Back to Rousseau!

There had been family councils and international negotiations concerning a name for this multimillionaire heiress. Many claims had been entered, and if they had all been granted, the little one would have been loaded down after the fashion of European royalty. Manifestly, it wouldn't do to give her the name Beauty; that was something that had to be earned—and suppose she failed to meet the test? Beauty's real name, Mabel, she didn't like—so that was out. Irma's own claims she renounced in favor of her mother, to whom it would mean so much. Irma was going to live most of her life in Europe, because that was what Lanny wanted; so should they not give a pining dowager in a Long Island palace whatever solace she could derive from having her name carried on? The Barnes clan also was entitled to consideration, having furnished the money. "Frances Barnes Budd" was a name not hard to say; but never, never was it to be "Fanny"! The Queen Mother of Shore Acres was helpless to understand how her once lovely name was being put to such base uses in these modern days.

II

Irma was reclining in the patio, enjoying the delight of holding the naked mite in her arms while it absorbed the sunshine of the Midi for a measured three minutes. Lanny came in, saying: "Uncle Jesse is over at the villa. Do you want to meet him?"

"Do you think I should?"

"You surely don't have to if you don't feel like it."

"Won't his feelings be hurt?"

"He's used to that." Lanny said it with a grin.

Irma had heard no little talk about this "Red sheep" of her mother-in-law's family. At first her curiosity hadn't been aroused, for she didn't take political questions to heart, and while she had no doubt that Communists were dreadful people, still, if that was what Jesse Blackless believed, he had to say it. Threats to the social order had never been real to Irma—at least not up to the time of the panic. During that convulsion she had heard many strange ideas discussed, and had begun to wonder about them. Now she said: "If you and your mother see him, I ought to see him too."

"Don't let him corrupt you," replied the husband, grinning again. He got fun out of arguing with his Red uncle, and used him for teasing other people.

Lanny went over to the villa and came back with a tall, odd-looking man, having an almost entirely bald head fairly baked by the sun—for he went about most of the time without a hat. He was dressed carelessly, as became a painter, with sandals, white duck trousers, and a shirt open at the throat. His face had many wrinkles, which he increased when he smiled in his peculiar twisted way; he was given to that kind of humor which consists in saying something different from what you mean, and which assumes understanding on the part of other people which they do not always possess. Jesse Blackless was ill-satisfied with the world in which he lived, and found his pleasure in reducing it to absurdity.

"Well, so this is Irma!" he said, looking down at her. She had covered up her bosom with the orange-colored peignoir of Chinese silk which she was wearing. Her vivid brunette color, which had come back quickly, should have pleased a painter; but Uncle Jesse painted only street urchins and poor beggar folk and workingmen with signs of hard toil on them.

"And this is the baby!" he said, peering into the well-shaded bassinet. He didn't offer any forbidden intimacies, but instead remarked: "Watch out for her—she'd be worth a lot to kidnapers." A sufficiently horrid idea.

The visitor seated himself in a canvas chair and stretched his long legs. His glance wandered from the young wife to the young husband and back again, and he said: "You made a lucky choice, Irma. A lot of people have tried to ruin him, but they haven't succeeded."

It was the first time Lanny had ever known his Red uncle to

pay anybody a compliment, and he valued it accordingly. Irma thanked the speaker, adding that she was sure his judgment was good.

"I know," declared the painter, "because I tried to ruin him myself."

"Have you given up hope?"

"There'd be no use in trying now, since he's married to you. I am a believer in economic determinism."

Lanny explained: "Uncle Jesse thinks he believes that everybody's behavior is conditioned by the state of his pocketbook. But he's a living refutation of his own theory. If he followed his pocketbook, he'd be painting portraits of the idle rich here on this coast, whereas he's probably been meeting with a group of revolutionary conspirators somewhere in the slums of Cannes."

"I'm a freak," said Uncle Jesse. "Nature produces only a few of these, and any statement of social causes has to be based upon the behavior of the mass."

So this pair took to arguing. Irma listened, but most of her thoughts were occupied with the personality of the man. What was he really like? Was he as bitter and harsh as he sounded, or was this only a mask with which he covered his feelings? What was it that had hurt him and made him so out of humor with his own kind of people?

III

The discussion lasted quite a while. They both seemed to enjoy it, even though they said sarcastic things, each about the other. The French word for abuse is "*injures*," which also means injuries, but no hard saying appeared to injure either of these men. Apparently they had heard it all before. Lanny's favorite remark was that his uncle was a phonograph; he put on a record and it ground out the old dependable tune. There was one called "dialectical materialism" and another called "proletarian dictatorship"—long words which meant nothing to Irma. "He wants to take my money

and divide it up among the poor," she thought. "How far would
it go, and how long would it take them to get rid of it?" She had
heard her father say this, and it sounded convincing.

They talked a great deal about what was happening in Russia.
Irma had been a child of nine at the time of the revolution, but
she had heard about it since, and here on the Riviera she had met
Russians who had escaped from the dreadful Bolsheviks, sometimes
with nothing but what they had on. You would be told that the handsome and distinguished-looking head waiter in a café was a former
Russian baron; that a night-club dancer was the daughter of a
one-time landowner. Did Uncle Jesse want things like that to happen in France and the United States? Irma tried to tell herself that
he didn't really mean it; but no, he was a determined man, and
there often came a grim look on his face; you could imagine him
willing to shoot people who stood in his way. Irma knew that the
Paris police had "detained" him a couple of times, and that he had
defied them. Apparently he was ready to pay whatever price his
revolution cost.

Presently he revealed the fact that he was taking steps to become
a citizen of France. He had lived in the country for thirty-five years
without ever bothering; but now it appeared that "the party" wanted
him to run for the Chamber of Deputies. He had made himself a
reputation as an orator. Said Lanny: "They want him to put on his
phonograph records for all France."

Irma, who was money-conscious, thought at once: "He's come to
get us to put up for his campaign." Lanny didn't have much money
since his father had got caught in the slump. Irma resolved: "I won't
help him. I don't approve of it." She had discovered the power of
her money during the Wall Street crisis, and was learning to enjoy it.

But then another point of view occurred to her. Maybe it would
be a distinguished thing to have a relative in the Chamber, even
if he was a Communist! She wasn't sure about this, and wished she
knew more about political affairs. Now and then she had that
thought about various branches of knowledge, and would resolve
to find out; but then she would forget because it was too much
trouble. Just now they had told her that she musn't get excited

about anything, because excitement would spoil her milk. A nuisance, turning yourself into a cow! But it was pleasant enough here in the sunshine, being entertained with novel ideas.

Lanny apparently agreed with his uncle that what the Russians were doing was important—for them. The dispute was over the question whether the same thing was going to happen in France and England and America. Lanny maintained that these countries, being "democracies," could bring about the changes peaceably. That was his way; he didn't want to hurt anybody, but to discuss ideas politely and let the best ideas win. However, Uncle Jesse kept insisting that Lanny and his Socialist friends were aiding the capitalists by fooling the workers, luring them with false hopes, keeping them contented with a political system which the capitalists had bought and paid for. Lanny, on the other hand, argued that it was the Reds who were betraying the workers, frightening the middle classes by violent threats and driving them into the camp of the reactionaries.

So it went, and the young wife listened without getting excited. Marriage was a strange adventure; you let yourself in for a lot of things you couldn't have foreseen. These two most eccentric families, the Budds and the Blacklesses! Irma's own family consisted of Wall Street people. They bought and sold securities and made fortunes or lost them, and that seemed a conventional and respectable kind of life; but now she had been taken to a household full of Reds and Pinks of all shades, and spiritualist mediums and religious healers, munitions makers and Jewish *Schieber*, musicians and painters and art dealers—you never knew when you opened your eyes in the morning what strange new creatures you were going to encounter before night. Even Lanny, who was so dear and sweet, and with whom Irma had entered into the closest of all intimacies, even he became suddenly a stranger when he got stirred up and began pouring out his schemes for making the world over—schemes which clearly involved his giving up his own property, and Irma's giving up hers, and wiping out the hereditary rights of the long-awaited and closely guarded Frances Barnes Budd!

IV

Uncle Jesse stayed to lunch, then went his way; and after the nap which the doctor had prescribed for the nursing mother, Irma enjoyed the society of her stepfather-in-law—if there is a name for this odd relationship. Mr. Parsifal Dingle, Beauty's new husband, came over from the villa to call on the baby. Irma knew him well, for they had spent the past summer on a yacht; he was a religious mystic, and certainly restful after the Reds and the Pinks. He never argued, and as a rule didn't talk unless you began a conversation; he was interested in things going on in his own soul, and while he was glad to tell about them, you had to ask. He would sit by the bassinet and gaze at the infant, and there would come a blissful look on his round cherubic face; you would think there were two infants, and that their souls must be completely in tune.

The man of God would close his eyes, and be silent for a while, and Irma wouldn't interrupt him, knowing that he was giving little Frances a "treatment." It was a sort of prayer with which he filled his mind, and he was quite sure that it 'affected the mind of the little one. Irma wasn't sure, but she knew it couldn't do any harm, for there was nothing except good in the mind of this gentle healer. He seemed a bit uncanny while sitting with Madame Zyszynski, the Polish medium, in one of her trances; conversing in the most matter-of-fact way with the alleged Indian spirit. "Tecumseh," as he called himself, was whimsical and self-willed, and would tell something or refuse to tell, according to whether or not you were respectful to him and whether or not the sun was shining in the spirit world. Gradually Irma had got used to it all, for the spirits didn't do any harm, and quite certainly Mr. Dingle didn't; on the contrary, if you felt sick he would cure you. He had cured several members of the Bienvenu household, and it might be extremely convenient in an emergency.

Such were Irma's reflections during the visits. She would ask him questions and let him talk, and it would be like going to church. Irma found it agreeable to talk about loving everybody, and thought that it might do some people a lot of good; they showed the need of it in their conversation, the traces they revealed of envy, hatred, malice, and all uncharitableness. Mr. Dingle wanted to change the world, just as much as any Bolshevik, but he had begun with himself, and that seemed to Irma a fine idea; it didn't threaten the Barnes fortune or the future of its heiress. The healer would read his mystical books, and magazines of what he called "New Thought," and then he would wander about the garden, looking at the flowers and the birds, and perhaps giving them a treatment—for they too had life in them and were products of love. Bienvenu appeared to contain everything that Mr. Dingle needed, and he rarely went off the estate unless someone invited him.

The strangest whim of fate, that the worldly Beauty Budd should have chosen this man of God to accompany her on the downhill of life! All her friends laughed over it, and were bored to death with her efforts to use the language of "spirituality." Certainly it hadn't kept her from working like the devil to land the season's greatest "catch" for her son; nor did it keep her from exulting brazenly in her triumph. Beauty's religious talk no more than Lanny's Socialist talk was causing them to take steps to distribute any large share of Irma's unearned increment. On the contrary, they had stopped giving elaborate parties at Bienvenu, which was hard on everybody on the Cap d'Antibes—the tradesmen, the servants, the musicians, the *couturiers*, all who catered to the rich. It was hard on the society folk, who had been so scared by the panic and the talk of hard times on the way. Surely somebody ought to set an example of courage and enterprise—and who could have done it better than a glamour girl with a whole bank-vault full of "blue chip" stocks and bonds? What was going to become of smart society if its prime favorites began turning their estates into dairy farms and themselves into stud cattle?

V

There came a telegram from Berlin: "Yacht due at Cannes we are leaving by train tonight engage hotel accommodations. Bess."

Of course Lanny wouldn't follow those last instructions. When friends are taking you for a cruise and paying all your expenses for several months, you don't let them go to a hotel even for a couple of days. There was the Lodge, a third house on the estate; it had been vacant all winter, and now would be opened and freshly aired and dusted. Irma's secretary, Miss Featherstone, had been established as a sort of female major-domo and took charge of such operations. The expected guests would have their meals with Irma and Lanny, and "Feathers" would consult with the cook and see to the ordering of supplies. Everything would run as smoothly as water down a mill-race; Irma would continue to lie in the sunshine, read magazines, listen to Lanny play the piano, and nurse Baby Frances when one of the maids brought her.

Lanny telephoned his old friend Emily Chattersworth, who took care of the cultural activities of this part of the Riviera. Her drawing-room was much larger than any at Bienvenu, and people were used to coming there whenever a celebrity was available. Hansi Robin always played for her, and the fashionable folk who cared for music and the musical folk who were socially acceptable would be invited to Sept Chênes for a treat. Emily would send Hansi a check, and he would endorse it over to be used for the workers' educational project which was Lanny's special hobby.

Just before sundown of that day Lanny and Irma sat on the loggia of their home, which looked out over the Golfe Juan, and watched the trim white *Bessie Budd* glide into the harbor of Cannes. They knew her a long way off, for she had been their home during the previous summer, and Lanny had taken two other cruises in her. With a pair of field-glasses they could recognize Captain Moeller, who had had a chance to marry them but had funked it. They could almost imagine they heard his large Prussian voice when it was time to slow down for passing the breakwater.

Next morning but one, Lanny drove into the city, with his little half-sister Marceline at his side and Irma's chauffeur following with another car. The long blue express rolled in and delivered five of their closest friends, plus a secretary and a nursemaid in a uniform and cap with blue streamers, carrying an infant in arms. It was on account of this last that the cruise was being taken so early in the year; the two lactant mothers would combine their dairy farms, put them on shipboard, and transport them to delightful places of this great inland sea, famed in story.

Just prior to the World War, Lanny Budd, a small boy traveling on a train, had met a Jewish salesman of electrical gadgets; they had liked each other, and the stranger had given Lanny his card. This small object had lain in a bureau drawer; and if, later on, Lanny hadn't happened to be rummaging in that drawer, how much would have been different in his life! He wouldn't have written to Johannes Robin, and Johannes wouldn't have come to call on him in Paris, and met Lanny's father, and with the father's money become one of the richest men in Germany. Lanny's half-sister wouldn't have met Hansi Robin, and shocked her family by marrying a Jewish musician. The yacht wouldn't have been called the *Bessie Budd*, and wouldn't have taken Lanny and his family on three cruises, and been the means of Lanny and Irma's getting married in a hurry. They mightn't have got married at all, and there wouldn't have been any honeymoon cruise to New York, or any Baby Frances, or any floating dairy farm! In short, if that business card, "*Johannes Robin, Agent, Maatschappij voor Electrische Specialiteiten, Rotterdam,*" had stayed covered up by Lanny Budd's neckties and handkerchiefs most of Lanny's life would have been missing!

VI

Two happy members of the prosperous classes welcoming five of their intimate friends on the platform of a railroad station. Everybody there knew who the Budds were, and knew that when they hugged and kissed people, and laughed and chatted with them gaily, the people must be wealthy and famous like themselves. A pleasant thing to have friends whom you can love and appreciate, and who will love and appreciate you. Pleasant also to have villas and motorcars and yachts; but many people do not have them, and do not have many dear friends. They know themselves to be dull and undistinguished, and feel themselves to be lonely; they stand and watch

with a sad envy the behavior of the fortunate classes on those few
occasions when they condescend to manifest their feelings in public.

Johannes Robin was the perfect picture of a man who has known
how to make use of his opportunities in this world. His black over-
coat of the finest cloth lined with silk; his black Homburg hat; his
neatly trimmed little black mustache and imperial; his fine leather
traveling-bags with many labels; his manner of quiet self-possession;
his voice that seemed to be caressing you—everything about him
was exactly right. He had sought the best of both body and mind
and knew how to present it to the rest of the world. You would
never hear him say: "Look at what I, Johannes Robin, have achieved!"
No, he would say: "What an extraordinary civilization, in which a
child who sat on the mud floor of a hut in a ghetto and recited ancient Hebrew texts while scratching his flea-bites has been able in
forty years to make so much money!" He would add: "I'm not
sure that I'm making the best use of it. What do you think?" That
flattered you subtly.

As for Mama Robin, there wasn't much you could do for her in
the way of elegance. You could employ the most skillful *couturier*
and give him *carte blanche* as to price, but Leah, wife of Jascha
Rabinowich, would remain a Yiddishe mother, now a grandmother;
a bit dumpier every year, and with no improvement in her accent,
whether it was Dutch or German or English she was speaking. All
she had was kindness and devotion, and if that wasn't enough you
would move on to some other part of the room.

The modern practice of easy divorces and remarriages makes com-
plications for genealogists. Lanny had grown tired of explaining
about his two half-sisters, and had taken to calling them sisters, and
letting people figure it out. The name of Marceline Detaze made it
plain that she was the daughter of the painter who had been killed
in the last months of the war; also it was possible to guess that Bessie
Budd Robin was the daughter of Lanny's father in New England.
On that stern and rock-bound coast her ancestors had won a hard
and honest living; so Bess was tall and her features were thin and
had conscientiousness written all over them. Her straight brown
hair was bobbed, and she wore the simplest clothes which the style-

makers would allow to come into the shops. She was twenty-two and had been married four years, but had put off having children because of her determination to play accompaniments for Hansi in exactly the way he wanted them.

Very touching to see how she watched every step he took, and managed him exactly as her mother at home managed a household. She carried his violin case and wouldn't let him pick up a suitcase; those delicate yet powerful fingers must be devoted to the stopping of violin strings or the drawing of a bow. Hansi was a piece of tone-producing machinery; when they went on tour he was bundled up and delivered on a platform, and then bundled up and carried to a hotel and put to bed. Hansi's face of a young Jewish saint, Hansi's soulful dark eyes, Hansi's dream of loveliness embodied in sound, drove the ladies quite beside themselves; they listened with hands clasped together, they rushed to the platform and would have thrown themselves at his feet, to say nothing of his head. But there was that erect and watchful-eyed granddaughter of the Puritans, with a formula which she said as often as it was called for: "I do everything for my husband that he requires—absolutely *everything!*"

The other members of the party were Freddi Robin's wife, and her baby boy, a month older than little Frances. Freddi was at the University of Berlin, hoping to get a degree in economics. Rahel, a serious, gentle girl, contributed a mezzo-soprano voice to the choir of the yacht; also she led in singing choruses. With two pianos, a violin, a clarinet, and Mr. Dingle's mouth-organ, they could sail the Mediterranean in safety, being able to drown out the voices of any sirens who might still be sitting on its rocky shores.

VII

If music be the food of love, play on! They were gathered in Lanny's studio at Bienvenu, which had been built for Marcel and in which he had done his best work as a painter. There were several of his works on the walls, and a hundred or so stored in a back room. The piano was the big one which Lanny had purchased for Kurt Meissner and which he had used for seven years before going back to Germany. The studio was lined with bookcases containing the library of Lanny's great-great-uncle. Here were all sorts of memories of the dead, and hopes of the living, with cabinets of music-scores in which both kinds of human treasures had been embodied and preserved. Hansi and Bess were playing Tchaikovsky's great concerto, which meant so much to them. Hansi had rendered it at his debut in Carnegie Hall, with Bess and her parents in the audience; a critical occasion for the anxious young lovers.

Next evening they went over to Sept Chênes to meet a distinguished company, most of the fashionable people who had not yet left the Côte d'Azur. The whole family went, including Irma and Rahel. Since it was only a fifteen-minute drive from Bienvenu, the young nursing mothers might have three hours and a half of music and social life; but they mustn't get excited. The two of them heartened each other, making bovine life a bit more tolerable. The feat they were performing was considered picturesque, a harmless eccentricity about which the ladies gossiped; the older ones mentioned it to their husbands, but the younger ones kept quiet, not wishing to put any notions into anybody's head. No Rousseau in our family, thank you!

Hansi and Bess played Lalo's *Symphonie Espagnole*, a composition which audiences welcome and which has to be in the repertoire of every virtuoso: a melancholy and moving *andante* over which the ladies may sigh; a *scherzando* to which young hearts may dance over flower-strewn meadows. It was no holiday for Bess, who wasn't sure if she was good enough for this fastidious company; but she got through it all right and received her share of compliments. Lanny, who knew the music well, permitted his eyes to roam over the audience, and wondered what they were making of it, behind the well-constructed masks they wore. What to them was the meaning of these flights of genius, these incessant calls to the human spirit, these unremitting incitements to ecstasy? Whose feet were swift enough to trip among these meadows? Whose spring was high enough to leap upon these mountain-tops? Who wept for these dying worlds? Who marched in these triumphal processions, celebrating the birth of new epochs?

The thirty-year-old Lanny Budd had come to understand his world, and no longer cherished any illusions concerning the ladies and gentlemen at a *soirée musicale*. Large, well-padded matrons who had been playing bridge all afternoon, and had spent so many hours choosing the fabrics, the jeweled slippers, the necklaces, brooches, and tiaras which made up their splendid ensemble—what fairy feet did they have, even in imagination? What tears did they shed for the lost hopes of mankind? There was Beauty's friend, Madame de Sarcé, with two marriageable daughters and an adored only son who had squandered their fortune in the gambling-palaces. Lanny doubted if any one of the family was thinking about music.

And these gentlemen, with their black coats and snowy shirt-fronts in which their valets had helped to array them—what tumults of exultation thrilled their souls tonight? They had all dined well, and more than one looked drowsy. Others fixed their eyes upon the smooth bare backs of the ladies in front of them. Close to the musicians sat Graf Hohenstauffen, monocled German financier, wearing a pleased smile all through the surging *finale;* Lanny had heard him tell Johannes Robin that he had just come from a broker's office where he had got the closing New York prices. In this April of 1930 there was a phenomenon under way which was being called "the little bull market"; things were picking up again, and the speculators were full of enthusiasms. Was the Graf converting Hansi's frenzied runs on the violin into movements of stocks and bonds?

However, there might be somebody who understood, some lonely heart that hid its griefs and lived in secret inner happiness. Someone who sat silent and abstracted after the performance, too shy to approach the players and thank them; who would go out with fresh hopes for a world in which such loveliness had been embodied in sound. In any case, Hansi and Bess had done their duty by their hostess, a white-haired *grande dame* who would always seem wonderful to them because it was in her château near Paris that they had met and been revealed each to the other.

VIII

It was considered a social triumph, but it was not sufficient for young people tinged with all the hues between pink and scarlet. In the Old Town of Cannes, down near the harbor, dwelt members of depressed classes, among whom Lanny had been going for years, teaching his ideas in a strange, non-religious Sunday school, helping with his money to found a center of what was called "workers' education." He had made many friends here, and had done all he could to break down the social barriers. As a result, the waiter in some fashionable café would say: *"Bon soir,* Comrade Lanny!" When he got out of his car to enter the Casino, or the Cercle Nautique, or some other smart place, he would be delayed by little street urchins running up to shake hands or even to throw their arms about him.

What would these people feel if they knew that the famous violinist who was Lanny's brother-in-law had come to town and given a recital for the rich but had neglected the poor? Unthinkable to go sailing off in a luxurious pleasure yacht without even greeting the class-conscious workers! Lanny's Socialist friend Raoul Palma, who conducted the school, had been notified of the expected visit, and had engaged a suitable hall and printed leaflets for the little street urchins to distribute. When Hansi Robin played in concert halls the rich paid as much as a hundred francs to hear him, but the workers would hear him for fifty centimes, less than a cent and a half in American money. From the point of view of Hansi's business manager it was terrible; but Hansi was a rich man's son and must be allowed to have his eccentricities. Wherever he went, the word would spread, and working-class leaders would come and beg his help. He was young and strong, and wanted to practice anyway, so why not do it on a platform for this most appreciative kind of audience?

Perhaps it was because they knew he was a "comrade," and read into his music things which were not there. Anyhow, they made a demonstration out of it, they took him to their hearts, they flew with him upon the wings of song to that happy land of the future where all men would be brothers and poverty and war only an evil memory. Hansi played no elaborate composition for them, he performed no technical feats; he played simple, soul-warming music: the *adagio* from one of the Bach solo sonatas, followed by Scriabin's *Prelude*, gently solemn, with very lovely double-stopping. Then he added bright and gay things: Percy Grainger's arrangement of *Molly on the Shore*, and when they begged for more he led them into a riot with Bazzini's *Goblins' Dance*. Those goblins squeaked and squealed, they gibbered and chattered; people had never dreamed that such weird sounds could come out of a violin or anything else, and they could hardly contain their laughter and applause until the goblins had fled to their caverns or wherever they go when they have worn themselves out with dancing.

When it was late, and time to quit, Bess struck the opening chords of the *Internationale*. It is the work of a Frenchman, and, pink or scarlet or whatever shade in between, everybody in that crowded hall seemed to know the words; it was as if a charge of electricity had passed through the chairs on which they sat. They leaped to their feet and burst into singing, and you could no longer hear the violin. "Arise, ye prisoners of starvation; arise, ye wretched of the earth!" The workers crowded about the platform, and if Hansi had let them they would have carried him, and Lanny, and Bess too, out to their car, and perhaps have hauled the car all the way to the Cap d'Antibes.

IX

The trim white *Bessie Budd* crept slowly beyond the breakwater of Cannes and through the Golfe Juan, passing that group of buildings with the red-tiled roofs which had been Lanny Budd's home since his earliest memory. Now for several months the yacht was to be his home. It carried five members and a small fraction of the Robin family—if that be the way to count an infant—and four members and two fractions of the Budd family: Lanny, his wife, and their baby; Beauty, her husband, and her daughter. This was the twelve-year-old Marceline's first yacht trip, and with her came the devoted English governess, Miss Addington; also Miss Severne, to look after

Baby Frances, with one of the nursemaids assisting. Finally there was
Madame Zyszynski and, it was hoped, Tecumseh with his troop of
spirits, requiring no cabin-space.

A windless morning, the sea quite still, and the shore quite close.
The course was eastward, and the Riviera glided past them like an
endless panorama. Lanny, to whom it was as familiar as his own garden, stood by the rail and pointed out the landmarks to his friends.
A most agreeable way of studying both geography and history!
Amusing to take the glasses and pick out the places where he had
played tennis, danced, and dined. Presently there was Monte Carlo,
a little town crowded onto a rock. Lanny pointed out the hotel of
Zaharoff, the munitions king, and said: "It's the time when he sits
out in the sunshine on those seats." They searched, but didn't see
any old gentleman with a white imperial! Presently it was Menton,
and Lanny said: "The villa of Blasco Ibáñez." He had died recently,
an exile from the tyranny in Spain. Yes, it was history, several thousand years of it along this shore.

Then came Italy; the border town where a young Socialist had
been put out of the country for trying to protest against the murder
of Matteotti. Then San Remo, where Lanny had attended the first international conference after the peace of Versailles. Much earlier,
when Lanny had been fourteen, he had motored all the way down
to Naples, in company with a manufacturer of soap from Reubens,
Indiana. Lanny would always feel that he knew the Middle Western
United States through the stories of Ezra Hackabury, who had carried little sample cakes of Bluebird Soap wherever he traveled over
Europe, giving them away to beggar children, who liked their smell
but not their taste. Carrara with its marbles had reminded Ezra of
the new postoffice in his home town, and when he saw the leaning
tower of Pisa he had remarked that he could build one of steel that
would lean further, but what good would it do?

A strange coincidence: while Lanny was sitting on the deck telling stories to the Robin family, Lanny's mother and her husband
had gone to the cabin of Madame Zyszynski to find out whether
Tecumseh, the Indian "control," had kept his promise and followed
her to the yacht. The Polish woman went into her trance, and right

away there came the powerful voice supposed to be Iroquois, but having a Polish accent. Tecumseh said that a man was standing by his side who gave the name of Ezra, and the other name began with H, but his voice was feeble and Tecumseh couldn't get it; it made him think of a butcher. No, the man said that he cleaned people, not animals. He knew Lanny and he knew Italy. Ask Lanny if he remembered—what was it?—something about smells in the Bay of Naples and about a man who raised angleworms. Mr. Dingle, doing the questioning, asked what that meant, but Tecumseh declared that the spirit had faded away.

So there was one of those incidents which cause the psychical researchers to prepare long reports. Beauty thought of Ezra Hackabury right away, but she didn't know that Lanny was up on the deck telling the Robins about him, nor did she know how the Bluebird Soap man had cited the smells of the Naples waterfront as proof that romance and charm in Italy were mostly fraudulent. But Lanny remembered well, and also that the gentleman from Indiana had told him about the strange occupation of raising angleworms and planting them in the soil to keep it porous.

What were you going to make out of such an episode? Was Mr. Hackabury really there? Was he dead? Lanny hadn't heard from him for years. He sat down and wrote a letter, to be mailed at Genoa, not mentioning anything about spirits, but saying that he was on his way to Naples, planning to retrace the cruise of the yacht *Bluebird*, and did his old friend remember the drive they had taken and the smells of the bay? And how was the man who raised angleworms making out? Lanny added: "Let me know how you are, for my mother and I often talk about your many kindnesses to us." He hoped that, if Ezra Hackabury was dead, some member of his family might be moved to reply.

X

They went ashore at Genoa, to inspect that very ancient city. They had in Lanny a cicerone who had wandered about the streets during several weeks of the Genoa Conference. A spice of excite-

ment was added by the fact that he wouldn't be allowed to enter
the country if he were identified. But local officers would hardly
know about that old-time misadventure, or cross-question fashionable people coming ashore from a private yacht; they could hardly
check every tourist by the records of the Fascist *militi* in Rome.

No question was raised. Italy was a poor country, and visitors
brought much-needed foreign exchange; the richer they were, the
more welcome—a rule that holds good in most parts of the world.
They engaged three cars and were driven about the town, which
is crowded between mountains and sea, and since it cannot float on
the latter is forced to climb the former. Ancient tall buildings
jammed close together; churches having façades with stripes of
white and black marble, and inside them monotonous paintings of
sorrowful Italian women with infants in their arms. Before the
shrines were wax images of parts of the body which had been
miraculously healed, displays not usually seen outside of hospitals.
Mr. Dingle might have been interested, but he had a deep-seated
prejudice against the Catholic system, which he called idolatrous.
Mr. Hackabury had had the same idea.

Lanny showed them the old Palazzo di San Giorgio, where the
conference had been held, a dingy and depressing place, in keeping
with the results of the assemblage. Lloyd George had made the
most inspiring promises of peace and prosperity to the representatives of twenty-nine nations; after which, behind the scenes, the
leaders had spent six weeks wrangling over what oil concessions
the Russians were to make to what nations. Lanny's father had been
here, trying to get a share; it had been his first fiasco, and the beginning of a chain of them for all parties concerned. Instead of peace
the nations had got more armaments and more debts. Instead of
prosperity had come a financial collapse in Wall Street, and all
were trembling lest it spread to the rest of the world.

XI

All this wasn't the most cheerful line of conversation for a sight-
seeing jaunt; so Lanny talked about some of the journalists and

writers whom he had met at this conference, and forbore to refer to the tragic episode which had cut short his stay in Genoa. But later, when Irma and Rahel had gone back to the yacht, he went for a stroll with Hansi and Bess, and they talked about the Italian Syndicalist leader who had set them to thinking on the subject of social justice. The young Robins looked upon Barbara Pugliese as a heroine and working-class martyr, cherishing her memory as the Italians cherish that virgin mother whose picture they never grow tired of painting. But the Fascist terror had wiped out every trace of Barbara's organization, and to have revealed sympathy for her would have exposed an Italian to exile and torture on those barren Mediterranean islands which Mussolini used as concentration camps.

When you talked about things like this you lost interest in ancient buildings and endlessly multiplied Madonnas. You didn't want to eat any of the food of this town, or pay it any foreign exchange; you wanted to shake its polluted dust from your feet. But the older people were here to entertain themselves with sight-seeing; so, take a walk, climb the narrow streets up into the hills where the flowers of springtime were thick and the air blew from the sea. These gifts of nature were here before the coming of the miserable Fascist braggart, and would remain long after he had become a stench in the nostrils of history. Try not to hate his strutting Blackshirts with their shiny boots, and pistols and daggers in their belts; think of them as misguided children, destined some day to pay with their blood for their swagger and bluster. "Father, forgive them, for they know not what they do!"

And when you come down from the heights and get on board the yacht again, keep your thoughts to your own little group, and say nothing to your elders, who have grown up in a different world. You cannot convert them; you can only worry them and spoil their holiday. Play your music, read your books, think your own thoughts, and never let yourselves be drawn into an argument! Not an altogether satisfactory way of life, but the only one possible in times when the world is changing so fast that parents and children may be a thousand years apart in their ideas and ideals.

3

And Their Adoption Tried

I

THE trim white *Bessie Budd* was among the Isles of Greece, where burning Sappho loved and sung, and where Lanny at the age of fourteen had fished and swum and climbed hills and gazed upon the ruins of ancient temples. The yacht stole through the Gulf of Corinth and made fast to a pier in the harbor of the Piraeus, now somewhat improved; the guests were motored to the city of Athens, and ascended the hill of the Acropolis on little donkeys which had not been improved in any way. They gazed at the most famous of all ruins, and Lanny told them about Isadora Duncan dancing here, and how she had explained to the shocked police that it was her way of praying.

The *Bessie Budd* anchored in the Channel of Atalante, and the experienced Lanny let down fishing-lines and brought up odd-appearing creatures which had not changed in sixteen years, and perhaps not in sixteen million. The guests were rowed ashore at several towns, and drank over-sweet coffee out of copper pots with long handles, and gazed at the strange spectacle of tall men wearing accordion-pleated and starched white skirts like those of ballet-dancers. They climbed the hills surmounted by ancient temples, and tried to talk in sign language to shepherds having shelters of brush built into little cones.

History had been made in these waters between Lanny's visits. German submarines had lurked here, British and French craft had hunted them, and a bitter duel of intrigue had been carried on over the part which Greece was to play. The Allies had landed an army at Salonika, and the *Bessie Budd* now followed in the wake of their

transports; her guests were driven about in a dusty old city of narrow crooked streets and great numbers of mosques with towering
minarets. The more active members of the party wandered over the
hills where the armies of Alexander had marched to the conquest of
Persia; through which the Slavs had come in the seventh century,
followed by Bulgars, Saracens, Gauls, Venetians, Turks.

There are people who have a sense of the past; they are stirred by
the thought of it, and by the presence of its relics; there are others
who have very little of this sense, and would rather play a game of
bridge than climb a hill to see where a battle was fought or a goddess
was worshiped. Lanny discovered that his wife was among these
latter. She was interested in the stories he told the company, but only
mildly, and while he and Hansi were studying the fragments of a
fallen column, Irma would be watching the baby lambs gamboling
among the spring flowers. "Oh, how charming!" Observing one of
them beginning to nuzzle its mother, she would look at her wristwatch and say: "Don't forget that we have to be back on board in
an hour." Lanny would return to the world of now, and resume the
delights of child study which he had begun long ago with Marceline.

II

When you live day and night on a yacht, in close contact with
your fellow-guests, there isn't much they can hide from you. It was
Lanny's fourth cruise with a Jewish man of money, but still he did
not tire of studying a subtle and complex personality. Johannes
Robin was not merely an individual; he was a race and a culture, a
religion and a history of a large part of human society for several
thousand years. To understand him fully was a problem not merely
in psychology, but in business and finance, in literature and language,
ethnology, archaeology—a list of subjects about which Lanny was
curious.

This man of many affairs could be tender-hearted as a child, and
again could state flatly that he was not in business for his health.
He could be frank to the point of dubious taste, or he could be

devious as any of the diplomats whom Lanny had watched at a dozen international conferences. He would drive a hard bargain, and then turn around and spend a fortune upon hospitality to that same person. He was bold, yet he was haunted by fears. He ardently desired the approval of his fellows, yet he would study them and pass judgments indicating that their opinion was not worth so very much. Finally, with his keen mind he observed these conflicts in himself, and to Lanny, whom he trusted, he would blurt them out in disconcerting fashion.

They were sitting on deck after the others had gone to bed; a still night, and the yacht gliding through the water with scarcely a sound. Suddenly the host remarked: "Do you know what this show costs every hour?"

"I never tried to estimate," said the guest, taken aback.

"You wouldn't, because you've always had money. I figured it up last night—about a hundred dollars every hour of the day or night It cost me several hours' sleep to realize it."

There was a pause. Lanny didn't know what to say.

"It's a weakness; I suppose it's racial. I can't get over the fear of spending so much!"

"Why do you do it, then?"

"I force myself to be rational. What good is money if you hoard it? My children don't want it, and their children won't know how to use it; and, anyhow, it mayn't last. I assume that I give my friends some pleasure, and I don't do any harm that I can think of. Can you?"

"No," replied the other.

"Of course I shouldn't mention it," said the host, "but you like to understand people."

"We'd all be happier if we did," replied Lanny. "I, too, am conscious of weaknesses. If I happened to be in your position, I would be trying to make up my mind whether I had a right to own a yacht."

III

Lanny went to bed thinking about this "racial" peculiarity. When he had first met Johannes Robin, the salesman had been traveling over Europe with two heavy suitcases full of electric curling-irons and toasters, and a "spiel" about promoting international trade and the spread of civilization. During the war he had made money buying magnetos and such things to be sold in Germany. Then he had gone in with Robbie Budd and bought left-over supplies of the American army. He had sold marks and bought shares in German industry, and now he was sometimes referred to as a "king" of this and that. Doubtless all kings, underneath their crowns and inside their royal robes, were hesitant and worried mortals, craving affection and tormented by fears of poison and daggers, of demons and gods, or, in these modern times, of financial collapses and revolutions.

Jascha Rabinowich had changed his name but had remained a Jew; which meant that he was race-conscious; he was kept that way by contempt and persecution. Part of the time he blustered and part of the time he cringed, but he tried to hide both moods. What he wanted was to be a man like other men, and to be judged according to his merits. But he had had to flee from a pogrom in Russia, and he lived in Germany knowing that great numbers of people despised and hated him; he knew that even in America, which he considered the most enlightened of countries, the people in the slums would call him a "sheeny" and a Christ-killer, while the "best" people would exclude him from their country clubs.

He talked about all this with Lanny, who had fought hard for his sister's right to marry Hansi. People accused the Jews of loving money abnormally. "We are traders," said Johannes. "We have been traders for a couple of thousand years, because we have been driven from our land. We have had to hide in whatever holes we could find in one of these Mediterranean ports, and subsist by buying something at a low price and selling it at a higher price. The penalty of failure being death has sharpened our wits. In a port it often happens that we buy from a person we shall never see again, and sell to some other person under the same conditions; they do not worry much about our welfare, nor we about theirs. That may be a limitation in our morality, but it is easy to understand."

Lanny admitted that he understood it, and his host continued:

"My ancestors were master-traders all the way from Smyrna to Gibraltar while yours were barbarians in the dark northern forests, killing the aurochs with clubs and spears. Naturally our view of life was different from yours. But when you take to commerce, the differences disappear quickly. I have heard that in your ancestral state of Connecticut the Yankee does not have his feelings hurt when you call him slick. You have heard, perhaps, of David Harum, who traded horses."

"I have heard also of Potash and Perlmutter," said Lanny, with a smile.

"It is the same here, all around the shores of this ancient sea which once was the civilized world. The Greeks are considered skillful traders; take Zaharoff, for example. The Turks are not easy to deceive, and I am told that the Armenians can get the better of any race in the world. Always, of course, I am referring to the professional traders, those who live or die by it. The peasant is a different proposition; the primary producer is the predestined victim, whether he is in Connecticut buying wooden nutmegs or in Anatolia receiving coins made of base metal which he will not be clever enough to pass on."

IV

Lanny sat with Madame Zyszynski, but the results he obtained were not of the best. Tecumseh, the noble redskin, was suspicious and inclined to be crotchety; he took offense when one did not accept his word, and Lanny had made the mistake of being too honest. The way to get results was to be like Parsifal Dingle, who welcomed the spirits quite simply as his friends, chatting with them and the "control" in an amiable matter-of-fact way. Apparently it was with the spirits as with healing: except ye be converted, and become as little children! . . .

What Tecumseh would do was to send messages to Lanny through

Parsifal. He would say: "Tell that smart young man that Marcel was here, and that he is painting spirit pictures, much more wonderful than anything he ever did on earth—but they will never be sold at auctions." Lanny wanted to know if Marcel objected to having his works sold; but for a long time the painter ignored his question. Then one day Tecumseh said, rather grudgingly, that it didn't really matter to Marcel; everything was sold in Lanny's world, and it was no use keeping beautiful things in a storeroom. This sounded as if the spirit world was acquiring a "pinkish" tinge.

Madame gave several séances every day. She had done it while she was earning her living on Sixth Avenue, and insisted that it didn't hurt her. She would accommodate anyone who was interested, and presently she was delving into the past of the Rabinowich family, telling about those members who had "passed over." It was a bit unsatisfactory, for there were many members of that family, and Jascha had lost track of them; he said that he never heard from them except when someone needed money for some worthy purpose, and all purposes were worthy. He said that the way to check on the identity of any member of his family in the spirit world would be that he was asking for money to be given to a son or daughter, a nephew or niece still on earth!

But there had been indeed an Uncle Nahum, who had peddled goods in Russian-Polish villages, and had been clubbed to death by the Black Hundreds. The realistic details of this event sounded convincing to Mama Robin, who had witnessed such an incident as a child and still had nightmares now and then as a result. Then it was Jascha's own father talking to him; when he mentioned that his beard had turned white faster on one side than on the other, and how he had kept his money hidden under a loose brick in the hearth, Lanny saw his urbane host look startled. Johannes said afterward that he had thought all this must be a fraud of some sort, but now he didn't know what to think. It was really unthinkable.

So it went on, all over the pleasure vessel. The gray-bearded and heavy-minded Captain Moeller condescended to try the experiment, and found himself in conversation with his eldest son, who had been a junior officer on a U-boat, and told how it felt to be suffocated at the bottom of the sea. Baby Frances's nursemaid, a girl with a Cockney accent who had got a few scraps of education at a "council school," learned to sit for long periods talking with her father, a Tommy who had been killed on the Somme, and who told her all about his early life, the name of the pub where he had made bets on horse races, and where his name was still chalked up on a board, along with that of other dead soldiers of the neighborhood.

How did Madame Zyszynski get such things? You could say that she sneaked about in the yacht and caught scraps of conversation, and perhaps rummaged about in people's cabins. But it just happened that she didn't. She was a rather dull old woman who had been first a servant and then the wife of the butler to a Warsaw merchant. She suffered from varicose veins and dropsy in its early stages. She understood foreign languages with difficulty and didn't bother to listen most of the time, but preferred to sit in her own cabin playing endless games of solitaire. When she read, it was the pictures in some cheap magazine, and the strange things she did in her trances really didn't interest her overmuch; she would answer your questions as best she could, but hardly ever asked any of you. She declared again and again that she did these things because she was poor and had to earn her living. She insisted, furthermore, that she had never heard the voice of Tecumseh, and knew about him only what her many clients had told her.

But what a different creature was this Indian chieftain! He was not the Tecumseh of history, he said, but an Iroquois of the same name. His tribe had been all but wiped out by smallpox. Now he ruled a tribe of spirits, and amused himself at the expense of his former enemies, the whites. He was alert, masterful, witty, shrewd— and if there was anything he didn't know, he would tell you to come back tomorrow and perhaps he would have it for you. But you had to be polite. You had to treat him as a social equal, and the best way to get along was to be a humble petitioner. "Please, Tecumseh, see if you can do me this great favor!"

V

What did it all mean? Was this really the spirit of an American aborigine dead more than two hundred years? Lanny didn't think so. After reading a number of books and pondering over it for months, he had decided that Tecumseh was a genius; something of the sort which had worked in William Shakespeare, producing a host of characters which the world accepted as more real than living people. In the case of the poet, this genius had been hitched up with his conscious mind, so that the poet knew what it was doing and could put the characters into plays and sell them to managers. But the genius in Madame Zyszynski wasn't hitched up; it stayed hidden in her unconscious and worked there on its own; a wild genius, so to speak, a subterranean one. What, old mole, work'st i' the earth so fast!

This energy played at being an Indian; also it gathered facts from the minds of various persons and wove stories out of them. It dipped into the subconscious mind of Lanny Budd and collected his memories and made them into the spirit of Marcel Detaze, painting pictures on the Cap d'Antibes or looking at ruins in ancient Greece. It dipped into the mind of Jascha Rabinowich and created the spirits of his relatives. Like children finding old costumes in a trunk, putting them on and making up stories about people they have heard of or read of in books—people alive or dead! Every child knows that you have to pretend that it's true, otherwise it's no fun, the imagination doesn't work. If you put on a bearskin, get down on your hands and knees and growl. If you put on the headdress of an Indian chieftain, stalk about the room and command the other children in a deep stern voice—even if it has a Polish accent!

All this seemed to indicate that there was some sort of universal pool of mindstuff, an ocean in which Lanny's thoughts and Madame Zyszynski's and other people's merged and flowed together. Figure yourself as a bubble floating on the surface of an ocean; the sun shines on you and you have very lovely colors; other bubbles float near, and you come together and form a cluster of bubbles—the guests of the yacht *Bessie Budd,* for example. One by one the bubbles break, and their substance returns to the ocean, and in due course becomes the substance of new bubbles.

This theory obliged you to believe that a medium had the power to dip into this mind substance and get facts to which the medium did not have access in any normal way. Was it easier to believe that than to believe that the spirits of dead persons were sending communications to the living? Lanny found it so; for he had lived long enough to watch the human mind develop along with the body and to decay along with it. In some strange way the two seemed to be bound together and to share the same fate. But don't fool yourself into thinking that you knew what the nature of that union was; how a thought could make a muscle move, or how a chemical change in the body could produce cheerful or depressed thoughts. Those questions were going to take wiser men than Lanny Budd to answer them; he kept wishing that people would stop robbing and killing one another and settle down to this task of finding out what they really were.

VI

The hundred-dollar-an-hour cruise was continued eastward, and presently they were approaching the Peninsula of Gallipoli, where so many Englishmen had paid with their lives for the blundering of their superiors. Great ships had gone down, and the beaches had been piled with mangled bodies. Among the many wounded had been the father of Lanny's *amie*, Rosemary Codwilliger, Countess of Sandhaven. He had "passed over" not long ago, and Lanny wondered, did his spirit haunt this place? He asked Tecumseh about it, and it wasn't long before Colonel Codwilliger was "manifesting"; but unfortunately Lanny hadn't known him very well, and must write to Rosemary in the Argentine to find out if the statements were correct.

They passed through the Dardanelles on a gusty, rainy afternoon, and the shores looked much like any other shores veiled in mist. Lanny and Bess walked for a while on deck, and then went into the saloon and played the Schubert four-hand piano sonata. Then Lanny came out again, for somewhere ahead was the Island of Prinkipo which had been so much in his thoughts at the Peace Conference eleven years before. It had been chosen as the place for a meeting with the Bolsheviks, in President Wilson's effort to patch up a truce with them. The elder statesmen had found it difficult to believe there existed a place with such a musical-comedy name.

It might as well have been a musical-comedy performance—such was Lanny's bitter reflection. The statesmen didn't go to Prinkipo, and when later they met the Russians at Genoa they didn't settle anything. They went home to get ready for another war—Lanny was one of those pessimistic persons who were sure it was on the way. He told people so, and they would shrug their shoulders. What could they do about it? What could anybody do? *C'est la nature!*

Perhaps it was the rain which caused these melancholy thoughts; perhaps the spirits of those tens of thousands of dead Englishmen and Turks; or perhaps of the dogs of Constantinople, which during the war had been gathered up and turned loose on this musical-comedy island to starve and devour one another. Under the religion of the country it was not permitted to kill them, so let them eat one another! The Prophet, born among a nomadic people, had loved the dog and praised it as the guardian of the tent; he had endeavored to protect it, but had not been able to foresee great cities with swarms of starveling curs and a dénouement of cannibalism.

The southern hills of this Sea of Marmora had been the scene of events about which Lanny had heard his father talking with Zaharoff. The munitions king had financed the invasion of Turkey by his fellow-Greeks, spending half his fortune on it, so he had said—though of course you didn't have to assume that everything he said was true. Anyhow, the Greeks had been routed and hosts of them driven into the sea, after which the victorious Turkish army had appeared before the British fortifications and the guns of the fleet. This critical situation had brought about the fall of the Lloyd George government and thus played hob with the plans of Robbie Budd for getting oil concessions. Robbie was one of those men who use governments, his own and others', threatening wars and sometimes waging them; while Lanny was an amiable playboy who traveled about on a hundred-dollar-an-hour yacht, making beautiful music, reading books of history and psychic research, and being troubled in his conscience about the way the world was going. He asked his friends very earnestly what ought to be done. Some thought they knew; but the trouble was, their opinions differed so greatly.

VII

The company went ashore in the crowded city, which had once been the capital of the Moslem world, and now was known as Istanbul. They got cars, as usual, and were driven about to see the sights. They visited the great cathedral of St. Sophia, and in the seraglio of the late sultan they inspected the harem, in which now and then a faithless wife had been strangled with a cord, tied in a sack, and set afloat in the Bosporus. They strolled through the bazaars, where traders of various races labored diligently to sell them souvenirs, from Bergama rugs to "feelthy postcards." Through the crowded street came a fire-engine with a great clangor; a modern one, painted a brilliant red—but Lanny saw in imagination the young Zaharoff riding the machine, busy with schemes to collect for his services. Were they still called *tulumbadschi?* And did they still charge to put out your fire—or to let it burn, as you preferred?

The unresting *Bessie Budd* stole northward along the coast of the immensely deep Black Sea, called by the ancient Greeks "friendly to strangers." The Soviet Union was in the middle of the Five-Year Plan, and miracles were confidently expected. The travelers' goal was Odessa, a city with a great outdoor stairway which they had seen in a motion picture. Their passports had been visaed and everything arranged in advance; they had only to make themselves known to Intourist, and they would have automobiles and guides and hotels to the limit of their supply of *valuta.*

"I have seen the future and it works." So Lincoln Steffens had said to Lanny Budd. Stef had had the eyes of faith, and so had Hansi and Bess and Rahel. When they looked at buildings much in need of repair and people wearing sneakers and patched sweaters, they said: "Wait till the new factories get going." They told the girl guides that they were "comrades," and they were taken off to inspect the latest styles in day nurseries and communal kitchens. They were motored into the country to visit a co-operative farm; when Hansi was asked about his occupation at home, he admitted that he was a violinist, and the people rushed to provide an instrument. All work on the place stopped while he stood on the front porch and played *Old Folks at Home* and *Kathleen Mavourneen* and Achron's *Hebrew Melody*. It was heart-warming; but would it help get tractors and reapers into condition for the harvest soon to be due?

VIII

Irma went on some of these expeditions, and listened politely to the enthusiasms of her friends; but to Mama Robin she confessed that she found "the future" most depressing. Mama shrugged her shoulders and said: "What would you expect? It's Russia." She had learned about it as a child, and didn't believe it could ever be changed. In the days of the Tsar people had been so unhappy they had got drunk and crawled away into some hole to sleep. The Bolsheviks had tried to stop the making of liquor, but the peasants had made it and smuggled it into the towns—"just like in America," said Mama. She would have preferred not to have these painful old memories revived.

Odessa had changed hands several times during the revolution and civil war. It had been bombarded by the French fleet, and many of its houses destroyed. One of the sights of the city was the Square of the Victims, where thousands of slain revolutionists had been buried in a common grave, under a great pyramid of stones. The young people went to it as to a shrine, while their elders sought entertainment without success. The young ones insisted upon visiting some of the many sanatoriums, which are built near bodies of water formed by silted-up river mouths. These too were shrines, because they were occupied by invalided workers. That was the way it was going to be in the future; those who produced the wealth would enjoy it! "They shall not build, and another inhabit; they shall not plant, and another eat." Thus the ancient Hebrew prophet, and it sounded so Red that in Canada a clergyman had been indicted by the grand jury for quoting it. Hansi and Rahel had the blood of these ancient prophets in their veins, and Bess had been taught that their utterances were the word of God, so this new religion came easily to them. It promised to save the workers, and Lanny hoped it would have better success than Mohammed had had in his efforts to help the watch-dogs of the tents.

Lanny was in his usual position, between the two sets of extremists. During this Russian visit he served as a sort of liaison officer to the Robin family. Johannes didn't dare to discuss Communism with any of his young people, for he had found that by doing so he injured his standing; he talked with Lanny, hoping that something could be done to tone them down. In the opinion of the man of money, this Bolshevik experiment was surviving on what little fat it had accumulated during the old regime. People could go on living in houses so long as they stood up, and they could wear old clothes for decades if they had no sense of shame—look about you! But the making of new things was something else again. Of course, they could hire foreign experts and have factories built, and call it a Five-Year Plan—but who was going to do any real work if he could put it off on somebody else? And how could any business enterprise be run by politicians? "You don't know them," said Johannes, grimly. "In Germany I have had to."

"It's an experiment," Lanny admitted. "Too bad it had to be tried in such a backward country."

"All I can say," replied the man of affairs, "is I'm hoping it doesn't have to be tried in any country where I live!"

IX

This was a situation which had been developing in the Robin family for many years, ever since Barbara Pugliese and Jesse Blackless had explained the ideals of proletarian revolution to the young Robins in Lanny's home: an intellectual vaccination which had taken with unexpected virulence. Lanny had watched with both curiosity and concern the later unfoldment of events. He knew how Papa and Mama Robin adored their two boys, centering all their hopes upon them. Papa made money in order that Hansi and Freddi might be free from the humiliations and cares of poverty. Papa and Mama watched their darlings with solicitude, consulting each other as to their every mood and wish. Hansi wanted to play the fiddle; very well, he should be a great musician, with the best teachers, everything to make smooth his path. Freddi wished to be a scholar, a learned person; very well, Papa would pay for everything, and give up his natural desire to have the help of one of his sons in his own business.

It had seemed not surprising that young people should be set afire with hopes of justice for the poor, and the ending of oppression and war. Every Jew in the world knows that his ancient prophets proclaimed such a millennium, the coming of such a Messiah. If Hansi and Freddi were excessive in their fervor, well, that was to be expected at their age. As they grew older, they would acquire discretion and learn what was possible in these days. The good mother and the hard-driving father waited for this, but waited in vain. Here was Hansi twenty-five, and his brother only two years younger, and instead of calming down they appeared to be acquiring a mature determination, with a set of theories or dogmas or whatever you chose to call them, serving as a sort of backbone for their dreams.

To the Jewish couple out of the ghetto the marriage of Hansi to Robbie Budd's daughter had appeared a great triumph, but in the course of time they had discovered there was a cloud to this silver lining. Bess had caught the Red contagion from Hansi, and brought to the ancient Jewish idealism a practicality which Johannes recognized as Yankee, a sternness derived from her ancestral Puritanism. Bess was the reddest of them all, and the most uncompromising. Her expression would be full of pity and tenderness, but it was all for those whom she chose to regard as the victims of social injustice. For those others who held them down and garnered the fruits of their toil she had a dedicated antagonism; when she talked about capitalism and its crimes her face became set, and you knew her for the daughter of one of Cromwell's Ironsides.

Lanny understood that in the depths of his soul Johannes quailed before this daughter-in-law. He tried to placate her with soft words, he tried to bribe her with exactly the right motor-car, a piano of the most exquisite tone, yachting-trips to the most romantic places of the seven seas, and not a single person on board who would oppose her ideas; only the members of her own two families and their attendants. "Look!" the poor man of millions seemed to be saying. "Here is Rahel with a baby who has to be nursed, and here is the lovely baby of your adored brother; here is this ship of dreams which exists for the happiness of all of you. It will go wherever you wish, and the service will be perfect; you can even break the rules of discipline at sea, you and Hansi can go into the forecastle and play music for the crew, or invite them up into the saloon once a week and play for them—in spite of the horror of an old martinet trained in the merchant marine of Germany. Anything, anything on earth, provided you will be gracious, and forgive me for being a millionaire, and not despise me because I have wrung my fortune out of the toil and sweat of the wage-slaves!"

This program of appeasement had worked for four years, for the reason that Bess had laid hold of the job of becoming a pianist. She had concentrated her Puritan fanaticism upon acquiring muscular power and co-ordination, in combining force with delicacy, so that the sounds she produced would not ruin the fine nuances, the exquisite variations of tone, which her more highly trained husband was achieving. But Johannes knew in his soul that this task wasn't going to hold her forever; some day she and Hansi both would consider themselves musicians—and they meant to be Red musicians, to play for Red audiences and earn money for the Red cause. They would make for themselves the same sort of reputation that Isadora Duncan had made by waving red scarves at her audiences and dancing the *Marseillaise*. They would plunge into the hell of the class struggle, which everyone could see growing hotter day by day all over Europe.

X

Besides Mama, the only person to whom Johannes Robin unbosomed himself of these anxieties was Lanny Budd, who had always been so wise beyond his years, a confidant at the age of fourteen, a counselor and guide at the age of nineteen. Lanny had brought Johannes together with his father, and listened to their schemes, and knew many of the ins and outs of their tradings. He knew that Johannes had been selling Budd machine guns to Nazi agents, to be used in the open warfare these people carried on with the Communists in the streets of Berlin. Johannes had asked Lanny never to mention this to the boys, and Lanny had obliged him. What would they do if they found it out? They might refuse to live any longer in the Berlin palace, or to travel in the hundred-dollar-an-hour yacht. Bess might even refuse to let it carry her name. Thus Jascha Rabinowich, standing in front of his private wailing wall. *Oi, oi!*

He was in the position only too familiar to the members of his race through two thousand years of the Diaspora: surrounded by enemies, and having to play them one against another, to placate them by subtle arts. Johannes had risen to power by his shrewdness as a speculator, knowing whom to pay for inside information and how to separate the true from the false. Having made huge sums out of the collapse of the mark, he had bought up concerns which were on the verge of bankruptcy. To hold them and keep them going meant, in these days of governmental interference with business, some sort of alliance with politicians; it meant paying them money which was close to blackmail and became ever closer as time passed. It meant not merely knowing the men who were in power, but guessing who might be in power next week, and making some sort of deal with them.

So it came about that Johannes was helping to maintain the coalition government of the Republic and at the same time supporting several of the ambitious Nazis; for, under the strain of impending national bankruptcy, who could tell what might happen? Knowing that his children were in touch with the Reds, and continually being importuned for money—who wasn't, that had money?—Johannes

would give them generous sums, knowing that they would pass
these on to be used for their "cause." Yet another form of insur-
ance! But do not let any of these groups know that you are giving
to the others, for they are in a deadly three-cornered war, each
against the other two.

All this meant anxious days and sleepless nights. And Mama, from
whom nothing could be hidden, would argue: "What is it for?
Why do we need so much money?" It was hard for her to understand that you must get more in order to protect what you had.
She and the children would join in efforts to get Papa away from
it all. For the past three summers they had lured him into a yachting-
trip. This year they had started earlier, on account of the two young
mothers, and they were hoping to keep him away all summer.

But it appeared that troubles were piling up in Berlin: business
troubles, political troubles. Johannes was receiving batches of mail
at the different ports, and he would shut himself up with his secretary and dictate long telegrams. That was one of his complaints
concerning the Soviet Union: letters might be opened, and telegrams were uncertain; you paid for them but couldn't be sure they
would arrive. Everything was in the hands of bureaucrats, and you
were wound up in miles of red tape—God pity the poor people who
had to get a living in such a world. Johannes, man of swift decisions, plowman of his own field, builder of his own road, couldn't
stand Odessa, and asked them to give up seeing the beautiful Sochi.
"There are just as grand palaces near Istanbul, and the long-distance
telephone works!"

XI

The *Bessie Budd* returned in her own wake, and in Istanbul its
owner received more telegrams which worried him. The yacht had
to wait until he sent answers and received more answers, and in the
end he announced that he couldn't possibly go on. There was serious trouble involving one of the banks he controlled. Decisions had
to be made which couldn't be left to subordinates. He had made a
mistake to come away in such unsettled times!—the Wall Street

crash had shaken all Europe, and little by little the cracks were revealing themselves. Johannes had to beg his guests to excuse him. He took a plane for Vienna, and from there to Berlin.

It had come to be that way now; there were planes every day between all the great capitals of Europe. You stepped in, hardly knew that you were flying, and in a few hours stepped out and went about your affairs. Not the slightest danger; but it tormented Mama to think of Jascha up there amid thunder and lightning, and so many things to bump into when you came down. They waited in Istanbul until a telegram arrived, saying that the traveler was safe in his own palace and that Freddi was well and happy, and sent love to all.

It was too late to visit the coast of Africa—the rains had come, and it was hot, and there would be mosquitoes. They made themselves contented on the yacht, and did not bother to go ashore. The dairy farm prospered; the ample refrigerators provided the two young mothers with fresh foods, and they in turn provided for the infants. The grandmothers hovered over the scene in such a flutter of excitement as made you think of humming-birds' wings. Really, it appeared as if there had never been two babies in the world before and never would be again. Grandmothers, mothers, babies, and attendants formed a closed corporation, a secret society, an organization of, by, and for women.

It was a machine that ran as by clockwork, and the balance wheel was the grave Miss Severne. She had been employed to manage only Baby Frances; but she was so highly educated, so perfectly equipped, that she overawed the Robins; she was the voice of modern science, speaking the last word as to the phenomena of infancy. Equally important, she had the English manner, she was Britannia which rules the waves and most of the shores; she was authority, and the lesser breeds without the law decided to come in. What one grandmother was forbidden to do was obviously bad form for the other to do; what little Frances's nursemaid was ordered to do was obviously desirable for little Johannes's nursemaid to do. So in the end Jerusalem placed itself under the British flag; Rahel made Miss Severne a present now and then, and she ran the whole enterprise.

Every morning Marceline was in Miss Addington's cabin, reciting her lessons. Mr. Dingle was in his cabin thinking his new thoughts and saying his old prayers. Madame Zyszynski was in hers, playing solitaire, or perhaps giving a "sitting." That left Hansi, Bess, and Lanny in the saloon, the first two working out their interpretation of some great violin classic, and Lanny listening critically while they played a single passage many times, trying the effect of this and that. Just what did Beethoven mean by the repetition of this rhythmic pattern? Here he had written *sforzando*, but he often wrote that when he meant *tenuto*, an expressive accent, the sound to be broadened—but be careful, it is a trick which becomes a bad habit, a meretricious device. They would discuss back and forth, but always in the end they deferred to Hansi; he was the one who had the gift, he was the genius who lived music in his soul. Sometimes the spirit caught them, they became not three souls but one, and it was an hour of glory.

These young people could never be bored on the longest yachting-cruise. They took their art with them, a storehouse of loveliness, a complex of ingenuities, a treasure-chest of delights which you could never empty. Lanny had stabbed away at the piano all his life, but now he discovered that he had been skimming over the surface of a deep ocean. Now he analyzed scientifically what before he had enjoyed emotionally. Hansi Robin had had a thorough German training, and had read learned books on harmony, acoustics, the history of music. He studied the personalities of composers, and he tried to present these to his audiences; he did not try to turn Mozart into Beethoven, or Gluck into Liszt. He would practice the most difficult Paganini or Wieniawski stuff, but wouldn't play it in public unless he could find a soul in it. Finger gymnastics were for your own use.

XII

Every afternoon, if the weather was right, the vessel would come to a halt, and the guests, all but Mama Robin, would emerge on the deck in bathing-suits; the gangway would be let down over the side, and they would troop down and plunge into the water. A sailor stood by with a life-belt attached to a rope, in case of accident; they were all good swimmers, but the efficient Captain Moeller took no chances and was always on watch himself. When they had played themselves tired, they would climb up, and the yacht would resume her course. The piano on little rubber wheels would be rolled out from the saloon, and Hansi and Bess would give an alfresco concert; Rahel would sing, and perhaps lead them all in a chorus. Twilight would fall, "the dusk of centuries and of song."

There was only one trouble on this cruise so far as concerned Lanny, and that was the game of bridge. Beauty and Irma had to play; not for money, but for points, for something to do. These ladies knew how to read, in the sense that they knew the meaning of the signs on paper, but neither knew how to lose herself in a book or apply herself to the mastering of its contents. They grew sleepy when they tried it; they wanted other people to tell them what was in books; and Irma at least had always been able to pay for the service. Now she had married a poor man, and understood it to mean that he was to keep her company. In the world of Irma Barnes the nursery rhyme had been turned about, and every Jill must have her Jack.

Lanny didn't really mind playing bridge—only there were so many more interesting things to do. He wanted to continue child study with the two specimens he had on board. He wanted to read history about the places he visited, so that a town would be where a great mind had functioned or a martyr had died. But Beauty and Irma were willing to bid five no trumps while the yacht was passing the scene of the battle of Salamis. They would both think it inconsiderate of Lanny if he refused to make a fourth hand because he wanted to write up his notes of the last séance with Madame Zyszynski. Lanny thought it was important to keep proper records, and index them, so that the statements of Tecumseh on one occasion could be compared with those on another. He had the books of Osty and Geley, scientists who had patiently delved into these phenomena and tried to evolve theories to explain them. This seemed much more important than whether Culbertson was right in his rules about the total honor-trick-content requirement of hands.

Irma had persuaded Rahel to prepare herself for life in the *beau monde,* and Lanny had helped to teach her. Then he had given the same sort of help to Marceline, who was going to be thirteen in a short while, and already was the most perfect little society lady you could imagine. Even on board a yacht she spent much time in front of the mirror, studying her charms and keeping them at their apex; surely she ought to be preparing to defend herself against those harpies with signaling-systems who would soon be trying to deprive her of her pocket-money. After she had been taught, Lanny could plead that he wasn't needed any more, and go back to the study of Liszt's four-hand piano compositions with Bess: the *Concerto Pathétique,* a marvel of brilliant color, turning two pianos into an orchestra; the *Don Juan Fantaisie,* most delightful of showpieces—Hansi came in while they were playing it, and said they really ought to give it on a concert stage. A memorable moment for two humble amateurs.

XIII

The *Bessie Budd* came to rest in the harbor of Cannes, and the company returned to Bienvenu for a few days. Beauty wished to renew her wardrobe—one gets so tired of wearing the same things. Lanny wished to renew the stock of music-scores—one's auditors get tired of hearing the same compositions. Also, there were stacks of magazines which had been coming in, and letters with news of one's friends. Lanny opened one from his father, and exclaimed: "Robbie's coming to Paris! He's due there now!"

"Oh, dear!" said the wife. She knew what was coming next.

"I really ought to see him, Irma. It's been eight months."

"It's been exactly as long since I've seen my mother."

"Surely if your mother were in Paris, I'd be offering to take you."

"It'll be so dreadfully lonesome on the yacht, Lanny!"

"I'll take a plane and join you at Lisbon in three or four days. You know Robbie's been in a crisis and I ought to find out how he's getting along."

Irma gave up, but not without inner revolt. She was going through such a trying ordeal, and people ought to do everything to make it easier for her. A violent change from being the glamour girl of Broadway, the observed of all observers, the darling of the columnists and target of the spotlights—and now to be in exile, almost in jail for all these months! Would anybody ever appreciate it? Would Baby appreciate it? Irma's observation of children suggested that Baby probably would not.

She thought of taking a couple of cars and transporting her half of the lactation apparatus up to Paris. But no, it would upset all the arrangements of the admirable Miss Severne; Baby might pick up a germ in the streets of a crowded city; it was so much safer out at sea, where the air was loaded with a stuff called ozone. And there was Rahel, with whom Irma had agreed to stick it out; knowing it would be hard, she had wanted to tie herself down, and had made a bargain.

"Another thing," Lanny said; "Zoltan Kertezsi should be in Paris and might help me to sell a picture or two."

"Oh, dear!" exclaimed the wife. "Do you still want to fool with that business?"

"A little cash would come in handy to both Beauty and me."

"I don't think it's kind of you, Lanny. There's no sense in your bothering to make money when I have it. If you have any time to sell, do please let me buy it!"

They had talked about this many times. Since Robbie couldn't afford to send Beauty her thousand dollars a month, Irma insisted upon putting it up. She wanted the life of Bienvenu to go on exactly as before. The cost was nothing to her, and she liked the people around her to be happy. She would send money to Lanny's account in Cannes, and then she didn't want anybody to talk or think about the subject. That her husband might actually enjoy earning a few thousand dollars by selling Marcel's paintings, or those of old masters, was something hard for her to make real to herself. It was harder still for Lanny to explain that he sometimes wanted to do other things than entertain an adored young wife!

4

I Can Call Spirits

I

FROM the windows of the Hotel Crillon Lanny Budd had looked
out upon quite a lot of history: the World War beginning, with
soldiers bivouacked in the Place de la Concorde; the war in progress, with enemy planes overhead and anti-aircraft firing; after the
armistice, with a great park of captured German cannon, and May
Day mobs being sabered by cuirassiers. In the hotel had lived and
worked a couple of hundred American peace-makers, all of them
kind to a very young secretary-translator and willing to assist with
his education. The only trouble was, they differed so greatly among
themselves that Lanny's mind had reached a state of confusion from
which it had not yet recovered.

Now the hotel had been restored to the system of private enterprise in which Robbie Budd so ardently believed and which he was
pleased to patronize regardless of cost. In view of his reduced circumstances, he might well have gone to a less expensive place, but
that would have been to admit defeat and to declass himself. No, he
was still European representative of Budd Gunmakers, still looking
for big deals and certain that Europe was going to need American
weapons before long. Keep your chin up, and make a joke out
of the fact that you have lost five or six million dollars. Everybody
knows that you had to be somebody to have that happen to you.

Here he was, comfortably ensconced in his suite, with a spare
room for Lanny; his whisky and soda and ice early in the morning,
his little portable typewriter and papers spread out on another table.
He was in his middle fifties, but looked younger than he had in
New York under the strain of the panic. He had got back his ruddy

complexion and well-nourished appearance; a little bit portly, but still vigorous and ready to tackle the world. Already he was in the midst of affairs; there was a Rumanian purchasing-commission in town, and a couple of Soviet agents—Robbie grinned as he said that he was becoming quite chummy with the "comrades"; he knew how to "talk their language," thanks to Lanny's help. He meant, not that he could speak Russian, but that he could speak Red.

Lanny told the news about the Dingles and the Robins, and Robbie in turn reported on the family in Newcastle. Amazing the way the head of the Budd tribe was holding on; at the age of eighty-three he insisted upon knowing every detail of the company's affairs; he sat in his study and ran the business by telephone. Esther, Lanny's stepmother, was well. "I really think she's happier since the crash," said the husband. He didn't add: "I have kept my promise to stay out of the market." Lanny knew he didn't break promises.

They talked about Wall Street, about that "little bull market" which had everybody so stirred up, a mixture of hope and fear currently known as the "jitters." When the *Bessie Budd* was setting out, the market had been booming, and Robbie in a letter had repeated his old formula: "Don't sell America short." Now stocks were slipping again, business going to pot, unemployment spreading; but Robbie had to keep up his courage, all America had to hold itself up by its bootstraps. The most popular song of the moment announced: "Happy days are here again."

II

They discussed Johannes Robin and his affairs, in which Robbie was deeply interested. He was going to Berlin on this trip: a subtle change in the relationship of the two associates, for in the old days it had been Johannes who came to Paris to see Robbie. The Jewish trader was on top; he hadn't lost any part of his fortune, and wasn't going to. He would never make Robbie Budd's mistake of being too optimistic about this world, for he had made most of his money by expecting trouble. Now he had sent a message, by Lanny, that he was going to help Robbie to come back; but it would have to be by the same judicious pessimism.

"He's a good sort," said Robbie, English-fashion. He knew, of course, that his old associate couldn't very well drop him, even if he had wished to, because Hansi and Bess had made them relatives. Moreover, Johannes was one of those Jews who desire to associate with gentiles and are willing to pay liberally for it.

Having had long talks with the financier on board the yacht, Lanny could tell what was in his mind. He considered that Germany was approaching the end of her rope; she couldn't make any more reparations payments, even if she wished. Taxation had about reached its limits, foreign credit was drying up, and Johannes couldn't see any chance of Germany's escaping another bout of inflation. The government was incompetent, also very costly to deal with; that, of course, was a money-man's polite way of intimating that it was corrupt and that he was helping to keep it so. Elections were scheduled for the end of the summer, and there would be a bitter campaign; sooner or later the various factions would fall to fighting, and that wouldn't help the financial situation any. Johannes was trimming his sails and getting ready for rough weather. He was taking some of his investments out of the country. Those he kept in Germany were mostly in industries which produced goods for export.

Lanny made a brief report upon the younger Robins, and the present condition of their political diseases. Fate had played a strange prank upon the business association known as "Robin and Robbie." The Robin half had got somewhat the worst of it, having two Reds and two Pinks, whereas Robbie had only one Red and one Pink, and didn't see either very often. The Robin half was considerate and never referred to the fact that the infection had come from the Robbie side. Johannes knew how his associate hated and despised Jesse Blackless, the man who had talked revolution to Lanny, and then to Hansi and Freddi, seducing these sensitive, idealistic minds away from their fathers.

Robbie wanted to know about Irma, and how she and Lanny

were making out. Very important, that; the father had found out last October what a convenient thing it was to have the Barnes fortune back of you. He hoped that Lanny wasn't going to fail to make a success of it. Lanny reported that he and Irma were getting along as well as most young couples he had known; better than some. Irma wanted a lot, and most of the things he was interested in didn't mean much to her, but they were in love with each other, and they found the baby a source of satisfaction. Robbie said you never got everything you wanted out of a marriage, but you could put up with a lot when it included a thumping big fortune. Lanny knew that wasn't the noblest view to take of the holy bonds of matrimony, but all he said was: "Don't worry. We'll make out."

III

One of Robbie's purposes was to see Zaharoff. The New England-Arabian Oil Company had managed to survive the panic, but Robbie and his associates at home needed cash and must find a buyer for their shares. Doubtless the old spider knew all about their plight, but Robbie would put up a bold front. As usual, he asked if his son would like to go along, and as usual the son wouldn't have missed it for anything. He had never given up the hope that somehow he might be able to help his father in his dealings with the retired munitions king of Europe.

Robbie phoned the old man's home, and learned that he was at his country estate, the Château de Balincourt in Seine-et-Oise, close to Paris. Robbie sent a telegram, and received an appointment for the next afternoon; he ordered a car through the hotel, and they were motored to the place, which had once belonged to King Leopold of Belgium. Now there was a new kind of kings in Europe, and one of them was this ex-fireman of Constantinople. A lodge-keeper swung back the gates for them, and they rolled down a tree-lined drive and were received at the door by an East Indian servant in native costume. All the servants were Hindus; an aged king wanted silence and secrecy, and one way was to have attendants who understood only a few simple commands. One of Zaharoff's married daughters lived with him, and no one came save by appointment.

The visitors were escorted into a drawing-room decorated in the lavish French fashion. On the walls were paintings, and Lanny had been invited to see them, so now he took the occasion. But it didn't last long, for the owner came in. His heavy shoulders seemed a bit more bowed than when Lanny had watched him, in his undershirt, burning his private papers in the drawing-room of his Paris house and setting fire to the chimney in the process. Now he wore an embroidered purple smoking-jacket, and his white mustache and imperial were neatly trimmed. He had become almost entirely bald.

"*Eh, bien, mon garçon?*" he said to Lanny.

Being at the beginning of his thirties, Lanny felt quite grown up, but understood that this might not impress one who was at the beginning of his eighties. "I was looking at your paintings," he remarked. "You have a fine Ingres."

"Yes; but I have looked at it for so many years."

"Paintings should be like old friends, Sir Basil."

"Most of my old friends are gone, and the younger ones are busy with their affairs. They tell me you have been making your fortune."

It was an allusion to Irma, and not exactly a delicate one; but Lanny knew that this old man was money-conscious. The duquesa, his companion, had tried tactfully to cure him of the defect, but without succeeding. Lanny was not surprised when Zaharoff added: "You will no longer have to be a picture-dealer, *hein?*"

He smiled and answered: "I get a lot of fun out of it."

The old man's remark was noted by Robbie, who had said on the way out that if Zaharoff knew that Lanny had the Barnes fortune behind him, he might expect to pay a higher price for the shares of the New England-Arabian Oil Company!

They seated themselves, and tea was served; for Robbie it was scotch and soda. The two men discussed the state of business in Europe and America, and Lanny listened attentively, as he had always done. One who found pleasure in buying and selling old masters could learn from the technique being here revealed. The

Knight Commander of the Bath of England and Grand Officer of the Légion d'Honneur of France was the very soul of courtesy, of suavity in manner; a bit deprecating, as if he were saying: "I am a very old man, and it would not be fair to take advantage of me." His soft voice caressed you and his smile wooed you, but at the same time his blue eyes watched you warily.

He was known as "the mystery man of Europe," and doubtless there had been mysteries enough about what he was doing in the political and financial worlds; but so far as his character was concerned, Lanny no longer found any mystery. An aged plutocrat had fought his way up in the world by many deeds of which he now did not enjoy the contemplation. He had intrigued and threatened, bribed and cajoled, made promises and broken them; by tireless scheming and pushing he had acquired the mastery of those great establishments which the various countries of Europe needed in order to wage their wars of power. But all the time he had remained in his soul a Greek peasant living among cruel oppressing Turks. He had been afraid of a thousand things: of his own memories, of the men he had thwarted and ruined, of slanderers, blackmailers, assassins, Reds—and, above all, of what he had helped to make Europe. A man who wanted to sell munitions, who wanted all the nations of the earth to spend their incomes upon munitions, but who didn't want any munitions shot off—at least not anywhere within his own hearing! Unaccountably the shooting continued, Europe seemed to be going from bad to worse, and Zaharoff's conversation revealed that he trusted nobody in power and had very little hope of anything.

A bitter, sad old man, he felt his powers waning, and had hidden himself away from dangers. He would soon be gone; and did he worry about where he was going? Or was it about what was going to become of his possessions? He mourned his beloved Spanish duquesa of the many names. Did he contemplate the possibility of being reunited to her? Lanny had something to say to him on that subject, but must wait until the two traders had got through with their duel of wits.

IV

It was Robbie Budd who had sought this interview, and he who would have to say what he had come for. Zaharoff, while waiting, would be gravely interested in what Robbie had to tell about the state of Wall Street and the great American financial world. The visitor was optimistic, sure that the clouds would soon blow over. Lanny knew that his father really believed that, but would Zaharoff believe that he believed it? No, the Greek would think that Robbie, having something to sell, was playing the optimist. Zaharoff, the prospective buyer, was a pessimist.

At last Robbie saw fit to get down to business. He explained that his father was very old, and the cares of the Budd enterprise might soon be on Robbie's shoulders. Budd's was largely out of munitions; it was making everything from needles to freight elevators. Robbie would no longer be in a position to travel—in short, he and his friends were looking for someone to take the New England-Arabian shares off their hands at a reasonable figure.

There it was; and Zaharoff's pessimism assumed the hues of the nethermost stage of Dante's inferno. The world was in a most horrible state; the Arabians were on the point of declaring a jihad and wiping out every European on their vast desolate hot peninsula; Zaharoff himself was a feeble old man, his doctors had given him final warning, he must avoid every sort of responsibility and strain —in short, he couldn't buy anything, and didn't have the cash anyhow.

A flat turn-down; but Lanny had heard a Levantine trader talk, and knew that Zaharoff's real purpose and desire would not be revealed until the last minute, when his two guests had their hats in their hands, perhaps when they were outside the front door. Meanwhile they mustn't show that they knew this; they mustn't betray disappointment; they must go on chatting, as if it didn't really mean very much to them, as if Robbie Budd had crossed the ocean to have one more look at Zaharoff's blue eyes, or perhaps at his very fine Ingres.

It was time for Lanny to mention the paintings, which he had been invited to inspect. He asked if he might stroll about the room, and the Knight Commander and Grand Officer rose from his seat and strolled with him, pointing out various details. Lanny said: "You know I am interested in the value of paintings, that being my business." The remark gave no offense; quite the contrary. The old man told the prices, which he had at his fingertips: a hundred thousand francs for this Fragonard, a hundred and fifty thousand for that David. "Before-the-war francs," he added.

They went into the great library, a magnificent room with a balcony all around it, having heavy bronze railings. Then they inspected the dining-room, in which was a startling Goya, the portrait of an abnormally tall and thin Spanish gentleman wearing brilliant-colored silks with much lace and jewelry. "An ancestor of my wife," remarked the old man. "She didn't care for it much; she found it cynical."

An opening which Lanny had been waiting for. "By the way, Sir Basil, here is something which might interest you. Have you ever tried any experiments with mediums?"

"Spiritualist mediums, you mean? Why do you ask?"

"Because of something strange which has been happening in our family. My stepfather interested my mother in the subject, and in New York they found a Polish woman with whom they held séances, and she gave them such convincing results that we brought her to the Riviera with us, and she has become a sort of member of our family."

"You think she brings you messages from—" The old man stopped, as if hesitating to say "the dead."

"We get innumerable messages from what claim to be spirits, and they tell us things which astonish us, because we cannot see how this old and poorly educated Polish woman can possibly have had any means of finding them out."

"There is a vast system of fraud of that sort, I have been told," said the cautious Greek.

"I know, Sir Basil; and if this were an alert-minded woman, I might think it possible. But she is dull and quite unenterprising. How could she possibly have known that the duquesa was fond of tulips, and the names of the varieties she showed me?"

"*What?*" exclaimed the host.

"She mentioned the names Bybloem and Bizarre, and spoke of Turkestan, though she didn't get it as the name of a tulip. She even gave me a very good description of the garden of your town house, and the number fifty-three. She was trying to get Avenue Hoche, but could only get the H."

Lanny had never before seen this cautious old man reveal such emotion. Evidently a secret spring had been touched. "Sit down," he said, and they took three of the dining-room chairs. "Is this really true, Lanny?"

"Indeed it is. I have the records of a hundred or more sittings."

"This concerns me deeply, because of late years I have had very strange feelings, as if my wife was in the room and trying to communicate with me. I have told myself that it could only be the product of my own grief and loneliness. I don't need to tell you how I felt about her."

"No, Sir Basil, I have always understood; the little I saw of her was enough to convince me that she was a lovely person."

"Six years have passed, and my sorrow has never diminished. Tell me—where is this Polish woman?" When Lanny explained about the yacht, he wanted to know: "Do you suppose it would be possible for me to have a séance with her?"

"It could be arranged some time, without doubt. We should be deeply interested in the results."

V

For half an hour or more the rich but unhappy old man sat asking questions about Madame Zyszynski and her procedure. Lanny explained the curious obligation of pretending to believe in an Iroquois Indian chieftain who spoke with a Polish accent. No easy matter for an intellectual person to take such a thing seriously; but Lanny told about a lady who had been his *amie* for many years prior to her death; she had sent him messages, including little details such as two lovers remember, but which would have no meaning for others: the red-and-white-striped jacket of the servant who attended them in the inn where they had spent their first night, the pear and apricot trees against the walls of the lady's garden. Such things might have come out of Lanny's subconscious mind, but even so, it was a curious experience to have somebody dig them up.

"I would like very much to try the experiment," said Zaharoff. "When do you think it could be arranged?"

"I will have to consult my mother and my stepfather. The yacht is on the way from Cannes to Bremen, and the plan is to go from there to America and return in the autumn. If you go to Monte Carlo next winter, we could bring Madame over to you."

"That is a long time to wait. Would it not be possible for me to bring her here for at least a trial? Perhaps the yacht may be stopping in the Channel?"

"We expect to stop on the English coast, perhaps at Portsmouth or Dover."

"If so, I would gladly send someone to England to bring her to me. I would expect to pay her, you understand."

"There is no need of that. We are taking care of her, and she is satisfied, so it would be better not to raise the question."

"This might mean a great deal to me, Lanny. If I thought that I was in contact with my wife, and that I had some chance of seeing her again, it would give me more happiness than anything I can think of." There was a pause, as if a retired munitions king needed a violent effort to voice such feelings. "I have met no one in any way approaching her. You have heard, perhaps, that I waited thirty-four years to marry her, and then she was spared to me barely eighteen months."

Lanny knew that Zaharoff and the duquesa had been living together during all those thirty-four years; but this was not to be mentioned. A young free lance could mention casually that he had had an *amie,* but the richest man in Europe had to look out for *chantage* and scandal-mongers—especially when the lady's insane husband had been a cousin to the King of Spain!

"If you want to make a convincing test," continued Lanny, "it would be better not to let Madame Zyszynski know whom she is to meet. She rarely asks questions, either before or after a sitting. She will say: 'Did you get good results?' and if you tell her: 'Very good,' she is satisfied. I should advise meeting her in some hotel room, with nothing to give her any clue."

"Listen, my boy," said the old man, with more eagerness than Lanny had ever seen him display in the sixteen years of their acquaintance, "if you will make it possible for me to see this woman in the next few days, I will come to any place on the French coast that you name."

"In that case I think I can promise to arrange it. I am to fly and join the yacht at Lisbon, and as soon as I can set a date, I will telegraph you. In the meantime, say nothing, and my father and I will be the only persons in the secret. I will tell my mother that I have a friend who wants to make a private test; and to Madame I won't say even that."

VI

To this long conversation Robbie Budd had listened in silence. He didn't believe in a hereafter, but he believed in giving the old spider, the old gray wolf, the old devil, whatever would entertain him and put him under obligations to the Budd family. When they rose to leave, Zaharoff turned to him and said: "About those shares: would you like me to see if some of my old-time associates would be interested in them?"

"Certainly, Sir Basil."

"If you will send me the necessary data concerning the company——"

"I have the whole set-up with me." Robbie pointed to his briefcase. "I have thirty-five thousand shares at my disposal."

"Are you prepared to put a price on them?"

"We are asking a hundred and twenty dollars a share. That represents exactly the amount of the investment."

"But you have had generous profits, have you not?"

"Not excessive, in view of the period of time and the work that I have put in on it."

"People are glad to get back the half of their investment these days, Mr. Budd."

"Surely not in oil, Sir Basil."

"Well, leave the documents with me, and I'll see what I can do and let you hear in the next few days."

They took their leave; and in their car returning to Paris, Robbie said: "Son, that was an inspiration! How did you think of it?"

"Well, it happened, and I thought he'd want to know."

"That business about the tulips really happened?"

"Of course."

"It was certainly most convenient. If that woman can convince him that the duquesa is sending him messages, there's nothing he won't do. We may get our price."

Lanny well knew that his father wasn't very sensitive when he was on the trail of a business deal; but then, neither is a spider, a wolf, or a devil. "I hope you do," he said.

"He means to buy the shares himself," continued Robbie. "It will take a lot of bargaining. Don't let him see too much of the woman until he pays up."

"The more he sees, the more he may want," countered the son.

"Yes, but suppose he buys her away from you entirely?"

"That's a chance we have to take, I suppose."

"My guess is he won't be able to believe that the thing is on the level. If he gets results, he'll be sure you told the woman in advance."

"Well," said the young idealist, "he'll be punishing his own sins. Goethe has a saying that all guilt avenges itself upon earth."

But Robbie wasn't any more interested in spirituality than he was in spirits. "If I can swing this deal, I'll be able to pay off the notes that I gave you and Beauty and Marceline."

"You don't have to worry about those notes, Robbie. We aren't suffering."

"All the same, it's not pleasant to know that I took the money which you had got by selling Marcel's paintings."

"If it hadn't been for you," said the young philosopher, "I

wouldn't have been here, Beauty would have married some third-rate painter in Montmartre, and Marceline wouldn't have been traveling about in a private yacht. I have pointed that out to them."

"All the same," said Robbie, "I came over here to sell those shares. Let's get as much of the old rascal's money as we can."

Lanny had made jokes about the firm of "R and R." In the days when his mother and Bess had been trying to find him a wife, there had been a firm of "B and B." Now he said: "We'll have a 'Z and Z.' "

VII

Back in Paris Lanny might have sat in at a conference and learned about the rearmament plans of the Rumanian government; but he had an engagement with Zoltan Kertezsi to visit the Salon and discuss the state of the picture market. The blond Hungarian was one of those happy people who never look a day older; always he had just discovered something new and exciting in the art world, always he wanted to tell you about it with a swift flow of words, and always his rebellious hair and fair mustache seemed to be sharing in his gestures. There wasn't anything first rate in the Salon, he reported, but there was a young Russian genius, Alexander Jacovleff, being shown at one of the galleries; a truly great draftsman, and Lanny must come and have a look right away. Also, Zoltan had come upon a discovery, a set of Blake water-color drawings which had been found in an old box in a manor-house in Surrey; they were genuine, and still fresh in color; nobody else on earth could have done such angels and devils; doubtless they had been colored by Blake's wife, but that was true of many Blakes. They ought to fetch at least a thousand pounds apiece——

Immediately Lanny began running over in his mind the names of persons who might be interested in such a treasure trove. It wasn't only because Zoltan would pay him half the commission; it was because it was a game that he had learned to play. No use for Irma to object, no use to think that the money she deposited to his account would ever bring him the same thrills as he got from putting through a deal.

"We shan't be able to get what we used to," said the friend. "You'd be astonished the way prices are being cut."

No matter; the pictures were just as beautiful, and if you kept your tastes simple, you could live and enjoy them. But the dealers who had loaded themselves up were going to have trouble paying their high rents; and the poor devils who did the painting would wander around with their canvases under their arms, and set them up in the windows of tobacco-shops and every sort of place, coming back two or three times a day and gazing at them wistfully, hoping that this might cause some passer-by to stop and take an interest.

Paris in the springtime was lovely, as always, and the two friends strolled along, feasting their eyes upon the chestnut blossoms and their olfactories upon the scents of flowerbeds. Zoltan was near fifty, but he acted and talked as young as his friend; he was full of plans to travel here and there, to see this and that. He was always meeting some delightful new person, discovering some new art treasure. Happy indeed is the man with whom business and pleasure are thus combined! A thousand old masters had made life easy for him, by producing works over which he could rave and feel proud when he secured one for some customer.

There were always wealthy persons on the hunt for famous works of art; and Zoltan would caution his Pink friend not to be too contemptuous in his attitude toward such persons. Many were ignorant and pretentious, but others were genuine art lovers who could be helped and encouraged; and that was not only good business, it was a public service, for many of these collections would come to museums in the end. Zoltan didn't know much about economics, and didn't bother his head with Lanny's revolutionary talk; he said that, no matter what happened, the paintings would survive, and people would want to see them, and there would be occupation for the man who had cultivated his tastes and could tell the rare and precious from the cheap and common.

VIII

Lanny rented a car and motored Zoltan out to have lunch with Emily Chattersworth at her estate, Les Forêts, where she spent the greater part of each year, a very grand place of which Lanny had memories from childhood. On this lawn under the great beech-trees he had listened to Anatole France exposing the scandals of the kings and queens of old-time France. In this drawing-room he had played the piano for Isadora Duncan, and had been invited to elope with her. Here also he had played accompaniments for Hansi, the day when Hansi and Bess had met and fallen irrevocably in love.

The white-haired châtelaine wanted to hear the news of all the families. She was interested in the story of Zaharoff and the duquesa, whom she had known. Emily had had a séance with Madame Zys-zynski, but hadn't got any significant results; it must be because she was hostile to the idea, and had frightened the spirits! She preferred to ask Zoltan's opinion of the Salon, which she had visited. Having a couple of paintings which no longer appealed to her taste, she showed them to the expert and heard his estimate of what they might bring. She told him not to hurry; she had lost a lot of money, as everybody else had, but apparently it was only a paper loss, for the stocks were still paying dividends. Lanny advised her not to count on that.

A young Pink wouldn't come to Paris without calling at the office of *Le Populaire* and exchanging ideas with Jean Longuet and Léon Blum. Lanny knew what they thought, because he read their paper, but they would want to hear how the workers' education movement was going in the Midi, and what the son of an American industrialist had seen in the Soviet Union. From a luncheon with Longuet, Lanny strolled to look at picture exhibitions, and then climbed the Butte de Montmartre to the unpretentious apartment where Jesse Blackless was in the midst of composing a manifesto to be published in *L'Humanité*, denouncing Longuet and his paper as agents and tools of capitalist reaction. When Jesse learned that his nephew had been to Odessa he began to ply him with questions, eager for every crumb of reassurance as to the progress of the Five-Year Plan.

Jesse lived here with his companion, a Communist newspaper employee. Theirs was a hard-working life with few pleasures; Jesse had no time to paint, he said; the reactionaries were getting ready to shut down upon the organized workers and put them out of business. The next elections in France might be the last to be held under the Republic. Lanny's Red uncle lived under the shadow of impending class war; his life was consecrated to hating the capitalist system and teaching others to share that feeling.

He was going into this campaign to fight both capitalists and Socialists. Lanny thought it was a tragedy that the labor groups couldn't get together to oppose enemies so much stronger than themselves. But there couldn't be collaboration between those who thought the change might be brought about by parliamentary action and those who thought that it would have to be done by force. When you used the last phrase to Jesse Blackless, he would insist that it was the capitalists who would use force, and that the attitude of the workers was purely defensive; they would be attacked, their organizations overthrown—the whole pattern had been revealed in Italy.

Lanny would answer: "That is just quibbling. The Communists take an attitude which makes force inevitable. If you start to draw a gun on a man, he knows that his life depends upon his drawing first."

Could capitalism be changed gradually? Could the job be done by voting some politicians out of office and voting others in? Lanny had come upon a quotation of Karl Marx, admitting that a gradual change might be brought about in the Anglo-Saxon countries, which had had parliamentary institutions for a long time. Most Reds didn't know that their master had said that, and wouldn't believe it when you told them; it seemed to give the whole Bolshevik case away. Jesse said that quoting Marx was like quoting the Bible: you could find anything you wanted.

They went on arguing, saying little that they hadn't said before. Presently Françoise came in, and they stopped, because she didn't share the carefree American sense of humor, and would get irritated with Lanny. He told her the good things about the Soviet Union;

and soon came Suzette, her young sister, married to one of the murderous taxi drivers of Paris. Uncle Jesse said this *garçon* had the
right solution of the social problem: to run over all the bourgeois,
while using Suzette to increase the Red population. They had a second baby.

The women set to work to prepare supper, and Lanny excused
himself and walked back to the Crillon to meet his father. When
Robbie asked: "What have you been doing?" he answered: "Looking at pictures." It was the truth and nothing but the truth—yet not
the whole truth!

IX

One other duty: a visit to the Château de Bruyne. Lanny had
promised Marie on her deathbed that he would never forget her two
boys. There wasn't much that he could do for them, but they were
friendly fellows and glad to tell him of their doings. He phoned to
the father, who came and motored him out. Denis de Bruyne, though
somewhat over seventy, was vigorous; his hair had become white,
and his dark, sad eyes and pale aristocratic features made him a person of distinction. He was glad to see Lanny because of the memories they shared.

On the way they talked politics, and it was curious to note how
the same world could appear so different to two different men.
Denis de Bruyne, capitalist on a modest scale, owner of a fleet of
taxicabs and employer of Suzette's husband—though he didn't know
it—agreed with Jesse Blackless that the Communists were strong in
Paris and other industrial centers and that they meant to use force if
they could get enough of it. Denis's conception of statesmanship was
to draw the gun first. He was a Nationalist, and was going to put up
money to keep Jesse and his sort from getting power. Lanny listened,
and this was agreeable to an entrepreneur who was so certain of his
own position.

Denis de Bruyne was worried about the state of his country, which
was in a bad way financially, having counted upon German reparations and been cheated out of most of her expectations. A French
Nationalist blamed the British business men and statesmen; Britain

was no true ally of France, but a rival; Britain used Germany to keep France from growing strong. Why did American business men further this policy, helping Germany to get on her feet, which meant making her a danger to France? Foreign investors had lent Germany close to five billion dollars since the end of the war: why did they take such risks?

Lanny replied: "Well, if they hadn't, how would Germany have paid France any reparations at all?"

"She would have paid if she had been made to," replied Denis. He didn't say how, and Lanny knew better than to pin him down. The men who governed France hadn't learned much by their invasion of the Ruhr and its failure; they still thought that you could produce goods by force, that you could get money with bayonets. It was useless to argue with them; their fear of Germany was an obsession. And maybe they were right—how could Lanny be sure? Certainly there were plenty of men in Germany who believed in force and meant to use it if they could get enough of it. Lanny had met them also.

Denis wanted to know what was going to be the effect of the Wall Street collapse upon French affairs. The season was beginning, and many of the fashionable folk were not here. Would the tourists fail to show up this summer? A question of urgency to the owner of a fleet of taxicabs! Lanny said he was afraid that Paris would have to do what New York had done—draw in its belt. When Denis asked what Robbie thought about the prospects, Lanny reported his father's optimism, and Denis was pleased, having more respect for Robbie's judgment than for Lanny's.

The Château de Bruyne was no great showplace like Balincourt and Les Forêts, but a simple country home of red stone; its title was a tribute to its age, and the respect of the countryside for an old family. It had been one of Lanny's homes, off and on, for some six years. The servants knew him, the old dog knew him, he felt that even the fruit trees knew him. Denis, *fils*, had got himself a wife of the right sort, and she was here, learning the duties of a châtelaine; they had a baby boy, so the two young fathers could make jokes about a possible future union of the families. Charlot, the younger brother, was studying to be an engineer, which meant that he might travel to far parts of the earth; incidentally, he was interested in politics, belonging to one of the groups of aggressive French patriots. Lanny didn't say much about his own ideas—he never had, for it had been his privilege to be the lover of Denis's wife, but not the corrupter of his sons. All that he could hope for was to moderate their vehemence by talking about toleration and open-mindedness.

The two young men—one was twenty-four and the other a year younger—looked up to Lanny as to an abnormally wise and brilliant person. They knew about his marriage, and thought it a coronation. In this opinion their mother would have joined, for she had had a Frenchwoman's thorough-going respect for property. The French, along with most other Europeans, were fond of saying that the Americans worshiped the dollar; a remark upon which Zoltan Kertezsi had commented in a pithy sentence: "The Americans worship the dollar and the French worship the sou."

5

From the Vasty Deep

I

LANNY rejoined the *Bessie Budd* at Lisbon, and they sailed again and put in at the yacht basin of Cowes. Awaiting them was a letter from Johannes, saying that he was tied up in some bad business, so no use hurrying to Bremen; also a letter from Rick, begging them to come to The Reaches for a few days; he and his wife hadn't seen them for a whole year. Lanny consulted Mama, and then "shot a wire" to Rick, inviting him to bring his wife and their oldest boy for a short cruise.

Friendship is a delightful thing when you have had the good judgment to choose the right friends. Eric Vivian Pomeroy-Nielson had come in the course of the years to be the most congenial of Lanny's friends. It could be doubted whether the younger man would have had the courage to stick to so many unorthodox ideas if it hadn't been for Rick's support. The baronet's son watched everything that went on in the world, analyzed the various tendencies, and set forth his understanding of them in newspaper articles which Lanny would clip and send to persons with whom he got into arguments. Not that he ever converted anybody, but he kept his cause alive.

Rick was only about a year and a half the elder, but Lanny was in the habit of deferring to him, which pleased Rick's wife and didn't altogether displease Rick. Whenever the Englishman wrote another play, Lanny was sure it was bound to make the long-awaited "hit." When it didn't, there was always a reason: that Rick persisted in dealing with social problems from a point of view unpopular with those who bought the best seats in theaters. The young playwright was fortunate in having parents who believed in him and gave him and his family a home while he wrote the truth as he saw it.

Nearly thirteen years had passed since a very young English flier had crashed in battle, and been found with a gashed forehead and a broken and badly infected knee. In the course of time he had learned to live with his lameness. He could go bathing from the special landing-place which Lanny had had made for him at Bienvenu; and now the carpenter of the *Bessie Budd* bolted two handles onto the landing-stage of the yacht's gangway, so that a man with good stout arms could lift himself out of the water without any help. He would unstrap his leg-brace, slide in, and enjoy himself just as if humanity had never been cursed with a World War.

II

Nina was her usual kind and lovely self, and as for Little Alfy— he had to be called that on account of his grandfather the baronet, but it hardly fitted him any more, for he had grown tall and leggy for his almost thirteen years. He had dark hair and eyes like his father's, and was, as you might have expected, extremely precocious; he knew a little about all the various political movements, also the art movements, and would use their patter in a fashion which made it hard for you to keep from smiling. He had thin, sensitive features and was serious-minded, which made him the predestined victim of Marceline Detaze, the little flirt, the little minx. Marceline didn't know anything about politics, but she knew some of the arts, including that of coquetry. Half French and half American, she also had been brought up among older people, but of a different sort. From the former Baroness de la Tourette, the hardware lady from Cincinnati, she had learned the trick of saying outrageous things with a perfectly solemn face and then bursting into laughter at a sober lad's look of bewilderment. Apparently Alfy never would learn about it.

The families had planned a match for these two by cable as soon as they had appeared on the scene. The parents made jokes about it, in the free and easy modern manner, and the children had taken up the practice. "I'll never marry you if you don't learn to dance better," Marceline would announce. Alfy, peeved, would respond: "You don't have to marry me if you don't want to." He would never have the least idea what was coming next. One time her feelings would be hurt, and the next time she would be relieved of a great burden; but whichever it was, it would turn out to be teasing, and Alfy would be like a man pursuing a will-o'-the-wisp on a dark night.

There had been dancing in Marceline's home ever since she was old enough to toddle about. So-called "society" dancing, Dalcroze dancing, Isadora Duncan dancing, Provençal peasant dancing, English and American country dancing—every sort that a child could pick up. Some kind of music going most of the time, and a phonograph and a radio so that she could make it to order. On the yacht, as soon as her lessons were finished, she would come running to where Hansi and Bess were practicing; she would listen for a minute to get the swing of it, then her feet would start moving and she would be dancing all over the saloon. She would hold out her hands to Lanny, and they would begin improvising; they had learned to read each other's signals, and once more, as in the old Dalcroze days, you saw music made visible.

No wonder Marceline could dance rings all around a lad who knew only that somnambulistic walking in time to jazz thumping which prevailed in fashionable society. Alfy would try his best, but look and feel like a young giraffe caught in an earthquake. "Loosen up, loosen up!" she would cry, and he would kick up his heels and toes in a most un-English manner. The girl would give him just enough encouragement to keep him going, but never enough to let him doubt who was going to call the tune in their household.

Lanny would see them sitting apart from the others while music was being played in the evening. Sometimes they would be holding hands, and he would guess that they were working out their problem in their own way. He recalled the days when he had paid his first visit to The Reaches, and had sat on the bank of the River Thames, listening to Kurt Meissner playing the slow movement of Mozart's D-minor concerto. How miraculous life had seemed to him, with one arm about Rosemary Codwilliger, pronounced Culliver, shivering with delight and dreaming of a marvelous future. Nothing had worked out as he had planned it; he reflected upon life, and how seldom it gives us what we expect. The young people come along, and clamor so loudly for their share, and have so little idea of the pain that awaits them. One's heart aches at the knowledge, but one cannot tell them; they have to have their own way and pay their own penalties.

III

The *Bessie Budd* cruised in waters frequented by vessels of every size, from ocean liners down to tiny sailboats. One more did not matter, provided you kept a lookout and blew your whistle now and then. They went up into the Irish Sea; the weather was kind, one day of blue sky succeeded another, and the air resounded with music and the tapping of feet upon the deck. Hansi and Bess practiced diligently, Beauty and Irma played bridge with Nina and Rahel, while Lanny and Rick sat apart and discussed everything that had happened to them during the past year.

Lanny had visited the great manufacturing-plant of his forefathers, and had been received as a prince consort in the Newcastle Country Club and in Irma's imitation French château on Long Island. Rick, meanwhile, had written a play about a young married couple who were divided over the issue of violence in the class struggle. Rick had written several plays about young people tormented by some aspect of this struggle. In the present opus the talk of his young idealist sounded much like that of Lanny Budd, while the ultra-Red wife might have had a private yacht named after her. Rick apologized for this, saying that a dramatist had to use such material as came to his hand. Lanny said that doubtless there were plenty of futile and bewildered persons like himself, but not many determined, hard-fighting rebels like Bess among the parasitic classes.

Rick had talked with editors and journalists in London, with statesmen, writers, and all sorts of people in his father's home. He knew about the upsurge of the Nazi movement in the harassed Fatherland. Not long ago he had had a letter from Kurt, who was always hoping to explain his country to the outside world; he sent newspaper clippings and pamphlets. The Germans, frantic with a sense of persecution, were tireless propagandists, and would preach to whoever might be persuaded to listen. But you rarely heard one of them set forth both sides of the case or admit the slightest wrong on his country's side.

They were put ashore in a small Irish harbor, and the young people took a ride in a jaunting car, while the ladies dickered with sharp-witted peasant women for quantities of hand-embroidered linen. They were put ashore in Wales, where the mountains did not seem imposing to one who had lived so close to the Alps. They visited the Isle of Man, and Lanny recalled a long novel which he had thought was tremendous in his boyhood, but which he now guessed to be no great shakes. They put into Liverpool, where they had arranged to receive mail, and among other things was a telegram from Robbie, who was back in Paris. "Sale concluded at eighty-three better than expected thanks to you sailing tomorrow good luck to the ghosts."

At his father's request Lanny had put off making the promised date with Zaharoff. Now he mailed a note, saying that the yacht was due on the French coast in a few days and he would wire an appointment. The *Bessie Budd* idled her way south again, and returned the Pomeroy-Nielsons to Cowes, from which place Lanny sent a wire to the Château de Balincourt, saying that he would bring his friend to a hotel in Dieppe on the following afternoon. He had explained to Mama Robin that he wished to meet a friend there, and she was pleased to oblige him. His mother and his stepfather were told that he desired to make a test with Madame, and to name no names until after it was over. As for the Polish woman, she was used to being bundled here and there for demonstrations of her strange gift.

I V

Dieppe is a thousand-year-old town with a church, a castle, and other sights for tourists; also it is a popular watering-place with a casino, so Lanny didn't have to think that he was inconveniencing his friends. The yacht was laid alongside a pier, and at the proper time he called a taxi and took his charge to the hotel. He had received an unsigned telegram informing him that "Monsieur Jean" would be awaiting him; at the desk he asked for this gentleman, and was escorted to the suite in which Zaharoff sat waiting, alone.

A comfortable chaise-longue had been provided for the medium and an armchair for each of the men. Since the old one had been thoroughly instructed, no talk was necessary. Lanny introduced him by the fictitious name, and he responded: "*Bon jour,*" and no more. Lanny said: "*Asseyez-vous, Madame,*" and not another word was spoken. The retired munitions king was inconspicuously dressed, and one who was not familiar with his photograph might have taken him for a retired business man, a college professor or doctor.

The woman began to shudder and moan; then she became still, and was in her trance. There was a long wait; Lanny, who kept telling himself that these phenomena were "telepathy," concentrated his mind upon the personality of María del Pilar Antonia Angela Patrocino Simón de Muguiro y Berute, Duquesa de Marqueni y Villafranca de los Caballeros. It was a personality which failed to live up to the magnificent-sounding names; a rather small, dark lady, very quiet, reserved, but kind. She had fitted the needs of an extremely exacting man of affairs; guarded him, cared for him, loved him, and, as Lanny knew, helped to raise his two nieces. Anyhow, he had adored her, and shown his pride in the restrained fashion which circumstances imposed upon him. For more than thirty-five years they had been inseparable, and a million memories of her must be buried in the old man's subconscious mind. Would the medium be able to tap them? If so, it might be embarrassing, and perhaps it would have been more tactful of Lanny to offer to withdraw. But Zaharoff had placed a chair, possibly with the idea that the younger man's help might be needed for the guiding of the experiment.

Suddenly came the massive voice of the Iroquois chieftain, speaking English, as always. "Hello, Lanny. So you are trying to bowl me out!" It certainly wasn't an Iroquois phrase, nor did it seem exactly Polish.

Said Lanny, very solemnly: "Tecumseh, I have brought a gentleman who is deeply sincere in his attitude to you."

"But he does not believe in me!"

"He is fully prepared to believe in you, if you will give him cause; and he will be glad to believe."

"He is afraid to believe!" declared the voice, with great emphasis. There was a pause; and then: "You are not a Frenchman."

"I have tried to be," said Zaharoff. Lanny had told him to answer every question promptly and truly, but to say no more than necessary.

"But you were not born in France. I see dark people about you, and they speak a strange language which I do not understand. It will not be easy for me to do anything for you. Many spirits come; you have known many people, and they do not love you; it is easy to see it in their faces. I do not know what is the matter; many of them talk at once and I cannot get the words."

V

From where Lanny sat he could watch the face of Madame, and saw that it was disturbed, as always when Tecumseh was making a

special effort to hear or to understand. By turning his eyes the observer could watch the face of the old munitions king, which showed
strained attention. On the arm of Lanny's chair was a notebook, in
which he was setting down as much as he could of what was spoken.

Suddenly the control exclaimed: "There is a man here who is trying to talk; to you, not to me. He is a very thin old man with a white
beard. He says, in very bad English, he was not always like that, he
had a black beard when he knew you. His name is like Hyphen; also
he has another name, Tidy; no, it is one name, very long; is it
Hyphen-tidies? A Greek name, he says, Hiphentides. Do you know
that name?"

"No," said Zaharoff.

"He says you lie. Why do you come here if you mean to lie?"

"I do not recall him."

"He says you robbed him. What is it he is talking about? He keeps
saying gall; you have gall; many sackfuls of gall. Is it a joke he is
making?"

"It must be." Zaharoff spoke with quiet decisiveness. Of all the
persons Lanny knew, he was the most completely self-possessed.

"He says it is no joke. Gall is something that is sold. A hundred
and sixty-nine sacks of gall. Also gum, many cases of gum. You were
an agent." Tecumseh began to speak as if he were the spirit, something which he did only when the communications came clearly.
"You took my goods and pledged them for yourself. Do you deny
it?"

"Of course I do."

"You did not deny it in the London court. You pleaded guilty.
You were in prison—what is it?—the 'Old' something, Old Basin? It
was more than fifty years ago, and I do not remember."

"Old Bailey?" ventured Lanny.

"That is it—Old Bailey. I was in Constantinople, and I trusted you.
You said you did not know it was wrong; but they were my goods
and you got the money——"

The voice died away; it had become querulous, as of an old man
complaining of something long forgotten. If it wasn't real it was
certainly well invented.

VI

Lanny stole a glance at the living old man, and it seemed to him there was a faint dew of perspiration on his forehead. From what Robbie had told him he was prepared to believe that the Knight Commander of the Bath and Grand Officer of the Legion of Honor had many recollections which he would not wish to have dragged into the light of day.

Said Tecumseh, after a pause: "I keep hearing the name Mugla. What is Mugla?"

"It is the village where I was born."

"Is that in Greece?"

"It is in Turkey."

"But you are not a Turk."

"My parents were Greeks."

"Somebody keeps calling you Zack. Then I hear Ryas. Is your name Ryas?"

"Zacharias is one of my names."

"There is a man here who says he is your uncle. Anthony; no, not that. I don't know these Greek names."

"I had an Uncle Antoniades."

"He says: 'Do you wish to talk to me?'"

"I do not especially wish it."

"He says: 'Ha, ha!' He does not like you either. You were in business with him, too. It was not so good. You made up wonderful stories about it. Do you write stories, or something like that?"

"I am not a writer."

"But you tell stories. All the spirits laugh when Uncle Antoniades says that. You have become rich and important and you tell stories about the old days. They tell stories about you. Do you wish to hear them?"

"That is not what I came for."

"There is a big strong man with a white beard; it looks like your own, only more of it. He gives the name Max. He speaks good English—no, he says it is not good, it is Yankee. Do you know the Yankee Max?"

"I don't recognize him."

"He says he is Maxim. You were in business with him, too."

"I knew a Maxim."

"You bought him out. He made millions, but you made tens of millions. There was no stopping you. Maxim says he did not believe in the future life, but he warns you, it is a mistake; you will be happier if you change all that materialism. Do you know what he means?"

"It does not sound like him."

"I have put off the old man. I was a strapping fellow. I could lick anybody in the Maine woods. I could lick anybody in Canada, and I did. I licked you once, you old snollygoster. Does that sound more like me?"

"Yes, I recognize that."

"I once wrote the emperor's name with bullets on a target. You haven't forgotten that, surely!"

"I remember it."

"All right, then, wake up, and figure out how you will behave in a better world. You cannot solve your problems as you used to do, putting your fingers in your ears."

A moment's pause. "He went away laughing," said Tecumseh. "He is a wild fellow. When he ate soup it ran down his beard; and it was the same with icecream. You do not like such manners; you are a quiet person, Zacharias—and yet I hear loud noises going on all around you. It is very strange! What are you?"

VII

The old Greek made no reply, and the voice of the control sank to a murmur, as if he was asking the spirits about this mystery. For quite a while Lanny couldn't make out a word, and he took the occasion to perfect his notes. Once or twice he glanced at the munitions king, who did not return the glance, but sat staring before him as if he were an image of stone.

"What is this noise I keep hearing?" burst out the Indian, suddenly. "And why are these spirits in such an uproar? A rattling and banging, and many people yelling, as if they were frightened. What is it that you do, Zacharias?"

Sir Basil did not speak.

"Why don't you answer me?"

"Cannot the spirits tell you?"

"It is easier when you answer my questions. Don't you like what these people are saying? It is not my fault if they hate you. Did you cheat them? Or did you hurt them?"

"Some thought that I did."

"What I keep hearing is guns. That is it! Were you a soldier? Did you fight in battles?"

"I made munitions."

"Ah, that is it; and so many people died. That is why they are screaming at you. I have never seen so many; never in the days when I commanded a tribe of the Six Nations, and the palefaces came against us. They had better guns and more of them, and my people died, they died screaming and cursing the invaders of our land. So men died screaming and cursing Zacharias the Greek. Do you run and hide from them? They come crowding after you, as if it was the first time they ever could get at you. They stretch out their hands trying to reach you. Do you feel them touching you?"

"No," said Zaharoff. For the first time Lanny thought there was a trace of quavering in his voice. Another quick glance revealed distinct drops of sweat on his forehead.

"It is like a battle going on—it gives me a headache, with all the smoke and noise. I see shells bursting away off, and men are falling out of the sky. No, no, keep back, he can't hear you, and there is no use yelling at me. Let somebody speak for you all. Any one of you. Come forward, you man, you with the ragged flag. What is it you want to say? No, not *you!* I don't want to talk to a man with the top of his head blown off. What sense can come out of only half a head? Keep your bloody hands off me—I don't care who you are. What's that? Oh, I see. All right, tell him. . . . I am the Unknown Soldier. I am the man they have buried by the Arc de Triomphe. They keep the undying flame burning for me, and they come and lay wreaths on my tomb. You came once and laid a wreath, did you not? Answer me!"

"I did." The munitions king's voice was hardly audible.

"I saw you. I see all who come to the tomb. I want to tell them to go away and stop the next war. I want to tell them something else that will not please them. Do you know my name?"

"Nobody knows your name."

"My name is Mordecai Izak. I am a Jew. Their Unknown Soldier is a Jew, and that would worry them very much. Are you a Jew?"

"I have been called that, but it is not so."

"I understand, brother. Many of us have had to do it."

There was a pause, and then Tecumseh was speaking. "They are all laughing. They tell me not to mind if you do not speak the truth. You are a very important man, they say. They push forward a little old woman. I cannot make out her name; it sounds like Haje —is that a woman's name? She says that she is the mother of your son. Is that possible?"

"It might be."

"She says that your name was Sahar. You changed it in Russia. It was a place called Vilkomir, a long, long time ago. She says your son is living; he is a very poor fellow. She says you have grand-children, but you do not wish to know it. Does that mean anything to you?"

"Possibly."

"The wounded men crowd her away. They do not let her talk. They are shouting again: 'There is blood on your money! You have a great deal of money, and there is a curse upon it. You murdered a man when you were young, but that is nothing, you have murdered all of us. We are waiting for you in the spirit world. We are the avengers—we, the men without faces, without bowels! Some day you will come to us——' "

The voice of Tecumseh had become shrill; and suddenly the aged Greek started to his feet. Two steps brought him to Lanny's side, and he said: "Give me the book." The younger man, taken aback, handed over his notebook; Zaharoff grabbed it and hastened, almost running, to the door, and went out, slamming it behind him.

VIII

That was the end of the séance. Not another word was spoken, but the medium began to moan pitiably. Lanny was prepared for trouble, because any sort of abrupt action always had a bad effect on her; it was something about which he had warned Zaharoff. Now she was seized by a sort of light convulsion, and sputum began to drip from her lips. Lanny ran and got a towel and wiped it away; he was frightened for a while, but gradually the moaning died, and after a space the woman opened her eyes.

"Oh, what is the matter?" she asked; and then, seeing the empty chair: "Where is the old gentleman?"

"He went away."

"He should not have done that. Something went wrong; I feel so bad."

"I am sorry, Madame. He was frightened."

"Did he hear something bad?"

"Very bad indeed."

"Somebody is dead?"

Lanny thought that was an easy way out. "Yes," he said. "He was not prepared for it and did not want to show his feelings."

"It is terribly bad for me. Tecumseh will be angry."

"I think he will understand, Madame."

"It made me so weak; and my head aches."

"I am sorry. I will call for a little wine, if you like."

"Please do."

Lanny ordered some wine and biscuits. She would not eat, but she sipped the wine, and after a while he helped her downstairs and into a taxi. He was interested to note that even under these rather sensational circumstances the woman did not press him with questions. It was her own feelings that she was concerned about. People should not treat her that way; they should be more considerate.

He helped her on board the yacht, and Baby Johannes's nursemaid, who had become her friend, helped her into bed. Beauty and the others were out seeing the sights of Dieppe, so Lanny went to his own cabin to write up his notes a second time before his memories grew cold.

A really striking experience! He couldn't judge about all the details—for example, the hundred and sixty-nine sacks of gall—but Zaharoff's behavior was proof of the general accuracy of the revelations. The young observer was clinging to his theory that these details had come out of the subconscious mind of Zacharias Basileos Zaharoff, formerly Sahar, who had given several names, several birthplaces and birthdates, according to his convenience at the moment. But what a subconscious mind for a man to carry about with him! Were those the things he thought about when he woke up in the small hours of the morning and couldn't get to sleep again? How much money would it take to compensate a man for having such memories and such feelings?

IX

Lanny could not forget that his own father was a manufacturer and salesman of munitions, and that he had bribed and deceived and had documents stolen in order to promote various deals. Did Robbie have a subconscious mind like that? Certainly he showed few signs of it. His cheeks were rosy, he was sleeping well (so he reported), and he seemed to have his zest for life. But was that all bluff? Was he holding himself up by his bootstraps? Lanny remembered how quickly and how angrily Robbie would leap to the defense of the munitions industry whenever he heard it attacked. That wasn't the sign of a mind perfectly at ease.

Lanny had learned his father's formulas in earliest childhood. Budd Gunmakers Corporation was one of the bulwarks of American national security, and what it did was a great patriotic service. To say that it worked for profit was the vilest demagogy, because it put the profits back into the business—that had been the family tradition for nearly a hundred years. To blame them for selling munitions to other countries in times of peace was mere nonsense, for you couldn't make munitions without skilled labor and you couldn't have such labor unless you gave it work to do and paid it wages to live. The government wouldn't order any large supplies in times of peace, but it expected to have a completely equipped plant running and ready to serve it in case of need. What could you do but follow the example of all other merchants and sell your goods whenever and wherever you could find customers?

There was a basic difference between Zacharias Basileos Zaharoff and Robbie Budd. Robbie really considered himself a patriot, and no doubt that is an excellent thing for a subconscious mind. On the other hand, Lanny had heard the old Greek say that he was a citizen of every country where he owned property. Did he want to enable each of his countries to fight his other countries? No, for Lanny had heard him, early in the year 1914, expressing his dread of war, in language which had surprised and puzzled a very young idealist. Robbie had joked about his attitude, saying that the old spider, the old wolf, the old devil wanted to sell munitions but didn't want them used.

But they had been used, and Zaharoff had had to live and see them used—and evidently that had been bad for his subconscious mind! Zaharoff had attended the Armistice Day ceremonies and laid a wreath on the tomb of the Unknown Soldier. He had thought about that soldier, and now Lanny knew what he had thought! Had he guessed that the national hero of France might be a Jew? Or was it that the national hero really had been a Jew? Was Zaharoff himself a Jew, or part Jew? Lanny didn't know, and wasn't especially interested. There were few people in Europe who didn't have Jewish blood, even those who despised the outcast race. For two thousand years the Jews had been scattered over the old Continent like thistledown in the wind; and the most carefully tended family trees don't always show what pollen has fallen upon them.

X

Lanny thought: What is the old man going to make of this? He can hardly believe that I planted it on him; that I knew about his uncle Antoniades! No, he will know that the thing must be genuine, and when he cools off he will realize that he wasn't quite a gentleman. Maybe he'll want to beg Tecumseh's pardon and have another try for the duquesa.

Lanny decided that this would be interesting; so he sat down and wrote a note to be mailed in Dieppe:

> My dear Sir Basil:
> I am truly sorry that the séance turned out to be so disturbing. I want to assure you that I am not telling anyone about it. I have seen many inaccuracies appear at sittings, and I have no interest in spreading them. You may count upon me in this.

Also he wrote a note to Rick, as follows:

> I wish you would see if you can find someone to do a job of research for me; that is, go through the records of Old Bailey prison during the 1870's and see if there is an entry of a prisoner by the name of Sahar, or Zahar, or Zaharoff. I enclose check for ten pounds to start it off, and if you will let me know the cost from time to time, I'll send more. Please say nothing about this, except to the dependable person you employ.

It wasn't going to be so easy to keep quiet about that afternoon's events. Beauty's curiosity had been aroused, and Irma's also. Fortunately Lanny had time to get over his own excitement, and to let Madame get over her bad feelings. He told his family that he had tried an experiment with someone who was interested, but the tests had not been conclusive, there were certain matters which had to be looked up, and then a second test might be made; he would tell them all about it later on. This was far from satisfactory, but he stuck to it, and pretty soon there were other séances, and other matters to talk about. Every now and then Beauty or Irma would say: "By the way, whatever became of that Dieppe affair?" Lanny would answer: "It hasn't been settled yet."

From Zaharoff he received no reply.

XI

The trim white *Bessie Budd* steamed away—or, to be exact, was propelled by crude oil, burning in a Diesel engine. At Bremerhaven the owner and his younger son were waiting, both proud and happy—the latter especially so, because he was a father and his fatherhood was new and shiny. How Freddi adored that gentle, sweet wife, and how he shivered with delight while gazing upon the mite of life which they had created! Nearly three months had passed since he had seen them both, and a newborn infant changes a lot in that time. The other Robins, including Bess and the nurse-maid, stood by when Freddi came aboard, sharing his happiness, of which he made quite a show, not being an Anglo-Saxon.

They all had a right to share, because this lovely infant was a prize exhibit of their dairy farm, so carefully supervised. Both father and grandfather had to certify themselves free of all diseases before they came on board, and there were to be no contaminating kisses, no demoralizing pettings, pokings, or ticklings. Wash your hands before you permit an infant to clutch your finger, for you can observe that the first thing he does is to convey your collected germs to his mouth.

Freddi had worked tremendously hard all year, and had got himself the coveted title of doctor. He was a handsome fellow, not quite so tall as his brother, but having the same large dark eyes and serious expression. He lacked Hansi's drive—he was never going to be a famous man, only an earnest student and teacher, a devoted husband and father. Not so Red as Hansi and Bess, but nearer to Lanny's shade; he still had hopes of the German Social-Democrats, in spite of the timidity and lack of competence they were displaying. Freddi had said that he was studying bourgeois economics in order to be able to teach the workers what was wrong with it. Already he and a couple of his young friends had set up a night school along the lines of Lanny's project in the Midi. A non-party affair, both the Socialists and the Communists took potshots at it, greatly to Freddi's disappointment. The workers were being lined up for class war, and there was no room for stragglers between the trenches.

Johannes had bad news for them. Business conditions in Germany were such that it was impossible for him to set out across the Atlantic. He wanted them to go without him, and the rest of the

Robin family were willing to do this because of the promises they had made. But the Budds knew that the purpose for which the yacht existed was to get Papa away from business cares, and they knew that the Robins would have a hard time enjoying themselves without him. Beauty talked it over with Lanny and his wife, and they agreed not to accept such a sacrifice. Irma would be sorry to miss seeing her mother, but, after all, it was easier to transport one stout queen mother across the ocean than to put a whole establishment ashore on Long Island. Irma said she really didn't have much pleasure in any sort of social life when she had to keep within four-hour time limits and have Miss Severne look grim if she came in hot and tired from any sort of exercise. Irma's smart young friends would all laugh at her and make jokes about cows. So it was better to stay on the yacht, where no explanations or apologies had to be made and where Rahel backed you up by her good example. "Jewish women seem to be much more maternal," said Irma. "Or is it because she is German?"

XII

It was decided that the *Bessie Budd* would loaf about in the North Sea and its adjoining waters so as to come back quickly and take its owner aboard whenever he was free. There would be regattas during the summer, and concerts and theaters in near-by cities and towns; art galleries to be visited—yes, one could think of worse ways of spending two or three months than on a luxury yacht based on Bremerhaven. The ship's library included Heine's *Nordseebilder*, also musical settings of some of these poems. Rahel would sing, Freddi would tootle, Hansi would scrape and scratch, Lanny and his sister would rumble and thump, Marceline would caper and prance, and Irma and Beauty and Johannes would raid the orchestra for a fourth hand at bridge.

The *Bessie Budd* steamed, or was propelled, to Copenhagen, where the party inspected the royal palace and attended a performance at the royal theater—the latter being comfortably within the young mothers' time limit. Lanny studied the sculptures in the Thorvald-

sen museum. Many interesting works of man to be seen, but not
many of nature in these low, flat islands and inlets, once the haunt
of fishermen and pirates. Having loaded themselves up with culture, they returned Johannes to Bremerhaven, and then set out
behind the Frisian islands, visiting Norderney, where a hundred
years previously an unhappy Jewish poet had written immortal
verses. *Sei mir gegrüsst, du ewiges Meer!*

Back to port, where the owner of the yacht joined them again,
bringing with him a large packet of mail. Included was a letter
from Rick to Lanny, as follows:

> With regard to your request concerning the Old Bailey, these
> records are not available, so I had a search made of the criminal
> reports in the *Times*. Under the date of January 13, 1873, ap-
> pears an entry numbered 61: "Zacharoff, Zacharia Basilius, agent
> pledging goods intrusted to him for sale." In the *Times* of
> January 17 appears a column headed "Criminal Court," begin-
> ning as follows: "Zacharia Basilius Zacharoff, 22, was indicted
> for that he, being an agent intrusted by one Manuel Hiphentides
> of Constantinople, merchant, for the purpose of sale with
> possession, among other goods, 25 cases of gum and 169 sacks
> of gall of the value together of £1000, did unlawfully and
> without any authority from his principal, for his own use make
> a deposit of the said goods as and by way of pledge."

Rick's letter gave a summary of the entire account, including the
statement: "Subsequently, by advice of his counsel, the prisoner
withdrew his plea of 'Not Guilty' and entered a plea of 'Guilty.' "
Rick added: "This is interesting, and I am wondering what use
you intend making of it. Let me add: Why don't your spirits give
you things like this? If they would do so, I would begin to take
them seriously!"

BOOK TWO

A Cloud That's Dragonish

6

Deutschland Erwache!

I

THE autumn storms begin early on the North Sea, and judging from his text the poet Heine had stayed to witness them. The storm rages and whips the waves, and the waves, foaming with fury and leaping, tower up, and the white water mountains surge with life, and the little ship mounts upon them, hasty-diligent, and suddenly plunges down into black wide-gaping abysses of flood. O sea! Mother of beauty, arise from the foam! Grandmother of love, spare mine!

But when you are running a floating dairy farm you cannot take chances of your stock's becoming seasick; you must put them on dry land before the equinoctial season and learn about storms from the pages of a book. Hansi and Bess had a concert tour, Freddi was going to apply the economic knowledge he had gained, and Lanny wanted to examine some pictures which might come on the market. Lanny, his wife, his mother, and her husband were urged to confer distinction and charm upon an oversized Berlin palace. "What else did I buy it for?" argued the proprietor.

To Lanny the young wife said privately: "Do you think it is a good thing for us to be associating with Jews all the time?"

The husband smiled. "You can meet anybody you want in that house. I assure you they will come."

"Maybe so; but won't they think there must be something wrong with us?"

"I assure you, my dear, they all know exactly what you are worth."

"Lanny, that's a horrid view to take of people!"

103

"You can save yourself a lot of unhappiness by taking my word about Europe. I have lived here most of my life." Lanny might have added: "Remember Ettore!" But he rarely permitted himself to mention the dashing Italian duca with whom she had once fancied herself in love.

"But, Lanny, we have been living off the Robins for nearly five months! Am I never going to spend any of my own money?"

"If your conscience worries you, give Freddi a good check for his new school. Nothing will please Johannes more."

"But if he wants that done, why doesn't he do it himself?"

"I think he may be afraid to; it would make too many enemies. But if you do it, he will have an alibi."

"Is he really that much of a coward, Lanny?"

The young husband chuckled. "Again I tell you, take my word about Europe!"

II

The German-Jewish money-lord had several of his guest-suites opened up, dusted, aired, and supplied with fresh flowers. He would have had them redecorated if there had been time. The one assigned to Irma and Lanny had a drawing-room with a piano in it; also a bedroom, dressing-room, and bath for each. Each dressing-room had a clothes closet which was almost a room and would hold all the imitations of Paris costumes which the *couturiers* of Berlin might persuade Irma to purchase. She didn't have gold bathroom fixtures and Lanny didn't have silver—one had to go to America for styles such as that; but they had drawings by Boucher and Fragonard, Watteau and Lancret on their walls, and Lanny knew these were genuine, for he and Zoltan had purchased them and divided a ten per cent commission. Irma found that rather embarrassing, but Lanny said: "It was what enabled me to dress properly while I was courting you!"

Next door to their suite was one for the baby and the dependable Miss Severne. Feathers had been telegraphed for, and was on hand to take charge of Irma's affairs: writing her letters, paying her bills, keeping track of her appointments. Johannes had provided an

English-speaking maid, ready to serve her from the moment of her arrival; indeed, he would have ordered a baby giraffe from the Hagenbeck zoo if he had thought that would have added to her happiness.

Feathers had only to telephone to the steward's office downstairs and a car would be at the door in a minute or two. There were theaters, operas, concerts, and cabaret entertainments for every sort of taste, high or low. The palace was in the fashionable district, convenient to everything, so the two young mothers had no trouble in keeping their schedules; lying back in the cushions of a limousine, they had time to recover from any excitement and thus avoid displeasing the head nurse. Their babies, being so well cared for, rarely cried at night, and, anyhow, that was the night nurse's affair. In the early morning hours this nurse would steal into Irma's bedroom, bringing Baby Frances for her first meal, and Irma would suckle her while still half asleep. Oh, yes, modern science can make life pleasant for those fortunate ones who have the price! Fond dreamers talk about making it that way for everybody, but the daughter of a utilities magnate would repeat an ancient question: "Who will do the dirty work?" She never found out who would, but she knew quite certainly who wouldn't.

Each member of the visiting party had his or her own idea of happiness. Miss Severne inquired concerning the English church in Berlin, and there she met persons near enough to her social station so that she could be happy in their company. Mr. Dingle discovered a New Thought group with a lecturer from America, and thus was able to supply himself with the magazines he had been missing. It is a fortunate circumstance about Christian Science and New Thought publications, that dealing with eternal truths they never get out of date. The only trouble is that, saying the same things, they are apt to become monotonous. Undeterred by this, Mr. Dingle began escorting Madame to a spiritualist church; they knew only a few words of the German language, but the spirits were international, and there were always living persons willing to help two foreigners.

III

The great city of Berlin, capital of the shattered Prussian dream. Triumphal arches, huge marble statues of Hohenzollern heroes, palaces of old-time princes and new-time money-lords; sumptuous hotels, banks that were temples of Mammon, department stores filled with every sort of luxury goods—and wandering about the streets, hiding in stone caves and cellars, or camping out in tents in vacant spaces, uncounted hordes of hungry, ill-clothed, fear-driven, and hate-crazed human beings. Out of a population of four million it might be doubted if there were half a million really contented. There was no street where you could escape the sight of pinched and haggard faces; none without beggars, in spite of the law; none where a well-dressed man could avoid the importunities of women and half-grown children, male or female, seeking to sell their bodies for the price of a meal.

Shut your eyes to these sights and your mind to these thoughts. The city was proud and splendid, lighted at night like the Great White Way in New York. The shop windows were filled with displays of elegance, and there were swarms of people gazing, and some buying. Tell yourself that the stories of distress were exaggerated; that the flesh of boys and girls had been for sale in Nineveh and Baghdad, and was now for sale in London and New York, though perhaps they used a bit more Anglo-Saxon hypocrisy. Prostitution has been the curse of great cities ever since they began; swarms of people come piling into them, lured by the hope of easy wealth, or driven from the land by economic forces which men have never learned to control.

This was something about which Freddi Robin should have been able to speak, he being now a duly certified Herr Doktor in the science of economics. He reported that the great university had left it still a mystery to students. The proper academic procedure was to accumulate masses of facts, but to consider explanations only historically. You learned that the three-stage pattern of primitive economic progress as taught by Friedrich List had been abandoned after the criticisms of anthropologists, and that Roscher's theory of national economics as a historical category had been replaced by the new historical school of Schmoller. It was all right for you to know that in ancient Rome the great estates, the latifundia, had been worked with slave labor, thus driving independent farmers to the city and herding them into ramshackle five-story tenements which often burned down. But if in the class you pointed out that similar tendencies were apparent in Berlin, you would be looked at askance by a professor whose future depended upon his avoidance of political controversy.

To be sure, they were supposed to enjoy academic freedom in Germany, and you might listen to a Catholic professor in one lecture hall and to a Socialist in the next; but when it came to promotions, somebody had to decide, and you could hardly expect the authorities to give preference to men whose teachings fostered that proletarian discontent which was threatening to rend the country apart. At any rate, that is the way Freddi Robin reported the situation in the great University of Berlin.

IV

The Budds arrived a week or so before the national elections in September 1930. The city was in an uproar, with posters and placards everywhere, hundreds of meetings each night, parades with bands and banners, crowds shouting and often fighting. The tension was beyond anything that Lanny had ever witnessed; under the pressure of the economic collapse events in Germany were coming to a crisis, and everybody was being compelled to take sides.

The young people wanted to see these sights. Hansi and Bess must attend a big Communist gathering the very night of their arrival, and the others went along out of curiosity. The great hall in the Moabit district was draped with red streamers and banners having the hammer and sickle in black. Also there were red carnations or rosettes in people's buttonholes. The crowd was almost entirely proletarian: pitiful pinched faces of women, haggard grim faces of men; clothing dingy, generally clean but so patched that

the original cloth was a matter of uncertainty; many a man had had
no new suit since the war.

The speakers raved and shouted, and worked the crowd into a
frenzy; the singing made you think of an army marching into battle. A quartet sang chants with hammering rhythms, the repetition
of simple words, like lessons repeated by children in school. Lanny
translated for his wife: "Be ready to take over! Be ready to take
over!"

Irma had learned a lot about this subject during her sojourn in
these two strange families; she had listened to Uncle Jesse, and to
Hansi and Bess arguing with Lanny, and now and then with Hansi's
father. They didn't want to kill anybody—not unless somebody
resisted. All they wanted was to reproduce in Germany what they
had done in Russia; to confiscate the property of the rich and reduce them to their own slum level. Johannes had smiled and said
they would make a museum out of his palace, and that would be
all right with him, he would buy another in London, and then one
in New York, and then one in Tahiti—by which time Russia would
have restored capitalism, and he would return to that region and
make his fortune all over again.

The financier made a joke of it, but it was no joke at this *Versammlung*. Not one single laugh in a whole evening; the nearest to
it was mocking jeers, hardly to be distinguished from cries of rage.
This was what they called the "proletariat," the creatures of the
slums, threatening to burst out, overcome the police, and raid the
homes of those whom they called "exploiters." The speakers were
seeking election to the Reichstag, where they would pour out the
same kind of tirades. Irma looked about her uneasily, and was glad
she had had the sense not to wear any of her jewels to this place.
It wasn't safe anyhow, for the National Socialists often raided the
crowds coming out from Red meetings, and there were fights and
sometimes shootings.

V

The Social-Democrats also were holding great meetings. They
were by far the largest party in the Republic, but had never had an

outright majority, either of votes or of representation; therefore they had not been able to have their way. If they had, would they have known what to do? Would they have dared trying to bring Socialism to the Fatherland? Hansi and Bess declared that they were paralyzed by their notions of legality; it was a party of office-holders, of bureaucrats warming swivel-chairs and thinking how to keep their jobs and salaries. They continued to call themselves Socialist and to repeat the party shibboleths, but that was simply bait for the voters. How to get Socialism they had no idea, and they didn't consider it necessary to find out.

Lanny, yearning after the orderly methods of democracy, considered that it was up to him to help this party. In days past he had brought letters of introduction from Longuet, and now he went to renew old acquaintanceships, and to prove his sincerity by making a contribution to the party's campaign chest. He took his family to one of the mass meetings, and certainly, if there was any tiredness or deadness, it didn't show on this public occasion. The hall was packed to the doors, banners and streamers were everywhere, and when the party's favorite orators made their appearance volumes of cheering rolled to the roof and back. These men didn't rave and threaten as the Communists did; they discussed the practical problems confronting the German workers, and denounced both groups of extremists for leading the people astray with false promises. It was a dignified meeting, and Irma felt more comfortable; there didn't seem to be anything to start a fight about.

On their way home the young people discussed what they had heard. Bess, who used the same phonograph records as Uncle Jesse, said that the party was old—a grandfather party—so it had the machinery for getting out the crowds. "But," she added, "those municipal councilors repeating their formulas make one think of stout, well-fed parrots dressed up in frock-coats."

"The Communists don't have any formulas, of course!" countered Lanny, not without a touch of malice. These two loved each other, but couldn't discuss politics without fighting.

Bess was referring to officials who had reported on their efforts to increase the city's milk supply and reduce its price. Lanny had found the Socialists discussing the same subject in New York; it was no unimportant matter to the women of the poor. "Of course it's dull and prosy," he admitted; "not so exciting as calling for the revolution next week——"

"I know," broke in the sister; "but while you're discussing milk prices, the Nazis are getting arms caches and making their plans to bring about the counter-revolution next week."

"And the reactionary princes conspiring with them, and the great capitalists putting up money to pay for the arms!" Thus Hansi, stepping onto dangerous ground, since his father was one of those capitalists. How much longer was that secret going to be kept in the Robin family?

VI

Lanny wanted to hear all sides; he wanted to know what the Nazis were doing and saying, if only so as to send Rick an account of it. Among his acquaintances in Berlin was Heinrich Jung, blue-eyed "Aryan" enthusiast from Upper Silesia. Heinrich had spent three years training himself to succeed his father as head forester of Graf Stubendorf's domain; but now all that had been set aside, and Heinrich was an official of the National Socialist German Workingmen's Party, high up in what they called the Hitler Youth. For seven or eight years he had been mailing propaganda to Lanny Budd in Bienvenu, having never given up hope that a pure-blooded "Aryan" would feel the pull of his racial ties.

Lanny called him on the telephone, and Heinrich was delighted and begged him to come to party headquarters. The visitor didn't consider it necessary to mention the fact that he was staying in the home of one of the most notorious of Jewish *Schieber*. It wouldn't really have mattered, for such eccentricities in an American didn't mean what they would have meant in a German. A German traveler had described America as "the land of unlimited possibilities," and rich, successful persons from that fabulous region walked the common earth of Europe as demigods. Even the Führer himself was in awe of them, having heard the report that they had not run away from the mighty German army. A bright feather in the cap of a young party official if he should bring in such a convert to the new religion of blood and soil.

The blue-eyed and fair-haired young Prussian had matured greatly in the three or four years since Lanny had seen him. He had his private office in the great Nazi building, and was surrounded by the appurtenances of power: files and charts, a telephone on his desk, and a buzzer to summon his subordinates. He wore the uniform of the Sturmabteilung, those party soldiers whose marching and drum-beating were by now among the familiar sights in German cities: brown shirt and trousers with black stripes, shiny black boots, red armband with the swastika in black. Handsome, smart, snappy—and keep out of their way, for they mean business. *Die Strasse frei den braunen Bataillonen!*

Heinrich stopped only long enough to ask after Lanny's wife and baby, about whom he had heard from Kurt. Then he began pouring out the story of the miracles which had been achieved by the N.S.D.A.P.—the initials of the party's German name—since those old days when a student of forestry had revealed it as a tiny shoot just pushing its head through the wintry soil. "Tall oaks from little acorns grow!" said Heinrich; having written it as an English copybook exercise in school.

A ladder was provided and Lanny was taken up to the topmost branches of that ever-spreading oak tree. The Hitler Youth constituted the branches where the abundant new growth was burgeoning; for this part of the tree all the rest existed. The future Germany must be taught to march and to fight, to sing songs of glory, hymns to the new Fatherland it was going to build. It must be well fed and trained, sound of wind and limb; it must know the Nazi creed, and swear its oath of loyalty to what was called the *Führerprinzip*, the faith that the individual exists for the state, and that the state is guided by one inspired leader. No matter from what sort of homes the young people came, the Nazis would make them all the same: perfect party members, obedient because it is a joy to obey, because the future belongs to those who are strong, confident, and united.

Lanny had seen this principle working in the soul of one sturdy young "Aryan," and now he discovered him as a machine engaged in turning out thousands of other specimens exactly like himself. A machine for making machines! On the wall was a map showing where the branch offices of this youth-machine were situated—and they weren't only in Germany, but in every city on earth where Germans lived. There were charts and diagrams, for in this land things are done scientifically, including Hitler propaganda. "*Deutschland Erwache!*" said a placard on Heinrich's wall. The Führer was a great deviser of slogans; he would retire to a secret place and there ponder and weigh many hundreds which came to his mind, and when he chose one, it would appear on posters and be shouted at meetings in every hamlet of the land. "Germany, Awake!"

VII

Lanny was touched by the pride with which the young official revealed and explained the complex organization he had helped to build; its various departments and subdivisions, each having an official endowed with one of those elaborate titles which Germans so dearly love. The head of the great machine was, of course, the one and only Adolf, *Partei- und oberster S.A. Führer, Vorsitzender der N.S.D.A.P.* Under him were adjutants and Secretariat and Chief of Staff, the *Reichsjugendführer* (who was Heinrich's superior) and his Staff Director, the Subdirectors of half a dozen different staffs, the Business Manager, the Secretary, the Presidium, the Reich Directorate.

Also there was a Political Organization, or rather two, P.O. 1 and P.O. 2—they had two of everything, except of the Führer. It made you dizzy merely to hear about all these obligations and responsibilities: the Foreign Division, Economic Policy Division, Race and Culture Division, Internal Political Division, Legal Division, Engineering-Technical Division, Labor Service Division; the Reich Propaganda Leaders Number 1 and Number 2, the Leaders of the Reich Inspection 1 and 2; the Investigation and Adjustment Committee—what a whopper of a title had been assigned to them: *Unter-suchungs- und Schlichtungsausschuss*, or USCHLA! But don't smile over it, for Heinrich Jung explains that the party is preparing to take over the destinies of the Fatherland, to say nothing of many decadent nations of Europe and elsewhere, and all this machinery and even more will be needed; the Gymnastics and Sports Committee, the Bureau Leader for the Press, the *Zentralparteiverlag*, the *Personalamt*, and much more.

Heinrich was responsible for the affairs of one department of the Hitler Youth, with twenty-one geographic sections throughout Germany. They maintained a school for future Nazi leaders, and published three monthlies and a semi-monthly. There were divisions dealing with press, culture, propaganda, defense-sport—they were learning not merely to fight the Young Communists, but to make a sport of it! Also there were the junior organizations, the *Deutsches Jungvolk* and the *Bund Deutscher Mädel*, and a *Studentenbund*, and a Women's League, and so on apparently without end. The polite Lanny Budd was glad in his heart that it was election time and that so many subordinates were waiting to receive orders from this overzealous expounder.

VIII

One thing a young party official would not fail to do for an old friend: to take him to the mighty *Versammlung* in the Sport-palast which was to climax the Nazi campaign. Here the Führer himself would make his final appeal to the German voters; and it would be like nothing ever seen in the world before. For several months this marvelous man had been rushing all over the land making speeches, many hundreds of them; traveling by airplane, or in his fast Mercédès car, wearing the tan raincoat in which Lanny had seen him in the old days; possibly not the same coat, but the same simple, devoted, inspired, and inspiring leader whose mission it was to revive Germany and then the whole world. *Heute gehört uns Deutschland und morgen die ganze Welt!*

Heinrich explained that seats would be difficult to obtain; there would be a line of people waiting at the doors of the Sportpalast from early morning to be sure of getting good places. There would of course be reserved seats for important persons, and Lanny accepted four tickets. He knew that none of the Robins would attend a Nazi meeting—it really wouldn't be safe, for someone might spit in their faces, or beat them if they failed to give the Nazi salute and shout *"Heil Hitler!"* Bess loathed the movement and its creed, and her curiosity had been fully satisfied by watching the Stormtroopers on the march and by occasional glances at their newspapers.

Well in advance of eight o'clock Lanny and his wife and Beauty and her husband were in their seats. Bands playing, literature-sellers busy, and armed squads keeping watch all over the enormous arena —Communists keep out! A display of banners and streamers with all the familiar slogans: "Down with Versailles!" "Freedom and Bread!" "Germany, Awake!" "An End to Reparations!" "Common Wealth before Private Wealth!" "Break the Bonds of Interest Slavery!" These last were the "radical" slogans, carried down from the old days; Robbie had said they were practically the same as those of the "money cranks" in the United States, the old-time Populists and Greenbackers; they appealed to the debtor classes, the small farmers, the little business men who felt themselves being squeezed by the big trusts. This Hitler movement was a revolt of the lower middle classes, whose savings had been wiped out by the inflation and who saw themselves being reduced to the status of proletarians.

To Irma they seemed much nicer-looking people than those she had seen at the other two meetings. The black-and-silver uniforms of the Schutzstaffel, who acted as ushers and guards, were new and quite elegant; these young men showed alertness and efficiency. Twenty or thirty thousand people singing with fervor were impressive, and Irma didn't know that the songs were full of hatred for Frenchmen and Poles. She knew that the Nazis hated the Jews, and this she deplored. She had learned to be very fond of one Jewish family, but she feared there must be something wrong with the others—so many people said it. In any case, the Germans had to decide about their own country.

Singing and speech-making went on for an hour or so; then came a roll of drums and a blast of trumpets in the main entrance, and all the men and women in the huge place leaped to their feet. *Der Führer kommt!* A regiment of Stormtroopers in solemn march, carrying flags with spearpoints or bayonets at the tips of the poles. The bands playing the magnificent open chords to which the gods march across the rainbow bridge into Valhalla at the close of *Das Rheingold*. Then the party leaders, military and magnificent, marching in the form of a hollow square, protecting their one and only leader. Someone with a sense of drama has planned all this; someone who has learned from Wagner how to combine music, scenery, and action so as to symbolize the fundamental aspirations of the human soul, to make real to the common man his own inmost longing.

Who was that genius? Everyone in the hall, with the possible exception of a few Lanny Budds, believed that it was the little man who marched in the center of that guard of honor; the simple man with the old tan raincoat, the one whom honors could not spoil, the one consecrated to the service of the Fatherland; one born of the common people, son of an obscure Austrian customs official; a corporal of the World War wounded and gassed; an obscure workingman, a dreamer of a mighty dream, of Germany freed and restored to her place among the nations, or perhaps above them.

He wore no hat, and his dark hair, long and brushed to one side, fell now and then across his pale forehead and had to be swept away. No fashion here, a plain man, just like you and me; one whose hand you can shake, who smiles in a friendly way at those who greet him. A storm of cheering arises, the *Heils* become like raindrops falling in a cloudburst—so many that you cannot hear the individual ones, the sounds become a union like the National Socialist German Workingmen's Party.

Lanny has never attended an old-fashioned American revival meeting, but his friend Jerry Pendleton from Kansas has told him about one, and here is another. Has someone from the American South or Middle West come over and taught these arts of stirring the souls of primitive people, of letting them take part in what is being done to them? Or is it something that rises out of the primitive soul in every part of the world? The speakers on this platform ask questions, and twenty thousand throats shout the answers. Only they do not shout: "Glory Hallelujah!" and "Bless the Lord!"; theirs are secular cries: "Down with Versailles!" "*Juda verrecke!*" and "*Deutschland erwache!*"

IX

Seven years since Lanny watched Charlie Chaplin come out upon the stage of a great beerhall in Munich; and here he is again, the same foolish little dark mustache, the same shy manner, humble, deprecating. But now he is stouter, he gets better food. Now, also, there are a score of spotlights centered upon him, telling everybody that appearances are deceptive, and that this is a special One. Banners and symbols, slogans and rituals, hopes and resolves, all have come out of his soul; he is the Messiah, the One appointed and sent to save the Fatherland in its hour of greatest trial.

He begins to speak, and Lanny knows every tone. Quiet at first, and the vast hall as still as the universe must have been before God created it. But soon the man of visions begins to warm up to his theme. The slogans which he has taught to all Germany work upon himself as others; they dominate his entire being; they are sparks from a white-hot flame which burns day and night within him. The flame of "Adi's" hatred of his miserable and thwarted life! Hatred of his father, the dumb petty bureaucrat who wanted to make his son like himself and wouldn't let him become an artist; hatred of the critics and dealers who wouldn't recognize his pitiful attempts at painting; hatred of the bums and wastrels in the flop-houses who wouldn't listen to his inspired ravings; hatred of the Russians and the French and the British and the Americans who wouldn't let an obscure corporal win his war; hatred of Marxists who betrayed Germany by a stab in the back; hatred of the Jews who made money out of her misery; hatred of all who now stood in the way of her destiny, who opposed Adi's party which was to save her from humiliation. All these hatreds had flamed forth from one thwarted soul and had set fire to the tinder-box which Germany had become—and here it was, blazing, blazing!

The Führer possessed no gleam of humor, no trace of charm. He was an uneducated man, and spoke with an Austrian country accent, not always grammatically. His voice was hoarse from a thousand speeches, but he forced it without mercy. He raved and shrieked; he waved his arms, he shook his clenched fists in the face of Germany's enemies. Perspiration poured from his pasty and rather lumpy countenance; his heavy hair fell down over his eyes and had to be flung back.

Lanny knew every gesture, every word. Adi hadn't learned a thing, hadn't changed a thing in seven years; he had merely said the same things a million times. His two-part book which Lanny had read with mingled dismay and laughter had become the bible of a new religion. Millions of copies had been sold, and extracts from it and reiterations of it had been printed in who could guess how many pamphlets, leaflets, and newspapers? Certainly well up in the billions; for some of the Nazi newspapers had circulations of hundreds of thousands every day, and in the course of years that mounts up. Heinrich told Lanny that they had held nearly thirty-five thousand meetings in Germany during the present campaign and quantities of literature had been sold at every one of them. Lanny, listening and watching the frenzied throng, remembered some lines from his poetry anthology, lines which had sounded melodious and exciting, but which he hadn't understood when he had read them as a boy:

> One man with a dream, at pleasure,
>   Shall go forth and conquer a crown;
> And three with a new song's measure
>   Can trample an empire down.

X

There had been an election to the Reichstag less than two and a half years before, and at that election the Social-Democrats had polled more than nine million votes, the Communists more than three million, and the Nazis less than one million. The two last-named parties had been active since then, and everyone agreed that conditions favored the extremists. The business collapse in America had made farm products unsalable there, and this had caused an immediate reaction in Germany; the peasants had their year's harvest to sell at a heavy loss. As for the workers, there were four million unemployed, and fear in the hearts of all the rest. These groups were sure to vote for a change—but of what sort?

Impossible to spend a week in a nation so wrought up and not come to share the excitement. It became a sort of sporting proposition; you chose sides and made bets to back yourself. After the fashion of humans, you believed what you hoped. Lanny became sure that the cautious, phlegmatic German people would prefer the carefully thought-out program of the Socialists and give them an actual majority so that they could put it into effect. But Johannes Robin, who thrived on pessimism, expected the worst—by which he meant that the Communists would come out on top. Red Berlin would become scarlet, or crimson, or whatever is the most glaring of shades.

The results astounded them all—save possibly Heinrich Jung and his party comrades. The Social-Democrats lost more than half a million votes; the Communists gained more than a million and a quarter; while the Nazis increased their vote from eight hundred thousand to nearly six and a half million: a gain of seven hundred per cent in twenty-eight months! The score in millions stood roughly, Social-Democrats eight and a half, Nazis six and a half, and Communists four and a half.

The news hit the rest of the world like a high-explosive shell. The statesmen of the one-time Allied lands who were so certain that they had Germany bound in chains; the international bankers who had lent her five billion dollars; the negotiators who, early in this year of 1930, had secured her signature to the Young Plan, whereby she bound herself to pay reparations over a period of fifty-eight years—all these now suddenly discovered that they had driven six and a half million of their victims crazy! War gains were to be confiscated, trusts nationalized, department stores communalized, speculation in land prevented, and usurers and profiteers to suffer the death penalty! Such was the Nazi program for the inside of

Germany; while for the outside, the Versailles treaty was to be denounced, the Young Plan abrogated, and Germany was to go to war, if need be, in order to set her free from the "Jewish-dominated plutocracies" of France, Britain, and America!

Lanny's host was unpleasantly surprised by these returns, but, after thinking matters over, he decided not to worry too much. He said that no soup is ever eaten as hot as it is cooked. He said that the wild talk of the Nazis was perhaps the only way to get votes just now. He had his private sources of information, and knew that the responsible leaders were embarrassed by the recklessness of their young followers. If you studied the Nazi program carefully you would see that it was full of all sorts of "jokers" and escape clauses. The campaign orators of Berlin had been promising the rabble "confiscation without compensation" of the great estates of the Junkers; but meanwhile, in East Prussia, they had got the support of the Junkers by pointing to the wording of the program: the land to be confiscated must be "socially necessary." And how easy to decide that the land of your friends and supporters didn't come within that category!

But all the same Johannes decided to move some more funds to Amsterdam and London, and to consult Robbie Budd about making more investments in America. Hundreds of other German capitalists took similar steps; and of course the Nazis found it out, and their press began to cry that these "traitor plutocrats" should be punished by the death penalty.

XI

The rich did not give up their pleasures on account of elections, nor yet of election results. The fashionable dressmakers, the milliners, the jewelers came clamoring for appointments with the famous Frau Lanny Budd, *geborene* Irma Barnes. They displayed their choicest wares, and skilled workers sat up all night and labored with flying fingers to meet her whims. When she was properly arrayed she sallied forth, and the contents of her trunks which Feathers had brought from Juan were placed at the disposal of the

elder Frau Budd, who dived into them with cries of delight, for they
had barely been worn at all and had cost more than anything she
had ever been able to afford in her life. A few alterations, to allow
for *embonpoint* attributable to the too rich fare of the yacht, and a
blond and blooming Beauty was ready to stand before kings—
whether of steel, coal, or chemicals, potash, potatoes, or *Renten-
marks*.

She did not feel humiliated to play second fiddle in the family,
for after all she was a grandmother; also, she had not forgotten the
lesson of the Wall Street collapse. Let Irma go on paying the family
bills and nursing the family infant, and her mother-in-law would
do everything in the power of a highly skilled social intriguer to
promote her fortunes, put her in a good light, see that she met the
right people and made the right impressions. Beauty would even
write to Irma's mother and urge her to come to Berlin and help in
this task; there must never be any rivalry or jealousy between them;
on the contrary, they must be partners in the duty of seeing that
Irma got everything to which her elegance, charm, and social position—Beauty didn't say wealth—entitled her.

Lanny, of course, had to play up to this role; he had asked for it,
and now couldn't back out. He had to let the tailors come and
measure him for new clothes, and stand patiently while they made
a perfect fit. No matter how bored he was, no matter how much he
would have preferred trying some of Hindemith's new compositions! His mother scolded him, and taught his wife to scold him;
such is the sad fate of kind-hearted men. When he and Irma were
invited to a dinner-party by the Prinz Ilsaburg zu Schwarzadler or
to a ball at the palace of the Baron von Friedrichsbrunn, it would
have been unthinkable to deprive Irma of such honors and a scandal
to let some other man escort her.

It wasn't exactly a scandal for Johannes Robin to escort the elder
Frau Budd, for it was known that he had a wife who was ill-
adapted to a fashionable career. Beauty, on the other hand, had
taken such care of her charms that you couldn't guess her years;
she was a gorgeous pink rose, now fully unfolded. Fashionable society was mistaken in its assumptions concerning her host and her-

self, for both this strangely assorted pair were happy with their respective spouses, and both spouses preferred staying at home—Mama Robin to watch over the two infants whom she adored equally, and Parsifal Dingle to read his New Thought publications and say those prayers which he was firmly assured were influencing the souls of all the persons he knew, keeping them free from envy, hatred, malice, and all uncharitableness. Parsifal himself had so little of these worldly defects that he didn't even know that it was a humiliation to have his wife referred to as the elder Frau Budd.

The Jew who had been born in a hut with a mud floor in the realm of the Tsar was proud to escort the Budd ladies about *die grosse Welt* of Berlin. He told them so with a frankness touched with humor and untouched with servility. He said that when he was with them his blood was pure and his fortune untainted. He said that many a newly arrived *Schieber* was paying millions of marks for social introductions which he, the cunning one, was getting practically free. He could say such things, not merely because Bess and Hansi had made their families one, but because he knew that Robbie Budd needed Johannes in a business way as much as Johannes needed Robbie's ladies in a social way. A fair deal, and all parties concerned understood it.

So the former Jascha Rabinowich of Lodz gave a grand reception and ball in honor of the two Damen Budd. Decorations were planned, a list of guests carefully studied, and the chefs labored for a week preparing fantastical foods; the reception-rooms of the marble palace which looked like a railway station came suddenly to resemble a movie director's dream of Bali or Brazil. Anyhow, it was a colossal event, and Johannes said that the magnates who came wouldn't be exclusively his own business associates, the statesmen wouldn't be exclusively those who had got campaign funds from him, and the members of the aristocracy wouldn't be exclusively those who owed him money. "Moreover," added the shrewd observer, "they will bring their wives and daughters."

XII

Lanny Budd, in his best bib and tucker, wandering about in this dazzling assemblage, helping to do the honors, helping to make people feel at home; dancing with any overgrown Prussian *Backfisch* who appeared to be suffering from neglect; steering the servitors of food toward any dowager whose stomach capacity hadn't been entirely met. Dowagers with large pink bosoms, no shoulder-straps, and perfectly incredible naked backs; servitors in pink-and-green uniforms with gold buttons, white silk gloves and stockings, and pumps having rosettes. Lanny has dutifully studied the list of important personages, so that he will know whom he is greeting and commit no *faux pas*. He has helped to educate his wife, so that she can live up to the majesty of her fortune. Never think that a social career is for an idler!

"Do you know General Graf Stubendorf?" inquires one of the enormous elderly Valkyries.

"I have never had the honor," replies the American. "But I have visited Seine Hochgeboren's home on many occasions."

"Indeed?" says Seine Hochgeboren. He is tall and stiff as a ramrod, with sharp, deeply lined features, gray hair not more than a quarter of an inch in length, a very bright new uniform with orders and decorations which he has earned during four years of never-to-be-forgotten war.

Lanny explains: "I have been for most of my life a friend of Kurt Meissner."

"Indeed?" replies the General Graf. "We consider him a great musician, and are proud of him at Stubendorf."

"I have spent many Christmases at the Meissner home," continues the young American. "I had the pleasure of listening to you address your people each year; also I heard your honored father, before the war."

"Indeed?" says Seine Hochgeboren, again. "I cannot live there any longer, but I go back two or three times a year, out of loyalty to my people." The gray-haired warrior is conveying to a former foe: "I cannot bear to live in my ancestral home because it has

become a part of Poland, and is governed by persons whom I consider almost subhuman. You and your armies did it, by meddling
without warrant in the affairs of Germany and snatching her hard-
won victory from her grasp. Then you went off and left us to be
plundered by the rapacious French and the shopkeeping British."

It is not a subject to be explored, so Lanny says some polite words
of no special significance and passes on, reflecting: "If Johannes
thinks he is winning that gentleman, he is surely fooling himself!"

XIII

But Lanny was making a mistake, as he discovered later in the
evening. The stiff aristocrat approached him and spoke again, in a
more cordial tone. "Mr. Budd, I have been realizing, I remember
you in Stubendorf. Also I have heard Meissner speak of you."

"Herr Meissner has treated me as if I were another of his sons,"
replied Lanny, modestly.

"*Ein braver Mensch*," said Seine Hochgeboren. "His sons have
rendered admirable service." He went on to speak of the family of
his Comptroller-General, upon whose capability and integrity he
depended as had his father before him. While hearing this formal
speech, Lanny guessed what must have happened. The dowager
Valkyrie had reminded the General Graf that this was the lucky
young *Taugenichts* who had married the fabulously wealthy heiress.
Not, as Seine Hochgeboren had supposed, some young snipe trying
to make himself important by claiming intimacy with one of a noble-
man's employees!

So here was a great aristocrat manifesting condescension, *noblesse
oblige*. He knew all about Mr. Budd, oh, of course! "Kurt Meissner
composed much of his music in your home, I have heard." He didn't
add: "Kurt Meissner was your mother's lover for many years, I
have heard." He talked about Kurt's compositions and showed that
he really knew about them; *echt deutsche Musik* which could be
praised without reserve. A young Franco-American who had built
a studio for a musical genius to work in could meet on equal terms

a Junker who had furnished a cottage for the genius to raise his family in.

Presently it came out that Lanny had served as a secretary-translator on the staff of the American Commission to Negotiate Peace. "I should be interested to talk to you about those Paris days," remarked the officer. "You might be able to explain some points about the American attitude which have always been a mystery to me."

"I should be pleased to do my best," said Lanny, politely. "You must realize that your beautiful *Schloss* made a great impression upon a small boy, and your father and yourself appeared to me as very grand personalities."

Seine Hochgeboren smiled graciously. He hadn't the slightest doubt that his father had been a grand personality, or that he was one now. "Are you planning to come to Stubendorf this Christmas?" he inquired.

"Kurt has been inviting us," was the reply. "I am not sure if we can arrange it."

"I would be happy if you and your wife would visit the *Schloss* as my guests," said the General Graf.

"Thank you very much," replied the younger man. "I should have to ask the Meissners to give us up."

"I think they would do so," the other suggested, dryly.

"I will let you know a little later. I must consult my wife." Another peculiarity of Americans—they consulted their wives instead of telling them! But of course when the wife was as rich as this one —what was her name?

XIV

They watched that valuable wife, dancing with a handsome young attaché of the American embassy staff. She was more than ever the young brunette Juno; some skilled *couturier* must have had the thought, for he had made her a gown of white silk chiffon with a hint of ancient Greece in it. For jewels she wore only her double rope of pearls; a fortune such as hers was beyond any quantity of stones to symbolize, and had better be left to the newspapers to proclaim. She danced with stately grace, smiled gently, and never chattered; yes, a young goddess, and an ornament to any *Schieber's* ballroom.

When the party was over, Lanny escorted her upstairs. She had promised to have no more than two glasses of champagne, and had kept her word, but was not a little excited by the presence of so many distinguished persons, all of whom had costumes, manners, and modes of speech calculated to impress the daughter of a one-time Wall Street errand-boy. She and her husband talked about this one and that while the maid helped her off with her gown. After she had rested for the required fifteen minutes, the baby was brought in for a nursing; quite a bundle now, nearly eight months old, and full of kicks and squirms and gurgles. She never needed any invitation, but took hold promptly, and while she worked away, Lanny told the mother about the invitation to Stubendorf. He had talked a lot about the "Christmas-card castle" with its snow-covered roofs gleaming in the early morning sunshine, and had made it seem as romantic to Irma as it had to him seventeen years ago.

"Shall we go?" she asked.

"If you would enjoy it."

"I think it would be ducky!" Then, after some reflection: "You and I really make a pretty good social team, don't we, Lanny!"

7

I Have Seen Tempests

I

THE results of the election had set Heinrich Jung in a seat of authority. He called Lanny on the telephone and poured out his exultation. There was no party but the N.S.D.A.P., and Heinrich was its prophet! Therefore, would Lanny come to his home some evening and meet his wife and one of his friends? Lanny said he would be happy to do so; he had just received a letter from Rick, saying that the German vote had made a great impression in England, and if Lanny would send a bunch of literature and some of his own notes as to the state of mind of the country, Rick could write an article for one of the weeklies. Lanny wanted to help his friend, and thought the English people ought to understand what the new movement signified. This, of course, was right down Heinrich's alley; he volunteered to assemble a load of literature—and even to have the article written and save Rick the bother!

Lanny left his wife in a comfortable family bridge game while he drove out to the suburbs toward Potsdam, where the young official lived in a modest cottage. Heinrich had chosen himself a proper *deutsches Mädel* with eyes as blue as his own, and according to the Nazi-Nordic principles they had set to work to increase the ruling race. They proudly showed two blond darlings asleep in their cribs, and one glance at Ilsa Jung was enough to inform Lanny that another would soon be added. There was a peculiarity of the Nazi doctrine which Lanny had observed already among the Italian Fascists. Out of one side of their mouths they said that the nation had to expand in order to have room for its growing population, while out of the other side they said that their population must be increased in order that they might be able to expand. In the land of Mussolini this need was known as *sacro egoismo*, and Lanny had tried in vain to puzzle out why a quality which was considered so offensive in an individual should become holy when exhibited by a group. He hoped that a day might come when nations would be gentlemen.

Heinrich had invited to meet his guest a sports director of one of the youth groups in Berlin. Hugo Behr was his name, and he was another exemplar of the Nordic ideal—which oddly enough a great many of the party leaders were not. There was a joke going the rounds among Berlin's smart intellectuals that the ideal "Aryan" was required to be as blond as Hitler, as tall as Goebbels, as slender as Göring, and so on, as far as your malicious memory would carry you. But Hugo had smooth rosy cheeks and wavy golden hair, and doubtless when in a gym costume presented a figure like that of a young Hermes. He had until recently been an ardent Social-Democrat, a worker in the youth movement in that party; not only could he tell all its scandals, but he knew how to present National Socialism as the only true and real Socialism, by which the German workers were to win freedom for themselves and later for the workers of the world.

The human mind is a strange thing. Both this pair had read *Mein Kampf* as their holy book, and had picked out what they wanted from it. They knew that Lanny had also read the book, and assumed that he would have picked out the same things. But Lanny had noted other passages, in which the Führer had made it clear that he hadn't the slightest interest in giving freedom to the workers of other nations or races, but on the contrary was determined to put them all to work for the benefit of the master race. "Aryan" was merely a fancy word for German—and for other persons of education and social position who were willing to join with the Nazis and help them to seize power.

However, Lanny wasn't there to convert two Nazi officials. He permitted Hugo Behr to speak to him as one comrade to another, and now and then he made notes of something which might be of interest to the reading public of Britain. Hugo was newer in the

movement than Heinrich, and more naïve; he had swallowed the
original Nazi program, hook, line, and sinker; that was the creed,
and when you had quoted it, you had settled the point at issue.
Lanny Budd, cynical worldling, product of several decadent cul-
tures, wanted to say: "How can Hitler be getting funds from von
Papen and the other Junkers if he really means to break up the
great landed estates of Prussia? How can he be getting funds from
Fritz Thyssen and the other steel kings if he means to socialize big
industry?" But what good would it do? Hugo doubtless thought
that all the party funds came from the pfennigs of the workers;
that banners and brassards, brown shirts and shiny boots, automatic
pistols and Budd machine guns were purchased with the profits
of literature sales! Heinrich, perhaps, knew better, but wouldn't
admit it, and Lanny wasn't free to name the sources of his own
information. Better simply to listen, and make careful notes, and
let Rick write an article entitled: "England, Awake!"

II

Right after the elections came a trial in Berlin of three officers
charged with having made Nazi propaganda in the army. It attracted a great deal of public attention, and Adolf Hitler appeared
as a witness and delivered one of his characteristic tirades, declaring that when his party took power the "November criminals,"
meaning the men who had established the Republic, would be
judged by a people's tribunal. "Heads will roll in the sand," he
said. Such language shocked the civilized German people, and
Johannes Robin took it as a proof of what he had been saying to
Lanny, that all you had to do was to give this fellow rope enough
and he would hang himself. There was a demand from many quar-
ters that Hitler be tried for treason; but probably the government
was of the same opinion as Johannes. Why hang a man who was
so ready to hang himself? The three officers were dismissed from
the army, and Adi went on making his propaganda—in the army
as everywhere else.

Lanny invited Hauptmann Emil Meissner to lunch with him, and they talked about these problems. Kurt's eldest brother, a World War veteran, had the younger's pale blue eyes and close-cropped straw-colored hair, but not his ardent temperament; he agreed with Lanny that Kurt had been led astray, and that the Führer was a dangerous fanatic. Emil was loyal to the existing government; he said that would always be the attitude of the army, and was the obligation of every officer, no matter how much he might disapprove the policies of the politicians in control.

"Would you obey the Nazis if they should take power?" inquired the American.

Emil shut his eyes for a moment, as if to hide the painful reaction which such a question caused in him. "I don't think it is necessary to contemplate that," he said.

Lanny replied: "The present election has made me do it." But he didn't press the point.

Emil placed his faith in Germany's symbol of loyalty, Feldmar-schall and now Präsident Paul Ludwig Hans Anton von Beneckendorff und von Hindenburg. The old commander had won the battle of Tannenberg, the one complete victory the Germans had gained, with the result that the people had idolized him all through the rest of the war. In every town they had set up huge wooden statues of him, and it had been the supreme act of patriotism to buy nails and drive them into this statue, the money going to the German Red Cross. The Hindenburg line had been another name for national security, and now the Hindenburg presidency was the same. But the stern old titan was now eighty-three years old, and his wits were growing dim; it was hard for him to concentrate upon complex matters. The politicians swarmed about him, they pulled him this way and that, and it was painful to him and tragic to those who saw it.

Emil Meissner had been on the old field marshal's staff during part of the war, and knew his present plight; but Emil was reserved in the presence of a foreigner, especially one who consorted with Jews and had a sister and a brother-in-law whose redness was notorious. On the other hand, an officer of the Reichswehr owed no love to Adolf Hitler, and reported that the President refused to recognize this upstart even as an Austrian, but persisted in referring to him as "the Bohemian corporal," and using the name of his father, which was Schicklgruber, a plebeian and humiliating name. *Der alte Herr* had steadily refused to meet Corporal Schicklgruber, because he talked too much, and in the army it was customary for a non-commissioned officer to wait for his superior to speak first.

Emil expressed his ideas concerning the disorders which prevailed in the cities of the Republic, amounting to a civil war between the two sets of extremists. The Reds had begun it, without doubt, and the Brownshirts were the answer they had got; but Emil called it an atrocious thing that anybody should be permitted to organize a private army as Hitler had done. Hardly a night passed that the rival groups didn't clash in the streets, and Emil longed for a courageous Chancellor who would order the Reichswehr to disarm both sides. The Nazi Führer pretended to deplore what his followers did, but of course that was nonsense; every speech he made was an incitement to more violence—like that insane talk about heads rolling in the sand.

So far two cultivated and modern men could agree over their coffee-cups. But Emil went on to reveal that he was a German like the others. He said that fundamentally the situation was due to the Allies and their monstrous treaty of Versailles; Germany had been stripped of everything by the reparations demands, deprived of her ships, colonies, and trade—and no people ever would starve gladly. Lanny had done his share of protesting against Versailles, and had argued for helping Germany to get on her feet again; but somehow, when he listened to Germans, he found himself shifting to the other side and wishing to remind them that they had lost the war. After all, it hadn't been a game of ping-pong, and somebody had to pay for it. Also, Germany had had her program of what she meant to do if she had won; she had revealed it clearly in the terms she had forced upon Russia at Brest-Litovsk. Also, there had been a Franco-Prussian War, and Germany had taken Alsace-Lorraine; there had been Frederick the Great and the partition of Poland; there had been a whole string of Prussian conquests—but you had better not mention them if you wanted to have friends in the Fatherland!

III

Three evenings a week Freddi and Rahel went to the school which they helped to support. Freddi taught a class in the history of economic theory and Rahel taught one in singing, both subjects important for German workers. Lanny went along more than once, and when the students old and young discovered that he lived in France and had helped with a school there, they wanted to hear about conditions in that country and what the workers were thinking and doing. Discussions arose, and Lanny discovered that the disciplined and orderly working people of Germany were not so different from the independent and free-spoken bunch in the Midi. The same problems vexed them, the same splits turned every discussion into a miniature war.

Could the workers "take over" by peaceable processes? You could tell the answer by the very words in which the speaker put the question. If he said "by parliamentary action," he was some sort of Socialist; if he said "by electing politicians," he was some sort of Communist. The former had the prestige of the greatest party of the Fatherland behind him, and quoted Marx, Bebel, and Kautsky. His opponent in the controversy took the Soviet Union for his model, and quoted Marx, Lenin, and Stalin. Between the two extremes were those who followed the recently exiled Trotsky, or the martyred Karl Liebknecht and "Red Rosa" Luxemburg. There were various "splinter groups" that Lanny hadn't heard of; indeed, it appeared that the nearer the rebel workers came to danger, the more they fought among themselves. Lanny compared them to people on a sinking ship trying to throw one another overboard.

At the school the "Sozis" were in a majority; and Lanny would explain to them his amiable idea that all groups ought to unite against the threat of National Socialism. Since he was a stranger, and Freddi's brother-in-law, they would be patient and explain that nobody could co-operate with the Communists, because they wouldn't let you. Nobody talked more about co-operating than the Communists, but when you tried it you found that what they meant was undermining your organization and poisoning the minds of your followers, the process known as "boring from within." Any Socialist you talked to was ready with a score of illustrations—and also with citations from Lenin, to prove that it was no accident, but a policy.

Members of the Social-Democratic party went even further; they charged that the Communists were co-operating with the Nazis against the coalition government in which the Social-Democrats were participating. That too was a policy; the Bolsheviks believed in making chaos, because they hoped to profit from it; chaos had given them their chance to seize power in Russia, and the fact that it hadn't in Italy did not cause them to revise the theory. It was easy for them to co-operate with Nazis, because both believed in force, in dictatorship; the one great danger that the friends of peaceful change confronted was a deal, more or less open, between the second and third largest parties of Germany. To Lanny that seemed a sort of nightmare—not the idea that it might happen, but the fact that the Socialists should have got themselves into such a state of hatred of another working-class party that they were willing to believe such a deal might be made. Once more he had to sink back into the role of listener, keep his thoughts to himself, and not tell Hansi and Bess what the friends of Freddi and Rahel were teaching in their school.

IV

Once a week the institution gave a reception; the Left intellectuals came, and drank coffee and ate great quantities of *Leberwurst* and *Schweizerkäse* sandwiches, and discussed the policies of the school and the events of the time. Then indeed the forces of chaos and old night were released. Lanny decided that every Berlin intellectual was a new political party, and every two Berlin intellectuals were a political conflict. Some of them wore long hair because it looked picturesque, and others because they didn't own a pair of scissors. Some came because they wanted an audience, and others because it was a chance to get a meal. But whatever their reason, nothing could keep them quiet, and nothing could get them to agree. Lanny had always thought that loud voices and vehement gestures marked the Latin races, but now he decided that it wasn't a matter of race at all, but of economic determinism. The nearer a country came to a crisis, the more noise its intellectuals made in drawing-rooms!

Lanny made the mistake of taking his wife to one of these gatherings, and she didn't enjoy it. In the first place, most of the arguing was done in German, which is rarely a very pleasant-sounding language unless it has been written by Heine; it appears to the outsider to involve a great deal of coughing, spitting, and rumbling in the back of the throat. Of course there were many who were able to speak English of a sort, and were willing to try it on Lanny's wife; but they wished to talk about personalities, events, and doctrines which were for the most part strange to her. Irma's great forte in social life was serenity, and somehow this wasn't the place to show it off.

She commented on this to her husband, who said: "You must understand that most of these people are having a hard time keeping alive. Many of them don't get enough to eat, and that is disturbing to one's peace of mind."

He went on to explain what was called the "intellectual proletariat": a mass of persons who had acquired education at heavy cost of both mind and body, but who now found no market for what they had to offer to the world. They made a rather miserable livelihood by hack-writing, or teaching—whatever odd jobs they could pick up. Naturally they were discontented, and felt themselves in sympathy with the dispossessed workers.

"But why don't they go and get regular jobs, Lanny?"

"What sort of jobs, dear? Digging ditches, or clerking in a store, or waiting on table?"

"Anything, I should think, so long as they can earn an honest living."

"Many of them have to do it, but it's not so easy as it sounds.

There are four million unemployed in Germany right now, and a job usually goes to somebody who has been trained for that kind of work."

Thus patiently Lanny would explain matters, as if to a child. The trouble was, he had to explain it many times, for Irma appeared reluctant to believe it. He was trying to persuade her that the time was cruelly out of joint, whereas she had been brought up to believe that everything was for the best in the best of all possible worlds. If people didn't get jobs and keep them, it must be because there was something wrong with those people; they didn't really want to work; they wanted to criticize and sneer at others who had been successful, who had worked hard, as Irma's father had done. He had left her secure. Who could blame her for wanting to stay that way, and resenting people who pulled her about, clamored in her ears, upset her mind with arguments?

It wasn't that she was hard of heart, not at all. Some pitiful beggar would come up to her on the street, and tears would start into her eyes, and she would want to give him the contents of her well-filled purse. But that was charity, and she learned that Lanny's friends all spurned this; they wanted a thing they called "justice." They required you to agree that the social system was fundamentally wrong, and that most of what Irma's parents and teachers and friends had taught her was false. They demanded that the world be turned upside down and that they, the rebels, be put in charge of making it over. Irma decided that she didn't trust either their capacity or their motives. She watched them, and announced her decision to her too credulous husband: "They are jealous, and want what we've got, and if we gave it to them they wouldn't even say thank you!"

"Maybe so," replied the husband, who had suffered not a few disillusionments himself. "It's no use expecting human beings to be better than they are. Some are true idealists, like Hansi and Freddi."

"Yes, but they work; they would succeed in any world. But those politicians, and intellectuals who want to be politicians but don't know how——"

Lanny laughed; he saw that she was beginning to use her own

head. "What you have to do," he cautioned, "is to consider principles and not individuals. We want a system that will give everybody a chance at honest and constructive labor, and then see that nobody lives without working."

V

The daughter of J. Paramount Barnes was forced to admit that there was something wrong, because her dividends were beginning to fall off. In the spring she had been hearing about the little bull market, which had sounded fine; but during the summer and fall had come a series of slumps, no less than four, one after another. Nobody understood these events, nobody could predict them. You would hear people say: "The bottom has been reached now; things are bound to take a turn." They would bet their money on it—and then, next day or next week, stocks would be tumbling and everybody terrified.

There came a letter from Irma's uncle Joseph, one of the trustees who managed her estate. He warned her about what was happening, and explained matters as well as he could; during the past year her blue-chip stocks had lost another thirty points, below the lowest mark of the great panic when she had been in New York. It appeared to be a vicious circle: the slump caused fear, and fear caused another slump. The elections in Germany had had a bad reaction in Wall Street; everybody decided there wouldn't be any more reparations payments. Mr. Joseph Barnes added that there hadn't really been any for a long time, and perhaps never had been, since the Germans first borrowed in Wall Street whatever they wished to pay. Irma didn't understand this very well, but gave the letter to Lanny, who explained it to her—of course from his Pink point of view.

One thing Uncle Joseph made plain: Irma must be careful how she spent money! Her answer was obvious: she had been living on the Robins for half a year, and when she went back to Bienvenu they would resume that ridiculously simple life. You just couldn't spend money when you lived in a small villa; you had no place to put things, and no way to entertain on a large scale. Lanny and his mother had lived on thirteen hundred dollars a month, whereas Irma had been accustomed to spend fifty times that. So she had no trouble in assuring her conscientious uncle that she would give heed to his advice. Her mother had decided not to come to Europe that winter; she was busy cutting down the expenses of the Long Island estate. Lanny read the letter and experienced the normal feelings of a man who learns that his mother-in-law is not coming to visit him.

VI

Heinrich Jung called Lanny on the telephone. "Would you like to meet the Führer?" he inquired.

"Oh, my gosh!" exclaimed Lanny, taken aback. "He wouldn't be interested in me."

"He says he would."

"What did you tell him about me?"

"I said that you were an old friend, and the patron of Kurt Meissner."

Lanny thought for a moment. "Did you tell him that I don't agree with his ideas?"

"Of course. Do you suppose he's only interested in meeting people who agree with him?"

Lanny had supposed something of the sort, but he was too polite to answer directly. Instead he asked: "Did you say that I might become a convert?"

"I said it might be worth while to try."

"But really, Heinrich, it isn't."

"You might take a chance, if he's willing."

Lanny laughed. "Of course he's an interesting man, and I'll enjoy meeting him."

"All right, come ahead."

"You're sure it won't injure your standing?"

"My standing? I went three times to visit him while he was a prisoner in the Landsberg fortress, and he is a man who never forgets a friend."

"All right, then, when shall we go?"

"The sooner the better. He's in Berlin now, but he jumps about a lot."

"You set the time."

"Are you free this afternoon?"

"I can get free."

Heinrich called again, saying that the appointment was for four o'clock, and he would be waiting for Lanny in front of the headquarters at three-thirty. When he was in the car and had given the address, he began, with some signs of hesitation: "You know, American manners are not quite the same as German. The Führer, of course, understands that you are an American——"

"I hope he won't expect me to say '*Heil Hitler!*' "

"Oh, no, of course not. You will shake hands with him."

"Shall I address him as '*Er*'?" Lanny had read a recent announcement of the introduction of this custom, previously reserved for royalty. It meant speaking in the third person.

"That will not be expected of a foreigner. But it is better if one doesn't contradict him. You know that he is under heavy pressure these days——"

"I understand." From many sources Lanny had heard that Adi was a highly excitable person; some even called him psychopathic.

"I don't mean that you have to agree with him," the other hastened to add. "It's all right if you just listen. He is very kind about explaining his ideas to people."

"Sure thing." Lanny kept a perfectly straight face. "I have read *Mein Kampf*, and this will be a sort of postscript. Five years have passed, and a lot has happened."

"Isn't it marvelous how much has come true!" exclaimed the faithful young "Aryan."

VII

The Partei- und oberster S.A. Führer, Vorsitzender der N.S.D.A.P., lived in one of those elegant apartment houses having a uniformed doorkeeper. The Führer was a vegetarian, and an abstainer from alcohol and tobacco, but not an ascetic as to interior decoration; on the contrary, he thought himself an artist and enjoyed fixing up his surroundings. With the money of Fritz Thyssen and other magnates he had bought a palace in Munich and made it over into a showplace, the Nazi Braune Haus; also for the apartment in Berlin he had got modernistic furniture of the utmost elegance. He lived with a married couple to take care of him, South Germans and friends of his earlier days. They had two children, and Adi was playing some sort of parlor game with them when the visitors were brought in. He kept the little ones for a while, talking to them and about them part of the time; his fondness for children was his better side, and Lanny would have been pleased if he had not had to see any other.

The Führer wore a plain business suit, and presented the aspect of a simple, unassuming person. He shook hands with his Franco-American guest, patted Heinrich on the back, and called for fruit juice and cookies for all of them. He asked Lanny about his boyhood on the Riviera, and the children listened with open eyes to stories about hauling the seine and bringing in cuttlefish and small sharks; about digging in one's garden and finding ancient Roman coins; about the "little Septentrion child" who had danced and pleased in the arena of Antibes a couple of thousand years ago. Adi Schicklgruber's own childhood had been unhappy and he didn't talk about it.

Presently he asked where Lanny had met Kurt Meissner, and the visitor told about the Dalcroze school at Hellerau. His host took this as a manifestation of German culture, and Lanny forbore to mention that Jaques-Dalcroze was a Swiss of French descent. It was true that the school had been built and endowed by a German patron. Said Hitler: "That kind of thing will be the glory of our National Socialist administration; there will be such an outburst of artistic and musical genius as will astound the world." Lanny noted that in all the conversation he took it for granted that the N.S.D.A.P. would soon be in control of Germany; he never said "if," he said "when"—and this was one of the subjects on which the visitor was surely not going to contradict him.

They talked about Kurt and his music, which was pure "Aryan," so the Führer declared; nothing meretricious, no corrupt foreign influences; life in France for so many years had apparently not affected the composer in the slightest. Lanny explained that Kurt had kept almost entirely to himself, and had seldom gone out unless one dragged him. He told about his life at Bienvenu, and the Führer agreed that it was the ideal way for an artist. "It is the sort of life I would have chosen; but, alas, I was born under a different star." Lanny had heard that he believed in astrology, and hoped he wouldn't get onto that subject.

VIII

What the Führer of all the Nazis planned was for this elegant and extremely wealthy young foreigner to go out to the world as a convert to the National Socialist ideas. To that end he laid himself out to be charming, for which he had no small endowment. He had evidently inquired as to Lanny's point of view, for everything he said was subtly directed to meeting that. Lanny was a Socialist, and Hitler, too, was a Socialist, the only true, practical kind of Socialist. Out of the chaos of competitive capitalism a new order was about to arise; an order that would endure, because it would be founded upon real understanding and guided by scientists. Not the evil, degenerate Socialism of the Marxists, which repudiated all that was most precious in human beings; not a Socialism poisoned with the delusion of internationalism, but one founded upon recognition of the great racial qualities which alone made such a task conceivable.

Patiently and kindly the Führer explained that his ideas of race were not German in the narrow sense. Lanny, too, was an "Aryan," and so were the cultured classes in America; theirs was a truly "Aryan" civilization, and so was the British. "I want nothing in the world so much as understanding and peace between my country and Britain, and I think there has been no tragedy in modern times so great as the war they fought. Why can we not understand one another and get together in friendship for our common task?

The world is big enough, and it is full of mongrel tribes whom we dare not permit to gain power, because they are incapable of making any intelligent use of it."

Hitler talked for a while about these mongrels. He felt quite safe in telling a young Franco-American what he thought about the Japanese, a sort of hairless yellow monkeys. Then he came to the Russians, who were by nature lazy, incompetent, and bloodthirsty, and had fallen into the hands of gutter-rats and degenerates. He talked about the French, and was careful of what he said; he wanted no enmity between France and Germany; they could make a treaty of peace that would last for a thousand years, if only the French would give up their imbecile idea of encircling Germany and keeping her ringed with foes. "It is the Polish alliance and the Little Entente which keep enmity between our peoples; for we do not intend to let those peoples go on ruling Germans, and we have an iron determination to right the wrongs which were committed at Versailles. You must know something about that, Mr. Budd, for you have been to Stubendorf, and doubtless have seen with your own eyes what it means for Germans to be governed by Poles."

Lanny answered: "I was one of many Americans at the Peace Conference who pleaded against that mistake."

So the Führer warmed to his visitor. "The shallow-minded call my attitude imperialism; but that is an abuse of language. It is not imperialism to recognize the plain evidence of history that certain peoples have the capacity to build a culture while others are lacking in it entirely. It is not imperialism to say that a vigorous and great-souled people like the Germans shall not be surrounded and penned in by jealous and greedy rivals. It is not imperialism to say that these little children shall not suffer all their lives the deprivations which they have suffered so far."

The speaker was running his hand over the closely cropped blond head of the little boy. "This *Bübchen* was born in the year of the great shame, that wicked Versailles *Diktat*. You can see that he is thin and undersized, because of the starvation blockade. But I have told him that his children will be as sturdy as his father was, because I intend to deliver the Fatherland from the possibility of blockades—and I shall not worry if my enemies call me an imperialist. I have written that every man becomes an imperialist when he begets a child, for he obligates himself to see to it that that child has the means of life provided."

Lanny, a Socialist not untainted with internationalism, could have thought of many things to answer; but he had no desire to spoil this most amiable of interviews. So long as a tiger was willing to purr, Lanny was pleased to study tigers. He might have been influenced by the many gracious words which had been spoken to him, if it had not been for having read *Mein Kampf*. How could the author of that book imagine that he could claim, for example, to have no enmity against France? Or had he changed his mind in five years? Apparently not, for he had formed a publishing-house which was selling his bible to all the loyal followers of the National Socialist German Workingmen's Party, and at the price of twelve marks per copy somebody was making a fortune.

IX

Lanny thought: "I am taking a lot of a busy man's time." But he knew that when you are calling on royalty you do not leave until you are dismissed; and perhaps it would be the same here. The children had been sent away, it being their suppertime; but still the Führer went on talking. Heinrich Jung sat leaning forward with an aspect of strained attention, and there was nothing for Lanny to do but follow his example.

The Führer retold the wrongs which had been done to his country; and as he went on he became more and more aroused, his voice swelled and he became the orator. Lanny remembered having read somewhere of Queen Victoria's complaining about her audiences with Gladstone: "He treats me as if I were a public meeting." Lanny found it somewhat embarrassing to be shouted at from a distance of six feet. He thought: "Good Lord, with this much energy the man could address all Germany!" But apparently Adolf Hitler had enough energy for all Germany and for a foreign visitor also; it was for him to decide how much to expend, and for the visitor to sit and gaze at him like a fascinated rabbit at a hissing snake.

Lanny had seen this same thing happen at several meetings. The Führer took fire from his own phrases; he was moved to action by his own eloquence. Now, now was the moment to overthrow these enemies of the Fatherland, to punish them for their crimes. Heads will roll in the sand! The orator forgot all about being sweet and reasonable for the benefit of a member of two of these enemy nations. Perhaps he thought that Lanny, having heard the whole story of Versailles, of reparations and starvation blockade and Ruhr invasion and Polish alliance and all the rest, must now be completely a convert. Away with the pretense that the Führer of the Nazis did not hate the French for their avarice, the British for their arrogance, the Americans for their upstart pretensions, the Bolsheviks for being bloodthirsty monsters, the Jews for being the spawn of hell. In short, he became that man of frenzy whom Lanny and Rick had first heard in the Bürgerbräukeller in Munich seven years ago. Lanny had said: "One must admit that he is sincere," and Rick had replied: "So are most lunatics."

How long this would have continued no one could say. The housekeeper opened the door and said: *"Verzeihung, mein Führer. Herr Strasser."* Behind her came, without delay, a large man in S.A. uniform. He had large, rather coarse features, a somewhat bulbous nose, a drooping mouth with deep lines at the sides. According to the practice with which Lanny was familiar he should have halted in the doorway, clicked his heels, given the Nazi salute, and said: *"Heil Hitler!"* Instead he came forward, remarking in a nonchalant way: *"Grüss Gott, Adolf."* This meant that he was an old friend, and also that he came from Bavaria.

The visitors were greatly startled by the Führer's response, delivered with the force of a blow: "You have not been conducting yourself as a friend, and therefore you have not been summoned as a friend!" The speaker rose to his feet and, pointing an accusing finger at the new arrival, went on: "Learn once for all, I have had enough of your insubordination! You continue at your peril!" It set the big man back on his heels, and his large mouth dropped open.

Would the Führer of the Nazis have attacked his subordinate in that abrupt and violent way if he had not already got steamed up? Impossible to say; but the astonishment and dismay of Herr Strasser were apparent. He opened his mouth as if to ask what was the matter, but then he closed it again, for he got no chance. Hitler was launched upon a tirade; he rushed at the man—not to strike him, but to thrust the accusing finger within a couple of inches of the big nose and shriek:

"Your intrigues are known! Your insolence is resented! Your public utterances are incitements to treason, and if you do not mend your ways you will be driven out. Go and join your brother's *Schwarze Front*, and the other disguised Communists and scoundrels! I—I, Adolf Hitler, am the Führer of the N.S.D.A.P., and it is for me to determine policies. I will not have opposition, I will not have argument, I will have obedience. We are in the midst of a war, and I demand loyalty, I demand discipline. *Zucht! Zucht! Zucht!*" It is one of those many German words which require a clearing of the throat, and the unfortunate Strasser flinched as if from a rain of small particles of moisture.

"Adolf, who has been telling you stories about me?" He forced the sentence in while the Führer caught his breath.

"I make it my business to know what is going on in my movement. Do you imagine that you can go about expressing contempt for my policies without word of it coming to me?"

"Somebody has been lying, Adolf. I have said only what I have said to you: that now is the time for action, and that our foes desire nothing but delay, so that they can weaken us by their intrigues——"

"They weaken us because of arrogance and self-will in my own party officials; because these presumptuous ones dare to set themselves up as authorities and thinkers. *I* think for the National Socialists, *I*—and I have ordered you to hold your tongue—*Maul halten*—and obey my orders, follow my policies and not your own stupid

notions. Your brother has turned himself into a criminal and an
outlaw because of that same arrogance——"

"Leave Otto out of it, Adolf. You know that I have broken with
him. I do not see him and have no dealings with him."

"*Ich geb' 'n Dreck d'rum!*" cried Adolf; he spoke that kind of
German. Talking to a Bavarian, he added: "*Das ist mir Sau-wurscht!*"

He rushed on: "You stay in the party and carry on Otto's agita-
tion in favor of discarded policies. I am the captain of this ship, and
it is not for the crew to tell me what to do, but to do what I tell
them. Once more, I demand unity in the face of our foes. Understand me, I command it! I speak as your Führer!"

Lanny thought he had never seen a man so beside himself with
excitement. Adolf Hitler's face had become purple, he danced about
as he talked, and every word was emphasized as with a hammer
blow of his finger. Lanny thought the two men would surely fight;
but no, presently he saw that the other was going to take it. Perhaps
he had seen the same thing happen before, and had learned to deal
with it. He stopped arguing, stopped trying to protest; he simply
stood there and let his Führer rave, let the storm blow itself out—
if it ever would blow itself out. Would the ocean ever be the same
after such a hurricane?

X

Lanny had learned much about the internal affairs of the Nazi
party from the conversation of Kurt and Heinrich. Also, during
the summer he had been getting the German papers, and these had
been full of a furious party conflict over the question of the old
program, which Hitler had been paring down until now there was
nothing left of it. Here in North Germany many of the Nazis took
the "Socialist" part of their label seriously; they insisted upon talking about the communizing of department stores, the confiscation
of landed estates, the ending of interest slavery, common wealth before private wealth, and so on. It had caused a regular civil war
in the party earlier in the year. The two Strasser brothers, Gregor
and Otto, had fought for the old program and had been beaten.

Gregor had submitted, but Otto had quit the party and organized a revolutionary group of his own, which the Hitlerites called the "Black Front" and which they were fighting with bludgeons and revolvers, just as they fought the Communists. Later on, immediately before the elections, there had been another attempt at internal revolution; the rebels had seized the offices of the Berlin party paper, *Der Angriff*, holding it by force of arms and publishing the paper for three days. A tremendous scandal, and one which the enemies of the movement had not failed to exploit.

So here was Gregor Strasser, Reich Organization Leader Number 1. A lieutenant in the World War, he had become an apothecary, but had given up his business in order to oppose the Reds and then to help Adi prepare for the Beerhall Putsch. He was perhaps the most competent organizer the party had, and had come to Berlin and built the Sturmabteilung by his efforts. Hitler, distrusting him as too far to the left, had formed a new personal guard, the Schutzstaffel, or S.S. So there were two rival armies inside the Nazi party of all Germany; which was going to prevail?

Lanny wondered, had Hitler really lost his temper or was this merely a policy? Was this the way Germans enforced obedience— the drill-sergeant technique? Apparently it was working, for the big man's bull voice dropped low; he stood meekly and took his licking like a schoolboy ordered to let down his pants. Lanny wondered also: why did the Führer permit a foreigner to witness such a demonstration? Did he think it would impress an American? Did he love power so much that it pleased him to exhibit it in the presence of strangers? Or did he feel so secure in his mastery that he didn't care what anybody thought of him? This last appeared to be in character with his procedure of putting his whole defiant program into a book and selling it to anybody in the world who had twelve marks.

Lanny listened again to the whole story of *Mein Kampf*. He learned that Adolf Hitler meant to outwit the world, but in his own good time and in his own way. He meant to suppress his land program to please the Junkers and his industrial program to please the steel kings, and so get their money and use it to buy arms for his S.A. and his S.S. He meant to promise everything to everybody and so get their votes—everybody except the *abscheulichen Bolschewisten* and the *verfluchten Juden*. He meant to get power and take office, and nobody was going to block him from his goal. If any *Dummkopf* tried it he would crush him like a louse, and he told him so.

When Strasser ventured to point out that Dr. Joseph Goebbels, the Führer's favorite propagandist, had said that he was developing a "legality complex," the Führer replied that he would deal with "Juppchen" at his own convenience; he was dealing now with Gregor Strasser, and telling him that he was not to utter another word of criticism of his Führer's policies, but to devote his energies to putting down the Reds and teaching discipline to his organization, which lacked it so shamefully. Adolf Hitler would do his own dickering with the politicians, playing them one against another, worming his way closer and closer to the chancellorship which was his goal—and in due course he would show them all, and his own friends would be ashamed of their blindness and presumption in having doubted their inspired leader.

So Lanny received a demonstration of what it meant to be a master of men. Perhaps that was what the Führer intended; for not until he had received the submission of his Reich Organization Leader Number 1 and had dismissed him did he turn again to his guest. "Well, Mr. Budd," he said, "you see what it takes to put people to work for a cause. Wouldn't you like to come and help me?"

Said Lanny: "I am afraid I am without any competence for such a task." If there was a trace of dryness in his tone the Führer missed it, for he smiled amiably, and seemed to be of the opinion that he had done a very good afternoon's work.

Long afterward Lanny learned from Kurt Meissner what the Führer thought about that meeting. He said that young Mr. Budd was a perfect type of the American privileged classes: good-looking, easy-going, and perfectly worthless. It would be a very simple task to cause that nation to split itself to pieces, and the National Socialist movement would take it in charge.

8

To Give and to Share

I

IN THE month of December Irma and Rahel completed the tremendous feat they had undertaken; having kept the pact they had made with each other and with their families, they were now physically and morally free. The condition of two lusty infants appeared to indicate that Rousseau and Lanny had been right. Little by little the greedy sucklings learned to take the milk of real cows instead of imitation ones; they acquired a taste for fruit juices and for prune pulp with the skins carefully removed. At last the young mothers could go to a bridge party without having to leave in the middle of it.

Marceline with her governess had returned to Juan at the end of the yacht cruise, and her mother had promised to join her for Christmas. Farewells were said to the Robin family, and Beauty and her husband went by train, taking the baby, Miss Severne, the nursemaid, and Madame. The General Graf Stubendorf's invitation to Lanny and Irma had been renewed, and Kurt had written that they should by all means accept; not only would it be more pleasant for Irma at the Schloss, but it would advantage the Meissners to have an old friend return as a guest of Seine Hochgeboren. Lanny noted this with interest and explained it to his wife; what would have been snobbery in America was loyalty in Silesia. The armies of Napoleon having never reached that land, the feudal system still prevailed and rank was a reality.

Stubendorf being in Poland, the train had to stop, and luggage and passports to be examined. The village itself was German, and only the poorer part of the peasantry was Polish. This made a situation full of tension, and no German thought of it as anything but a truce. What the Poles thought, Lanny didn't know, for he couldn't talk with them. In Berlin he had shown his wife a comic paper and a cartoon portraying Poland as an enormous fat hog, being ridden by a French army officer who was twisting the creature's tail to make it gallop and waving a saber to show why he was in a hurry. Not exactly the Christmas spirit!

Irma Barnes Budd explored the feudal system, and found it not so different from the South Shore of Long Island. She was met at the train by a limousine, which would have happened at home. A five-story castle didn't awe her, for she had been living in one that was taller and twice as broad. The lady who welcomed her was certainly no taller or broader than Mrs. Fanny Barnes, and couldn't be more proud of her blood. The principal differences were, first, that the sons and daughters of this Prussian family worked harder than any young people Irma had ever known; and, second, there were uniforms and ceremonies expressive of rank and station. Irma gave close attention to these, and her husband wondered if she was planning to introduce them into the New World.

Visiting his father's home in Connecticut, Lanny had discovered that being married to a great heiress had raised his social status; and now he observed the same phenomenon here. Persons who through the years had paid no particular attention to him suddenly recognized that he was a man of brilliant parts; even the Meissner family, whom he had known and loved since he was a small boy, appeared to be seized with awe. Whereas formerly he had shared a bed in Kurt's small room, he was now lodged in a sumptuous suite in the castle; the retainers and tenants all took off their hats to him, and he no longer had to hear the *gräflichen* ideas explained second-hand by Herr Meissner, but got them from the horse's mouth, as the saying is.

It was unfortunate that the ideas no longer impressed him as they did in the earlier years. The General Graf was a typical Junker, active in the Nationalist party; his policies were limited by the interests of his class. He did not let himself be influenced by the fact that his estate was now in Poland; that was a temporary matter.

soon to be remedied. He supported a tariff on foodstuffs so that the German people would pay higher prices to landowners. He wanted his coal mined, but he didn't want to pay the miners enough so that they could buy his food. He wanted steel and chemicals and other products of industry, which required swarms of workers, but he blamed them for trying to have a say as to the conditions of their lives, or indeed whether they should live at all.

II

Fortunately it wasn't necessary to spend much time discussing politics. There was a great deal of company, with music, dancing, and feasting. If the country products couldn't be sold at a profit they might as well be eaten at home, so everyone did his best, and it was astounding how they succeeded. Modern ideas of dietetics, like Napoleon, hadn't penetrated the feudalism of Upper Silesia. It was the same regimen which had startled Lanny as a boy: a preliminary breakfast with *Dresdener Christstollen,* a sort of bun with raisins inside and sugar on top; then at half-past ten the "fork breakfast," when several kinds of meat were eaten—but without interfering with anybody's appetite for lunch. An afternoon tea, only it was coffee, and then an enormous dinner of eight or ten courses, served with the utmost formality by footmen in satin uniforms. Finally, after cards, or music and dancing, it was unthinkable that one should go to bed on an empty stomach. That meant six meals a day, and it produced vigorous and sturdy young men, but when they came to middle age they had necks like bulls' and cheeks like pelicans' and eyes almost closed by fat in the lids.

One discovery Lanny made very quickly: this was the life for which his wife had been created. Nobody shouted at her, nobody confused her mind with strange ideas; everybody treated her as a person of distinction. and found her charming, even brilliant. A world in which serenity and poise counted; a world which didn't have to be changed! The Gräfin became a second mother to her, and she was invited to visit so many distinguished families, she might have been carried through the entire winter without spending any of her money. One aspect of the feudal system appeared to be that most of its ruling members were bored on their estates, and eager for visitors, provided they were of proper station. They all had bursting larders, with a host of servants trained to put meals on tables. Do come and enjoy your share!

III

What Lanny really wanted was to spend the time with his boyhood chum. Kurt now lived with his own family in a stone cottage on the outskirts of the village of Stubendorf, all of which belonged to Seine Hochgeboren. Lanny met for the first time Kurt's gentle and devoted young wife, and three little blond "Aryans" produced according to the Schicklgruber prescription. Irma went along on the first visit as a matter of courtesy, and also of curiosity, for she had heard how this wonderful *Komponist* had been Beauty Budd's lover for some eight years; also, she had heard enough about Kurt's adventures in Paris during the Peace Conference to make him a romantic figure.

Kurt hadn't changed much in the four years since Lanny had seen him. The war had aged him prematurely, but from then on he seemed to stay the same: a grave and rather silent man, who chose to speak to the world through his art. He worshiped the classic German composers, especially the "three B's." Each of these had written a few four-hand piano compositions, and in the course of the years others of their works had been arranged in this form, so now there were more than a hundred such available. Lanny had ordered a complete collection from one of the dealers in Berlin; not often can one make a Christmas present which will give so much pleasure to a friend! The two of them wanted to sit right down and not get up even for meals. Irma couldn't see how it was possible for human fingers to stand the strain of so much pounding; she couldn't see how human ears could take in so many notes. She had to remind them of an engagement at the Schloss; whereupon Kurt leaped up at once, for Seine Hochgeboren must not be kept waiting, even for Bach, Beethoven, and Brahms.

In return for his pension and his home it was Kurt's duty to play for his patron, and to assemble, rehearse, and conduct a small orchestra for special occasions such as this Christmas visit. He did this with scrupulous fidelity, as the young Haydn had done for the great Prince Esterhazy of Vienna. It wasn't an onerous job, for of late years Seine Hochgeboren came only rarely. To his people living under the Poles he made a formal address, full of Christmas cheer, but also of quiet unbending faith that God would somehow restore them to their Fatherland. *Deutsche Treue und Ehre* acquired a special meaning when used by those living in exile.

That was what the National Socialist movement meant to Kurt Meissner. He and his young wife listened with eager attention while Lanny told about his meeting with Adolf Hitler; then Herr Meissner asked to have the story told to his family, and later on the lord of the Schloss wanted his friends to hear it. They questioned the visitor closely as to just what Adi's program now was; and of course Lanny knew what was in their minds. Had the Führer of the Nazis really dropped that crazy Socialist stuff with which he had set out on his career? Could he be depended upon as a bulwark against Bolshevism, a terror so real to the people on Germany's eastern border? Would he let the landowners alone and devote himself to rearming the country, and forcing the Allies to permit the return of Stubendorf and the other lost provinces, the Corridor and the colonies? If the Germans in exile could be sure of these things, they might be willing to support him, or at any rate not oppose him actively.

IV

Kurt had composed a symphony, which he called *Das Vaterland*. He and his adoring wife had copied out the parts for an orchestra of twenty pieces, and Kurt had engaged musicians from the near-by towns, of course at the Graf's expense. They had been thoroughly drilled, and now played the new work before a distinguished company on Christmas night. This was the high point of Lanny's visit, and indeed of his stay in Germany. In his boyhood he had taken

Kurt Meissner as his model of all things noble and inspiring; he had predicted for him a shining future, and felt justified when he saw all the *hochgeboren Herrschaften* of Kurt's own district assembled to do him honor.

During the composer's time in Bienvenu his work had been full of bitterness and revolt, but since he had come home he had apparently managed to find courage and hope. He didn't write program music, and Lanny didn't ask what the new work was supposed to signify; indeed, he would rather not be told, for the military character of much of the music suggested it was meant for the Nazis. It pictured the coming of a deliverer, it portrayed the German people arising and marching to their world destiny; at its climax, they could no longer keep in march tempo, but broke into dancing; great throngs of them went exulting into the future, endless companies of young men and maidens, of that heroic and patriotic sort that Heinrich Jung and Hugo Behr were training.

The music didn't actually say that, and every listener was free to make up his own story. Lanny chose to include youths and maidens of all lands in that mighty dancing procession. He remembered how they had felt at Hellerau, in the happy days before the war had poisoned the minds of the peoples. Then internationalism had not been a *Schimpfwort,* and it had been possible to listen to Schubert's C-major symphony and imagine a triumphal procession shared by Jews and Russians, by young men and maidens from Asia and even from Africa.

Irma was much impressed by the welcome this music received. She decided that Kurt must be a great man, and that Beauty should be proud of having had such a lover, and of having saved him from a French firing-squad. She decided that it was a distinguished thing to have a private orchestra, and asked her husband if it wouldn't be fun to have one at Bienvenu. They must be on the lookout for a young genius to promote.

Lanny knew that his wife was casting around in her mind for some sort of career, some way to spend her money that would win his approval as well as that of their friends. She had timidly broached the idea of becoming a *salonnière,* like Emily. He had felt compelled to point out that this was a difficult thing to do, for it was better to have no salon at all than to have a second-rate one, and the eminent persons who frequent such assemblages expect the hostess not merely to have read their books but to have understood them. It isn't enough to admire them extravagantly—indeed they rather look down on you unless you can find something wrong with their work.

Now Lanny had to mention that musical geniuses are apt to be erratic, and often it is safer to know them through their works. One cannot advertise for one as for a butler or a chef; and suppose they got drunk, or took up with the parlor-maid? Lanny said that a consecrated artist such as Kurt Meissner would be hard to find. Irma remarked: "I suppose they wouldn't be anywhere but in Germany, where everybody works so hard!"

V

Among the guests they had met at the Schloss was an uncle of their host, the Graf Oldenburg of Vienna. The Meissners had told them that this bald-headed old Silenus was in financial trouble; he always would be, it having been so planned by the statesmen at Paris, who had cut the Austro-Hungarian Empire into small fragments and left a city of nearly two million people with very little hinterland to support it. The Graf was a gentleman of the old school who had learned to dance to the waltzes of the elder Strauss and was still hearing them in his fancy. He invited Irma and Lanny to visit him, and mentioned tactfully that he had a number of fine paintings. Since it was on their way home, Lanny said: "Let's stop and have a look."

It was a grand marble palace on the Ringstrasse, and the reception of the American visitors was in good style, even though the staff of servants had been cut, owing to an outrageous law just passed by the city administration—a graduated tax according to the number of your servants, and twice as high for men as for women! But a Socialist government had to find some way to keep going. Here was a city with great manufacturing power and nowhere to export its goods. All the little states surrounding it had put up tariff barriers, and all efforts at a customs union came to naught. Such an agreement with Germany seemed the most obvious thing in the world, but everybody knew that France would take it as an act of war.

An ideal situation from the point of view of a young art expert with American dollars in the bank! The elderly aristocrat, his host, was being hounded by his creditors, and responded promptly when Lanny invited him to put a price on a small-sized Jan van Eyck representing the Queen of Heaven in the very gorgeous robes which she perhaps was now wearing, but had assuredly never seen during her sojourn on earth.

Among Irma's acquaintances on Long Island was the heiress of a food-packing industry; and since people will eat, even when they do nothing else, Brenda Spratt's dividends were still coming in. She had appeared fascinated by Lanny's accounts of old masters in Europe and his dealings in them; so now he sent her a cablegram informing her that she could obtain a unique art treasure in exchange for four hundred and eighty thousand cans of spaghetti with tomato sauce at the wholesale price of three dollars per case of forty-eight cans. Lanny didn't cable all that, of course—it was merely his way of teasing Irma about the Long Island plutocracy. Next day he had a reply informing him at what bank he could call for the money. A genuine triumph of the soul of man over the body, of the immortal part over the mortal; and incidentally it would provide Lanny Budd with pocket-money for the winter. He invited his wife to state whether her father had ever done a better day's business at the age of thirty-one.

The over-taxed swells of Vienna came running to meet the American heiress and to tell her brilliant young husband what old masters they had available. Irma might have danced till dawn every night, and Lanny might have made a respectable fortune, transferring culture to the land of his fathers. But what he preferred was meeting Socialist writers and party leaders and hearing their stories of suffering and struggle in this city which was like a head without a body. The workers were overwhelmingly Socialist, while the peasants of the country dis icts were Catholic and reactionary. To add to the confusion, the Hitlerites were carrying on a tremendous drive, telling the country yokels and the city hooligans that all their troubles were due to Jewish profiteers.

The municipal government, in spite of near-bankruptcy, was going bravely ahead with a program of rehousing and other public services. This was the thing of which Lanny had been dreaming, the socialization of industry by peaceful and orderly methods, and he became excited about it and wished to spend his time traveling about looking at blocks of workers' homes and talking to the people who lived in them. Amiable and well-bred people, going to bed early to save light and fuel, and working hard at the task of making democracy a success. Their earnings were pitifully small, and when Lanny heard stories of infant mortality and child malnutrition and milk prices held up by profiteers, it rather spoiled his enjoyment of stately banquets in mansions with historic names. Irma said: "You won't let yourself have any fun, so we might as well go on home."

VI

It wasn't much better at Bienvenu, as the young wife was soon to learn. The world had become bound together with ties invisible but none the less powerful, so that when the price of corn and hogs dropped in Nebraska the price of flowers dropped on the Cap d'Antibes. Lanny explained the phenomenon: the men who speculated in corn and hogs in Chicago no longer gave their wives the money to buy imported perfumes, so the leading industry of the Cap went broke. Leese, who ran Bienvenu, was besieged by nieces and nephews and cousins begging to be taken onto the Budd staff. There was a swarm of them already, twice as many as would have been employed for the same tasks on Long Island; but in the Midi they had learned how to divide the work, and nobody ever died from overexertion. Now there were new ones added, and it was a delicate problem, because it was Irma's money and she was entitled to have a say. What she said was that servants oughtn't to be permitted to bother their employers with the hard-luck stories of their relatives. Which meant that Irma still had a lot to learn about life in France!

The tourists didn't come, and the "season" was slow—so slow that it began to stop before it got started. The hotelkeepers were frightened, the merchants of luxury goods were threatened with ruin, and of course the poor paid for it. Lanny knew, because he went on helping with that Socialist Sunday school, where he heard stories which spoiled his appetite and his enjoyment of music, and troubled his wife because she knew what was in his thoughts—that she oughtn't to spend money on clothes and parties while so many children weren't getting enough to eat.

But what could you do about it? You had to pay your servants, or at any rate feed them, and it was demoralizing if you didn't give them work to do. Moreover, how could you keep up the prices of foods except by buying some? Irma's father and uncles had fixed it firmly in her mind that the way to make prosperity was to spend; but Lanny seemed to have the idea that you ought to buy cheap foods and give them to the poor. Wouldn't that demoralize the poor and make parasites of them? Irma thought she saw it happening to a bunch of "comrades" on the Riviera who practically lived on the Budd bounty, and rarely said "Thank you." And besides, what was to become of the people who raised the more expensive foods? Were they going to have to eat them?

Life is a compromise. On Sunday evening Lanny would go down into the Old Town of Cannes and explain the wastes of the competitive system to a group of thirty or forty proletarians: French and Provençal, Ligurian and Corsican, Catalan and even one Algerian. On Monday evening he would take his wife and mother to Sept Chênes and play accompaniments for a singer from the Paris opera at one of Emily's soirées. On Tuesday he would spend the day helping to get ready for a dinner-dance at Bienvenu, with a colored jazz band, Venetian lanterns with electric lights all over the lawns, and the most fashionable and titled people coming to do honor to the daughter of J. Paramount Barnes. Yes, there were still some who had money and would not fail in their economic duty! People who had seen the storm coming and put their fortune into bonds; people who owned strategic industries, such as the putting up of canned spaghetti for the use of millions who lived in tiny apartments in cities and had never learned how to make tomato sauce!

VII

Robbie Budd came visiting that winter. He had some kind of queer deal on; he was meeting with a former German U-boat commander who had entered the service of a Chinese mandarin, and this latter had been ousted and now wanted Budd machine guns so as to get back. He had got the support of some bankers in French Indo-China, but they didn't want to buy French munitions, for fear of publicity—a shady affair all round, but Robbie explained with a grin that one had to pick up money where one could these days. No chance to sell any of the products of peace in Europe now!

He told the same stories of hard times which his son had heard in Berlin and Vienna. There were breadlines in all the American cities, and on street corners one saw men, and some women, stamping their feet and holding out apples in their half-frozen hands. The price of apples having slumped, this was a way to get rid of them; a nickel apiece, Mister, and won't you help a poor guy get a cup of coffee? There was no way to count the unemployed, but everybody agreed that the number was increasing and the situation was terrible. Robbie thanked God for the Great Engineer whom he had helped to elect President; that harassed man was standing firm as a rock, insisting that Congress should balance the budget. If it was done, business would pick up in the end. It always had and always must.

Robbie had paid off one-half of the notes which he had given to Lanny, Beauty, and Marceline as security for the money turned over to him during the Wall Street panic. He had invested a hundred and fifty thousand dollars for the three of them in United States government bonds, and now tried to persuade them to shift it to stocks. They discussed the matter for an hour or so, sitting in front of a blazing fire of cypress wood in the drawing-room of the home. Beauty wavered, but Lanny said "No," and said it again and again.

"Look where steel is now!" exclaimed the father.

"But," argued the younger man, "you said exactly the same thing when you were here last time. You were sure it couldn't go lower."

He took his father on a tour of the civilized world. Where was

there a nation that had money to buy American steel? Britain,
France, Germany—all could make more than they could market, and
the smaller nations were kept going only by the fears of their creditors. Here was Robbie, himself a steel man, reduced to selling to
Chinese mandarins and South American revolutionists! Russia wanted
steel desperately, but had to learn to make it for herself because
she had no foreign exchange and nobody would trust her. "And you
talk about steel 'coming back'!" exclaimed the son.

Robbie couldn't answer, but neither could he change. He knew
that Lanny got his ideas out of his Pink and Red papers—which he
kept in his own study, so as not to offend the eyesight of his relatives and friends. All these papers had a vested interest in calamity;
but they couldn't be right, for if so, what would become of Robbie's
world? He said: "Have it your way; but mark what I tell you, if
only Hoover can hold out against inflationary tendencies, we'll be
seeing such a boom as never was in the world before."

VIII

Lanny returned to the delights of child study. Truly a marvelous
thing to watch a tiny organism unfolding, in such perfect order
and according to schedule. They had a book which told them what
to expect, and it was an event when Baby Frances spoke her first
word two full weeks ahead of time, and a still greater thrill when she
made her first effort to get up on her feet. All, both friends and
servants, agreed that they had never seen a lovelier female infant,
and Lanny, with his imaginative temperament, fell to speculating as
to what might become of her. She would grow up to be a fine young
woman like her mother. Would it be possible to teach her more
than her mother knew? Probably not; she would have too much
money. Or would she? Was there any chance of a benevolent revolution on the Viennese model, compelling her to do some useful
work?

He had the same thought concerning his half-sister, who was
ripening early in the warm sunshine of the Midi and in the pleasure-
seeking of its fashionable society. Marceline was going to be a beauty

like her mother; and how could she fail to know it? From earliest childhood she had been made familiar with beauty-creating and beauty-displaying paraphernalia: beauty lotions, beauty creams, beauty powders and paints, all put up in such beautiful receptacles that you couldn't bear to throw them away; clothing designed to reveal beauty, mirrors in which it was to be studied, conversation concerning the effects of it upon the male for whom it was created. Self-consciousness, sex-consciousness were the very breath of being of this young creature, paused on tiptoe with excitement, knowing by instinct that she was approaching the critical period of her life.

The prim Miss Addington was troubled about her charge, but Beauty, who had been that way herself, took it more easily. Lanny, too, had been precocious at that age, and so could understand her. He would try to teach her wisdom, to moderate her worldly desires. He would talk about her father, endeavoring to make him effective as an influence in her life. The pictures made him a living presence, but unfortunately Marceline did not know him as a poor painter on the Cap, working in a pair of stained corduroy trousers and an old blue cap. She knew him as a man of *renommée*, a source of income and a subject of speculation; his example confirmed her conviction that beauty and fame were one. To receive the attentions of other persons was what she enjoyed. Important persons, if possible—but anyone was better than no one!

IX

Amid this oddly assorted family Parsifal Dingle went on living his quietest life. He had the firm faith that it was impermissible to argue with people; the only thing was to set an example, and be certain that in due course it would have its effect. He took no part in any controversy, and never offered an opinion unless it was asked for. He sought nothing for himself, because, he said, everything was within him. He went here and there about the place, a friend of the flowers and the birds and the·dogs. He read a great deal, and often closed his eyes; you wouldn't know whether he was praying or asleep. He was kind to everybody, and treated rich and poor the same; the servants revered him, having become certain that he was some kind of saint. His fame spread, and he would be asked to come and heal this person and that. The doctors resented this, and so did the clergy of the vicinity; it was unsanctioned, a grave violation of the proprieties.

At least an hour every day Mr. Dingle spent with Madame Zyszynski, and often Beauty was with him. The spirits possessed the minds of this pair, and the influence of the other world spread through the little community. Beauty began asking the spirits' advice, and taking it in all sorts of matters. They told her that these were dangerous times, and to be careful of her money. The spirit of Marcel told her this, and so did the spirit of the Reverend Blackless—so he referred to himself. Beauty had never taken his advice while he was living, but assumed he would be ultra-wise in the beyond. As economy was what Lanny wanted her to practice, he felt indebted to the shades. Being a talkative person, Beauty told her friends about her "guides," and Bienvenu acquired a queerer reputation than it had ever had, even when it was a haunt of painters, munitions buyers, and extra-marital couples.

Lanny would try his luck with a séance now and then. The character of his spirit life underwent a change; Marie receded into the background and her place was taken by Marcel and Great-Great-Uncle Eli Budd. These two friends of his boyhood told him much about themselves, and held high converse with each other in the limbo where they dwelt; just so had Lanny imagined them after their death, and it confirmed his idea that he was getting an ingenious reconstruction of the contents of his own mind. Now and then would appear some fact which he hadn't known before; but he argued that he might have heard it and forgotten it. He had had many intimate talks with both his former relatives, and surely couldn't remember every detail.

His theory was confirmed by the fact that he received a cordial letter from Mr. Ezra Hackabury, who was trying to keep out of bankruptcy in the town of Reubens, Indiana. Terrible times, he reported; but he hoped people would still have to have kitchen soap. The question was being answered in monthly sales reports, and meanwhile Mr. Hackabury pitched horseshoes behind the barn, as in the old days, and wondered if Lanny had kept up his skill in this art. When Lanny wrote what the spirits had said, the soapman replied that it was with him as it had been with Mark Twain: the report of his death was exaggerated. In the course of a year and a half of intercourse with Tecumseh, Lanny had recorded several cases of the chieftain's failure to distinguish between the living and the dead, and Lanny drew from this fact the conclusion which satisfied his own mind—at the same time overlooking a number of other facts which didn't. In this behavior he had the example of many leading men of science.

X

So passed a pleasant period in the well-cushioned limousine in which Lanny Budd was rolling through life. He was unhappy about the sufferings of the world, but not so unhappy that he couldn't eat the excellent meals which the servants of both the villa and the Cottage prepared; not so unhappy that he couldn't read the manuscripts which Rick sent him, and the first draft of a *Silesian Suite* which Kurt submitted. He taught his Pink class, and argued with the young Reds who came to bait him—and at the same time to borrow money when they got into trouble. He spent his own funds, and some of Irma's, playing patron to the social discontent of the Midi; but Irma didn't mind especially, because she had the money, and had the instinctive feeling that the more the family was dependent upon her, the more agreeable they would make themselves. Who eats my bread, he sings my song!

A surprising incident. One afternoon Lanny was in his studio, playing that very grand piano which he had bought for Kurt, but which was beginning to show the effects of a decade of sea air. A sunshiny afternoon of spring; Lanny had the doors and windows open, and was filling the surrounding atmosphere with the strains of Rubinstein's *Waltz Caprice*. The telephone rang, for they now had phones in all the buildings on the estate; to Irma it had seemed ridiculous to have to send a servant every time she wished to invite

Beauty over to the Cottage for lunch, or when she wanted to tell Lanny to come swimming. Now a servant was calling from the villa, reporting that there was an elderly gentleman who said his name was "Monsieur Jean." Lanny wasn't usually slow, but this time he had to have the name repeated. Suddenly he remembered the town of Dieppe.

The Knight Commander of the Bath and Grand Officer of the Legion of Honor had held off for the better part of a year, until Lanny had given up the idea of hearing from him. It seemed hard to believe, for Zaharoff was bound to know that he had got something real at that séance—and how could he bear not to get more? At last he had decided to give way, and characteristically he wasn't taking half-measures; he had come in person, the first time he had ever thus honored the Budd family. He honored very few persons in that manner.

"Monsieur Jean" was alone. He had seated himself on the edge of a straight chair, as if he wasn't sure that he would be welcomed; he had kept his walking-stick, and was leaning on it with both hands folded over it. The cold blue eyes met Lanny's. Was Lanny mistaken in thinking that there was an anxious look on the face of the old spider, the old wolf, the old devil? Anyhow, the younger man greeted his caller with cordiality, and the latter said quickly: "For a long time I have known that I owed you an apology."

"Don't bother about it, Monsieur Jean," said the younger man. He used that name because some servant might overhear. "I realized that you were upset. Several times in these séances I have been told things which didn't happen to be true, and which would have been embarrassing if there had been others present." Nothing could have been more tactful.

"I should have written to you," continued the other. "But I put it off, thinking you might come to see me."

"I had no way of knowing what your wishes would be." To himself Lanny added: "You were trying other mediums, to see if you could get what you want!"

"I decided that the proper thing to do was to make my apologies in person. I will make them to the medium, if she is still with you."

"She is." Lanny would wait, and make the old man ask for what he wanted.

"Do you suppose it would be possible for me to see her again?"

"You mean, to try another séance?"

"I would esteem it a great favor."

"I can't answer for her, Monsieur Jean. As I explained at the time, it causes her distress if anything goes wrong. She was very much upset."

"I realize that. I am thoroughly prepared now, and can give you my word that nothing of the sort will happen again. Whatever comes, I will 'take it,' as you Americans say."

"Perhaps," suggested Lanny, "you might prefer to sit with her alone?"

"If she will trust me, that would be better. You may tell her that I will pay her generously."

"I would beg you not to mention that. We have a financial arrangement with her, and her time is ours."

"Surely it would be proper for me to pay a portion of the cost?"

"There is no need to raise the question. The amount is small—and you may not get the results you want."

"If I should get them, and if I might see her now and then, you will surely let me make some financial arrangement?"

"We can talk about that by and by. First, I will see if I can persuade her to give you another sitting."

"You have not told her about me?"

"I haven't told anybody. You remember I wrote you that that was my intention."

"You have been very kind, Lanny, and I shall never forget it."

XI

It wasn't an easy matter to persuade Madame Zyszynski. She was still angry with "that rude old gentleman." What he had done to her was unforgivable. But Lanny told her that the rude old gentleman had been extremely unhappy, and something had come from Tecumseh which had broken him down; it had taken him nearly

a year to get over it. But now he was penitent, and had given his
word, and Lanny felt sure he would keep it. Madame was used to
trusting Lanny—she was a lonely old woman, and had adopted him
as her son in her imagination. Now she said she would give Monsieur
Jean another chance to behave, but first Lanny must explain to him
the physical shock which he had caused her, that she had been ill
and depressed for days, and so on. Tecumseh would doubtless be
extremely angry, and would scold the sitter without the least regard to his dignity.

Lanny dutifully went back and delivered these messages; and the
armament king of Europe solemnly agreed to humble his pride before the chieftain of the Iroquois. Lanny said: "I don't know what
he really is, but he acts like a personage, and you have to treat him
that way. You have given him offense, and you will have to pretend
that you are petitioning for pardon." Lanny said it with a smile,
but the Knight Commander and Grand Officer was serious; he replied that if it would get him a message from the source desired
he would submit to torture from real Indians.

So Lanny took him down to his studio, and showed him some of
Marcel's paintings· on the walls—though he probably didn't have
much mind for art just then. The medium came in, and said: *"Bon
jour, monsieur."* Zaharoff answered: *"Bon jour, madame,"* and they
seated themselves in the two chairs which Lanny had moved into
place for them. He waited until he saw the woman going into her
trance successfully; then he went out, closing the studio door behind him.

Beauty and Irma had been in to Cannes for shopping. They came
back; and of course it would no longer be possible to keep the secret
from them. No need to, anyhow, for the matter would doubtless
be settled this time; the duquesa would "come through," or Zaharoff
would give up. Lanny took them into his mother's room and told
them who had attended Madame's séance in Dieppe. Both the ladies
were excited, for Zaharoff was the same kind of royalty as Irma,
and sovereigns do not often meet their social equals. "Oh, do you
think he'll stay for dinner?" inquired Beauty.

Anyhow, the ladies would dress; but not too much, for Monsieur

Jean wouldn't be dressed. Lanny explained the reason for the name. Then he walked up and down on the loggia in front of the villa, watching the sun set behind the dark mountains across the Golfe Juan. Many times he had watched it, as far back as his memory went. He had seen war come, and vessels burning and sinking in that blue expanse of water. He had watched the tangled fates of human beings woven on these grounds; love and hate, jealousy and greed, suffering and fear; he had seen people dancing, laughing and chatting, and more than once crying. Marcel had sat here with his burned-off face, meeting his friends in the protecting darkness. Here, too, Kurt had played his music, Rick had outlined his plays, and Robbie had negotiated big munitions deals. Now Lanny walked, waiting to hear if the spirit of a noble Spanish lady was going to speak to her Greek husband through the personality of an American redskin, dead a couple of centuries and using the vocal cords of a Polish peasant woman who had been a servant in the home of a Warsaw merchant. One thing you could say about life, it provided you with variety!

XII

The old man came up from the studio alone, walking with his head thrust forward, as he always did, as if smelling his way. Lanny went to meet him, and he said, with unwonted intensity: "My boy, this is really a disturbing thing!"

"You got some results?"

"I got what certainly seemed results. Tell me, are you convinced of this woman's honesty?"

"We are all convinced of that."

"How long have you known her?"

"For some eighteen months."

"You think she is really in a trance when she pretends to be?"

"She would have to be a skilled actress if that were not true; we have watched her closely, and we don't think she is intelligent enough to fool us."

"You are sure she doesn't know who I am?"

"I can't imagine how she could have found out. No one but my father knew about the matter, and you know that my father is not a loose talker. When you wrote me the appointment, I took the precaution to tear up your letter and throw it into the sea."

"Lanny, it was just as if my wife was sitting in the next room, sending me messages. You can understand how important this is to me."

"It is important to all of us, for we all get communications like that."

"She reminded me of things from my childhood, and from hers; things we both knew but which nobody else knows—at least, not that I can think of."

They went inside, for it grows chilly on the Riviera the moment the sun is down. The old man wanted to know all that Lanny thought about these phenomena, the most mysterious which confront the modern thinker. When Lanny told him of the books of Geley and Osty, Zaharoff took out his notebook and jotted down the names; also the two great volumes of Pierre Janet—he promised to study them all. His education had been neglected, but now he would try to find out about the subconscious mind and its powers, so different from those of a munitions king! He had missed a great deal, and was only beginning to be aware of it when life was ebbing.

The ladies came in: two most elegant ladies, about whom he had heard; concerning Irma nothing but good. He was extraordinarily courteous; he hoped for a favor from them, and asked it as a humble petitioner: would they graciously permit Madame Zyszynski to visit him in Monte Carlo if he would send his car for her and send her back? Beauty said: "Why, certainly. That is, of course, if Madame is willing, and I am sure she will be."

"We got along all right this time," said Zaharoff. And Lanny, not untrained in observation, perceived that the old spider, likewise not untrained, was watching for some hint of the fact that Beauty knew of the earlier fiasco. Since Beauty didn't know what had happened on that occasion, it was easy for her to appear innocent. Not that it would have been difficult, anyhow!

Lanny went down to the studio for the purpose of consulting Madame and found her pleased with the old gentleman's new humility. She said she would be willing to visit his hotel, and Lanny went back and made a date. Zaharoff excused himself from dinner, saying that he ate very little and that his mind was full of the things he had heard.

He went out to his car and was driven away. Beauty said to Irma: "That poor old man! He has so much money, yet he can't get the one thing in the world he wants!" After saying it, the mother-in-law wondered if it mightn't sound a wee bit tactless!

9

Land Where My Fathers Died

I

I RMA had promised her mother to visit Long Island that summer and exhibit the new heiress of the Barnes and Vandringham clans. Johannes Robin had said that they would make it another yachting-trip, but now he wrote sorrowfully that it was impossible for him to leave Berlin; financial conditions were becoming desperate, and he would have to be on hand every day and perhaps every hour. With a princely gesture he offered the Budd family the yacht with all expenses paid, but perhaps he knew that they would not accept such a favor.

Irma said: "We might rent it from him." They talked about the idea for a while, but they knew the young Robins wouldn't come, they would feel it their duty to stick by their mother and father. Freddi would prefer to carry on the school, for workers don't have vacations—when they stop work, their pay stops, and this was happening to great numbers of them. Hansi and Bess were helping by playing at low-priced concerts in large halls for the people. A violinist doesn't promote his reputation by that kind of thing, but he helps his conscience.

There were plenty of persons who would have been pleased to be offered a free yachting-trip, but Irma admitted that it might be a bore to be with a small group for so long a time; better to be footloose, and free to change friends as well as places. The efficient Bureau International de Voyage, which now consisted of Mr. and Mrs. Jerry Pendleton and nobody else, was happy to supply them with information concerning steamers from Marseille to New York. There were sumptuous Mediterranean cruises on which one could book for the return trip; there were steamers making so-called de luxe tours around the world, coming by way of the Suez Canal and Gibraltar to New York. De luxe was what Irma Barnes desired, and it was pleasant to learn that the choicest suites of these floating hotels were vacant on account of hard times. Irma chose the best for herself and Lanny, and a near-by one for Miss Severne, the nursemaid, and the baby; also a second-class passage for her maid, and for the demoted Feathers, whose duty it now was to run all the errands and accept all humiliations.

Early in May the party embarked, and Lanny found himself returned suddenly into that café society from which he had fled a year and a half ago. Ten to twelve million dollars had been expended to provide a sea-going replica of the Great White Way, and by expertly contrived advertising exactly the right sort of crowd had been lured on board. This floating hotel included a swimming-pool deep enough for high diving, a game room, a gymnasium with instructors, a squash court, a playground for children, an arcade with beauty parlors and luxury shops, several bars and barber-shops used mainly by ladies, a jazz band and a small orchestra, a motion-picture theater, and a grill room where you could order anything you wanted if you became hungry in between the elaborate regular meals. Here were people one had met at first nights on Broadway, in the swanky night clubs and the Park Avenue penthouses. A sprinkling of sight-seers and curiosity-seekers from the "sticks," which meant any place west of Seventh Avenue; people who had "made their pile" in hogs or copper and put it into bonds, and wished to get away from the troubles of their world. They had expected the depression to be over by the time they got back, but they had miscalculated.

Before the vessel docked at Marseille word had got about that Irma Barnes and her husband were coming on board; so there was a crowd lined up by the rail to spot them and watch them. Once upon a time it had been rude to stare, but that time was gone with the daisies. Several old friends rushed up to greet Irma, and to be introduced to the lucky young prince consort; so right away the pair were plunged into the midst of events: supper parties, bridge parties, dancing, sports of one sort or another. So much gossip to hear and to impart, so many new people to meet and play with! Everybody's cabin was loaded with souvenirs; everybody had stories of places visited. But on the whole it had been rather a bore, you know; they would be glad to get back home, where you could play golf and ride and motor, and get rid of the people who bored you.

II

Living under the feudal system, Irma had found herself impressed by the idea of being exclusive; but here she was back in the easygoing world which was much less trouble and much more fun. All sorts of people wanted to know her, and how was she to find out who they were or what they wanted? It might be an expert thief, trying to find out what jewels she wore and where she kept them; it might be a blackmailer on the watch for something he could put to use; there was a good chance of its being a cardsharp, for swarms of them preyed upon the passengers of ocean liners. Irma and a New York acquaintance played against a couple of ladies with manners and costumes beyond criticism; quite probably the pair had some means of signaling other than the bids which were a part of the game and which everybody studied and argued about. They proposed a dollar a point for stakes, and Irma didn't mind; she didn't mind especially when she found that her side was a couple of thousand dollars in the hole at the end of an afternoon. Her partner broke down and wept, saying she didn't have the money, so Irma paid for both, and didn't like it when Lanny insisted that all three women were probably in cahoots.

Also there was the question of liquor. The young people were drinking all the time, and how they managed to carry it was a problem. Lanny said: "Why not choose some friends who know something to talk about?" But those were older persons, and Irma could only listen. Presently along would come some of her own set and carry her off to a gaily decorated bar; or they would order drinks while they were playing shuffleboard on deck. Lanny could no longer say: "You have the health of our baby to think of." He was put in the unpleasant position of the sober man at a feast; he was a wet blanket, a sorehead, a grouch. Irma didn't say these things, but others said them behind her back, and looked them; you had either to play the game or antagonize people. Lanny decided that he would be glad when his wife was under the sheltering wing of Fanny Barnes, who had the right to scold her daughter and exercised it.

Among the conveniences on board this movable city was a broker's office where you could get quotations and gamble in your favorite stocks; also a daily newspaper which reported what was happening in Wall Street and the rest of the world. Shortly before the vessel reached New York it was learned that the troubles in Vienna had come to a climax; there was a failure of the Creditanstalt, biggest bank in the city. Next day the panic was spreading to Germany. Lanny heard people say: "All right. It's time they had some troubles." But others understood that if Germany couldn't pay reparations, Britain and France would soon be unable to pay their debts to the United States. These financial difficulties traveled like waves of sound; they met some obstruction and came rolling back. The world had become a vast sounding-board, filled with clashing echoes hurled this way and that. Impossible to guess what was coming next!

III

The Statue of Liberty stood, erect and dignified, holding her torch immovable; in bright sunlight she appeared quite sober. Lanny wondered: was she "on the wagon," or did she, like so many of his acquaintances in café society, never get drunk until night? It was still the time of Prohibition, and you couldn't buy anything on the ship after she had passed the three-mile limit; but everybody knew that as soon as you stepped ashore you could get whatever you wanted.

Fanny Barnes, accompanied by her brother Horace, was waiting on the pier for the first sight of the most precious of all babies. When gangplanks were lowered and the family procession came down, she took the soft warm bundle in her arms, and Lanny saw the first tears he had ever seen in what he had thought were hard, worldly eyes. She refused to put the bundle down, but carried it off to the waiting car and sat there, breaking every rule which Miss Severne had laid down for the hygienic and psychological protection of infants. Lanny saw the Englishwoman watching with disapproval; he feared that a first-class row was pending, for the head nurse had explained many times that she was a professional person and considered that her services were superfluous if her advice was disregarded.

They left Feathers to attend to the customs formalities and to bring Irma's maid and the nursemaid and the bags in another car. The family drove away in state, with Miss Severne in front with the chauffeur, so that she wouldn't be so aware of a grandmother coddling and cuddling a fourteen-month-old child, poking a finger at her and talking nonsense. That went on all the way across Fourteenth Street, and through the slums of New York's East Side, over a great bridge, and on the new speedway. Lanny recognized what a serious action he had committed in keeping the precious creature in Europe—and what a fight he was going to have to get her back there!

Plenty of news to talk about: family affairs, business affairs, and all their friends who had got married, or died, or been born. Presently Uncle Horace Vandringham was telling Lanny about stocks. They were down again—very bad news from Germany, and rumors that the trouble might spread to Britain. The one-time market manipulator gave it as his opinion that prices had just about reached bottom; the very same words that Robbie Budd had said: "Look where steel is now!" Uncle Horace had written Irma, begging her to put up a little money, so that he might get back into the game; he would go fifty-fifty with her—it was a crime to waste the expert knowledge which he had spent a lifetime in acquiring. Irma had said no, and had told her husband that she would continue to say it and not let herself be bothered with importunities.

I V

Life at Shore Acres was taken up where it had been left off. The question of Baby Frances was settled quickly, for the head nurse came to Irma, who had employed her; she didn't say that Irma had been raised wrong, or that grandmothers were *passées*, but simply that modern science had made new discoveries and that she had been trained to put them into practice. Irma couldn't dream of losing that most conscientious of persons, so she laid down the law to her mother, who took it with surprising meekness. Likewise, Uncle Horace made only the feeblest of tentatives in the direction of Wall Street. Lanny perceived that they had had family consultations; the haughty Fanny was going to be the ideal mother-in-law, her brother was going to make himself agreeable at all costs, and everybody in the house was to do the same—in the hope that a prince consort might be persuaded to settle down in his palace and enjoy that state of life to which it had pleased God to call him.

All that Lanny and his royal spouse had to do was to be happy, and they had the most expensive toys in the world to play with. The estate had been created for that purpose, and thousands of skilled workers had applied their labor and hundreds of technicians had applied their brains to its perfection. If the young couple wanted to ride there were horses, if they wanted to drive there were cars, if they wanted to go out on the water there were sailboats and launches. There were two swimming-pools, one indoors and one out, besides the whole Atlantic Ocean. There were servants to wait upon them and clean up after them; there were pensioners and courtiers to flatter and entertain them. The world had been so contrived that it was extremely difficult for the pair to do any sort of useful thing.

Playmates came in swarms: boys and girls of Irma's set who were "lousy with money"—their own phrase. Irma had romped and danced with them from childhood, and now they were in their twenties, but lived and felt and thought as if still in their teens. The depression had hit many of them, and a few had had to drop out, but most were still keeping up the pace. They drove fast cars, and thought nothing of dining in one place and dancing fifty miles away; they would come racing home at dawn—one of them would be assigned to drive and would make it a point of honor not to get drunk. The boys had been to college and the girls to finishing-schools, where they had acquired fashionable manners, but no ideas that troubled them. Their conversation was that of a secret society: they had their own slang and private jokes, so that if you didn't "belong," you had to ask what they were talking about.

It was evident to all that Irma had picked up an odd fish, but they were willing enough to adopt him; all he had to do was to take them as they were, do what they did, and not try to force any ideas upon them. He found it interesting for a while; the country was at its springtime best, the estates of Long Island were elaborate and some of them elegant, and anybody who is young and healthy enjoys tennis and swimming and eating good food. But Lanny would pick up the newspaper and read about troubles all over the world; he would go into the swarming city where millions had no chance to play and not even enough to eat; he would look at the apple-sellers, and the breadlines of haggard, fear-driven men—many with clothes still retaining traces of decency. Millions wandering over the land seeking in vain for work; families being driven from their farms because they couldn't pay the taxes. Lanny wasn't content to read the regular newspapers, but had to seek out the Pink and Red ones, and then tell his wealthy friends what he had found there. Not many would believe him, and not one had any idea what to do about it.

Nobody seemed to have such ideas. The ruling classes of the various nations watched the breakdown of their economy like spectators in the neighborhood of a volcano, seeing fiery lava pour out of the crater and dense clouds of ashes roll down the slopes, engulfing vine-yards and fields and cottages. So it had been when the younger Pliny had stood near Mt. Vesuvius some nineteen hundred years back, and had written to the historian Tacitus about his experience:

"I looked behind me; gross darkness pressed upon our rear, and came rolling over the land after us like a torrent. We had scarce sat down, when darkness overspread us, not like that of a moonless or cloudy night, but of a room when it is shut up, and the lamp put out. You could hear the shrieks of women, the crying of children, and the shouts of men; some were seeking their children, others their parents, others their wives or husbands, and only distinguishing them by their voices; one lamenting his own fate, another that of his family; some praying to die, from the very fear of dying; many lifting their hands to the gods; but the great part imagining that there were no gods left anywhere, and that the last and eternal night was come upon the world."

V

By way of the automobile ferry from Long Island to New London, Connecticut, Lanny drove his wife to his father's home, and they spent a week with the family. The town of Newcastle had been hard hit by the depression: the arms plant was shut down entirely; the hardware and elevator and other plants were running only three days a week. The workers were living on their savings if they had any; they were mortgaging their homes, and losing their cars and radio sets because they couldn't meet installment payments. There were a couple of thousand families entirely destitute, and most of them were Budd workers, so it was a strain upon the consciences and pocketbooks of all members of the ruling family. Esther was working harder than even during the World War; she was chairman of the finance committee of the town's soup kitchens and children's aid, and went about among the women's clubs and churches telling harrowing stories and making the women weep, so that private charity might not break down entirely.

That was a crucial issue, as her husband told her. If America was forced to adopt the British system of the dole, it would be the end of individual initiative and private enterprise. Robbie seemed to his son like the anchor-man of a tug-of-war team, his heels dug into the ground, his teeth set, the veins standing out purple in his forehead with the effort he was making to keep his country from moving the wrong way. Robbie had been down to Washington to see President Hoover, his hero and the captain of his team. The Great Engineer was literally besieged; all the forces of disorder and destruction—so he considered them and so did Robbie—were trying to pry him from his stand that the budget must be balanced, the value of the dollar maintained, and business allowed to "come back" in due and regular course.

The cities and the counties, nearing the end of their resources, were clamoring for Federal aid; the returned soldiers had organized to demand a bonus for the services they had rendered overseas while the business men at home were filling their pocketbooks. So the agitators charged, frothing at the mouth, and they had forced their bill through Congress over the President's veto. Poor Herbert went on making speeches about the American system of "rugged indi- vidualism"; it was heartening to him to have a solid business man, one who had been an oil man like himself, come in and tell him that he was saving civilization.

Esther, of course, had to believe her husband; she told all the club ladies and church ladies that they were saving civilization, and they put in their dimes or their dollars, and gathered together and knitted sweaters or cooked and served hot soup. But every slump in Wall Street threw more men out of work in Newcastle, and the ladies were at their wit's end. When Irma wrote a check for five thousand dollars for the children, tears of gratitude ran down the cheeks of Lanny's stepmother. He had given her great sorrow in years past, but now his credit rating was triple-A. Even his Pinkness had been made respectable by the crimson hues of Bess, concerning whom the mother inquired with deepest anxiety.

The Newcastle Country Club was giving a costume dance for charity. You paid twenty-five dollars for a ticket, and if you weren't there you were nobody. Irma and Lanny had to drive to a near-by city, since everybody who knew how to sew in Newcastle was already at work on costumes. But it was all right, for that city likewise had its smokeless factory chimneys. Several women worked day and night, and as a result the visiting pair appeared as a very grand Beatrice and Benedick in red-and-purple velvet with gold linings. A delightful occasion, and when it was over, Irma and Lanny presented the costumes to the country club's dramatics committee, for Irma said that if you folded them and carried them in the car they'd be full of creases and not fit to use again.

VI

Not much fun visiting a factory town in times like these. But it was the Budd town, and in prosperous days everybody had been cordial to the young couple and their friends, even the Jewish ones. So now it was necessary to stay, and give sympathy and a little help, and have receptions held in their honor, and shake hands and chat with innumerable Budds—not even Lanny could remember them all, and had to "bone up" as if it were for a college examination. Also they played golf and tennis at the country club, and swam and went sailing in delightful June weather. The countryside put on a show of wild roses, and all nature told them not to worry too much, that life was going on.

Also they had to pay a visit to the president of Budd Gunmakers. The old man had told Lanny that he would probably never see him again; but here he was, still holding on, still running the company by telephone. His hands shook so that it was painful to watch; his cheeks hung in flaps so that he seemed to have twice as much yellow skin as was needed to cover his shrinking form; but he was the same grim Puritan, and still questioned Lanny to make sure he had not forgotten his Bible texts. He had heard about Baby Frances, of course, and said he had carried out his promise to put her in his will, though he didn't know if he really had any property any more, or if Budd stocks would be worth the paper. He pinned the pair down on whether they were going to have another try for a son, and Irma told him they were leaving it to the Lord; this wasn't so, but Lanny didn't contradict her, and afterward she said it would have been a shame to worry that old man so close to the grave.

Everybody knew that he couldn't hold on much longer, and there was an underground war going on for control of the company; a painful struggle between Robbie and his oldest brother Lawford, that silent, morose man who was in charge of production, and whom Lanny and Irma saw only when they attended the First Congregational Church. The old grandfather had not said whom he wished to have succeed him, and of course nobody liked to ask him. For some time Lawford had been seeking out the directors and presenting his side of the case, which involved telling them of the blunders which Robbie had committed—or what Lawford considered blunders. Naturally, this made it necessary for Robbie to defend himself, and it was an ugly situation. Robbie thought he had the whip hand so far. His father had renewed his contract as European sales representative for another five years, so if Lawford got the presidency they'd have to pay a pretty price to buy Robbie out.

VII

The business situation in Germany went from bad to worse. Robbie received a letter from Johannes, saying that it looked like the end of everything. Foreign loans were no more, and Germany couldn't go on without them. Johannes was taking more money out of the country, and asking Robbie's help in investing it. Robbie told his son in strict confidence—not even Irma was allowed to know —that President Hoover had prepared a declaration of a moratorium on international debts; he was still hesitating about this grave step; would it help or would it cause more alarm? The French, who had not been consulted, would probably be furious.

The declaration was issued soon after the young couple had returned to Shore Acres, and the French were furious, but the Germans were not much helped. In the middle of July the great Danat Bank failed in Berlin, and there was terror such as Lanny had witnessed in New York. Chancellor Brüning went to Paris to beg for help, and Premier Laval refused it; France was now the strongest

European power financially, and was sitting on her heap of gold, lending it only for the arming of Poland and her other eastern allies —which were blackmailing her without mercy. Britain had made the mistake of trying to buttress German finances, and now her own were shaky as a result. "We're not that sort of fools," wrote young Denis de Bruyne to Lanny, who replied: "If you let the German Republic fall and you get Hitler, will that help you?" Young Denis did not reply.

Such were the problems faced by the statesmen while two darlings of fortune were having fun all over the northeastern states. Invitations would come, and they would order their bags packed, step into their car in the morning, drive several hours or perhaps all day, and step out onto an estate in Bar Harbor or Newport, the Berkshires or the Ramapo Hills, the Adirondacks or the Thousand Islands. Wherever it was, there would be a palace—even though it was called a "cottage" or a "camp." The way you knew a "camp" was that it was built of "slabs," and you wore sport clothes and didn't dress for dinner; but the meal would be just as elaborate, for nobody stayed anywhere without sending a staff of servants ahead and having all modern conveniences, including a dependable bootlegger. Radios and phonographs provided music for dancing, and if you didn't have the right number for games, you called people on the long-distance telephone and they motored a hundred miles or more, and when they arrived they bragged about their speed. Once more Lanny thought of the English poet Clough, and his song attributed to the devil in one of his many incarnations: "How pleasant it is to have money, heigh ho! How pleasant it is to have money!"

These young people still had it, though the streams were drying up. The worst of the embarrassments of a depression, as it presented itself to the daughter of J. Paramount Barnes, was that so many of her friends kept getting into trouble and telling her about it. A truly excruciating situation: in the midst of a bridge game at Tuxedo Park the hostess received a telephone call from her broker in New York, and came in white-faced, saying that unless she could raise fifty thousand dollars in cash by next morning she was "sunk." Not everybody had that much money in the bank, and especially not in times when rumors were spreading about this bank and that. Irma saw the eyes of the hostess fixed upon her, and was most uncomfortable, because she couldn't remedy the depression all by herself and had to draw the line somewhere.

Yes, it wasn't all fun having so much money. You didn't want to shut yourself up in yourself and become hard-hearted and indifferent to others' suffering; but you found yourself surrounded by people who wanted what you had and didn't always deserve it, people who had never learned to do anything useful and who found themselves helpless as children in a crisis. Of course they ought to go to work, but what could they do? All the jobs appeared to be filled by persons who knew how to do them; right now there were said to be six, or eight, or ten million people looking for jobs and not finding any. Moreover, Lanny and Irma didn't seem to be exactly the right persons to be giving that sort of advice!

VIII

The first of July was a time for dividends, and many of the biggest and most important corporations "passed" them. This gave a shock to Wall Street, and to those who lived by it; Irma's income was cut still more, and the shrinkage seemed likely to continue. The news from abroad was as bad as possible. Rick, who knew what was going on behind the scenes, wrote it to his friend. The German Chancellor was in London, begging for funds, but nobody dared help him any further; France was obdurate, because the Germans had committed the crime of attempting to set up a customs union with Austria. But how could either of these countries survive if they couldn't trade?

All Lanny's life it had been his habit to sit and listen to older people talking about the state of the world. Now he knew more about it than most of the people he met, even the older ones. While Irma played bridge, or table tennis with her young friends who had acquired amazing skill at that fast game, Lanny would be telling the president of one of the great Wall Street banks just why he had blundered in advising his clients to purchase the bonds of Fascist

Italy, or trying to convince one of the richest old ladies of America that she wasn't really helping to fight Bolshevism when she gave money for the activities of the Nazis in the United States. Such a charming, cultivated young German had been introduced to her, and had explained this holy crusade to preserve Western civilization from the menace of Asiatic barbarism!

It was a highly complicated world for a devout Episcopalian and member of the D.A.R. to be groping about in. A great banking fortune gave her enormous power, and she desired earnestly to use it wisely. Lanny told her the various radical planks of the Nazi program, and the old lady was struck with dismay. He told her how Hitler had been dropping these planks one by one, and she took heart again. But he assured her that Hitler didn't mean the dropping any more than he had meant the planks; what he wanted was to get power, and then he would do whatever was necessary to keep it and increase it. Lanny found it impossible to make this attitude real to gentle, well-bred, conscientious American ladies; it was just too awful. When you persisted in talking about it, you only succeeded in persuading them that there must be something wrong with your cynical self.

IX

Lanny just couldn't live with these overstuffed classes all the time; he became homesick for his Reds and Pinks, and went into the hot, teeming city and paid another visit to the Rand School of Social Science. He told them what he had been doing for workers' education on the Riviera, and made a contribution to their expenses. The word spread quickly that here was the bearer of a Fortunatus purse, and everybody who had a cause—there appeared to be hundreds of them—began writing him letters or sending him mimeographed or printed appeals for funds. The world was so full of troubles, and there were so few who cared!

Also he sent in a subscription to the *New Leader*, and got a weekly dose of the horrors of the capitalist system, which had developed such marvelous powers of production and was unable to use them;

which left millions to starve while a few parasites fattened themselves in luxury. This paper would lie on the table in his room, and
Irma would see the prominent headlines and say: "Oh, dear! Are
you still reading that stuff?" It irritated her to be referred to as a
parasite and to have Lanny say: "But that's what we are," and go on
to prove it.

Several of the workers' groups and labor unions had summer
camps where their members could spend a vacation. Lanny went
to have a look at one of them, having the idea that he ought to
know the workers at first hand. But he made the mistake of taking
his wife along, which spoiled matters. Irma did her best, but she
didn't know how to unbend. The place was crowded, and mostly
they were Jews; their dress was informal and their manners hearty;
they were having a good time in their own way, and didn't mind if
it was different from her way; they didn't look up to royalty, and
didn't enjoy being looked at as a zoo. In short, as an effort to bridge
the social chasm the visit was a flop.

On the same South Shore of Long Island with the Barnes estate
is the resort known as Coney Island. Lanny had heard about it
but had never seen it, and Irma had only vague memories from a
time in childhood when her father had taken her. On a hot Sunday
afternoon the perverse idea occurred to one of their smart crowd:
"Let's go and see Coney!" It really was a spectacle, they insisted;
the world's premier slumming-tour—unless you went to Shanghai or
Bombay on one of those de luxe cruises.

Two motor-carloads of them drove to the resort, which is a long
spit of land. It was hard to find a place to park, and they had to
walk a couple of miles; but they were young, and were out for fun.
There must have been a million people at the resort, and most of
them crowded onto the wide stretch of beach; it was barely possible
to move about for the swarms of people lying or sitting in the sand,
sweltering in the blazing sunshine. If you wanted to know the ele-
mentary facts about the human animal, here was the place to see
exactly how fat they were, or how skinny, how hairy, how bow-
legged, how stoop-shouldered, how generally different from the
standards established by Praxiteles. You could discover also how

they stank, what raucous noises they made, what a variety of ill-odored foods they ate, and how utterly graceless and superfluous they were.

To the fastidious Lanny Budd the worst thing of all was their emptiness of mind. They had come for a holiday, and wanted to be entertained, and there was a seemingly endless avenue of devices contrived for the purpose. For prices from a dime up you could be lifted on huge revolving wheels, or whirled around sitting on brightly painted giraffes and zebras; you could ride in tiny cars which bumped into one another, you could walk in dark tunnels which were a perpetual earthquake, or in bright ones where sudden breezes whipped up the women's skirts and made them scream; you could be frightened by ghosts and monsters—in short, you could have a thousand fantastic things done to you, all expressive of the fact that you were an animal and not a being with a mind; you could be humiliated and made ridiculous, but rarely indeed on Coney Island could you be uplifted or inspired or taught any useful thing. Lanny took this nightmare place as an embodiment of all the degradations which capitalism inflicted upon the swarming millions of its victims. Anything to keep them from thinking.

Thus a young Pink; and he got himself into a red-hot argument with a carload of his young companions, who had drawn their own conclusions from this immersion in carnality. Irma, who monopolized a half-mile of ocean front, was disgusted that anyone should be content to squat upon ten or a dozen square feet of it. Her childhood playmate, Babs Lorimer, whose father had once had a "corner" in wheat, drew political conclusions from the spectacle and wondered how anybody could conceive of the masses' having anything to say about the running of government. "Noodles" Winthrop—his name was Newton—whose widowed mother collected a small fraction of a cent from everyone who rode to Coney Island on a street railway, looked at the problem biologically, and said he couldn't imagine how such hordes of ugly creatures had survived, or why they desired to. Yet look at the babies they had!

X

With the members of Irma's immediate family Lanny found that he was getting along surprisingly well. The domineering Fanny Barnes was set in her opinions, but for the most part these had to do with questions of manners and taste and family position; she didn't give much thought to politics and economics. Pride was her leading motive; she lived in the faith that her Protestant Episcopal God had assigned to her family a specially precious strain of blood. She had the firm conviction that bearers of this blood couldn't do anything seriously wrong, and she found ways to persuade herself that they hadn't. She had made up her mind to make the best of this son-in-law whom fate had assigned to her, and presently she was finding excuses for him. Did someone call him a Socialist? Well, he had been reared in Europe, where such ideas didn't mean what they did in America. Hadn't some distinguished Englishman —Fanny couldn't recall who it was—declared: "We are all Socialists now"?

For Lanny as a prince consort there was really quite a lot to be said. His manners were distinguished and his conversation even more so. He didn't get drunk, and he had to be urged to spend his wife's money. The uncertainty about his mother's marriage ceremony hadn't broken into the newspapers, and he was received by his father's very old family. So the large and majestic Queen Mother of Shore Acres set out to butter him with flattery and get from him the two things she ardently desired: first, that he should help Irma to produce a grandson to be named Vandringham; and second, that they should leave Baby Frances at Shore Acres to be reared in the Vandringham tradition.

Uncle Horace, that pachyderm of a man who moved with such astonishing energy, proved to be an equally complaisant relative. He had a sense of humor, with more than a trace of mischief in it. He was amused to hear Lanny "razz" the American plutocracy, and especially those representatives of it who came to the Barnes estate. The fact that he himself had been knocked down and out had diminished his admiration for the system and increased his

pleasure in seeing others "get theirs." He chuckled at Lanny's Pinkish jokes, and took the role of an elderly courtier "playing up" to
a newly crowned king. Did he hope that Lanny might some day
persuade Irma to let him have another fling in the market? Or was
he merely making sure of holding onto the comfortable pension
which she allowed him? Anyhow, he was good company.

XI

The echoes of calamity came rolling from Germany to England.
Trade was falling off, factories closing, unemployment increasing;
doubts were spreading as to the soundness of the pound sterling,
for a century the standard of value for all the world; investors were
taking refuge in the dollar, the Dutch florin, the Swiss franc. Rick
told about the situation in his country; boldness was needed, he
said—a capital levy, a move to socialize credit; but no political party
had the courage or the vision. The Tories clamored to balance the
budget at any cost, to cut the dole, and the pay of the school-
teachers, even of the navy. It was the same story as Hoover with
his "rugged individualism." Anything to save the gold standard and
the power of the creditor class.

At the beginning of September the labor government fell. An
amazing series of events—the labor Prime Minister, Ramsay Mac-
Donald, and several of his colleagues in the old Cabinet went over
to the Tories and formed what he called a "National" government
to carry out the anti-labor program. It had happened before in
Socialist history, but never quite so dramatically, so openly; Rick,
writing about it for one of the leftist papers, said that those who
betrayed the hopes of the toiling masses usually managed to veil
their sell-out with decorous phrases, they didn't come out on the
public highway to strip themselves of their old work-clothes and
put on the livery of their masters.

Rick was a philosopher, and tried to understand the actions of
men. He said that the ruling classes couldn't supply their own quota
of ability, but were forced continually to invade the other classes
for brains. It had become the function of the Socialist movement

to train and equip lightning-change artists of politics, men who understood the workers and how to fool them with glittering promises and then climb to power upon their shoulders. In Italy it had been Mussolini, who had learned his trade editing the principal Socialist paper of the country. In France no fewer than four premiers had begun their careers as ardent revolutionaries; the newest of them was Pierre Laval, an innkeeper's son who had driven a one-horse omnibus for his father, and while driving had read Socialist literature and learned how to get himself elected mayor of his town.

For what had these men sold out their party and their cause? For cash? That played a part, of course; a premier or prime minister got considerably more than a Socialist editor, and learned to live on a more generous scale. But more important yet was power: the opportunity to expand the personality, to impress the world, to be pictured and reported in the newspapers, to hold the reins and guide the national omnibus. A thousand flatterers gather round the statesman, to persuade him that he is indispensable to the country's welfare, that danger lies just ahead, and that he alone can ride in the whirlwind and direct the storm.

Rick sent his friend a bunch of clippings, showing how the man who had once lost his seat in the House of Commons for his convictions had now become the hero and darling of those who had unseated him. The entire capitalist press had rallied behind him, praising his action as the greatest of public services. "He will find that he is their prisoner," wrote Rick. "He can do nothing but what they permit; he can have no career except by serving them."

Rick mailed this letter; but before the steamer reached New York, the cables brought word that the prisoner of the Tories had failed. Britain was off the gold standard, and the pound sterling had lost about twenty per cent of its value! It happened to be the twenty-first of September, a notable day in Wall Street history, for it marked two years from the high point of the big bull market. In those two years American securities had lost sixty per cent of their value; and now came this staggering news, causing another drop! "Look where steel is *now!*" said Lanny Budd to his father over the telephone.

XII

In the midst of this world chaos Pierre Laval, innkeeper's son, paid a visit to Germany to see what could be done for that frantic government. The boy driver had grown up into a short, stocky man with black hair always awry, with somber, rather piratical features and a thick black mustache. He had made a lot of money, a tremendous aid to a political career. Of his Socialist days he kept one souvenir: he always wore the little four-in-hand wash ties which had been the fashion in his youth, and had been cheap because he could wash them himself. In France it was well for a statesman to retain some proletarian eccentricity; that he sold out his convictions mattered less, for the people had become so cynical about public men that they hoped only to find the least dishonest.

With Laval traveled Aristide Briand, his Foreign Minister, another innkeeper's son and another Socialist who had changed his mind. He had been a member of twenty-one cabinets—which had required not a little flexibility. But he had labored with genuine conviction to make peace between France and Germany. Now he was an old man, bowed and gray; the glorious organ voice was broken and the strong heart was soon to break. He was still pleading for peace, but he was the prisoner of Laval; and anyhow it was too late. Ancient hatreds and fears had prevailed, and now Germany was in a desperate plight, and France in a worse one, but couldn't realize it.

A curious whim of history: Briand meeting with Hindenburg! The washerwoman's child and the East Prussian aristocrat; old-time enemies, now both nearing their graves; each thinking about his country's safety, and helpless to secure it. *Der alte Herr* talking about the menace of revolution in Germany; not the respectable kind which would put the Kaiser's sons on the throne, but a dangerous gutter-revolution, an upsurge of the *Lumpenproletariat*, led by the one-time odd-job man, the painter of picture postcards, the "Bohemian corporal" named Schicklgruber. Briand demanding the dropping of the Austro-German customs-union project, while Hindenburg pleaded for a chance for his country to sell goods.

Briand denouncing the Stahlhelm and the new pocket-battleships, while Hindenburg complained that France was not keeping her promise to disarm. Hindenburg begging for loans, while Briand explained that France had to keep her gold reserve as the last bulwark of financial security in Europe. No, there wasn't much chance of their getting together; the only one who could hope to profit by the visit was the aforesaid "Bohemian corporal," whose papers were raving alike at the French visitors and at the German politicians who licked their boots to no purpose.

Adolf Hitler Schicklgruber wouldn't attack Hindenburg, for Hindenburg was a monument, a tradition, a living legend. The Nazi press would concentrate its venom upon the Chancellor, a Catholic and leader of the Center party, guilty of the crime of signing the Young Plan which sought to keep Germany in slavery until the year 1988. Now Hoover had granted a moratorium, but there was no moratorium for Brüning, no let-up in the furious Nazi campaign.

Lanny Budd knew about it, because Heinrich Jung had got his address, presumably from Kurt, and continued to keep him supplied with literature. There was no one at Shore Acres who could read it but Lanny himself; however, one didn't need to know German, one had only to look at the headlines to know that it was sensational, and at the cartoons to know that it was a propaganda of cruel and murderous hate. Cartoons of Jews as monsters with swollen noses and bellies, of John Bull as a fat banker sucking the blood of German children, of Marianne as a devouring harpy, of the Russian bear with a knife in his teeth and a bomb in each paw, of Uncle Sam as a lean and sneering Shylock. Better to throw such stuff into the trash-basket without taking off the wrappers.

But that wouldn't keep the evil flood from engulfing Germany, it wouldn't keep millions of young people from absorbing a psychopath's view of the world. Lanny Budd, approaching his thirty-second birthday, wondered if the time hadn't come to stop playing and find some job to do. But he kept putting it off, because jobs were so scarce, and if you took one, you deprived somebody else of it—someone who needed it much more than you!

10

Conscience Doth Make Cowards

I

OCTOBER and early November are the top of the year in the North Atlantic states. There is plenty of sunshine, and the air is clear and bracing. A growing child can toddle about on lawns and romp with dogs, carefully watched by a dependable head nurse. A young mother and father can enjoy motoring and golf, or going into the city to attend art shows and theatrical first nights. Irma had been taken to the museums as a child, but her memories of them were vague. Now she would go with an expert of whom she was proud, and would put her mind on it and try to learn what it was all about, so as not to have to sit with her mouth shut while he and his intellectual friends voiced their ideas.

This pleasant time of year was chosen by Pierre Laval for a visit to Washington, but it wasn't because of the climate. The Premier of France came because there were now only two entirely solvent great nations in the world, and these two ought to understand and support each other. Germany had got several billion dollars from America, but had to have more, and France didn't want her to get them until she agreed to do what France demanded. The innkeeper's son was received with cordiality; excellent dinners were prepared for him, and nobody brought up against him his early Socialistic opinions. Robbie Budd reported that what Laval wanted was for the President to do nothing; to which Robbie's flippant son replied: "That ought to suit Herbert Hoover right down to the ground."

A few days later came the general elections in Britain. Ramsay MacDonald appealed to the country for support, and with all the great newspapers assuring the voters that the nation had barely escaped collapse, Ramsay's new National government polled slightly less than half the vote and, under the peculiarities of the electoral system, carried slightly more than eight-ninths of the constituencies. Rick wrote that Ramsay had set the Labor party back a matter of twenty-one years.

Robbie Budd didn't worry about that, of course; he was certain that the rocks had been passed and that a long stretch of clear water lay before the ship of state. Robbie's friend Herbert had told him so, and who would know better than the Great Engineer? Surely not the editors of Pink and Red weekly papers! But Lanny perversely went on reading these papers, and presently was pointing out to his father that the British devaluation of the pound was giving them a twenty per cent advantage over American manufacturers in every one of the world's markets. Odd as it might seem, Robbie hadn't seen that; but he found it out by cable, for the Budd plant had a big hardware contract canceled in Buenos Aires. One of Robbie's scouts reported that the order had gone to Birmingham; and wasn't Robbie hopping!

II

Mr. and Mrs. Lanny Budd took passage on a German steamer to Marseille; a spick-and-span, most elegant steamer, brand-new, as all German vessels had to be, since the old ones had been confiscated under the treaty of Versailles. One of the unforeseen consequences of having compelled the Germans to begin life all over again! Britain and France didn't like it that their former foe and ever-present rival should have the two fanciest ocean liners, the blue-ribbon holders of the transatlantic service; also the two most modern warships—they were called pocket-battleships, because they weren't allowed to weigh more than ten thousand tons each, but the Germans had shown that they could get pretty nearly everything into that limit.

This upstart nation was upstarting again, and outdistancing everybody else. The Germans filled the air with outcries against persecutions and humiliations, but they had gone right ahead borrowing money and putting it into new industrial plant, the most modern, most efficient, so that they could undersell all competitors. You might not like Germans, but if you wanted to cross the ocean, you liked a new and shiny boat with officers and stewards in new uniforms, and the cleanest and best table-service. They were so polite, and at the same time so determined; Lanny was interested in talking with them and speculating as to what made them so admirable as individuals and so dangerous as a race.

Right now, of course, they were in trouble, like everybody else. They had the industrial plant, but couldn't find customers; they had the steamships, but it was hard to get passengers! The other peoples blamed fate or Providence, economic law, the capitalist system, the gold standard, the war, the Reds—but Germans everywhere blamed but one thing, the Versailles *Diktat* and the reparations it had imposed. Every German was firmly set in the conviction that the Allies were deliberately keeping the Fatherland from getting on its feet again, and that all their trouble was a direct consequence of this. Lanny would point out that now there was a moratorium on all their debts, not only reparations but post-war borrowings, so it ought to be possible for them to recover soon. But he never knew that argument to have the slightest effect; there was a national persecution complex which operated subconsciously, as in an individual.

Since there were so few passengers, Lanny had a week in which to study the ship and those who manned it. Knowing Germany so well, he had a passport to their hearts. He could tell the officers that he had been a guest of General Graf Stubendorf; he could tell the stewards that he had talked with Adolf Hitler; he could tell the crew that he was a brother-in-law of Hansi Robin. The vessel was a miniature nation, with representatives of all the various groups in about the right proportions. Some of the officers had formerly served in the German navy, and some of those who tended the engines had rebelled against them and made the Socialist revolution. In between were the middle classes—stewards, barbers, clerks, radio men, petty officers—all of whom worked obsequiously for tips but would work harder for love if you whispered: "*Heil Hitler!*"—even though you said it in jest.

Irma couldn't understand Lanny's being interested to talk to such people, and for so long a time. He explained that it was a sociological inquiry; if Rick had been along he would have written an article: "The Floating Fatherland." It was a question of the whole future of Germany. How deeply was the propaganda of Dr. Joseph Goebbels taking effect? What were the oilers thinking? What did the scullerymen talk about before they dropped into their bunks? There were dyed-in-the-wool Reds, of course, who followed the Moscow line and were not to be swerved; but others had become convinced that Hitler was a genuine friend of the people and would help them to get shorter hours and a living wage. Arguments were going on day and night, an unceasing war of words all over the ship. Which way was the balance swinging?

Important also was what Capain Rundgasse said. As the physician has a bedside manner, so the captain of a passenger liner has what might be called a steamer-chairside manner. He talked with two wealthy and fashionable young Americans, saying that he could understand why they were worried by the political aspect of his country; but really there was no need for concern. Fundamentally all Germans were German, just as all Englishmen were English, and when it was a question of the welfare and safety of the Fatherland all would become as one. That applied to the deluded Socialists, and even to the Communists—all but a few criminal leaders. It applied to the National Socialists especially. If Adolf Hitler were to become Chancellor tomorrow, he would show himself a good German, just like any other, and all good Germans would support him and obey the laws of their country.

III

Bienvenu seemed small and rather dowdy when one came to it from Shore Acres. But it was home, and there were loving hearts here. Beauty had spent a quiet but contented summer, or so she said. That most unlikely of marriages was turning out one of the best; she couldn't say enough about the goodness and kindness of Parsifal Dingle—that is, not enough to satisfy herself, although she easily satisfied her friends. She was trying her best to become spiritual-minded, and also she had the devil of *embonpoint* to combat. She consoled herself with the idea that when you were well padded, you didn't develop wrinkles. She was certainly a blooming Beauty.

Madame Zyszynski had been two or three times to visit Zaharoff at Monte Carlo; then he had gone north to the Château de Balincourt, and had written to ask if Beauty would do him the great favor of letting Madame come for a while. She had spent the month of August there, and had been well treated, and impressed by the grandeur of the place, but rather lonely, with those strange Hindu servants to whom she couldn't talk. When she was leaving, the old gentleman had presented her with a diamond solitaire ring which must have cost twenty or thirty thousand francs. She was proud of it, but afraid to wear it and afraid it might be stolen, so she had asked Beauty to put it away in her safe-deposit box.

Lanny took up the subject of child study again. He would have liked to find out if Baby Frances would discover the art of the dance for herself; but this was not possible, because Marceline was there, dancing all over the place, and nothing could keep her from taking a tiny toddler by the hands and teaching her to caper and jump. Every day the baby grew stronger, and before that winter was over there was a pair of dancers, and if the phonograph or the piano wasn't handy, Marceline would sing little tunes and sometimes make up words about Baby and herself.

Sophie and her husband would come over for bridge with Beauty and Irma; so Lanny was left free to catch up on his reading or to run over to Cannes to his workers'-education project. The workers hadn't had any vacation, but were right where he had left them. Intellectually they had gained; nearly all could now make speeches, and as a rule they made them on the subject of Socialism *versus* Communism. While they all hated Fascism, they didn't hate it enough to make them willing to get together to oppose it. They were glad to hear Lanny tell about the wonderland of New York; many had got it mixed up with Utopia, and were surprised to hear that it was not being spared by the breakdown of capitalism. Bread-

lines and apple-selling on the streets of that city of plutocrats—
sapristi!

I V

Another season on the Riviera: from the point of view of the
hotelkeepers the worst since the war, but for people who had
money and liked quiet the pleasantest ever. The fortunate few had
the esplanade and the beaches to themselves; the sunshine was just
as bright, the sea as blue, and the flowers of the Cap as exquisite.
Food was abundant and low in price, labor plentiful and willing—
in short, Providence had fixed everything up for you.

When Irma and Beauty Budd emerged from the hands of *mo-
distes* and *friseurs*, all ready for a party, they were very fancy
showpieces; Lanny was proud to escort them and to see the attention they attracted. He kept himself clad according to their standards, did the honors as he had been taught, and for a while was
happy as a young man *à la mode*. His wife was deeply impressed
by Emily Chattersworth, that serene and gracious hostess, and was
taking her as a model. Irma would remark: "If we had a larger
house, we could entertain as Emily does." She would try experiments, inviting this eminent person and that, and when they came
she would say to her husband: "I believe you and I could have a
salon if we went about it seriously."

Lanny came to recognize that she was considering this as a career. Emily was growing feeble, and couldn't go on forever; there
would have to be someone to take her place, to bring the fashionable French and the fashionable Americans together and let them
meet intellectuals, writers and musicians and statesmen who had
made names for themselves in the proper dignified way. As a rule
such persons didn't have the money or time to entertain, nor were
their wives up to it; if you rendered that free service, it made you
"somebody" in your own right.

Lanny had said, rather disconcertingly, that she didn't know
enough for the job; since which time Irma had been on watch. She
had met a number of celebrities, and studied each one, thinking:
"Could I handle you? What is it you want?" They seemed to like

good food and wine, like other people; they appreciated a fine house and liked to come into it and sun themselves. Certainly they liked beautiful women—these were the suns! Irma's dressing-room in the Cottage was rather small, but it contained a pier-glass mirror, and she knew that what she saw there was all right. She knew that her manner of reserve impressed people; it gave her a certain air of mystery, and caused them to imagine things about her which weren't really there. The problem was to keep them from finding out!

Each of the great men had his "line," something he did better than anybody else. Lanny assumed that you had to read his book, listen to his speeches, or whatever it was; but Irma made up her mind that this was her husband's naïveté. *He* would have had to, but a woman didn't. A woman observed that a man wanted to talk about himself, and a woman who was good at listening to that was good enough for anything. She had to express admiration, but not too extravagantly; that was a mistake the gushy woman made, and the man decided that she was a fool. But the still, deep woman, the Mona Lisa woman, the one who said in a dignified way: "I have wanted very much to know about that—please tell me more," she was the one who warmed a celebrity's heart.

The problem, Irma decided, was not to get them to talk, but to get them to stop! The function of a *salonnière* was to apportion the time, to watch the audience and perceive when it wanted a change and bring about the change so tactfully that nobody noticed it. Irma watched the technique of her hostess, and began asking questions; and this was by no means displeasing to Emily, for she too was not above being flattered and liked the idea of taking on an understudy. She showed Irma her address-book, full of secret marks which only her confidential secretary understood. Some meant good things and some bad.

V

Lanny perceived that this developing interest in a salon was based upon a study of his own peculiarities. He had always loved Emily

CONSCIENCE DOTH MAKE COWARDS 195

and enjoyed her affairs, having been admitted to them even as a boy, because he had such good manners. What Irma failed to note was that Lanny was changing: the things which had satisfied him as a boy didn't necessarily do so when he had passed his thirty-second birthday, and when the capitalist system had passed its apogee. He would come home from one of Emily's soirées and open up a bunch of mail which was like a Sophoclean chorus lamenting the doom of the House of Oedipus. The front page of a newspaper was a record of calamities freshly befallen, while the editorial page was a betrayal of fears of others to come.

For years the orthodox thinkers of France had congratulated that country upon its immunity from depressions. Thanks to the French Revolution, the agriculture of the country was in the hands of peasant proprietors; also the industry was diversified, not concentrated and specialized like that of Germany, Britain, and America. France had already devalued her money, one step at a time; she possessed a great store of gold, and so had escaped that hurricane which had thrown Britain off the gold standard, followed by a dozen other countries in a row.

But now it appeared that the orthodox thinkers had been wishful. Hard times were hitting France; unemployment was spreading, the rich sending their money abroad, the poor hiding what they could get in their mattresses or under the oldest olive tree in the field. Suffering and fear everywhere—so if you were a young idealist with a tender heart, how could you be happy? Especially if your doctrines persuaded you that you had no right to the money you were spending! If you persisted in keeping company with revolutionists and malcontents who were only too ready to support your notions—and to draw the obvious conclusion that, since your money didn't belong to you, it must belong to them! As a rule they asked you to give it for the "cause," and many were sincere and would really spend it for the printing of literature or the rental of meeting-places. That justified them in their own eyes and in yours, but hardly in the eyes of the conservative-minded ladies and gentlemen whom your wife expected to invite to a salon!

Some five years had passed since Lanny had begun helping work-

ers' education in the Midi, and that was time enough for a generation of students to have passed through his hands and give him some
idea of what he was accomplishing. Was he helping to train genuine
leaders of the working class? Or was he preparing some careerist
who would sell out the movement for a premiership? Sometimes
Lanny was encouraged and sometimes depressed. That is the fate of
every teacher, but Lanny had no one of experience to tell him so.

Bright lads and girls revealed themselves in the various classes,
and became the objects of his affection and his hopes. He found
that, being children of the Midi, they all wanted to learn to be
orators. Many acquired the tricks of eloquence before they had got
any solid foundation, and when you tried to restrain them and
failed, you decided that you had spoiled a good mechanic. Many
were swept off their feet by the Communists, who for some reason
were the most energetic, the most persistent among proletarian agitators; also they had a system of thought wearing the aspect and
using the language of science, and thus being impressive to young
minds. Lanny Budd, talking law and order, peaceable persuasion,
gradual evolution, found himself pigeon-holed as *vieux jeu*, or in
American a "back number." "Naturally," said the young Reds,
"you feel that way because you have money. You can wait. But
what have we got?"

This was true enough to trouble Lanny's mind continually. He
watched his own influence upon his proletarian friends and wondered, was he really doing them good? Or were the preachers of
class struggle right, and the social chasm too wide for any bridge-
builder? What community of feeling or taste could survive between the exquisite who lived in Bienvenu and the roustabout's son
who lived in the cellar of a tenement in the Old Town of Cannes?
Was it not possible that in coming to the school well dressed, and
speaking the best French, Lanny was setting up ideals and standards
which were as apt to corrupt as to stimulate?

His friends at the school saw him driving his fancy car, they saw
him with his proud young wife; for though she came rarely, they
knew her by sight and still more by reputation. And what would
that do to youths at the age of susceptibility? Would it teach them

to be loyal to some working-class girl, some humble, poorly dressed comrade in their movement? Or would it fill them with dreams of rising to the heaven where the elegant rich ladies were kept? Lanny, surveying his alluring spouse, knew that there was in all the world no stronger bait for the soul and mind of a man. He had taken that bait more than once in his life; also he knew something about the four Socialists who had become premiers of France, and knew that in every case it had been the hand of some elegant siren which had drawn him out of the path of loyalty and into that of betrayal.

VI

There stood unused on the Bienvenu estate a comfortable dwelling, the Lodge, which Lanny had built for Nina and Rick. He begged them to come and occupy it this season; he had some important ideas he wanted to discuss. But Rick said the pater had been hit too hard by the slump, which seemed to have been aimed at landowners all over the world. Lanny replied with a check to cover the cost of the tickets; it had been earned by the sale of one of Marcel's pictures, and there were a hundred more in the storeroom. Also, Lanny explained, the vegetable garden at Bienvenu had been enlarged, so as to give some of Leese's cousins a chance to earn their keep. Come and help to eat the stuff!

Mother and father and the three children came; and after they had got settled, Lanny revealed what he had in mind: to get some more money out of the picture business (perhaps Irma would want to put some in) to found a weekly paper, with Rick as editor. They would try to wake up the intellectuals and work for some kind of co-operative system in Europe before it was too late. Lanny said he didn't know enough to edit a paper himself, but would be what in America was called an "angel."

Rick said that was a large order, and did his friend realize what he was letting himself in for? The commercial magazine field was pretty crowded, and a propaganda paper never paid expenses, but cost like sin. Lanny said: "Well, I've spent my share on sin, and I might try something else for a change."

"One can't publish a paper in a place like Cannes," declared Rick. "Where would you go?"

"I've wondered if it mightn't be possible to bring out a paper in London, and at the same time in Paris in French?"

"You mean with the same contents?"

"Well, practically the same."

"I should say that might be done if the paper were general and abstract. If you expect to deal with current events, you'd find the interests and tastes of the two peoples too far apart."

"The purpose would be to bring them together, Rick. If they read the same things, they might learn to understand each other."

"Yes, but you're trying to force them to read what they don't want. The paper would seem foreign to both sides; your enemies would call it that and make it appear still more so."

"I don't say it would be easy," replied the young idealist. "What makes it hard is exactly what makes it important."

"I don't dispute the need," Rick said. "But it would cost a pile of money. A paper has to come out regularly, and if you have a deficit, it goes on and on."

"Would you be interested in it as a job?" persisted the other.

"I'd have to think it over. I've come down here with a mind full of a play."

That was the real trouble, as it turned out. There was no use imagining that anybody could edit a paper as a sideline; it was a full-time job for several men, and Rick would have to give up his life's ambition, which was to become a dramatist. He had had just enough success to keep him going. That, too, was an important task: to force modern social problems into the theater, to break down the taboo which put the label of propaganda upon any effort to portray that class struggle which was the basic fact of the modern world. Rick had tried it eight or ten times, and said that if he had put an equal amount of energy and ability into portraying the sexual entanglements of the idle rich, he could have joined that envied group and had plenty of entanglements. But he was always thinking of some wonderful new idea which no audience would be able to resist; he had one now, and so the Franco-British weekly would have to wait until the potential editor had relieved his mind.

Lanny said: "If it's a good play, maybe Irma and I will back it." He always included his wife, out of politeness, and the same motive would cause her to come along.

"That costs money, too," was Rick's reply. "But at least, if the play falls flat, you don't have to produce it again the next week and the week after."

VII

Zaharoff was back at his hotel in Monte, and would send his car for Madame Zyszynski, and write notes expressing his gratitude to the family. He said he wished there were something he could do in return; and apparently he meant it, for when Robbie Budd came into possession of a block of New England-Arabian stock, he came to see the old man, who bought the stock at Robbie's own price. It wasn't a large amount, but Lanny said it was a sign that the duquesa really was "coming through."

Beauty was devoured by curiosity about these séances, and questioned Madame every time she came back; but the medium stuck to her story that she had no idea of what happened when she was in her trance. Evidently Tecumseh was behaving well, for when she came out she would find the sitter gracious and considerate. She always had tea with the maid of Sir Basil's married daughter, and sometimes the great man himself asked questions about her life and ideas. Evidently he was reading along the lines of spiritualism, but he never said a word about himself, nor did he mention the duquesa's name.

Beauty thought it was poor taste for a borrower to keep the owner so entirely in the dark; and perhaps the idea occurred to Sir Basil, for he called Lanny on the telephone and asked if he could spare time to run over and see him. Lanny offered to drive Madame on the next trip, and Zaharoff said all right; Lanny might attend the séance if it would interest him. That was certainly an advance, and could only mean that Zaharoff had managed to make friends with the Iroquois chieftain and his spirit band.

"All flesh is grass, and all the goodliness thereof is as the flower

of the field." So Lanny's stern grandfather had quoted, at the time
when Lanny was making a scandal in Newcastle by falling in love
with a young actress. The playboy thought of it now as he sat and
watched this man who might be as old as Grandfather Samuel. His
suave manners were a mask and his soul a bundle of fears. He had
fought so hard for wealth and power, and now he sat and watched
infirmity creeping over him and everything slipping out of his
grasp. "Then I looked on all the works that my hands had wrought,
and on the labor that I had labored to do: and, behold, all was van-
ity and vexation of spirit, and there was no profit under the sun."

Secretiveness was the breath of the munitions king's being. For
nearly a year he had had Tecumseh and the spirits to himself, and
if he had told anyone what was happening it hadn't come to Lanny's
ears. But he couldn't hold out indefinitely, because his soul was
racked with uncertainties. Was it really the duquesa who was sending him messages? Or was it merely a fantasy, a cruel hoax of somebody or something unknown? Lanny had attended many séances,
and was continually studying the subject. The old man had to know
what he made of it.

The sitting itself was rather commonplace. Evidently the munitions king and the spirit of his dead wife had become established
on a firm domestic basis. She came right away, as she would have
done if he had called her from the next room. She didn't have much
to talk about—which probably would have been the case if her
"grass" had not withered and blown away. The only difference was
that Zaharoff would have known the "grass" for what it was; but
this imitation grass, this mirage, this painting on a fog—what was it?
She assured him that she loved him—of which he had never had any
doubt. She assured him that she was happy—she had said it many
times, and it was good news if it was she.

As to the conditions of her existence she was vague, as the spirits
generally are. They explain that it is difficult for mortal minds to
comprehend their mode of being; and that is a possibility, but also
it may be an evasion. The duquesa had given evidence of her reality, but now she seemed to wish that he should take it as settled;
that made her happier—and of course he sought to make her happy.

But afterward he tormented himself with doubts. Should he tor-
ment her with them?

She greeted Lanny and talked to him. She had come to him first,
with messages to her husband, and now she thanked him for delivering them. It was exactly as if they had been together in the garden
of the Paris mansion. She reminded him of it, and of the snow-
white poodles shaved to resemble lions. She had escorted him into
the library, and he, a courteous youth, had understood that she
might have no more time for him, and had volunteered to make
himself happy with a magazine. Did he remember what it was? She
said: *La Vie Parisienne,* and he remembered. He darted a glance at
Zaharoff, and thought he saw the old white imperial trembling.
"Tell him that that is correct," insisted the Spanish duquesa with a
Polish accent. "He worries so much, *pauvre chéri.*"

The spirit talked about the unusually wet weather, and about the
depression; she said that both would end soon. Such troubles did
not affect her, except as they affected those she loved. She knew
everything that was happening to them; apparently she knew whatever she wanted to know. Lanny asked her politely, could she bring
them some fact about the affairs of her ancient family which her
husband had never known, but which he might verify by research;
something that was in an old document, or hidden in a secret vault
in a castle; preferably something she hadn't known during her own
lifetime, so that it couldn't have been in the subconscious mind of
either of them?

"Oh, that subconscious mind!" laughed the Spanish lady. "It is
a name that you make yourself unhappy with. What is mind when
it isn't conscious? Have you ever known such a thing?"

"No," said Lanny, "because then it would be conscious. But what
is it that acts like a subconscious mind?"

"Perhaps it is God," was the reply; and Lanny wondered: had
he brought with him some fragment of the subconscious mind of
Parsifal Dingle, and injected it into the subconscious mind which
called itself María del Pilar Antonia Angela Patrocino Simón de
Muguiro y Berute, Duquesa de Marqueni y Villafranca de los
Caballeros?

VIII

When the séance was over, the maid invited Madame into another room to have tea; and Sir Basil had tea and a long talk with Lanny. He wanted to know what the younger man had learned and what he now believed. Lanny, watching the aging and anxious face, knew exactly what was wanted. Zaharoff wasn't an eager scientist, loving truth for truth's sake; he was a man tottering on the edge of the grave, wanting to believe that when he departed this earth he was going to join the woman who had meant so much to him. And what was Lanny, a scientist or a friend?

He could say, quite honestly, that he didn't know; that he wavered, sometimes one way, sometimes the other. Then he could go on to waver in the right direction. Certainly it had seemed to be the duquesa speaking: not the voice, but the mind, the personality, something which one never touches, never sees, but which one comes to infer, which manifests itself by various modes of communication. The duquesa speaking over a telephone, for example, and the line in rather bad condition!

Zaharoff was pleased. He said he had been reading the books. "Telepathy?" he said. "It seems to me just a word they have invented to save having to think. What is this telepathy? How would it work? It cannot be material vibrations, because distance makes no difference to it. You have to suppose that one mind can dip into another mind at will and get anything it wants. And is that easier to credit than survival of the personality?"

Said Lanny: "It is reasonable to think that there might be a core of the consciousness which survives for a time, just as the skeleton survives the body." But he saw that this wasn't a pleasing image to the old gentleman, and hastened to add: "Maybe time isn't a fundamental reality; maybe everything which has ever existed still exists in some form beyond our reach or understanding. We have no idea what reality may be, or our own relationship to it. Maybe we make immortality for ourselves by desiring it. Bernard Shaw says that birds grew wings because they desired and needed to fly."

The Knight Commander and Grand Officer had never heard of *Back to Methuselah,* and Lanny told him about that metabiological panorama. They talked about abstruse subjects until they were like Milton's fallen angels, in wand'ring mazes lost; also until Lanny remembered that he had to take his wife to a dinner-party. He left the old gentleman in a much happier frame of mind, but he felt a little guilty, thinking: "I hope Robbie doesn't have any more stocks to sell him!"

IX

Lanny found his wife dressing, and while he was doing the same she told him some news. "Uncle Jesse was here."

"Indeed?" replied Lanny. "Who saw him?"

"Beauty was in town. I had quite a talk with him."

"What's he doing?"

"He's absorbed in his election campaign."

"How could he spare the time to come here?"

"He came on business. He wants you to sell some of his paintings."

"Oh, my God, Irma! I can't sell those things, and he knows it."

"Aren't they good enough?"

"They're all right in a way; but they're quite undistinguished— there must be a thousand painters in Paris doing as well."

"Don't they manage to sell their work?"

"Sometimes they do; but I can't recommend art unless I know it has special merit."

"They seemed to me quite charming, and I should think a lot of other people would like them."

"You mean he brought some with him?"

"A whole taxicab-load. We had quite a show, all afternoon; that, and the Comintern, and that—what is it?—diagrammatical?—"

"Dialectical materialism?"

"He says he could make a Communist out of me if it wasn't for my money. So he tried to get some of it away from me."

"He asked you for money?"

"He may be a bad painter, dear, but he's a very good salesman."

"You mean you bought some of those things?"

"Two."

"For the love of Mike! What did you pay?"

"Ten thousand francs apiece."

"But, Irma, that's preposterous! He never got half that for a painting in all his life."

"Well, it made him happy. He's your mother's brother, and I like to keep peace in the family."

"Really, darling, you don't have to do things like that. Beauty won't like it a bit."

"It's much easier to say yes than no," replied Irma, watching in the mirror of her dressing-table while her maid put the last touches to her coiffure. "Uncle Jesse's not a bad sort, you know."

"Where are the paintings?" asked the husband.

"I put them in the closet for the present. Don't delay now, or we'll be late."

"Let me have just a glance."

"I didn't buy them for art," insisted the other; "but I do like them, and maybe I'll hang them in this room if they won't hurt your feelings."

Lanny got out the canvases and set them up against two chairs. They were the regular product which Jesse Blackless turned out at the rate of one every fortnight whenever he chose. One was a little gamin, and the other an old peddler of charcoal; both sentimental, because Uncle Jesse really loved these poor people and imagined things about them which fitted in with his theories. Irma didn't have such feelings, but Lanny had taught her that she ought to, and doubtless was trying. "Are they really so bad?" she asked.

"They aren't any bargain," he answered.

"It's only eight hundred dollars, and he says he's broke on account of putting everything into the campaign. You know, Lanny, it might not be such a bad thing to have your uncle a member of the Chamber."

"But such a member, Irma! He'll make himself an international scandal. I ought to have mentioned to you that he's gone into a working-class district and is running against a Socialist."

"Well," said the young wife, amiably, "I'll help the Socialist, too, if you wish it."

"You'll take two horses, and hitch one to the front of your cart and one to the back, and drive them as hard as you can in opposite directions."

Irma wasn't usually witty; but now she thought of Shore Acres, and said: "You know how it is, I've been paying men right along to exercise my horses."

X

Alfred Pomeroy-Nielson the younger was at school in England; he came to Bienvenu for the Easter vacation, and he and Marceline took up their life at the point where they had dropped it on board the *Bessie Budd*, a year and a half ago. Meanwhile they had been getting ready for each other, and at the same time making important discoveries about themselves.

The daughter of Marcel Detaze and Beauty Budd, not quite fourteen, was at that point "where the brook and river meet, womanhood and childhood fleet." Like the diving-champion on the end of a springboard, with every muscle taut, the body poised in the moment of swaying forward, so she presented herself above the swimming-pool of fashion, pleasure, and so many kinds of glory. She had gazed into it as a fascinated spectator and now was getting ready to plunge—much sooner than any member of her family knew or desired. That was her secret; that was the meaning of the fluttering heart, the flushed cheeks, the manner of excitement—she couldn't wait to begin to live!

Marceline loved her mother, she adored her handsome and fashionable half-brother, she looked with awe upon the blooming Juno who had come recently into her life, surrounded by a golden aura, talked about by everybody, pictured in the newspapers—in short, a queen of plutocracy, that *monde* which Marceline had been taught to consider *beau, grand, haut, chic, snob, élégant, et d'élite*. She was going to show herself off in it, and no use trying to change her mind. Men were beginning to look at her, and she was not failing to notice that or to know what it meant. Hadn't it been in the conversation of all the smart ladies since she had begun to understand the meaning of words? Those ladies were growing old, they were on the way out—and Marceline was coming, it was her turn!

And now this English lad, of almost the same age as herself, and destined, in the family conversation, to become her life partner. Maybe so, but first there were a few problems to be settled; first it was necessary to determine who would be the boss in that family. Alfy was serious, like his father; extremely conscientious, more reticent than seemed natural in one so young, and tormented by a secret pride. Marceline, on the other hand, was impulsive, exuberant, talkative, and just as proud in her own way. Each of these temperaments was in secret awe of the other; the natural strangeness of a youth to a maid and of a maid to a youth accentuated their differences and offended their self-esteem. Was he scorning her when he was silent? Was she teasing him when she laughed? Exasperation was increased by arrogance on both sides.

It is the English custom, when two boys fall to pommeling each other, to form a ring and let them fight it out. Now it appeared to be the same with the sex-war. Rick said: "They'd better settle it now than later." He gave advice only when it was asked, and poor Alfy was proud even with his father. It was up to a man to handle his own women!

Marceline, on the other hand, fled to her mother and had weeping-fits. Beauty tried to explain to her the peculiar English temperament, which makes itself appear cold but really isn't. The short vacation was passing, and Beauty advised her daughter to make it up quickly; but Marceline exclaimed: "I think they are horrid people, and if he won't have better manners I don't want to have anything more to do with him." The French and the English had been fighting ever since the year 1066.

XI

Oddly enough, it was the man from Iowa who served as international mediator. Parsifal Dingle never meddled in anybody's affairs, but talked about the love of God, and perhaps it was a coincidence that he talked most eloquently when he knew that two persons were at odds. God was all and God was love; God was alive and God was here; God knew what we were doing and saying and thinking, and when what we did was not right, we were deliberately cutting ourselves off from Him and destroying our own happiness. That was the spiritual law; God didn't have to punish us, we punished ourselves; and if we humbled ourselves before Him, we exalted ourselves before one another. So on through a series of mystical statements which came like a message from a much better world.

All this would have been familiar doctrine to the forebears of either of these young people. Perhaps ideas have to be forgotten in order to become real again; anyhow, to both Marceline and Alfy this strange gentleman was the originator or discoverer of awe-inspiring doctrines. A rosy-cheeked, cherubic gentleman with graying hair and the accent of the prairies. Once when he wanted to bathe his hands on board the sailboat he had used what he called a "wawsh-dish," which Alfy thought was the funniest combination of words he had ever heard.

But apparently God didn't object to the Iowa accent, for God came to him and told him what to do. And when you thought of God, not somewhere up in the sky on a throne, but living in your heart, a part of yourself in some incomprehensible way, then suddenly it seemed silly to be quarreling with somebody who was a friend of the family, even if not your future spouse! Better to forget about it—at least to the extent of a game of tennis.

Beauty thought how very convenient, having a spiritual healer in the family! She thought: "I am an unworthy woman, and I must try to be like him and love everybody, and value them for their best qualities. I really ought to go to Lanny's school, and meet some of those poor people, and try to find in them what he finds." She would think these thoughts while putting on a costly evening-gown which

Irma had given her after two or three wearings; she would be escorted to a party at the home of the former Baroness de la Tourette, and would listen to gossip about a circus-rider who had married an elderly millionaire and was cutting a swath on this Coast of Pleasure. The ladies would tear her reputation to shreds, and Beauty would enjoy their cruel cleverness and forget all about the fact that God was listening to every word.

A complicated world, so very hard to be good in!

BOOK THREE

Blow, Winds, and Crack Your Cheeks

11

'Tis Woman's Whole Existence

I

THE betrayal of the British labor movement had entered like a white-hot iron into the flesh of Eric Vivian Pomeroy-Nielson. He had brooded over it and analyzed its causes; he had filled his soul with images of it; and the result was to be a drama called *The Dress-Suit Bribe*. No literary title, dignified and impartial, but a fighting title, a propaganda title.

The central figure was a miner's son who had escaped from the pits by becoming a secretary of his union. He had a wife who had been a schoolteacher, somewhat above him in station. They had no children, because the labor movement was to be their child. At the opening of the play he was a newly elected member of Parliament. There were characters and episodes recalling his early days of fervor and idealism, but now we saw him absorbed in the not very edifying details of party politics, the maneuvers for power, the payment of past obligations in the hope of incurring more.

The leisure-class woman in the story had no doubt been modeled on Rosemary, Countess of Sandhaven, Lanny's old flame; one of those women touched by the feminist movement who did not permit themselves to love deeply because it would interfere with their independence, their enjoyment of prominence and applause. She was a political woman who liked to wield power; she set out to seduce a labor leader, not because she wanted to further the interests of her Tory group, but because she enjoyed playing with a man and subjecting him to her will. She tried to teach him what she called common sense, not merely about love, but about politics and all the affairs of the world they lived in. She didn't mind breaking the heart

211

of a wife whom she considered an inferior and superfluous person; if in the process she broke up a labor union, that was an incidental gain.

It was a "fat" part for an actress, and at Lanny's suggestion Rick had endowed the woman with an American mother; a common enough phenomenon in London society, this would make the role possible for Phyllis Gracyn. Lanny's old friend and playmate had been starred in two plays which had "flopped" on Broadway through no fault of her own; so she was in a humble frame of mind, and when Lanny wrote her about Rick's play she cabled at once, begging to be allowed to see the script. The part had been written for her— even to allowing for traces of an American accent.

Lanny had become excited about the play, and had talked out every scene with his friend, both before and after it was put down on paper. Irma and Beauty read it, and Emily and Sophie, and of course Rick's wife; these ladies consulted together, and contributed suggestions as to how members of the *grand* and *beau* and *haut monde* felt and behaved. So the play became a sort of family affair, and there was small chance of anything's being wrong with its atmosphere and local color. After Emily had read the entire script, she offered to put in five thousand dollars on the same terms as the rest of them, and Sophie, the ex-baroness, was not to be outdone.

The play would be costly to produce, on account of the money atmosphere. If you want actors to look like workingmen or labor leaders, you can hire them cheaply, but if you want one who can play the Chancellor of the Exchequer, you have to dip into your own. Rick, who by now had considerable experience, estimated the total at thirty thousand dollars, and the figure sounded familiar to Lanny, because that had been the cost of Gracyn's first production, the sum for which she had thrown him over. Now he would take a turn at being the "angel"; a higher, celestial kind, for whom she wouldn't have to act anywhere but on the stage.

II

The play was finished early in April, and the family went north, with Alfy returning to school. Lanny and Irma motored the mother and father as far as Paris, starting several days ahead; for Zoltan Kertezsi was there, and they wanted to see the spring Salon through his expert eyes; also there were plays to be seen, of interest to professionals such as they were about to become. As it happened, France was in the midst of a furious election campaign, and when you had an uncle running for the Chamber of Deputies, you were interested to see the show. Hansi and Bess had consented to come and give a concert for the benefit of his campaign, so it would be a sort of family reunion.

The Hungarian art expert was his usual serene and kindly self. He had just come back from a trip to the Middle West, where, strange as it might seem, there were still millionaires who enjoyed incomes and wanted to buy what they called "art paintings." Lanny had provided Zoltan with photographs of the Detazes which were still in the storeroom, and three had been sold, at prices which would help toward the production of *The Dress-Suit Bribe*. Irma insisted upon putting up a share of the money, not because she knew anything about plays, but because she loved Lanny and wanted him to have his heart's desires.

She took the same tolerant attitude toward political meetings. If Lanny wanted to go, she would accompany him, and try to understand the French language shouted in wildly excited tones. Jesse Blackless was running as candidate in one of those industrial suburbs which surrounded Paris with a wide Red band. Under the French law you didn't have to be a resident of your district but had to be a property-owner, so the Red candidate had purchased the cheapest vacant lot he could find. He had been carefully cultivating the constituency, speaking to groups of workers every night for months on end, attending committee meetings, even calling upon the voters in their homes—all for the satisfaction of ousting a Socialist incumbent who had departed from the "Moscow line." Irma didn't understand these technicalities, but she couldn't help being thrilled to find this newly acquired uncle the center of attention on a platform, delivering a fervid oration which drove the crowd to frenzies of delight. Also she couldn't fail to be moved by the sight of Hansi Robin playing for the workers of a foreign land and being received as a comrade and brother. If only they hadn't been such 'terrible-looking people!

III

All this put Lanny in a peculiar position. He attended his uncle's *réunion*, but didn't want him to win and told him so. Afterward they repaired with a group of their friends to a café where they had supper and argued and wrangled until the small hours of the morning. A noisy place, crowded and full of tobacco smoke; Irma had been taken to such haunts in Berlin, London, and New York, so she knew that this was how the intelligentsia lived. It was supposed to be "bohemian," and certainly it was different; she could never complain that her marriage had failed to provide her with adventures.

By the side of the millionairess sat a blond young Russian, speaking to her in English, which made things easier; he had just come out of the Soviet Union, that place about which she had heard so many terrible stories. He told her about the Five-Year Plan, which was nearing completion. Already every part of its program had been overfulfilled; the great collective farms were sowing this spring more grain than ever before in Russian history; it meant a complete new era in the annals of mankind. The young stranger was quietly confident, and Irma shivered, confronting the doom of the world in which she had been brought up. From the attitude of the others she gathered that he was an important person, an agent of the Comintern, perhaps sent to see that the campaign followed the correct party line; perhaps he was the bearer of some of that "Moscow gold" about which one heard so much talk!

Across the table sat Hansi and Bess; and presently they were telling the Comintern man details about the situation in Germany. Elections to the diets of the various states had just been held, and the parties of the two extremes had made tremendous gains; the middle classes were being wiped out, and with them the middle-class point of view. Hansi said that the battle for the streets of the German cities, which had been waged for the last two or three years, was going against the Communists; their foes had the money and the arms. Hansi had witnessed a battle in broad daylight in Berlin. A squad of Stormtroopers had been marching with their *Hakenkreuz* banners and a fife and drum, and passing a co-operative store they had hurled stones through the windows; the men inside had rushed out and there had been a general clubbing and stabbing. The Jewish violinist hadn't stayed to see the outcome. "I don't suppose I ought to use my hands to beat people," he said, spreading them out apologetically.

"Poor Hansi!" thought Irma. He and Freddi were unhappy, having discovered how their father was dealing with all sides in this German civil war. The Nazis were using Budd machine guns in killing the workers, and how could that have come about without the firm of "R & R" knowing about it? The boys hadn't quarreled with their father—they couldn't bear to—but their peace of mind was gone and they were wondering how they could go on living in that home.

Also Irma thought: "Poor Lanny!" She saw her husband buffeted between the warring factions. The Reds were polite to him in this crowd because he was Jesse's nephew, and also because he was paying for the supper, a duty he invariably assumed. He seemed to feel that he had to justify himself for being alive: a person who didn't enjoy fighting, and couldn't make up his mind even to hate wholeheartedly.

Yet he couldn't keep out of arguments. When the Communist candidate for the Chamber of Deputies put on his phonograph record and remarked that the Social-Democrats were a greater barrier to progress than the Fascists, Lanny replied: "If you keep on asking for it, Uncle Jesse, you may have the Fascists to deal with."

Said the phonograph: "Whether they mean to or not, they will help to smash the capitalist system."

"Go and tell that to Mussolini!" jeered Lanny. "You've had ten years to deal with him, and how far have you got?"

"He knows that he's near the end of his rope."

"But we're talking about capitalism! Have you studied the dividend reports of Fiat and Ansaldo?"

So they sparred, back and forth; and Irma thought: "Oh, dear, how I dislike the intelligentsia!"

But she couldn't help being impressed when the elections came off, and Zhess Block-léss, as the voters called him, showed up at the top of the poll in his district. On the following Sunday came a run-off election, in which the two highest candidates, who happened to be the Red and the Pink, fought it out between them. Uncle Jesse came to Irma secretly to beg for funds, and she gave him two thousand francs, which cost her seventy-nine dollars. As it happened, the Socialist candidate was a friend of Jean Longuet, and went to Lanny and got twice as much; but even so, Zhess Block-léss came out several hundred votes ahead, and Lanny had the distinction of having an uncle who was a member of the Chamber of Deputies of the French Republic. Many a young man had made his fortune from such a connection, but all Lanny could expect was a few more *additions*—that is to say, accounts for food and wine consumed by parties in restaurants.

IV

The Pomeroy-Nielsons had gone to London, where Rick was engaging a stage director and a business manager. The Budds and the Robins went for a visit to Les Forêts, where Emily Chattersworth had just arrived. Hansi and Bess played for her; and later, while Bess and Lanny practiced piano duets, Irma sought out the hostess to ask her advice about the problems of a Pink husband and a Red uncle-in-law.

Mrs. Chattersworth had always been open-minded in the matter of politics; she had allowed her friends and guests to believe and say what they chose, and as a *salonnière* had been content to steer the conversation away from quarrels. Now, she said, the world appeared to be changing; ever since the war it had been becoming more difficult for gentlemen—yes, and ladies, too—to keep their political discussions within the limits of courtesy. It seemed to have begun with the Russian Revolution, which had been such an impolite affair. "You have to be either for it or against it," remarked Emily; "and whichever you are, you cannot tolerate anyone's being on the other side."

Said Irma: "The trouble with Lanny is that he's willing to tolerate anybody, and so he's continually being imposed upon."

"I watched him as a little boy," replied her friend. "It seemed very sweet, his curiosity about people and his efforts to understand them. But like any virtue, it can be carried to extremes."

Lanny's ears would have burned if he could have heard those two women taking him to pieces and trying to put him together according to their preferences. The wise and kind Emily, who had been responsible for his marriage, wanted to make it and keep it a success, and she invited the young people to stay for a while so that she might probe into the problem. Caution and tact were necessary, she pointed out to the young wife, for men are headstrong creatures and do not take kindly to being manipulated and maneuvered. Lanny's toleration for Reds and Pinks was rooted in his sympathy for suffering, and Irma would love him less if that were taken out of his disposition.

"I don't mind his giving money away," said Irma. "If only he didn't have to meet such dreadful people—and so many of them!"

"He's interested in ideas; and apparently they come nowadays from the lower strata. You and I mayn't like it, but it's a fact that they are crashing the gates. Perhaps it's wiser to let in a few at a time."

Irma was willing to take any amount of trouble to understand her husband and to keep him entertained; she was trying to acquire ideas, but she wanted them to be safe, having to do with music and art and books and plays, and not politics and the overthrowing of the capitalist system. "What he calls the capitalist system," was the way she phrased it, as if it were a tactical error to admit that such a thing existed. "I've made sure that he'll never be interested in my friends in New York," she explained. "But he seems to be impressed by the kind of people he meets at your affairs, and if you'll show me how, I'll do what I can to cultivate them—before it's too late. I mean, if he goes much further with his Socialists and Communists, the right sort of people won't want to have anything to do with him."

"I doubt if that will happen," said Emily, smiling. "They'll tolerate him on your account. Also, they make allowances for Americans— we're supposed to be an eccentric people, and the French find us entertaining, much as Lanny finds his Reds and Pinks."

V

The husband wasn't told of this conversation, or others of the kind which followed; but he became aware, not for the first time in his life, of female arms placed about him, exerting a gentle pressure in one direction and away from another. Not female elbows poked into his ribs, but soft, entwining arms; a feeling of warmth, and perhaps a contact of lips, or whispered words of cajolement: darling, and dear, and intimate pet names which would look silly in print and sound so from any but a chosen person. Never: "Let's not go there, dear," but instead: "Let's go here, dear." And always the "here" had to do with music or pictures, books or plays, and not with the overthrow of the so-called, alleged, or hypothetical capitalist system.

Under Emily's guidance Irma decided that she had made a mistake in discouraging Lanny's efforts as an art expert. To be sure, it seemed silly to try to make more money when she had so much, but the prejudices of men had to be respected; they just don't like to take money from women, and they make it a matter of prestige to earn at least their pocket-money. Irma decided that Zoltan Kertezsi was an excellent influence in her husband's life. So far she had looked upon him as a kind of higher servant, but now decided to cultivate him as a friend.

"Let's stay in Paris a while, dear," she proposed. "I really want to understand about pictures, and it's such a pleasure to have Zoltan's advice."

Lanny, of course, was touched by this act of submission. They went to exhibitions, of which there appeared to be no end in Paris.

Also, there were private homes having collections, and Zoltan possessed the magic keys that opened doors to him and his guests. Pretty soon Irma discovered that she could enjoy looking at beautiful creations. She paid attention and tried to understand the points which Zoltan explained: the curves of mountains or the shape of trees which made a balanced design in a landscape; the contrasting colors of an interior; the way figures had been placed and lines arranged so as to lead the eye to one central feature. Yes, it was interesting, and if this was what Lanny liked, his wife would like it, too. Marriage was a lottery, she had heard, and you had to make the best of what you had drawn.

VI

"Zaharoff's house on the Avenue Hoche contains some gay and bright Bouchers," remarked Lanny. "He's not apt to be there, but the servants know me, so no doubt we can get in."

The three of them called at the white-stone mansion with the glass-covered window-boxes full of flowers. The tottery old butler was still on duty, and the beautiful portraits still hung in the drawing-room where Sir Basil had burned his private papers and set fire to his chimney. The butler reported that his master was at the château and seldom came to town now; but no one knew when he might come, and he continued the custom which had prevailed ever since Lanny had known him, of having a full-course dinner prepared every evening, enough for himself and several guests. If after a certain hour he had not arrived, the servants ate what they wanted and gave the rest to worthy poor. The duquesa's *by bloemen* and *bizarres* still bloomed in her garden, fifteen springtimes after she had shown them to Lanny. "They have their own kind of immortality," she had said; and these words had been repeated to him by an old Polish woman in a Mother Hubbard wrapper, then living in a tenement room on Sixth Avenue, New York, with the elevated railroad trains roaring past the windows.

There were old masters worth seeing at Balincourt, and Lanny telephoned and made an appointment to bring his wife and his friend. He motored them out on a day of delightful sunshine, and the Knight Commander and Grand Officer received the party with every evidence of cordiality. He had discovered that Lanny's wife was kind, and any lonely old man appreciates the attentions of a beautiful young woman. He showed them his David and his Fragonard, his Goya, his Ingres, and his Corots. These also had their kind of immortality, a magical power to awaken life in the souls of those who looked at them. Zaharoff had told Lanny that he was tired of them, but now it appeared that the fires of the young people's appreciation warmed up the dead ashes of his own.

The Hungarian expert never failed to have something worth while to say about a painting, and Zaharoff didn't fail to recognize that what he said was right; they talked about prices, which were of interest to them both, and important to Zoltan—one never knew what might come of such a contact. Lanny said: "This is the man who has taught me most of what I know about art." Zoltan, flushing with pleasure, replied: "This from the stepson of Marcel Detaze!"

They talked about that painter, of whom Zaharoff had heard. He asked questions, and in his mind the seed of an idea fell and began to germinate. Perhaps this was a way to get more of Madame Zyszynski's time! Buy a Detaze!

Tea was served on the terrace in front of the château. A beautiful view of formal gardens and distant forest, and when Lanny commented on it, Zaharoff said: "My wife chose this place and I bought it from King Leopold of Belgium."

He didn't go any further, but Lanny knew the story, and on the drive back to Paris entertained his passengers with the scabrous details. The King of the Belgians, a tall, magnificent personage wearing a great square-cut white beard, had been wont to roam the highways and byways of Paris in search of likely pieces of female flesh. The sixty-five-year-old monarch had chanced upon the sixteen-year-old sister of one of the famous *demi-mondaines* of the city and had sent a procuress to buy her; he had taken her to live in Hungary for a while, had fallen madly in love with her and brought her back to Paris, and purchased this splendid château for her home. He hadn't been content with it, but had insisted upon remodeling a great part, tearing out the ceiling of his lady's bedroom and making it two stories tall, like a church. The four windows facing the bed had draperies which had cost twenty thousand francs; the coverlet of English point lace had cost a hundred and ten thousand—the pre-war kind of francs! Her bathroom was of massive porphyry and her tub of silver; in the basement was a swimming-pool of gold mosaic. Lanny, who had never had a bath here, wondered if the very proper Duquesa Marqueni had retained these Byzantine splendors.

VII

Another of the homes which the trio visited was the town house of the Duc de Belleaumont, a member of the old French nobility who had married a cattle-king's daughter from the Argentine and so was able to live in the state of his forefathers. The palace stood on a corner near the Parc Monceau, and had an impressive white marble exterior and about thirty rooms, many of them spacious. It was decorated with that splendor which the French have cultivated through centuries. Every piece of furniture, every tapestry and statue and vase was worthy of separate study. A crystal cross set with sixteenth-century gold-enamel reliquaries, an inlaid Louis Seize writing cabinet, a set of translucent azure ginger jars from ancient China—such things moved Zoltan Kertezsi to raptures. The total effect was somewhat like a museum, but this does not trouble anyone in France, and has been known to occur on Long Island, too.

The family was away, and the furniture was under dust-covers, but Zoltan knew the caretaker, who, being sure of a generous tip, exhibited anything in which they expressed interest. The idea occurred to Irma that the depression might have affected the market for Argentine beef, and she inquired whether the place could be rented; the reply was that Madame should consult the agent of M. le Duc. Irma did so, and learned that a properly accredited family might lease the residence for the sum of a million francs per year.

"Why, Lanny, that's nothing!" exclaimed Irma. "Less than forty thousand dollars."

"But what on earth would you do with it?"

"Wouldn't you like to live in Paris and be able to entertain your friends?"

"But you've got one white elephant on your hands already!"

"Be sensible, darling, and face the facts. You don't like Shore Acres, or the people who come to it. You want to live in France."

"But I've never asked for a palace!"

"You want your friends about you, and you want to do things for them. All your life you've taken it for granted that somebody will do the entertaining, and you enjoy the benefits. You're delighted to go to Sept Chênes and meet intellectual and cultivated people. You hear famous musicians, you hear poets read their work —and apparently you think that kind of pleasure grows on trees, you don't even have to pick the fruit, it comes already cut up in little cubes and served on ice! Hasn't it occurred to you that Emily's health is failing? And some day you won't have your mother, or Sophie, or Margy—you'll be dependent on what your wife has learned."

He saw that she had thought it all out, and he guessed that she had consulted the other ladies. Naturally, they would approve, because it would provide good fun for them. "You'll be taking a heavy load on your shoulders," he objected, feebly.

"It won't be so easy in a foreign country; but I'll get help, and I'll learn. It will be my job, just as it has been Emily's."

"What will you do with Shore Acres?"

"Let's try this place for a year. If we like it, perhaps we can buy it, and sell Shore Acres; or if mother wants to go on living there, she can cut down on the staff. If this depression goes on, they'll be glad to work for their keep, and that'll be fair."

"But suppose your income goes on dropping, Irma!"

"If the world comes to an end, how can anybody say what he'll do! Anyhow, it can't do us any harm to have a lot of friends."

VIII

It was a compromise she was proposing; she would live in France, as he desired, but she would live according to her standards. In order to stop her, he would have to say a flat no, and he didn't have the right to say that. It was her money, and all the world knew it.

There was nothing very novel to Lanny Budd in the idea of living in Paris. He had spent a winter here during the Peace Conference, and another during the period of his *vie à trois* with Marie de Bruyne. Paris offered every kind of art and entertainment, and it was centrally situated; roads and cars had been so improved that you could reach London or Geneva or Amsterdam in a few hours. They could step into their car in the morning and be in Bienvenu by nightfall. "Really, it'll be about the same as commuting," said Irma.

What astonished him was the zest with which she set to work, and the speed with which she put the job through. She was the daughter of J. Paramount Barnes, and all her life she had been used to hearing decisions made and orders given. As soon as Lanny gave his consent she seated herself at the telephone and put in a call for Jerry Pendleton in Cannes. "How's business?" she asked, and when the familiar cheery voice informed her that it was dead and buried, she asked if he would like to have a job. He answered that he would jump for it, and she said: "Jump for the night express, and don't miss your hold."

"But darling!" objected Lanny. "He doesn't know anything about running a palace!"

"He's honest, he's lived in France for fifteen years, and employed some help. It won't take him long to learn the ropes."

When the red-headed ex-lieutenant from Kansas arrived, she put it up to him. He would become steward, or perhaps *Contrôleur-Général*, like Herr Meissner in Stubendorf. "Put on lots of side," she advised, "and be taken at your own valuation." He would engage a first-class major domo and a butler who would know what was done and what wasn't. He would be paid enough so that he could have his own car, and run down to see his family now and then.

Jerry Pendleton had once undertaken to tutor Lanny Budd without any preparation, and now he was taking another such chance. No time even to read a book on the duties of a *Contrôleur-Général!* Go right to work; for the "season" was soon to begin, and Irma wanted what she wanted when she wanted it. The elaborate inventory of the contents of the palace was made and checked and signed on every page; the lease was signed, the money paid, and the keys delivered. Emily's butler had a brother who was also in the profession, and knew everything there was to know about Paris society. Also he knew servants, enough for an emergency staff, and they came and took off the dust-covers and got things ready with American speed.

Irma and her prince consort and her *Contrôleur-Général* moved into their new home, and it was but a few hours before the newspapers had got word of it, and the doorbell was ringing and the flashlight bulbs of the photographers exploding. Lanny saw that his wife was once more getting her money's worth; they were back in café society, with the spotlight centered upon them. Paris was going to have a new hostess, a famous one. The marble steps of the palace were worn by the feet of chauffeurs and lackeys leaving calling cards with distinguished names on them, and the side entrance bell was ringing to announce the presence of *bijoutiers* and *couturiers* and *marchands de modes*.

Irma said: "Your mother must come and help us." So Lanny wrote at once, and that old war-mare said "Ha, ha!" and scented the battle afar off. It would have been a mortal affront to invite one mother-in-law and not the other, so Irma sent a cablegram to Shore Acres, and that older and more experienced charger dropped all her plans and took the first steamer. Even Emily came to town for a few days, bringing her calling lists with the secret symbols. Feathers sat by her side with a stenographer's notebook, collecting pearls of information which dropped from the lips of the most esteemed of Franco-American hostesses.

In short, Lanny Budd found himself in the midst of a social whirlwind; and it would have been cruelly unkind of him not to like it. Once more the ladies were in charge of his life, and what they considered proper was what he did. He listened to their talk and he met the people they brought for him to meet; if he wanted to play the piano it had to be done at odd moments between social engagements; while, as for sitting down in a splendid library and burying himself in a book—well, it was just too selfish, too solitary, too inconsiderate of all those persons who wanted to pay their attentions to the lessee of so much magnificence.

IX

The election results had given a tremendous jolt to the conservative elements in France. The party of Jesse Blackless had gained only two seats, but the party of Léon Blum had gained seventeen, while the "Radicals" had gained forty-eight. To be sure that word didn't mean what it meant in the United States; it was the party of the peasants and the small business men, but it was expected to combine with the Socialists, and France would have a government of the left, badly tainted with pacifism, and likely to make dangerous concessions to the Germans. The groups which had been governing France, the representatives of big industry and finance capital, popularly known as the *mur d'argent,* the "wall of money," were in a state of great alarm.

One of Lanny's duties in Paris was to keep in touch with his ex-family, the de Bruynes. Having now a suitable home of his own, he invited them to dinner and they came, father, two sons, and the young wife of Denis *fils.* Irma hadn't met them before, but had heard a lot about them, and felt herself being fascinatingly French when she welcomed the family of her husband's former mistress. They, for their part, appeared to take it as a matter of course, which made it still more French. They were people of high culture and agreeable manners, so Irma was pleased to assist in carrying out the death-bed promises which Lanny had made to the woman who had done so much to prepare him to be a good and satisfactory husband.

They talked about politics and the state of the world. That was what this splendid home was for; so that Lanny wouldn't have to meet his friends in crowded cafés, where they were jostled and could hardly hear one another's voices, but might sit in comfort and express themselves with leisure and dignity. It was Irma's hope that the things said would take on something of the tone of the surroundings; and certainly this appeared to be true with the de Bruynes, who were Nationalists, all four of them, and in a state of great concern as to the trend of the country and its position in the world.

Said the proprietor of a great fleet of taxicabs, speaking with some hesitation to a hostess from overseas: "I am afraid that the people of your country do not have a clear realization of the position in which they have placed my country."

"Do feel at liberty to speak freely, Monsieur," replied Irma, in her most formal French.

"There is a natural barrier which alone can preserve this land from the invasion of barbarians, and that is the River Rhein. It was our intention to hold and fortify it, but your President Veelson"— so they called him, ending with their sharp nasal "n"—"your President Veelson forced us back from that boundary, onto ground which is almost indefensible, no matter how hard we may try with our Maginot line. We made that concession because of your President's pledge of a protective agreement against Germany; but your Congress ignored that agreement, and so today we stand well-nigh defenseless. Now your President Oovay has declared a moratorium on reparations, so that chapter is at an end—and we have received almost nothing."

Lanny wanted to say: "You received twenty-five billions of francs under the Dawes plan, and the products have glutted the world markets." But he had learned in Denis's home that it was futile to argue with him, and it would be no less so in the palace of the Duc de Belleaumont, one of Denis's financial associates.

"You do not feel that there is any possibility of trusting the German Republic?" inquired Irma, trying hard to perfect her political education.

"When one says Germany today, Madame, one means Prussia; and to these people good faith is a word of mockery. For such men as Thyssen and Hugenberg, and for the Jewish money-lenders, the name 'Republic' is a form of camouflage. I speak frankly, because it is all in the family, as it were."

"Assuredly," said the hostess.

"Every concession that we make is met by further demands. We have withdrawn from the Rheinland, and no longer have any hold upon them, so they smile up their sleeves and go on with their rearming. They waited, as you have seen, until after our elections, so as not to alarm us; then, seeing the victory of the left, they overthrow their Catholic Chancellor, and we see a Cabinet of the Barons, as it is so well named. If there is a less trustworthy man in all Europe than Franz von Papen, I would not know where to seek him."

Irma perceived that you might invite a French Nationalist to the most magnificent of homes and serve him the best of dinners, but you would not thereby make him entirely happy. Practicing her new role of *salonnière*, she brought the young people into the conversation; but this succeeded no better, for it turned out that Charlot, the young engineer, had joined the Croix de Feu, one of the patriotic organizations which did not propose to surrender *la patrie* either to the Reds or to the Prussians. The Croix de Feu used the technique of banners and uniforms and marching and singing as did the Fascists of Italy and the Nazis of Germany; but Lanny said: "I'm afraid, Charlot, you won't get so far, because you don't make so many promises to the workers."

"They tell the people falsehoods," said the young Frenchman, haughtily; "but we are men of honor."

"Ah, yes," sighed his old friend; "but how far does that go in politics?"

"In this corrupt republic, no distance at all; but we have set out to make France a home for men who mean what they say."

Lanny spoke no more. It made him sad to see his two foster sons —they were supposed to be something like that—going the road of Fascism; but there was nothing he could do about it. He knew that their mother had shared these tendencies. They were French patriots, and he couldn't make them internationalists, or what he called "good Europeans."

X

Having had such a dose of reaction, he had to have one of hope. He said to Irma: "I really ought to call on Léon Blum, and perhaps take him out to lunch. Would you care to come along?"

"But Lanny," she exclaimed, "what is this house for?"

"I didn't suppose you'd want to have him here."

"But dear, what kind of home will it be if you can't bring your friends?"

He saw that she was determined to be fair. He guessed that she had talked the matter out with the wise Emily, and was following the latter's program. If one's husband must have vices, let him have them at home, where they may be toned down and kept within limits. After all, Léon Blum was the leader of the second largest political party in France; he was a scholar and a poet, and had once had a fortune. In the old days, as a young aesthete, he had been a frequenter of Emily's salon; now he had exchanged Marcel Proust for Karl Marx, but he remained a gentleman and a brilliant mind. Surely one might invite him to lunch, and even to dinner—if the company was carefully chosen. Emily herself would come; and Lanny knew from this that the matter had been discussed.

He took the good the gods had provided him. The Socialist leader sat in the same chair which Denis de Bruyne had filled, and maybe he felt some evil vibrations, for he spoke very sadly. In the midst of infinite corruption he was trying to believe in honesty; in the midst of wholesale cruelty he was trying to believe in kindness. The profit system, the blind competitive struggle for raw materials and markets, was wrecking civilization. No one nation could change this by itself; all must help, but someone must begin, and the voice of truth must be heard everywhere. Léon Blum spoke tirelessly in the Chamber, he wrote daily editorials for *Le Populaire*, he traveled here and there, pleading and explaining. He would do it at the luncheon table of a friend, and then stop and apologize, smiling and saying that politics ruined one's manners as well as one's character.

He was a tall slender man with the long slim hands of an artist; a thin, sensitive face, an abundant mustache which made him a joy

to the caricaturists of the French press. He had been through campaigns of incredible bitterness; for to the partisans of the French
right it was adding insult to injury when their foes put up a Jew as
their spokesman. It made the whole movement of the workers a
part of the international Jewish conspiracy, and lent venom to all
Fascist attacks upon France. "Perhaps, after all, it is a mistake that
I try to serve the cause," said the statesman.

He was ill content with the showing which his party had made
at the polls. A gain of seventeen was not enough to save the day.
He said that immediate and bold action was required if Europe was
to be spared the horrors of another war. He said that the German
Republic could not survive without generous help from France. He
said that the "Cabinet of the Barons" was a natural answer to the
cabinet of the bigot, Poincaré, and to that of the cheat, Laval. Blum
was standing for real disarmament of all the nations, including
France, and he had been willing to split his party rather than to
yield on that issue. Said Irma, after the luncheon: "We won't ever
invite him and the de Bruynes at the same time!"

XI

From the time her decision was taken to rent the palace, Irma's
mind was occupied with the problem of a party which *tout Paris*
would attend; a sort of housewarming—Lanny said that a building
of that size, made of white marble, would require a lot of cordiality
to affect its temperature. His wife wanted to think of something
original. Parties were so much alike. People ate your food and drank
your wine, often too much of it; they danced, or listened to a
singer they had heard many times at the opera and been bored by.
Lanny quoted an old saying: "Gabble, gobble, git."

Irma insisted that *tout Paris* would expect something streamlined
and shiny from America. Couldn't they think of something? The
husband tried various suggestions: a performing elephant from the
circus, a troop of Arabian acrobats he had seen in a cabaret—their
black hair was two feet long and when they did several somersaults

in one leap they brought down the house. "Don't be silly, dear," said the wife.

He thought of an idea to end all ideas. "Offer a prize of a hundred thousand francs for the most original suggestion for a party. That will start them talking as nothing ever did." He meant it for burlesque, but to his amusement Irma was interested; she talked about it, speculating as to what sort of suggestions she would get, and so on; she wasn't satisfied until she had asked Emily, and been assured that it might be a good idea for Chicago, but not for Paris. Even after Irma dropped it, she had a hankering, and said: "I believe my father would have done it. He didn't let people frighten him away from things."

It would have to be a conventional soirée. The young Robins would come and play—a distinguished thing to furnish the talent from your own family, and have it the best. Fortunately the Paris newspapers did not report Communist doings—unless it was a riot or something—therefore few persons knew that Hansi had assisted in electing Zhess Block-léss to the Chamber of Deputies. (Already that body had met, and the new member, refusing to be intimidated by the splendid surroundings, had put on his old phonograph record, this time with a loud-speaker attachment, so that his threats against the *mur d'argent* had been heard as far as Tunisia and Tahiti, French Indo-China and Guiana.)

Lanny was fascinated to observe his young wife functioning in the role which she had chosen for herself. She was not yet twenty-four, but she was a queen, and had found out how queens conduct themselves. No worry, no strain, no sense of uncertainty. Being an American, she could without sacrifice of dignity ask the chef or the butler how things were done in France; then she would say whether or not they were going to be done that way in her home. She spoke with quiet decision, and the servants learned quickly to respect her; even the new *Contrôleur-Général* was impressed, and said to Lanny: "By heck, she's a whiz!"

When the great day arrived, she didn't get excited, like many hostesses, and wear herself out so that she couldn't enjoy her own triumph; no chain smoking of cigarettes, no coffee or nips of brandy to keep her going. Nor did she put responsibilities off on her mother or mother-in-law; that would be a bad precedent. She said: "This is my home, and I want to learn to run it." She had thought everything out, and had lists prepared; she summoned the servitors before her and checked off what had been done and gave them their final instructions. She had learned to judge them in two or three weeks. Jerry was a "brick," and anything he undertook was just as good as done. Ambroise, the butler, was conscientious, but had to be flattered; Simone, the housekeeper, was fidgety and lacking in authority; Feathers had always been a fool and would get rattled in any emergency. Having checked everything, Irma took a long nap in the afternoon.

At about nine in the evening the shiny limousines began rolling up before the palace, and a stream of immaculate guests ascended the white marble stairs, covered with a wide strip of red velvet carpet. It was the cream of that international society which made its headquarters in the world's center of fashion. Many of them had met Irma in New York or on the Riviera, in Berlin, London, Vienna, or Rome. Others were strangers, invited because of their position; they came because of curiosity as to a much-talked-about heiress. They would see what sort of show she put on, and were prepared to lift an eyebrow and whisper behind a fan over the slightest wrong detail.

But there wasn't much to quarrel with. The young Juno was good to look at, and the best artists had been put to work on her. The prevailing fashions favored her; they had gone back to natural lines, with high waists. The décolletage for backs was lower; in fact, where the back of the dress might have been there was nothing but Irma; but it was enough. Her dark brown hair was in masses of curls, and that looked young and wholesome. Her gown of pale blue silk chiffon appeared simple, but had cost a lot, and the same was true of her long rope of pearls.

The daughter of the utilities king was naturally kind; she liked people, and made them feel it. She did the honors with no visible coaching. She had taken the trouble to learn who people were, and if she had met them before, she remembered where, and had something friendly to say. If they were strangers, she assumed that they were welcoming her to Paris and thanked them for their courtesy. At her side stood a good-looking young fellow, *bon garçon*, son of his father—Budd Gunmakers, you know, quite a concern in America. In the background was a phalanx of older women: the two mothers, large and splendid, and Mrs. Chattersworth, whom everyone knew. In short, *tout comme il faut*, viewed by *tout le monde*.

XII

A modest-appearing young Jewish violinist came forward, and with his wife accompanying him played César Franck's violin sonata; French music, written in Paris by a humble organist and teacher who had lived obscurely among them until an omnibus had killed him; now they honored him, and applauded his interpreter. As an encore Hansi played Hubay's *Hejre Katy*, fiery and passionate; when they applauded again, he smiled and bowed, but did not play any more. His sister-in-law, Rahel Robin, whom nobody had ever heard of, came to the piano, and with Lanny Budd accompanying and her husband playing a clarinet obbligato, sang a couple of Provençal peasant songs which she herself had arranged. She had a pleasing voice, and it was a sort of homelike family affair; you wondered if they were showing themselves off, or if they were saving money.

Certainly they hadn't saved on the food and drink, and that is important at any party. In the ball-room a smart colored band played jazz, and in the other rooms the young wife and the young husband moved here and there, chatting with this one and that. Madame Hellstein, of the international banking-house, with her daughter Olivie, now Madame de Broussailles; Lanny had told his wife: "I might have married her, if Rosemary hadn't written me a note at the critical moment!" So, naturally, Irma was interested to look her over. A lovely daughter of Jerusalem—but she was growing stout! "These Jewish women all do," thought Irma.

And then one of Zaharoff's married daughters, who also had looked upon the son of Budd as a *parti*. And old M. Faure, rich importer of wines and olive-oil who had bought paintings of nude ladies from Zoltan. A traveling maharajah who bought ladies—but from another dealer! A Russian grand duke in exile; a crown prince from one of the Scandinavian lands; a couple of literary lions, so that you wouldn't appear to be snobbish. Lanny had been a dear and hadn't asked for any Reds or Pinks; they wouldn't appreciate the honor, he said.

Irma wasn't clever; but that is a quality for the "outs," whereas she was among the "ins." She was serene and gracious, and as she moved among this elegant company little shivers of happiness ran over her and she thought: "I am getting away with it; it is truly *distingué*"—this being one of the first French words she had learned. Lanny, thirty-two and world weary, thought: "How hard they all try to keep up a front and to be what they pretend!" He thought: "All the world's a stage, and all the men and women merely players"—these being among the first words of Shakespeare he had learned.

He knew much more about these players than his wife did. He had been hearing stories from his father and his business friends, from his mother and her smart friends, from his Red uncle, from Blum and Longuet and other Pinks. This lawyer for the Comité des Forges who had all the secrets of *la haute finance* hidden in his skull; this financier, paymaster for the big banks, who had half the members of the Radical party on his list; this publisher who had taken the Tsar's gold before the war and now was a director of Skoda and Schneider-Creusot! Who would envy these men their stage roles? The whole show was tolerable to the players only because of the things they didn't know, or which they thrust into the back of their minds. Lanny Budd, treading the boards, playing acceptably his part as prince consort, enjoyed it with one-half his mind, while the other half wondered: how many of his guests could bear to dance if they knew what would be happening to them ten years from now?

12

Pleasure at the Helm

I

THE *Dress-Suit Bribe* was in rehearsal in London, and if Lanny could have had his own way, he would have been there to watch every moment. But Irma had her new white elephant on her hands, and had to get some use of it; several weeks would have to pass before she would feel justified in going away and leaving its staff of servants idle. Meanwhile, she must invite people to come, at any hour from noon to midnight. Supposedly she was doing it because she wanted to see them, but the real reason was that she wanted them to see her. And having offered them hospitality, she was under obligation to accept theirs; she would be forever on the go, attending social affairs or getting ready for future affairs.

Always she wanted company; and Lanny went along, because it had been his life's custom to do what he didn't want to do rather than to see a loved one disappointed and vexed. His wife was attaining her uttermost desire, she was standing on the apex of the social pyramid; and what could it mean to her to climb down and go off to London to watch a dozen actors and actresses rehearsing all day on an empty stage, the women in blouses and the men with their coats off on a hot day? The fact that one of these women was Phyllis Gracyn didn't increase her interest, and Lanny mustn't let it increase his too much!

He persuaded the young Robins to stay for a while; he much preferred their company to that of the fashionable folk. They would play music every morning, and at odd times when social duties permitted. Nothing was allowed to interfere with Hansi's violin practice; it was his task to master one great concert piece

after another—which meant that he had to fix in his head hundreds
of thousands of notes, together with his own precise way of
rendering each one. Nobody who lived near him could keep from
being touched by his extraordinary conscientiousness. Lanny
wished he might have had some such purpose in his own life,
instead of growing up an idler and waster. Too late now, of course;
he was hopelessly spoiled!

II

Sitting in the fine library of the Duc de Belleaumont, filled with
the stored culture of France, Lanny had a heart-to-heart talk with
his half-sister, from whom he had been drifting apart in recent
years. She was one who had expected great things of him, and had
been disappointed. It wasn't necessary that he should agree with
her, she insisted; it was only necessary that he should make up his
mind about anything, and stick to it. Lanny thought that he had
made up his mind as to one thing: that the Communist program,
applied to the nations which had parliamentary institutions, was a
tactical blunder. But it would be a waste of time to open up this
subject to Bess.

She had something else she wanted to talk about: the unhappiness
which was eating like a cancer into the souls of the members of
the Robin family. They had become divided into three camps; each
husband agreeing with his own wife, but with none of the other
members of the family; each couple having to avoid mentioning
any political or economic problem in the presence of the others.
With affairs developing as they now were in Germany, that meant
about every subject except music, art, and old-time books. Johannes
read the *Börsenzeitung*, Hansi and Bess read the *Rote Fahne*, while
Freddi and Rahel read *Vorwärts;* each couple hated the very
sight of the other papers and wouldn't believe a word that was in
them. Poor Mama, who read no newspaper and had only the vaguest
idea what the controversy was about, had to serve as a sort of
liaison officer among her loved ones.

There was nothing so unusual about this. Lanny had lived in disagreement with his own father for the greater part of his life; only it happened that they both had a sense of humor, and took it out in "joshing" each other. Jesse Blackless had left home because he couldn't agree with his father; now he never discussed politics with his sister, and always ended up in a wrangle with his nephew. The majority of radicals would tell you the same sort of stories; it was a part of the process of change in the world. The young outgrew their parents—or it might happen that leftist parents found themselves with conservative-minded children. "That will be my fate," opined the playboy.

In the Robin family the problem was made harder because all the young people took life so seriously; they couldn't pass things off with teasing remarks. To all four of them it seemed obvious that their father had enough money and to spare, and why in the name of Karl Marx couldn't he quit and get out of the filthy mess of business plus politics in which he wallowed? Just so the person who has never gambled cannot understand why the habitué hangs on, hell-bent upon making up his night's losses; the teetotaler cannot understand the perversity which compels the addict to demand one more nip. To Johannes Robin the day was a blank unless he made some money in it. To see a chance of profit and grab it was an automatic reflex; and besides, if you had money you had enemies trying to get it away from you, and you needed more of it in order to be really safe. Also you got allies and associates; you incurred obligations to them, and when a crisis came they expected you to play a certain part, and if you didn't you were a shirker. You were no more free to quit than a general is free to resign in the midst of a campaign.

The tragedy is that people have lovable qualities and objectionable ones, impossible to separate. Also, you have grown up with them, and have become attached to them; you may be under a debt of gratitude, impossible to repay. If the young Robins were to lay down the law: "Either you quit playing at *Gross Kapital* in Germany, or we move out of your palace and sail no more in your yacht"—they might have had their way. But how much would have been left of Johannes Robin? Where would they have taken him, and what would they have done with him? Lanny had put such pressure on his father in the matter of playing the stock market, and had got away with it. But in the case of Johannes it was much more; he would have had to give up everything he was doing, every connection, associate, and interest except his children and their affairs. Said Lanny to Bess: "Suppose he happened to dislike music, and thought the violin was immoral—what would you and Hansi do about it?"

"But nobody could think that, Lanny!"

"Plenty of our Puritan forefathers thought it; I've a suspicion that Grandfather thinks it right now. Very certainly he thinks it would be immoral to keep business men from making money, or to take away what they have made."

So Lanny, the compromiser, trying to soothe the young people, and persuade them that they could go on eating their food in the Berlin palace without being choked. Including himself, here were five persons condemned to dwell in marble halls—and outside were five millions, yes, five hundred millions, looking upon them as the most to be envied of all mortals! Five dwellers begging to be kicked out of their marble halls, and for some strange reason unable to persuade the envious millions to act! More than a century ago a poet, himself a child of privilege, had called upon them to rise like lions after slumber in unvanquishable number; but still the many slept and the few ruled, and the chains which were like dew retained the weight of lead!

III

The dowager queen of Vandringham-Barnes had gone down to Juan in order to be with the heir apparent. A dreadful thing had happened in America, something that sent a shudder of horror through every grandmother, mother and daughter of privilege in the civilized world. In the peaceful countryside of New Jersey a criminal or gang of them had brought a ladder and climbed into the home of the flyer Lindbergh and his millionaire wife, and had carried off the nineteen-month baby of this happy young couple. Ransom notes had been received and offers made to pay, but apparently the kidnapers had taken fright, and the body of the slain infant was found in a near-by wood. It happened that this ghastly discovery fell in the same week that the President of the French republic was shot down by an assassin who called himself a "Russian Fascist." The papers were full of the details and pictures of both these tragedies. A violent and dreadful world to be living in, and the rich and mighty ones shuddered and lost their sleep.

For a full generation Robbie Budd's irregular family had lived on the ample estate of Bienvenu and the idea of danger had rarely crossed their minds, even in wartime. But now it was hard to think about anything else, especially for the ladies. Fanny Barnes imagined kidnapers crouching behind every bush, and whenever the wind made the shutters creak, which happened frequently on the Côte d'Azur, she sat up and reached out to the baby's bed, which had been moved to her own room. Unthinkable to go on living in a one-story building, with windows open, protected only by screens which could be cut with a pocket-knife. Fanny wanted to take her tiny namesake to Shore Acres and keep her in a fifth-story room, beyond reach of any ladders. But Beauty said: "What about fire?" The two grandmothers were close to their first quarrel.

Lanny cabled his father, inquiring about Bub Smith, most dependable of bodyguards and confidential agents. He was working for the company in Newcastle, but could be spared, and Robbie sent him by the first steamer. So every night the grounds of Bienvenu would be patrolled by an ex-cowboy from Texas who could throw a silver dollar into the air and hit it with a Budd automatic. Bub had been all over France, doing one or another kind of secret work for the head salesman of Budd Gunmakers, so he knew the language of the people. He hired a couple of ex-poilus to serve as daytime guards, and from that time on the precious mite of life which was to inherit the Barnes fortune was seldom out of sight of an armed man. Lanny wasn't sure if it was a good idea, for of course all the Cap knew what these men were there for, and it served as much to advertise the baby as to protect her. But no use telling that to the ladies!

Bub came by way of Paris, so as to consult with Lanny and Irma.

He had always been a pal of Robbie's son, and now they had a
confidential talk, in the course of which Bub revealed the fact that
he had become a Socialist. A great surprise to the younger man,
for Bub's jobs had been among the most hardboiled, and Bub himself, with his broken nose and cold steely eyes, didn't bear the
appearance of an idealist. But he had really read the papers and the
books and knew what he was talking about, and of course that
was gratifying to the young employer. The man went down to the
Cap and began attending the Socialist Sunday school in his free
time, becoming quite a pal of the devoted young Spaniard, Raoul
Palma.

That went on for a year or more before Lanny discovered what
it was all about. The bright idea had sprung in the head of Robbie
Budd—to whom anarchists, Communists, and kidnapers were all
birds of a feather. Robbie had told Bub that this would be a quick
and easy way to get in touch with the underworld of the Midi;
so before stepping onto the steamer, Bub had got himself a load
of Red literature, and all the way across had been boning up as if
for a college entrance examination. He had "passed" with Lanny,
and then with Raoul and the other comrades, who naturally had
no suspicions of anybody coming from Bienvenu. It was somewhat
awkward, because Bub was also maintaining relations with the
French police; but Lanny didn't know just what to do about it.
It was one more consequence of trying to live in the camps of two
rival armies getting ready for battle.

IV

Hearing and thinking so much about the Lindbergh case had had
an effect upon Irma's maternal impulses; she decided that she
couldn't do any more traveling without having at least a glimpse
of Baby. She proposed that they hop into the car and run down
to Bienvenu—the weather was hot there, and they could have a
swim, also. The young Robins hadn't seen Baby for more than
a year; so come along! Hansi had been motored to Paris by Bess,
in her car; now the couples "hopped" into two cars, and that eve-

ning were in Bienvenu, with Irma standing by the bedside of her
sleeping darling, making little moaning sounds of rapture and hardly
able to keep from waking the child.

The next two days she had a debauch of mother emotions,
crowding everything into a short time. She didn't want anybody
else to touch the baby; she washed her, dressed her, fed her, played
with her, walked with her, talked to her, exclaimed over every baby
word she managed to utter. It must have been bewildering to a
twenty-seven-month child, this sudden irruption into her well-
ordered life; but she took it serenely, and Miss Severne permitted
some rules to be suspended for a brief period.

Lanny had another talk with Bub Smith, keeper of the queen's
treasure and sudden convert to the cause of social justice. Bub
reported on his experiences at the school, and expressed his appreciation of the work being done there; a group of genuine idealists,
he said, and it was a source of hope for the future. Lanny found
it a source of hope that an ex-cowboy and company guard should
have seen the light and acknowledged his solidarity with the
workers.

Also Bub told about conditions in Newcastle, where some kind
of social change seemed impossible to postpone. There wasn't
enough activity in those great mills to pay for the taxes and upkeep, and there was actual hunger among the workers. The people
had mortgaged their homes, sold their cars, pawned their belongings; families had moved together to save rent; half a dozen people
lived on the earnings of a single employed person. So many New
Englanders were proud and wouldn't ask for charity; they just
withdrew into a corner and starved. Impossible not to be moved
by such distress, or to realize that something must be done to get
that great manufacturing plant to work again.

Bub Smith had always been close to Robbie Budd, and so this
change of mind appeared important. There was no secret about it,
the man declared; he had told Mr. Robert how he felt, and Mr.
Robert had said it would make no difference. Lanny thought that,
too, was important; for some fifteen years or so he had been hoping
that his father would see the light, and now apparently it was

beginning to dawn. In a letter to Robbie he expressed his gratification; and Robbie must have had a smile!

V

The young people had their promised swim, diving off the rocks into that warm blue Mediterranean water. Afterward they sat on the shore and Bub lugged a couple of heavy boxes from the car, one containing Budd automatics and other weapons, the other containing several hundred rounds of ammunition. Bub had brought a liberal supply from Newcastle, enough to stave off a siege by all the bandits in France. He said the family ought to keep in practice, for they never knew when there might be an uprising of the Fascists or Nazis, and "we comrades" would be the first victims. He was shocked to learn that neither Hansi nor Freddi had ever fired a gun in his life, and hadn't thought of the possible need. The ex-guard wanted to know, suppose their revolution went wrong and the other side appeared to be coming out on top?

He showed them what he would propose to do about it. He threw a corked bottle far out into the water, then popped off the cork with one shot from an army service revolver. He threw out a block of wood and fired eight shots from a Budd .32 automatic, all in one quick whir, and not one of the shots struck the water; Bub admitted that that took a lot of practice, because the block jumped with every hit, and you had to know how far it would jump in a very small fraction of a second. He did it again to show them that it was no accident. He couldn't do it a third time, because the block of wood had so much lead in it that it sank.

Lanny couldn't perform stunts like that, but he was good enough to hit any Nazi, Bub said. All the targets were either Nazis or Fascists, for the guard had made up his mind that trouble was coming and no good fooling yourself. He wanted Hansi to learn to shoot, but Hansi said he would never use his bowing hand for such a nerve-shattering performance. Bess would have to protect him; she had learned to shoot when a child, and proved that she had not forgotten. Then it was Freddi's turn, and he tried it, but had a hard time keeping his eyes open when he pulled the trigger. The consequences of this pulling upon a Budd automatic were really quite alarming, and to a gentle-souled idealist it didn't help matters to imagine a member of the National Socialist German Workingmen's Party in the line of the sights.

Lanny, who had been used to guns all his life, had no idea of the effect of these performances upon two timid shepherd boys out of ancient Judea. Hansi declared that his music didn't sound right for a week afterward; while as for the younger brother, the experiment had produced a kind of moral convulsion in his soul. To be sure, he had seen guns being carried in Berlin and elsewhere by soldiers, policemen, S.S.'s and S.A.'s; but he had never held one in his hand, and had never realized the instantaneous shattering effect of an automatic. Calling the targets a portion of the human anatomy had been a joke to an ex-cowboy, but Freddi's imagination had been filled with images of mangled bodies, and he kept talking about it for some time afterward. "Lanny, do you really believe we are going to see another war? Do you think you can live through it?"

Freddi even talked to Fanny Barnes about the problem, wondering if it mightn't be possible to organize some sort of society to teach children the ideal of kindness, in opposition to the dreadful cruelty that was now being taught in Germany. The stately Queen Mother was touched by a young Jew's moral passion, but she feared that her many duties at home would leave her no time to organize a children's peace group in New York. And besides, wasn't Germany the country where it needed to be done?

VI

Fanny set up a great complaint concerning the heat at Bienvenu; she became exhausted and had to lie down and fan herself and have iced drinks brought to her. But Beauty Budd, that old Riviera hand, smiled behind her *embonpoint*, knowing well that this was one more effort—and she hoped the last—to carry Baby Frances away. Beauty took pleasure in pointing out the great numbers of brown and healthy babies on the beaches and the streets of Juan; she pointed to Lanny and Marceline as proof that members of the less tough classes could be raised here successfully. Baby herself had developed no rashes or "summer complaints," but on the contrary rollicked in the sunshine and splashed in the water, slept long hours, ate everything she could get hold of, and met with no worse calamity than having a toe nipped by a crab.

So the disappointed Queen Mother let her bags be packed and stowed in the trunk of Lanny's car, and herself and maid stowed in the back seat, from which she would do as much driving as her polite son-in-law would permit. On the evening of the following day they delivered her safely in London, and obtained for her a third-row seat on the aisle for the opening performance of *The Dress-Suit Bribe*, a play of which she wholly disapproved and did not hesitate to say so. Next day when most of the London critics agreed with her, she pointed out that fact to the author, who, being thirty-four years of age, ought to have sowed his literary wild oats and begun to realize the responsibilities he owed to his class which had built the mighty British Empire. The daughter of the Vandringhams and daughter-in-law of the Barneses was as Tory as the worst "diehard" in the House of Lords, and when she encountered a propagandist of subversion she wanted to say, in the words of another famous queen: "Off with her head!"—or with "his."

But not all the audience agreed with her point of view. The house divided horizontally; from the stalls came frozen silence and from the galleries storms of applause. The critics divided in the same way; those with a pinkish tinge hailed the play as an authentic picture of the part which fashionable society was playing in politics, an indictment of that variety of corruption peculiar to Britain, where privileges which would have to be paid for in cash in France or with office in America, go as a matter of hereditary right or of social prestige. In any case it was power adding to itself, "strength aiding still the strong."

It was the kind of play which is automatically labeled propaganda and therefore cannot be art. But it was written from inside knowledge of the things which were going on in British public life and it told the people what they needed to know. From the first night the theater became a battleground, the high-priced seats were only half filled but the cheap ones were packed, and Rick said: "It's a question whether we can pay the rent for two or three weeks, until it has a chance to take hold."

Lanny replied: "We'll pay, if I have to go and auction off some pictures." No easy matter raising money with hard times spreading all over the world; but he telephoned all the fashionable people he knew, begging them to see the play, and he cajoled Margy, Dowager Lady Eversham-Watson, to have a musicale and pay the Robin family a couple of hundred pounds to come and perform: the money to go for the play. Irma "chipped in," even though in her heart she didn't like the play. As for Hansi, he wrote to his father, who put five hundred pounds to his son's credit with his London bankers—a cheap and easy way to buy peace in his family, and to demonstrate once again how pleasant it is to have money, heigh ho!

In one way or another they kept the play going. Gracyn, to whom it gave such a "fat" part, offered to postpone taking her salary for two weeks. Lanny wrote articles for the labor papers, pointing out what the production meant to the workers, and so they continued to attend and cheer. The affair grew into a scandal, which forced the privileged classes to talk about it, and then to want to know what they were talking about. In the end it turned out that Eric Vivian Pomeroy-Nielson had a "hit"—something he had been aiming at for more than ten years. He insisted on paying back all his friends, and after that he paid off some of the mortgages of "the Pater," who had been staking him for a long time. The main thing was that Rick had managed to say something to the British people, and had won a name so that he would be able to say more.

VII

The Robins were begging the Budds to take a little run into Germany. Yachting time was at hand, and they had persuaded

Papa to put the *Bessie Budd* into commission again; they wanted so much to get him away from the worries of business—and who could do it so well as the wonderful Lanny Budd and his equally wonderful wife? Lanny might even be able to persuade him to retire for good; or perhaps to take a long cruise around the world, where he couldn't be reached by friends or foes.

Germany was in the midst of a hot election campaign. A new Reichstag was being chosen; the "Cabinet of the Barons," otherwise known as the "Monocle Cabinet," was asking for popular support. Elections were always interesting to Lanny, and the young people urged him to come and see. But Irma had another maternal seizure; she said "Let's run down to Juan again, and come back for a cruise at the end of the campaign." Lanny said: "Any way you want it."

So the party broke up. Fanny took a steamer to New York, the Robins took the ferry to Flushing, and the Budds took one to Calais. They sent a telegram to the palace in Paris, and dinner was ready when they arrived. Irma observed: "It's nice to have your own place; much nicer than going to a hotel." Lanny saw that she wished to justify herself for having spent all that money, so he admitted that it was "nicer." Jerry was there, and with a lot of checks ready for her to sign; he wanted her to go over the accounts, but she was sure they were all right, and she signed without looking. The three went to a cabaret show, very gay, with music and dancing and a scarcity of costumes; some of it made Irma blush, but she was trying to acquire the cosmopolitan tone.

The following evening they were at Bienvenu again. Baby was bigger and brighter; she knew more words; she remembered what you had taught her. She was growing a mind! "Oh, Lanny, come see this, come see that!" Lanny would have been glad to settle down to child study, and to swimming and target-shooting with Bub, and talking to the workers at the school; but they had made a date with the Robins; and also there came a letter from Pietro Corsatti, who was at Lausanne, reporting the conference for his paper. He said: "A great show! How come you're missing it?"

At this time there were two of Europe's international talk-fests being held on the same Swiss lake. For many years such gatherings had been Lanny's favorite form of diversion; he had attended a dozen, and had met all the interesting people, the statesmen and writers, the reformers and cranks. Irma had never been to one, but had heard him tell about them, and always in glowing terms. Now he proposed: "Let's stop off on our way to Berlin."

"O.K. by me!" said Irma.

VIII

They followed the course of the River Rhone, every stage of which had some memory of Marie de Bruyne: the hotels where she and Lanny had stopped, the scenery they had admired, the history they had recalled. But Lanny judged it better for Irma to have her own memories, unscented by the perfume of any other woman. They climbed into the region of pine-trees and wound through rocky gorges where the air was still and clear. Many bridges and a great dam, and it was Lake Leman, with Geneva, home of the League of Nations, an institution which for a few years had been the hope of mankind, but now appeared to have fallen victim to a mysterious illness. Since the beginning of the year a great Conference on Arms Limitation, with six hundred delegates from thirteen nations, had been meeting here, and was to continue for a year longer; each nation in turn would bring forward a plea to limit the sort of weapon which it didn't have or didn't need, and then the other nations would show what was wrong with that plan.

Farther up the lake was Lausanne, where the premiers and foreign ministers were gathered to debate the ancient question of reparations. Lanny Budd greeted his friend Pete and other journalists whom he had been meeting off and on since the great peace conference thirteen summers ago. They remembered him and were glad to see him; they knew about his gold-embossed wife and her palace in Paris; they knew about Rick and his play. Here was another show, and a fashionable young couple was taken right behind the scenes.

Lausanne is built on a mountainside, with each street at a different level. The French had a hotel at the top, the British one at the bottom, and the other nations in between; the diplomats ascended or descended to have their wrangles in one another's suites, and the newspapermen wore themselves thin chasing the various controversies up hill and down. Such, at any rate, was Corsatti's description. The statesmen were trying to keep their doings secret, and Pete declared that when one saw you he dived into his hole like a woodchuck. Your only chance was to catch one of them in swimming.

It was good clean fun, if you were a spectator who liked to hear gossip and ferret out mysteries, or a devil-may-care journalist with an expense account which you padded freely. The food was of the best, the climate delightful, the scenery ditto, with Mont Blanc right at your back door—or so it seemed in the dustless Alpine air. You would be unhappy only if you thought about the millions of mankind whose destiny was being gambled with by politicians. The gaming-table was a powder-keg as big as all the Alps, and the players had no thought but to keep their own country on top, their own class on top within their country, and their own selves on top within their class.

IX

The statesmen had to drop the Young Plan, by which Germany had been bound to pay twenty-five billion dollars in reparations. But France couldn't give up the hope of getting something; so now with incessant wrangling they were adopting a plan whereby at the end of three years Germany was to give bonds for three billion marks. But most observers agreed that this was pure futility; Germany was borrowing, not paying. Germany was saying to the bankers of the United States: "We have five billions of your money, and if you don't save us you will lose it all!" The people of Germany were saying: "If you don't feed us we shall vote for Hitler, or worse yet for Thälmann, the Bolshevik." The statesmen of Germany were saying: "We are terrified about what will happen"—and who could say whether they were really terrified or only pretending? Who could trust anybody in power, anywhere in all the world?

Robbie Budd had told his son a story, which he said all business men knew. A leather merchant went to his banker to get his notes renewed and the banker refused to comply with the request. The leather merchant told his troubles and pleaded hard; at last he asked: "Were you ever in the leather business?" When the banker replied: "No," the other said: "Well, you're in it now." And that, opined Pietro Corsatti, was the position of the investing public of the United States; they were in the leather business in Germany, in the steel and coal and electrical and chemical businesses, to say nothing of the road-building business and the swimming-pool business. Nor was it enough to renew the notes; it was necessary to put up working capital to keep these businesses from falling into ruins and their workers from turning Red!

Irma knew that this was the "great world" in which her career was to be carried on, so she listened to the gossip and learned all she could about the eminent actors in the diplomatic drama. Lanny had met several of the under-secretaries, and these realized that the wealthy young couple were entitled to be introduced to the "higher ups." Irma was told that next winter would probably see more negotiations in Paris, and it was her intention that these important personages should find her home a place for relaxation and perhaps for private conferences. Emily herself couldn't have done better.

Lanny observed his wife "falling for" the British ruling class. Many Americans did this; it was a definite disease, known as "Anglomania." Upper-class Englishmen were tall and good-looking, quiet and soft-spoken, cordial to their friends and reserved to others; Irma thought that was the right way to be. There was Lord Wickthorpe, whom Lanny had once met on a tally-ho coach driving to Ascot; they had both been youngsters, but now Wickthorpe was a grave diplomat, carrying a brief-case full of responsibility— or so he looked, and so Irma imagined him, though Lanny, who had been behind many scenes, assured her that the sons of great families didn't as a rule do much hard work. Wickthorpe was

divinely handsome, with a tiny light brown mustache, and Irma
said: "How do you suppose such a man could remain a bachelor?"

"I don't know," said the husband. "Margy can probably tell you.
Maybe he couldn't get the girl he wanted."

"I should think any girl would have a hard time refusing what
he has."

"It can happen," replied Lanny. "Maybe they quarrel, or something goes wrong. Even the rich can't always get what they want."
Lanny's old "Pink" idea!

X

The assembled statesmen signed a new treaty of Lausanne, in
which they agreed to do a number of things, now that it was too
late. Having signed and sealed, they went their various ways, and
Irma and Lanny motored out of Switzerland by way of Basle, and
before dinner-time were in Stuttgart. A bitterly fought election
campaign had covered the billboards with slogans and battle-cries
of the various parties. Lanny, who got hold of a newspaper as soon
as he arrived anywhere, read the announcement of a giant
Versammlung of the Nazis to be held that evening, the principal
speaker being that Reich Organization Leader Number One who
had received such a dressing-down from his Führer in Lanny's
presence some twenty months ago. Lanny remarked: "I'd like to
hear what he's saying now."

"Oh, dear!" exclaimed Irma. "Such a bore!" But she didn't want
to be left in a hotel room alone, so she said: "Let's not stay too late."

During those twenty months a Franco-American playboy had
been skipping over the world with the agility conferred by rail-
roads and motor-cars, airplanes, steamships, and private yachts. He
had been over most of western Europe, England, and New England. He had read books on many subjects, he had played thousands
of musical compositions, looked at as many paintings, been to many
theaters, danced in many ball-rooms, and swum in many seas; he
had chatted with his friends and played with his baby, eaten the
choicest of foods, drunk the best wines, and enjoyed the love of a

beautiful and fashionable wife. In short, he had had the most delightful sort of life that the average man could imagine.

But meantime the people of Germany had been living an utterly different life; doing hard and monotonous labor for long hours at low wages; finding the cost of necessities creeping upward and insecurity increasing, so that no man could be sure that he and his family were going to have their next day's bread. The causes of this state of affairs were complex and hopelessly obscure to the average man, but there was a group which undertook to make them simple and plain to the dullest. During the aforementioned twenty months the customs official's son from Austria, Adi Schicklgruber, had been skipping about even more than Lanny Budd, using the same facilities of railroad trains and motor-cars and airplanes. But he hadn't been seeking pleasure; he had been living the life of an ascetic, vegetarian, and teetotaler, devoting his fanatical energies to the task of convincing the German masses that their troubles were due to the Versailles *Diktat*, to the envious foreigners who were strangling the Fatherland, to the filthy and degraded Jews, and to their allies the international bankers and international Reds.

Say the very simplest and most obvious things, say them as often as possible, and put into the saying all the screaming passion which one human voice can carry—that was Adolf Hitler's technique. He had been applying it for thirteen years, ever since the accursed treaty had been signed, and now he was at the climax of his efforts. He and his lieutenants were holding hundreds of meetings every night, all over Germany, and it was like one meeting; the same speech, whether it was a newspaper print or cartoon or signboard or phonograph record. No matter whether it was true or not—for Adi meant literally his maxim that the bigger the falsehood, the easier to get it believed; people would say you wouldn't dare make up a thing like that. Imagine the worst possible about your enemies and then swear that you knew it, you had seen it, it was God's truth and you were ready to stake your life upon it—shout this, bellow this, over and over, day after day, night after night. If one person states it, it is nonsense, but if ten thousand join in it becomes an indictment, and when ten million join in it becomes history. The

Jews kill Christian children and use their blood as a part of their
religious ritual! You refuse to believe it? But it is a well-known
fact; it is called "ritual murder." The Jews are in a conspiracy to
destroy Christian civilization and rule the whole world. It has all
been completely exposed in the *Protocols of the Elders of Zion;*
the party has printed these, the Führer has guaranteed their authen-
ticity, the great American millionaire Henry Ford has circulated
them all over America. Everybody there knows that the charges
are true, the whole world knows it—save only the Jew-lovers, the
Jew-kissers, the filthy Jew-hirelings. *Nieder mit den Juden!*

XI

So here was another huge mass meeting, such crowds that you
could hardly get in, and two rich Americans having to climb to
distant seats in a gallery. But it was all right, for there were loud-
speakers, a wonderful device whereby one small figure on a platform could have the voice of a score of giants, while a dissenter
became a pigmy, uttering a squeak like a mouse. The radio was a
still more marvelous invention; that feeble little "crystal set" with
earphones which Robbie Budd had brought to Bienvenu ten years
ago had become the most dominating of psychological forces,
whereby one man could indoctrinate a hundred million. Learned
technicians of the mind had evolved methods of awakening curiosity, so that the millions would listen; and no matter how much
anyone disagreed, he was powerless to answer back. The dream
of every dictator was to get exclusive control of that colossal instrument, so that never again in all history would it be possible
to answer back. Then what you said would become the truth and
the only truth—no matter how false it might have been previously!
He who could get and hold the radio became God.

Once more Lanny observed the application of the art of moving
the mass mind. Adolf Hitler taught that the masses did not think
with their brains but with their blood; that is to say, they did not
reason but were driven by instincts. The most basic instinct was the
desire to survive and the fear of not surviving; therefore Adolf

Hitler told them that their enemies desired to destroy them and that he alone could and would save them; he told them that they were the *Herrenvolk*, the master race, designed by nature to survive and to rule all other races of the earth. The second basic instinct was hunger, and they had suffered it, and he promised them that under his leadership Germany would break into the storehouses of the world's plenty; the Fatherland would have *Lebensraum*, the space in which to expand and grow. The third basic instinct is sex, and he told them that they were destined to populate the earth, and that every pure-blooded Aryan *Mädchen* was the predestined mother of blond heroes; that was what she was created for, and no permission was needed for her to begin; a wise Fatherland would provide for her care and give all honor to her and her offspring.

All these instincts added up into pride and victory over the foes of Germany. *"Sieg Heil!"* they shouted; and the party had invented an elaborate ritual to embody these concepts and to thrill the dullest soul. At the futile Beerhall Putsch which Lanny had witnessed in Munich there had been carried banners, and these banners had been riddled with bullets and stained with the blood of martyrs; that made them holy, and Adolf Hitler had carried them all over Germany, and upon public platforms had performed the ceremony of touching the new banners with the old; that made all the Nazi banners holy, and worthy of being stained with the blood of martyrs. So now when they were carried all hearts beat high, and all good party members longed for a chance to become martyrs and have a new *Horst Wessel Lied* sung about them. Shrill trumpets proclaimed the entry of these banners, drums beat and fifes shrilled and a bodyguard of heroes marched into the hall with faces solemn and grim.

To the speakers' platform ascended large, heavy Gregor Strasser; not humbled and browbeaten as Lanny had last seen him, but bursting with assurance of power. He was one of the original party leaders, and had helped Adolf to keep alive in the early days. He had believed in the early program with all its promises for the overthrow of the rich and the setting up of the disinherited. Did he believe in them still, when he knew that the Führer no longer meant them? You could never have guessed it from listening to his speech, for he seemed to have but one rule: to think of everything that ten thousand Württembergers could possibly want, and promise it to them, to be delivered on the day when they would elect the candidates of the N.S.D.A.P.

Lanny said: "That's surely the way to get out the vote!"

Irma, who didn't understand what the orator was promising, and had to judge by gestures and tones, remarked: "It is surprising how much like Uncle Jesse he sounds."

"Don't let either of them hear that!" chuckled the husband.

XII

It was a political campaign of frenzied hate, close to civil war. Troops of armed men marched, glaring at other troops when they passed, and ready to fly at the others' throats; in the working class districts they did so, and bystanders had to flee for their lives. The conservatives, who called themselves Democrats and Nationalists, had their *Stahlhelm* and their *Kampfring*, the Nazis had their S.S.'s and S.A.'s, the Sozis had their *Reichsbanner*, and the Communists their *Rotfront*, although the last named were forbidden to wear uniforms. The posters and cartoons, the flags and banners, all had symbols and slogans expressive of hatred of other people, whether Germans of the wrong class, or Russians, French, Czechs, Poles, or Jews. Impossible to understand so many kinds of hatreds or the reasons for them. Irma said: "It's horrible, Lanny. Let's not have any more to do with it."

She had met charming people in Berlin, and now Johannes gave her a reception, and they all came; when they found that she didn't like politics they said they didn't blame her, and talked about the music festivals, the art exhibitions, the coming yacht regattas. The Jewish money-lord tried to keep friendly with everybody, and he knew that many who would not ordinarily darken his door were willing to come when a celebrated American heiress was his guest. According to his custom, he did not try to hide this, but on the contrary made a point of mentioning it and thanking her. She knew that this Jewish family had risen in the world with the help of the Budds; but so long as they showed a proper gratitude and didn't develop a case of "swelled head," it was all right for the help to continue.

German big business men came, and their wives, still bigger as a rule. German aristocrats came, tall, stiff gentlemen wearing monocles, and their *Damen* who seemed built for the stage of Bayreuth. All had long titles, and left off none of the *vons* and *zus;* Irma had trouble in telling Herr vons from Herr Barons, Herr Grafen from Erlauchts, and Erlauchts from Durchlauchts.

Graf Stubendorf came, reported on affairs at home, and cordially renewed his invitation for next Christmas, or for the shooting season earlier. The new Chancellor came; tall and thin-faced, the smartest of diplomats and most elegant of Catholic aristocrats, he lived entangled in a net of intrigue of his own weaving. A son of the Russian ghetto might have been overwhelmed by the honor of such a presence, but Johannes took it as the payment of a debt. The gentlemen of the fashionable Herren Klub hadn't been able to raise enough money to save their party, so the Chancellor had had to come to the Jew for help.

Irma found him charming, and told her husband, who remarked: "There is no greater rascal in all Europe. Franz von Papen was put out of the United States before we entered the war because he was financing explosions in munitions plants."

"Oh, darling!" she exclaimed. "You say such horrid things! You can't really know that!"

Said the young Pink: "He didn't have sense enough to burn his check-stubs, and the British captured his ship on the way home and published all the data."

13

Even to the Edge of Doom

I

THE cruise of the *Bessie Budd* began. Not a long cruise, never more than a week at a time in these disturbed days. They stopped to fish and swim, and they sent out upon the North Sea breezes a great deal of romantic and delightful music. The seamen and the fishermen who glided by in the night must have been moved to wonder, and perhaps some young Heine among them took flight upon the wings of imagination. Far on the Scottish rock-coast, where the little gray castle towers above the raging sea, there, at the high-arched window, stands a beautiful frail woman, tender-pellucid and marble-pale, and she plays the harp and sings, and the wind sweeps through her long tresses and carries her dark song over the wide storming sea.

Resting from such flights of fancy the solicitous Lanny Budd had quiet talks with his host, hoping by gentle and tactful intervention to lessen the strain of that family conflict which had been revealed to him. Johannes explained, in much the same words that Robbie Budd had used when Lanny was a small boy, that the business man did not think merely of the money he was making or might make; he acquired responsibilities to thousands of investors, not all of them greedy idlers, but many aged persons, widows, and orphans having no means of support but their shares of stock; also to workingmen whose families starved unless the weekly pay envelopes were filled. It was a libel upon business administrators to suppose that they had no sense of duties owed to other people, even though most of these people were strangers.

"Moreover," said Johannes, "when a man has spent his life learning to pursue a certain kind of activity, it is no easy matter to persuade him to drop it at the height of his powers. Difficulties, yes; but he has expected them, and takes them as a challenge, he enjoys coping with them and showing that he can master them. To give up and run away from them is an act of cowardice which would undermine his moral foundations; he would have no use for himself thereafter, but would spend his time brooding, like an admiral who veered about and deserted his fleet.

"My children have their own moral code," continued the money master, "and they have the task of convincing me that it applies to my case. They wish to build a new and better world, and I would be glad if they could succeed, and if I saw any hope of success I would join them. I ask for their plans, and they offer me vague dreams, in which as a man of affairs I see no practicality. It is like the end of *Das Rheingold:* there is Valhalla, very beautiful, but only a rainbow bridge on which to get to it, and while the gods may be able to walk on a rainbow, my investors and working people cannot. My children assure me that a firmer bridge will be constructed, and when I ask for the names of the engineers, they offer me party leaders and propagandists, speechmakers who cannot even agree among themselves; if it were not for what they call the capitalist police they would fall to fighting among themselves and we should have civil war instead of Utopia. How can my two boys expect me to agree with them until they have at least managed to agree between themselves?"

Lanny was sad to have no answer to this question. He had already put it to his sister, and she could say only that she and her husband were right, while Freddi and Rahel were wrong. No use putting the question to the other pair, for their answer would be the same. Neither couple was going to give way—any more than Lanny himself was going to give up his conviction that it was the program of the Communists which had caused the development of Fascism and Nazism—or at any rate had made possible its spread in Italy and Germany. Only in the Scandinavian and Anglo-Saxon lands, where democratic institutions were firmly rooted, had neither Reds nor anti-Reds been able to make headway.

II

So there wasn't any chance of persuading Johannes Robin to retire to a monastery or even to a private yacht right now. He didn't
pretend to know what was going to happen in Germany, but he
knew that these were stormy times and that he, the admiral, would
stand by his fighting fleet. He would protect his properties and
keep his factories running; and if, in order to get contracts and
concessions it was necessary to make a present to some powerful
politician, Johannes would bargain shrewdly and pay no more than
he had to. That had been the way of the world since governments
had first been invented, and a Jewish trader, an exile barely tolerated
in a strange land, had to be satisfied with looking out for his own.
His sons felt more at home in Germany and dreamed of trying to
change it; but for the child of the ghetto it was enough that he
obeyed the law. "Not very noble," he admitted, sadly; "but when
the nobler ones come to me for help, they get it."

The world was in a bad way and getting worse. Banks were
failing all over the United States, and unemployment increasing
steadily. A presidential election was due in November, and the
political parties had held their conventions and made their nomina-
tions; the Republicans had endorsed the Great Engineer and all
that he had done, while the Democrats nominated the Governor
of New York, Franklin Roosevelt by name. Johannes asked if
Lanny knew anything about this man, and Lanny said no; but
when the yacht picked up some mail, there was Robbie's weekly
letter, a cross between a business man's report and one of the
lamentations of Jeremiah. Robbie said that the Democratic candidate was a man wholly without business experience, and moreover
an invalid, his legs shriveled by infantile paralysis. Surely these times
called for one at least physically sound; the presidency was a man-
killing job, and this Roosevelt, if elected, couldn't survive it for a
year. But he wasn't going to be elected, for Robbie and his friends
were pulling off their coats, to say nothing of opening their purses.

"I suppose Robbie will be asking you for a contribution!"
chuckled the irreverent son, and the other replied: "I have **many**

interests in America." Lanny recalled the remark he had once heard
Zaharoff make: "I am a citizen of every country where I have
investments."

III

They discussed conditions in Germany, living on borrowed capital and sliding deeper and deeper into the pit. The existing government had no popular support, but was run by the Herren Klub,
an organization of big business men, aristocrats, and "office gen-
erals," having some twenty branches throughout Germany. Its two
most active politicians were Chancellor von Papen and General von
Schleicher, and they were supposed to be colleagues, but neither
could trust the other out of his sight. Now Papen was in office, and
Schleicher was trading secretly with the Nazis for their support
to turn him out. Nobody could trust anybody, except the eighty-
five-year-old monument of the Junkerdom, General von Hindenburg. Poor *alte Herr*, when the burdens of state were dumped upon
him he could only answer: *"Ich will meine Ruhe haben!"*—I must
have my rest.

Johannes judged it certain that the Nazis would make heavy
gains at the coming elections, but he refused to worry about this.
He had several of them on his payroll, but what he counted upon
most was the fact that Hitler had gone to Düsseldorf and had a
long session with Thyssen and other magnates of the Ruhr. They
wanted the Red labor unions put down, and Hitler had satisfied
them that he was ready to do the job. You might fool one or two
of those tough steel-men, but not many; they knew politicians, and
dealt with one crop after another; it was part of the game of conducting industry in a world full of parliaments and parties. A
nuisance, but you learned to judge men and saw to it that none
got into power who couldn't be trusted. The same thing applied to
the great landlords of Prussia; they wanted above all things a bulwark against Bolshevism, and were willing to pay a heavy price
for that service. These two powers, the industrialists of the west and
the landed gentry of the east, had governed Germany since the
days of Bismarck and would go on doing so.

"But aren't you afraid of Hitler's anti-Semitism?" asked Lanny.

"*Herrgott!*" exclaimed the owner of the *Bessie Budd*. "I was brought up in the midst of pogroms, and what could I do then? It is said that there once lived a Jew called Jesus, and other Jews had him executed by the Romans; such things happened ten thousand times, no doubt; but because of this one time my poor people have to be spat upon and clubbed and stabbed to death. What can any of us do, except to pray that it will not break out in the street where we live?"

"But they threaten it wholesale, Johannes!"

"It is a means of getting power in a world where people are distracted and must have some one to blame. I can only hope that if ever the Nazis come into office they will have real problems to deal with, so that the spotlight will be turned away from my unfortunate people."

IV

Irma had voted to keep out of German political affairs, but that couldn't be arranged entirely. There was the workers' school, in which Freddi was so deeply interested, and which had been more or less modeled upon Lanny's own project. When they came back to Berlin Lanny's wife played bridge while he went with Freddi and Rahel to a reception at which he met the teachers and friends of the enterprise, heard its problems discussed, and told them how things were going in the Midi.

In his way of thinking Lanny was nearer to these young Socialists than to any other group; yet what a variety of opinion there was among them, and how difficult to get them together on any program of action! A few days before the election the von Papen government had effected a *coup d'état* in the state of Prussia, which includes Berlin; the premier and the principal officials, all Social-Democrats, were turned out of office and threatened with arrest if they attempted to resist—which they did so feebly that it amounted to submission. As a result, the Socialists were buzzing like a swarm of bees whose hive has been upset; but alas, they appeared to be bees which had lost their stingers! The Communists had proposed a general strike of the workers and called upon the Socialists to co-operate with them; but how could anybody co-operate with Communists? They would take advantage of an uprising to seize the reins themselves; they would turn upon their allies as they had done with Kerensky in Russia. The Socialists were more in fear of the Communists than of the reactionaries; they were afraid of acting like Communists, of looking like Communists, of being called Communists.

So the Cabinet of the Barons seized control of the Berlin police and all the other powers of the local government. How different it had been twelve years ago during the "Kapp Putsch"! Then the workers hadn't waited for their leaders, they had known instantly what to do—drop their tools and come into the streets and show their power. But now, apparently, they had lost interest in the Republic. What good had it done them these twelve years? It couldn't prevent hard times and unemployment, it couldn't even make promises any more! It was so chained by its own notions of legality that it couldn't resist the illegality of others.

Lanny listened to the discussions of these Berlin intellectuals. They came from all classes, brought together by community of ideas. They had the keenest realization of danger to the cause of freedom and social justice. They all wanted to do something; but first they had to agree what to do, and apparently they couldn't; they talked and argued until they were exhausted. Lanny wondered, is this a disease which afflicts all intellectuals? Is it a paralysis which accompanies the life of the mind? If so, then it must be that the thinkers will be forever subject to the men of brute force, and Plato's dream of a state ruled by philosophers will remain forever vain.

Lanny thought: "Somebody ought to lead them!" He wanted to say: "My God, it may be settled this very night. Your republic will be dead! Let's go now, and call the workers out!" But then he thought: "What sort of a figure would I cut, taking charge of a German revolution? I, an American!" He settled back and listened to more arguments, and thought: "I'm like all the others. I'm an intellectual, too! I happen to own some guns, and know how to use them—but I wouldn't!"

V

There was a teacher of art at the school, by name Trudi Schultz, very young, herself a student at an art school, but two or three evenings a week she came to impart what she knew to the workers, most of them older than herself. She was married to a young commercial artist who worked on a small salary for an advertising concern and hated it. Both Trudi and Ludi Schultz were that perfect Aryan type which Adolf Hitler lauded but conspicuously was not; the girl had wavy fair hair, clear blue candid eyes, and sensitive features which gave an impression of frankness and sincerity. Lanny watched her making sketches on a blackboard for her class, and it seemed to him that she had an extraordinary gift of line; she drew something, then wiped it out casually, and he hated to see it go.

She was pleased by his interest and invited him to come and see her work. So, on another evening while Irma played bridge, Lanny drove Freddi and Rahel to a working class quarter of the city where the young couple lived in a small apartment. Lanny inspected a mass of crayon drawings and a few water-colors, and became interested in what he believed was a real talent. This girl drew what she saw in Berlin; but she colored it with her personality. Like Jesse Blackless she loved the workers and regarded the rich with moral disapprobation; that made her work "propaganda," and hard to sell. But Lanny thought it ought to appeal to the Socialist press and offered to take some with him and show it to Léon Blum and Jean Longuet. Of course the Schultzes were much excited— for they had heard about Lanny's having selected old masters for the palace of Johannes Robin, and looked upon the wealthy young American as a power in the art world.

Lanny, for his part, was happy to meet vital personalities in the workers' movement. More and more he was coming to think of art as a weapon in the social struggle, and here were young people who shared his point of view and understood instantly what he said.

He had traveled to many far places, while they knew only Berlin and its suburbs and the countryside where they sometimes had walking trips; yet they had managed to get the same meaning out of life. More and more the modern world was becoming one; mass production was standardizing material things, while the class struggle was shaping the minds and souls of workers and masters. Lanny had watched Fascism spread from Italy to Germany, changing its name and the color of its shirts, but very little else; he heard exactly the same arguments about it here in Berlin as in Paris, the Midi, and the Rand School of Social Science in New York.

These five young people, so much alike in their standards and desires, talked out of their hearts in a way that Lanny had not had a chance to do for some time. All of them were tormented by fears of what was coming in Europe, and groping to determine their own duty in the presence of a rising storm of reaction. What were the causes of the dreadful paralysis which seemed to have fallen upon the workers' movement of the world?

Trudi Schultz, artist-idealist, thought that it was a failure of moral forces. She had been brought up in a Marxist household, but was in a state of discontent with some of the dogmas she had formerly taken as gospel; she had observed that dialectical materialism didn't keep people from quarreling, from being jealous, vindictive, and narrow-minded. Socialists talked comradeship, but too often they failed in the practice of it, and Trudi had decided that more than class consciousness was needed to weld human beings into a social unity.

Freddi Robin, who had a scholar's learning in these matters, ventured the opinion that the identification of Social-Democracy with philosophic materialism was purely accidental, due to the fact that both had originated in nineteenth-century Germany. There was no basic connection between the two, and now that modern science had moved away from the old dogmatic notion of a physical atom as the building material of all existence, it was time for the Socialists to find themselves a philosophy which justified creative effort and moral purpose.

The eager girl student was glad to hear someone say that, in the long philosophical terms which made it sound right to a German. She said that she had observed this error working in everyday life. Men who preached that matter and force were the bases of life, the sole reality, were tempted to apply this dogma in their own lives; when they got a little power they thought about keeping it, and forgot their solidarity with the humble toilers. People had to believe in moral force, they had to let love count in the world, they had to be willing to make sacrifices of their own comfort, their own jobs and salaries, yes, even their lives, if need be. It was lack of that living spirit of brotherhood and solidarity which had made it possible for Otto Braun, Social-Democratic Premier of the Prussian state, and Karl Severing, Minister of the Interior, to bow to the threats of monocled aristocrats, and slink off to their villas without making the least effort to rouse the people to defend their republic and the liberties it guaranteed them.

Lanny thought: "Here, at last, is a German who understands what freedom means!"

VI

On a Sunday, the last day of July, more than thirty-seven million citizens of the German Republic, both men and women, went to the polls and registered their choice for deputies to represent them in the Reichstag. As compared with the elections of two years previously, the Socialists lost some six hundred thousand votes, the Communists gained as many, while the Nazis increased their vote from six and a half million to fourteen million. They elected two hundred and thirty deputies out of a total of six hundred and eight—outnumbering the Socialists and Communists, even if combined, which they wouldn't. So from then on it became impossible for anyone to govern Germany without Adolf Hitler's consent.

There began a long series of intrigues and pulling of wires behind the scenes. Johannes would report events to Lanny, and also to Lanny's father, who had come over for a conference with his associate and went for a short cruise on the *Bessie Budd*. The politicians of the right, who had polled less than five per cent of the vote, nevertheless hung on to power, trying to persuade Hitler to come into their cabinet, so that they might flatter him and smooth him down as had been done with MacDonald in England. They would offer him this post and that; they would try to win his followers away from him—and Adi would summon the waverers to his presence and scream at them hysterically. When he couldn't get his way he would threaten suicide, and his followers never knew whether he meant it or not.

A great event in Berlin life when the haughty old Field Marshal consented to receive the "Bohemian corporal." Hitler was driven to the Wilhelmstrasse, with crowds cheering him on the way. He had lunch with von Papen, the Chancellor whose post he was demanding, and when he was escorted into the presence of Hindenburg he was so nervous that he stumbled over a rug; he started one of his orations, just like Gladstone before Queen Victoria, and had to be stopped by his old commander. Hindenburg told him that he would not turn over the chancellorship to a man whose followers practiced terrorism and systematic violations of the law; he thought the vice-chancellorship was enough for such a man. But Hitler refused it, demanding full power. The aged Junker stormed, but the ex-corporal had been brought up on that, and all he would reply was: "Opposition to the last ditch." Said Hindenburg: *"Ich will meine Ruhe haben!"*

There began a new wave of terrorism; attacks upon Reds of all shades by the Nazi Stormtroopers in and out of uniform. Irma heard about it and began begging Lanny to cease his visits among these people; she tried to enlist Robbie's help, and when that failed she wanted to leave Berlin. What was this obscure tropism which drove her husband to the companionship of persons who at the least wanted to get his money from him, and frequently were conspiring to involve him in dangerous intrigues? What had they ever done for him? What could he possibly owe them?

Lanny insisted that he had to hear all sides. He invited Emil Meissner to lunch—not in the Robin home, for Emil wouldn't come there. Kurt's oldest brother was now a colonel, and Lanny wanted to know what a Prussian officer thought about the political deadlock. Emil said it was deplorable, and agreed with Lanny that the Nazis were wholly unfitted to govern Germany. He said that if von Papen had been a really strong man he would never have permitted that election to be held; if the Field Marshal had been the man of the old days he would have taken the reins in his hands and governed the country until the economic crisis had passed and the people could settle into a normal state of mind.

"But wouldn't that mean the end of the Republic?" asked Lanny.

"Republics come and go, but nations endure," said Oberst Meissner.

VII

Heinrich Jung called up, bursting with pride over the triumph of his party. He offered to tell Lanny the inside story, and Lanny said: "But I am consorting with your enemies." The other laughed and replied: "Then you can tell *me* the inside story!" He seemed to take the view that Lanny, an American, was above the battle. Was it that a young Nazi craved the admiration of a foreigner? Was there in his secret heart some pleasure in free discussion, the expression of unbiased opinion which he did not get from his party press? Or was it that Lanny was so rich, and looked like a figure out of a Hollywood movie?

The Jung family had been increased again. "More Junkers," said Lanny, with what seemed a pun to him. Heinrich's salary had been increased and he had moved into a larger home. He had invited Hugo Behr, and the three of them sat for a couple of hours sipping light beer and settling the destiny of Germany and its neighbors. Lanny was interested to observe that there were disagreements among Nazi intellectuals, as elsewhere; the two names of Hitler's party covered widely different and inconsistent points of view. Heinrich was the National and Hugo was the Socialist, and while they agreed in worship of the Führer and in the certainty that he could do no wrong, they differed as to the party's immediate policies as well as its ultimate goal. It seemed to the visitor that the split had widened greatly since he had last met the pair. Hugo, the convert from Marxism, had brought over with him the attitude of workingclass consciousness and the program of socialization; whereas Heinrich, son of one of Graf Stubendorf's employees, had the mentality of a Prussian state servant to whom *Ordnung und Zucht* were the breath of being.

Lanny thought there was drama in this, and that it might pay an English playwright to come to Berlin and study what was going on. He had suggested the idea to Rick, who hadn't thought the Nazi movement important enough; but maybe the recent vote would change his mind! Anyhow, Lanny was interested to listen to two young zealots, setting out to make the world over in the image of their inspired leader; it pleased him to take a mental crowbar and insert it in the crack between their minds and make it wider and deeper. Just how deep would it go before they became aware of it themselves?

Lanny couldn't tell them what he knew. He couldn't say to Hugo: "Your Führer is in the thick of negotiations with Thyssen, and Krupp von Bohlen, and Karl von Siemens, and others of the greediest industrialists of your country. He is making fresh promises of conservatism and legality. He will do anything to get power, and anything to keep it. You and your friends are just so many pawns that he moves here and there and will sacrifice when his game requires it." No, for they would ask: "How do you know this?" And he couldn't reply: "Fritz Thyssen told my father yesterday." They would assume that he had got the stories from Johannes Robin, a Jew, which would mean to them two things: first, that the stories were lies, and second, that some Nazi patriots ought to visit the Robin palace by night and smash all its windows and paint *Juda verrecke!* on its front door.

No, among Catholics one did not question the purity of the Holy Virgin, and among Nazis one didn't question the honor of the Führer. When he said in his book that he would have no honor, he meant as regards his foes; but for his *Parteigenossen* he was a loving shepherd, to be followed after the manner of sheep. All that Lanny could do was to ask impersonal questions. "How can the Führer get commercial credits, if Germany defaults in payments on her bonds? I don't mean reparations, but the bonds of private investors." Hugo Behr, naïve young Socialist, didn't even know that there were such bonds. Lanny said: "I have several of them in a safe-deposit box in Newcastle, Connecticut. I bought them because I wanted to help your Socialist republic."

"It is a bourgeois fraud!" said the ex-Marxist; and that settled all Lanny's claims.

VIII

Kurt had written, begging Irma and Lanny to come for a visit. Lanny had never been to Stubendorf except at Christmas time, and he thought it would be pleasant to see the country in midsummer. They drove with a speed greater than the wind over the splendid level roads of Prussia, past fields where gangs of Polish immigrant women labored on the potato crops. The roads were lined with well-tended fruit trees, and Irma said: "We couldn't do that in America. People would steal all the fruit." She had never seen vast fields so perfectly cultivated: every inch of ground put to use, no such thing as a weed existing, and forests with trees planted in rows like orchards. She renewed her admiration for the German *Volk.*

They stayed at the Schloss, even though the Graf was not at home. Kurt had a new "Junker," and so had his brother's family and his sister's. Herr Meissner was feeble, but able to talk politics; he renewed his complaints of corruption and incompetence of the Polish government under which he was forced to live. Just now there was wrangling over religious questions; the old problem of the relations of church and state was being fought over with bitterness inherited through six centuries or more. There were Polish Lutherans and German Lutherans who couldn't and wouldn't say the Lord's prayer together. There were Polish Catholics trying to polonize German Catholics. There was the Volhynian Russian church, and the Uniat church which was half-way between Russian Orthodox and Roman Catholic—they accepted the Pope, but their priests married and had large families. Superimposed upon all this was a new Polish ecclesiastical system, which subjected all the churches to the government. Herr Meissner, soon to depart from this earth, found the making of a proper exit as complicated a problem as had ever confronted him while staying on.

Lanny had been looking forward to having a frank talk with his old chum. He wanted to tell Kurt what he had learned about the Nazi political machine, and make one last effort to get him out of it. But he realized that it would be a waste of effort. Kurt was in a state of exultation over the election results, for which he had been hoping for ten years and working for five. He considered that Germany was being redeemed, and he was composing a *Victory March* to end all marches. Lanny decided sadly that it was better to play piano duets and consider politics as beneath the notice of inspired musicians.

He and Irma had intended to return to Berlin for another cruise; but there came a telegram from Miss Severne, who was under strict orders to report the slightest sign of indisposition on the part of her charge. She reported a digestive disturbance and a temperature of 101; that didn't mean much in a child, and the nurse was sure it wasn't serious, but Irma fell into a panic right away—she was a neglectful and selfish mother who had run away from her responsibilities, amusing herself all over Europe. She wanted to take a plane; but Lanny said: "By the time you get to an airport and arrange for one we can be half way home. You spell me and we'll drive straight through."

So they did, and reached Juan in a little over two days—not so bad considering the mountains in Austria and Italy. Twice on the way they stopped to telephone, and when they arrived they found that the fire was all out. Was it the magic of Parsifal Dingle, or just the natural tendency of very young children to get over a fever as quickly as they get it? There was no way to know; suffice it that Lanny's stepfather had done his best, and Miss Severne had done hers, and Baby Frances was well—and ready to take full advantage of a reformed and penitent mother! Irma was so happy to prattle and dance and play with her darling that she couldn't understand how she had ever wanted to be fashionable.

I X

They settled down to domestic life. In the evening Sophie and her husband would come over to play bridge with Irma and Beauty. Marceline had begun attending a private school, where fashionable young ladies didn't learn very much but were watched and kept out of mischief. That left Lanny free to read the magazines which had accumulated in his absence, and to play the music that took his fancy; also to attend the workers' school and tell them what he had learned in England and Germany, and advise them how to avoid the misfortunes which had befallen their comrades in these countries.

The only trouble was, the data appeared so complicated and the conclusions so uncertain. "MacDonaldism" appeared to indicate the futility of "gradualness" and legality; the moment you mentioned it, up popped some young Red to say: "You see what happens when the workers put their trust in parliaments!" When you mentioned Hitler, right away a wrangle started as to what had caused him. Was he an agent of German heavy industry, and a proof that capitalism would not submit peaceably to any form of limitation upon its rule? Or were the Nazis a product of the fears which Bolshevism had inspired in the *Kleinbürgertum*—the small business men, the petty officials, the white collar workers who had no unions and couldn't protect their status?

You could take either side of this debate, produce a mass of facts to prove your case, and come out feeling certain that you had won. The uncomfortable person was the one like Lanny, who wanted the whole truth, and could see that there was some of it on both sides. Nobody could look at an issue of a Nazi newspaper without seeing that they were exploiting the fear of Red Russia to the limit; on the other hand, who could look at Hitler's Braune Haus with its costly equipment, or see the Stormtroopers marching with their shiny new uniforms and weapons—and not know that this movement was being financed by big money of some sort. *Gross Kapital* was afraid of Russia, just as the white collar workers were; but *Gross Kapital* was exploiting all the workers, and these two groups couldn't agree on any domestic policies. Sooner or later the Nazis would have to make up their minds which master they meant to serve.

There lay the drama of present day events in Germany, and Lanny strove to explain it to the French workers and to such of their leaders as he met. Hitler sat in his study in Berlin, or in Munich, or in the retreat which he had bought for himself in the mountains, and the Nazi chieftains came to him and argued and pulled him this way and that; he thought it over, and chose whatever course seemed to him to open the way to power. He was as slippery as an eel, and as quick to move, and nobody could say what he was going to do until he had done it. The one thing you could say for sure was that National Socialism was power without conscience; you might call it the culmination of capitalism, or a degenerate form of Bolshevism—names didn't matter, so long as you understood that it was counter-revolution.

The important question was, whether this same development was to be expected in every country. Was the depression going to wipe out the middle classes and drive them into the arms of demagogues? Were the workers being driven to revolt, and would their attempts be met by the overthrow of parliaments? Were the Communists right in their seemingly crazy idea that Fascism was a necessary stage in the breakdown of capitalism?

Apparently the question was up for answer in the land which Lanny and Irma called theirs. The ex-service men who had gone overseas to fight for their country had come back to find the jobs and the money in the hands of others. Now they were unemployed, many of them starving, and they gathered in Washington demanding relief; some brought their destitute families and swarmed upon the steps of the Capitol or camped in vacant lots beside the Potomac. The Great Engineer fell into a panic and could think of nothing to do but turn the army loose on them, kill four, and burn the tents and pitiful belongings of all. The "bonus men" were driven out, a helpless rabble, no one caring where they went, so long as they stopped bothering politicians occupied with getting re-elected.

To Lanny this appeared the same thing as the Cabinet of the

Barons, seizing control of Prussia and ruling Germany with only a few votes in the Reichstag. It was Poincairé occupying the Ruhr for the benefit of the Comité des Forges; it was Zaharoff sending an army into Turkey to get oil concessions. It was the same type of men all over the world. They tried to grab one another's coal and steel and oil and gold; yet, the moment they were threatened by their wage slaves anywhere, they got together to fight against the common peril. Do it with the army, do it with gangsters, do it with the workers' own leaders, buying them or seducing them with titles, honors, and applause!

Lanny could see that clearly; and it is a pleasure to the mind to discover unity in the midst of variety. But then the thought would come to him: "My father is one of these men, and so are his father and his brothers. My sister's father-in-law is one, and so was my wife's father, and all the men of her family." That spoiled the pleasure in Lanny's mind.

X

Two or three weeks passed, and ambition began to stir once more in the soul of Irma Barnes Budd. There was that splendid palace in Paris, for which she was paying over eighty thousand francs rent per month, and nearly as much for upkeep, whether she used it or not. Now it was autumn, one of the delightful seasons in la Ville Lumière. The *beau monde* came back from the mountains and the sea, and there were the autumn Salons, and operas and concerts and all the things that Lanny loved; there were balls and parties, an automobile show and other displays of luxury. The young couple set out in their car, and Sophie and her husband in theirs, and Beauty and her husband in hers. Mr. Dingle didn't mind wherever she took him, for, strange as it might seem, God was in Paris, and there were people there who knew Him, even in the midst of the rout of pleasure-seeking.

Margy, Dowager Lady Eversham-Watson, came from London, bringing Nina and Rick for a short holiday. Rick was a celebrity now, and the hostesses were after him. Also General Graf Stubendorf was invited, in return for his hospitality, and to Lanny's surprise he accepted. Others of the fashionable Berliners came, and it was hands across the Rhein again—but Lanny was no longer naïve, and couldn't persuade himself that this was going to keep the peace among the great European powers. The Conference on Arms Limitation was still arguing at Geneva, and facing complete breakdown. The statesmen and fashionable folk, even the army men, would wine and dine one another and be the best of friends; but they would go on piling up weapons and intriguing, each against all the others—until one day an *alerte* would be sounded, and you would see them all scurrying back to their own side of the river, or mountains, or whatever the boundary line might be.

It didn't take Irma long to become the accomplished hostess. With Emily Chattersworth and the other ladies coaching her, she played her part with dignity and success; everybody liked her, and the most fastidious denizens of St. Germain, *le gratin,* could find no fault in her. She wasn't presuming to attempt a salon—that would take time, and perhaps might grow as it were by accident. Meanwhile she gave elegant entertainments with no sign of skimping, at a time when all but a few were forced to that least pardonable of improprieties.

For three years the business prophets had been telling the world that the slump was only temporary, that prosperity was just around the corner. But apparently it was a round house. Apparently some devil had got into the economic structure and was undermining it. In Wall Street, at the culmination of a furious political campaign, there was a new wave of bank failures; dividends seemed to have stopped, and now interest on bonds was stopping. Irma's income for the third quarter of the year had fallen to less than a hundred thousand dollars. She said to her husband: "We'll have a splurge for the rest of this lease and then go back and crawl into our storm-cellar."

He answered: "All right," and let it go at that. He knew that he couldn't change Irma's idea that she was helping to preserve the social order by distributing money among domestic servants, wine merchants, florists, dressmakers, and all the train that came to the side-door of this palace—as they had come in the days of Marie

Antoinette a hundred and fifty years ago. It hadn't succeeded in saving feudalism, and Lanny doubted if it was going to save capitalism; but there was no use upsetting anybody ahead of time!

Lanny worried because his life was too easy; he had worried about that for years—but how could he make it hard? Even the harsh and bitter Jesse Blackless, *député de la république française*, couldn't forget the fact that he owed his election to Irma's contributions, and that sooner or later he would have to be elected again. Even Jean Longuet, man of letters as well as Socialist editor, didn't presume to question the judgment of a wealthy young American who brought him some drawings by a German art student. He said he would be delighted to use them, and Trudi Schultz was made happy by a modest honorarium from *Le Populaire.* She had no idea that the money came out of a contribution which Lanny had made to the war-chest of that party organ.

XI

Hitler's program of "opposition to the last ditch" had forced the dissolution of the Reichstag, and a new election campaign was going on. It was hard on Adolf, for he couldn't get the money which such an effort required, and when the election took place, early in November, it was found that he had lost nearly two million votes in three months. Johannes Robin was greatly relieved, and wrote that it was the turning of the tide; he felt justified in his faith in the German people, who couldn't be persuaded to entrust their affairs to a mentally disordered person. Johannes said that the Führer's conduct since the setback showed that he couldn't control himself and ought to be in an institution of some sort.

Two days after the German elections came those in the United States. Robbie Budd had his faith in the American people, and he clung to it up to 7:00 p.m. on the Tuesday after the first Monday of November 1932, but then it was completely and irremediably shattered. The Great Engineer, Robbie's friend and idol, went down in ignominious defeat, and "that man Roosevelt" carried all the states but six. One that he failed to carry was Robbie's home state, and a rock-ribbed Republican could thank God for that small atom of self-respect left to him! Adi Hitler might be a mental case, but he had the wisdom of Jove compared with Roosevelt as Robbie saw him; a candidate who had gone on a joy-ride about the country, promising everything to everybody—completely incompatible things such as the balancing of the budget and a program of government expansion which would run the public debt up to figures of the sort used by astronomers.

Both Robbie and Johannes made it a practice to send Lanny carbon copies of their letters containing comments on public affairs. For the first time since the World War the Jewish trader was the optimist. He repeated his favorite culinary formula, that no soup is ever eaten as hot as it is cooked. He offered to prove his faith in the land of the pilgrims' pride by letting Robbie buy more Budd shares for him; but Robbie wrote in the strictest confidence—typing the letter himself—that Budd's might soon be closing down entirely; only Hoover's wise and merciful Reconstruction Finance Corporation had kept it from having to default on its bonds.

Under the American system, four months had to elapse between Roosevelt's election and his taking of power. Robbie thought that would be a breathing-spell, but it proved to be one of paralysis; nothing could be done, and each side blamed the other. Herbert was sure that Franklin wanted to see the country go to wreck in order that he might have the glory of saving it. Anyhow, there it was, wave after wave of bank failures, and people hiding their money in mattresses, business men buying gold because of the expected inflation, and people in Europe who had shipped their money to America now calling it back. Seventeen million workers were said to be without jobs—a world record!

XII

Meanwhile the deadlock in Germany continued. The Socialists had lost another big chunk of votes to the Communists, and they hated each other more than ever. Hitler had another interview with Hindenburg, and demanded the chancellorship, but didn't get it.

The Nazi extremists were infuriated by Hitler's "legality complex," and clamored for him to seize power. There was another violent quarrel between the Führer and his Reich Organization Leader Number One, Gregor Strasser; the former threatened suicide again, and the latter threatened to resign from the party and set up a new one of his own.

Strasser began intriguing with the gentlemen of the Herren Klub, who were ready to make a deal with anybody who could deliver votes. General von Schleicher wanted to supplant von Papen, who was supposed to be his friend and ally; he had the bright idea of a cabinet which would combine the extreme Junkers with the extreme Nazis—they could browbeat Hitler, because his party was bankrupt, his paymasters had drawn the purse-strings, and he himself was in a state of distraction. Schleicher and Strasser combined would threaten another dissolution of the Reichstag and another election, with the certainty that without money the Nazi vote would be cut in half. Such was the X-ray picture of German politics which Johannes Robin sent to his trusted friends; he didn't say in so many words that both the conspirators had come to him for funds, but he said that he hadn't got the above information at second hand.

This deal apparently went through. When the members of the Budd family drove to Bienvenu to spend Christmas, the "office general" was Chancellor of the German Republic, Gregor Strasser had broken with Hitler and was being talked of for a cabinet post, and Hitler had been browbeaten into consenting to an adjournment of the Reichstag until January.

From Connecticut and from Long Island came Christmas letters in which you could see that the writers had labored hard to think of something cheerful to say. Irma, reading them, said to her husband: "Maybe we'd better close up the palace and save money, so that we can take care of my mother and your father if we have to."

"Bless your heart!" replied the prince consort. "You've hired that white elephant until April, so you might as well ride him that long."

"But suppose they get really stuck, Lanny!"

"Robbie isn't playing the market, and I don't suppose your mother is, so they can't be broke entirely."

Irma thought for a while, then remarked: "You know, Lanny, it's really wonderful the way you've turned out to be right about business affairs. All the important people have been wrong, while you've hit the nail on the head."

Said the young Pink: "It's worth going through a depression to hear that from one's wife!"

14

The Stormy Winds Do Blow

I

BACK in Paris during the month of January Lanny would receive every morning a copy of the Berlin *Vorwärts*, twenty-four hours late; he would find on the front page details of the political situation, displayed under scare headlines and accompanied by editorial exhortations. All from the Socialist point of view, of course; but Lanny could check it by taking a stroll up the Butte de Montmartre and hearing the comments of his deputy-uncle, based on the reading of *L'Humanité*, the paper which Jaurès had founded but which now was in the hands of the Communists. This paper also had its Berlin news, set off with scare headlines and editorial exhortations. Because *L'Humanité* got its stories by wire, Lanny would sometimes swallow the antidote ahead of the poison.

"You see!" the Red uncle would exclaim. "The Social-Democrats haven't a single constructive proposal. They only denounce what we propose!"

"But you do some denouncing also, Uncle Jesse."

"The workers know our program; and every time there's an

election, the Socialist bureaucrats lose half a million or a million
votes, and we gain them."

"But suppose there aren't any more elections, Uncle Jesse. Suppose Hitler takes power!"

"He can't do any harm to our monolithic party. We have educated and disciplined our members and they will stand firm."

"But suppose he outlaws your organization!"

"You can't destroy a party that has several hundred thousand
members, and has polled four or five million votes."

"Don't make the mistake of underestimating your enemy."

"Well, if necessary we'll go underground. It has happened before,
and you may be sure that we have made plans—in France as well as
in Germany."

"I hope you're not mistaken, Uncle Jesse." Lanny said it and
meant it. He argued against the Communists, but was only half-
hearted about it, because after all, they were a workers' party, and
nobody could be sure they mightn't be needed. The first Five
Year Plan of the Soviet Union had been completed with success,
and all the Reds were exulting over it; the Pinks couldn't fail to
be impressed, and many wavered and wondered if maybe the Russian way might be the only way. Anyhow, they had a right to be
heard; Lanny did what he could to persuade both sides to stop
quarreling, and he set them an example by refusing to let them quarrel with him.

I I

Any time he was in doubt about what was really happening in
Germany he had only to write to Johannes Robin. A letter from
the Jewish money-master was like a gust of wind blowing away a
fog and revealing the landscape. It disclosed the German nation
traveling upon a perilous path, with yawning abysses on every side,
earthquakes shaking the rocks loose and volcanoes hurling out
clouds of fiery ashes. Assuredly neither of the Plinys, uncle or
nephew, had confronted more terrifying natural phenomena than
did the Weimar Republic at the beginning of this year 1933.

The ceaselessly aggressive Nazis were waging daily and nightly battles with the Communists all over the country. And meantime the two ruling groups, the industrialists of the west and the landlords of the east, were concentrating their attention upon getting higher tariffs to protect their interests; one hundred per cent wasn't enough in these days of failing markets. The workers, who wanted lower prices for goods and for food, had refused time after time to vote for candidates of these groups; but with less than five per cent of the votes, the reactionary politicians still clung to power, playing one faction against another, using cajolements mixed with threats.

Chancellor von Schleicher had begun wooing the labor unions, calling himself the "social general," and pointing out to the moderates among Socialists and Catholics how much worse things would be if either set of extremists came in. By such blandishments he lost favor with the paymasters of the Ruhr, who wanted the labor unions broken and were listening to the siren song of Hitler, promising this service. Also there was the problem of *Osthilfe,* a scandal hanging over the heads of the landed aristocrats of East Prussia. Huge public funds had been voted to save the farmers from ruin, but the owners of the big estates, the powerful aristocrats, had managed to get most of the money, and they had used it for other purposes than land improvements. Now hardly a day passed that the Socialist and Communist press didn't print charges and demand investigations.

Papen and Schleicher still pretended to be friends, while scheming to cut each other's throats. Schleicher had ousted Papen by a deal with the Nazis, and two could play at that game. Papen, the "gentleman jockey," was the most tireless of wirepullers. A pale blond aristocrat with a thin, lined face wearing a perpetual smile, he went from one secret meeting to another telling a different story to everybody—but all of them carefully calculated to injure his rival.

"Papen has had a meeting with Hitler at the home of Thyssen's friend, Baron von Schroeder," wrote Johannes, and Lanny didn't need to ask what that meant. "I am told that Papen and Hugenberg have got together;"—that, too, was not obscure. Hugenberg, the "silver fox," had come to one of the Robin soirées; a big man with a walrus mustache, brutal but clever; leader of the Pan-German group and owner of the most powerful propaganda machine in the world, practically all of the big capitalist newspapers of Germany, plus U.F.A., the film monopoly. "Papen is raising funds for Hitler among the industrialists," wrote Johannes. "I hear that the Führer has more than two million marks in notes which he cannot meet. It is a question whether he will go crazy before he becomes chancellor!"

III

The Nazis held one of their tremendous meetings in the Sport-palast, and Hitler delivered one of his inspired tirades, promising peace, order, and restoration of self respect to the German people. The conservative newspapers in Paris published his promises and half believed them; they were far more afraid of the Reds than of the Nazis, and Lanny found that Denis de Bruyne was inclined to look upon Hitler as a model for French politicians. Even Lanny himself began hesitating; he was so anxious to be sure that he was right. Hitler was calling upon Almighty God to give him courage and strength to save the German people and right the wrongs of Versailles. Lanny, who had protested so energetically against those wrongs, now wondered if it mightn't be possible for Hitler to scare France and Britain into making the necessary concessions, and then to settle down and govern the country in the interest of those millions of oppressed "little people" for whom he spoke so eloquently.

The son of Robbie Budd and husband of Irma Barnes might waver, but the German workers didn't. A hundred thousand of them met in the Berlin Lustgarten, clamoring for the defense of the Republic against its traitor enemies. "Something is going to pop," wrote Johannes, American fashion. "*Der alte Herr* is terrified at the prospect of having the *Osthilfe* affair discussed in the Reichstag. Schleicher is considering with the labor unions the idea of refusing to resign and holding on with their backing. I am told that the Catholics have assented, but the Socialists are afraid it wouldn't be legal. What do you think?" Lanny knew that his old friend was

teasing him, and didn't offer any opinion on German constitutional
law.

Johannes didn't say what he himself was doing in this crisis, but
Lanny guessed that he was following his program of keeping friendly
with all sides. Certainly he possessed an extraordinary knowledge of
the intrigues. Now and then Lanny would call him on the long
distance telephone, a plaything of the very rich, and Johannes would
speak a sort of camouflage. He would say: "My friend Fränzchen
wants to be top dog, but so does his friend the publisher, and their
schemes will probably fall through because they can't agree." Lanny
understood that this meant Papen and Hugenberg; and when
Johannes added: "They may harness up the Wild Man and get
together to drive him," Lanny had no trouble guessing about that.
Presently Johannes said: "They are telling the Old Gent that the
General is plotting a *coup d'état* against him." It was like reading
a blood and thunder novel in instalments, and having to wait for
the next issue. Would the rescue party arrive in time?

I V

On the thirtieth of January the news went out to a startled world
that President von Hindenburg had appointed Adolf Hitler Chancellor of the German Republic. Even the Nazis were taken by surprise;
they hadn't been invited to the intrigues, and couldn't imagine by
what magic it had been brought about that their Führer's enemies
suddenly put him into office. Franz von Papen was Vice-Chancellor,
and Hugenberg was in the Cabinet; in all there were nine reactionaries against three Nazis, and what could that mean? · The newspapers outside Germany were certain that it meant the surrender
of Hitler; he was going to be controlled, he was going to be
another Ramsay MacDonald. They chose not to heed the proclama-
tion which the Führer himself issued, telling his followers that the
struggle was only beginning. But the Stormtroopers heeded, and
turned out, exultant, parading with torchlights through Unter den
Linden; seven hundred thousand persons marched past the Chancellery, with Hindenburg greeting them from one window and Hitler

from another. The Communist call for a general strike went unheeded.

So it had come: the thing which Lanny had been fearing for the past three or four years. The Nazis had got Germany! Most of his friends had thought it unlikely; and now that it had happened, they preferred to believe that it hadn't. Hitler wasn't really in power, they said, and could last but a week or two. The German people had too much sense, the governing classes were too able and well trained; they would tone the fanatic down, and the soup would be eaten cool.

But Adolf Hitler had got, and Adolf Hitler would keep, the power which was most important to him—that of propaganda. He was executive head of the German government, and whatever manifesto he chose to issue took the front page of all the newspapers. Hermann Göring was Prussian Minister of the Interior and could say to the world over the radio: "Bread and work for our countrymen, freedom and honor for the nation!" Dwarfish little Jupp Goebbels, President of the Propaganda Committee of the Party, found himself Minister of Propaganda and Popular Enlightenment of the German Republic. The Nazi movement had been made out of propaganda, and now it would cover Germany•like an explosion.

Hitler refused to make any concessions to the other parties, and thus forced Hindenburg to dissolve the Reichstag and order a new election. This meant that for a month the country would be in the turmoil of a campaign. But what a different campaign! No trouble about lack of funds, because Hitler had the funds of the nation, and his tirades were state documents. Goebbels could say anything he pleased about his enemies and suppress their replies. Göring, having control of the Berlin police, could throw his political opponents into jail and nobody could even find out where they were. These were the things of which Adi Schicklgruber had been dreaming ever since the end of the World War; and where else but in the Arabian Nights had it happened that a man awoke and found such dreams come true?

V

Lanny Budd lived externally the life of a young man of fashion. He accompanied his wife to various functions, and when she entertained he played the host with dignity. Having been married nearly four years, he was entitled to enjoy mild flirtations with various charming ladies of society; they expected it, and his good looks and conversation gave him reason to expect success. But instead, he would pick out some diplomat or man of affairs and disappear into the library to discuss the problems of Europe. These gentlemen were impressed by a young man's wide range of knowledge, but they thought he was unduly anxious concerning this new movement of Nazism; they had learned what a French revolution was, and a Russian one, but had difficulty in recognizing a revolution that happened in small instalments and under ingenious camouflage. Hardly a man of wealth and importance in France who didn't accept Nazism as a business man's answer to Bolshevism. When they read in the papers that Communists were being shot pretty freely throughout Germany, they shrugged their French shoulders and said: *"Eh, bien?* Do the Reds complain of illegality?"

Lanny ran up a large telephone bill calling his friends in Berlin. It was his one form of dissipation, and Irma learned to share it; she would take the wire when he got through and ask Rahel about the baby, or Mama about anything—for Mama's Yiddish-English was as delightful as a vaudeville turn. Lanny was worried about the safety of his friends, but Johannes said: *"Nu, nu!* Don't bother your head. I have assurances that I cannot tell you about. I wear the Tarnhelm."

He would retail the latest smart trick of those Nazis, whose cleverness and efficiency he couldn't help admiring. "No, they will not outlaw the Communist party, because if they did, the vote would go to the Sozis, and there would be the same old deadlock in the Reichstag. But if they let the Communist deputies be elected, and then exclude them from their seats, the Nazis may have a majority of what is left! What is it that you say about skinning a cat? There are nine ways of doing it?"

How long would a Jew, even the richest, be allowed to tell the inmost secrets of the Führer over the telephone to Paris? Lanny wondered about that, and he wondered about the magic cap which Johannes thought he was wearing. Might he not be fooling himself, like so many other persons who put their trust in political adventurers? Who was there among the Nazi powers who had any respect for a Jew, or would keep faith with one for a moment after it suited his purpose? To go to a rich *Schieber* to beg money for a struggling outcast party was one thing; but to pay the debt when you had got the powers of the state into your hands—that was something else again, as the Jews said in New York.

Lanny worried especially about Hansi, who was not merely of the hated race, but of the hated party, and had proclaimed it from public platforms. The Nazi press had made note of him; they had called him a tenth-rate fiddler who couldn't even play in tune. Would they permit him to go on playing out of tune at Red meetings? The Stormtroopers were now turned loose to wreak their will upon the Reds, and how long would it be before some ardent young patriot would take it into his head to stop this Jewish swine from profaning German music?

Lanny wrote, begging Hansi to come to Paris. He wrote to Bess, who admitted that she was afraid; but she was a granddaughter of the Puritans, who hadn't run away from the Indians. She pointed out that she and her husband had helped to make Communists in Berlin, and now to desert them in the hour of trial wouldn't be exactly heroic, would it? Lanny argued that a great artist was a special kind of being, different from a fighting man and not to be held to the military code. Lanny wrote to Mama, telling her that it was her business to take charge of the family in a time like this. But it wasn't so easy to manage Red children as it had been in the days of Moses and the Ten Commandments.

However, there was still a Providence overseeing human affairs. At this moment it came about that a certain Italian diva, popular in Paris, was struck by a taxicab. The kind Providence didn't let her be seriously hurt, just a couple of ribs broken, enough to put her out of the diva business for a while. The news appeared in the papers while Lanny and Irma were at Bienvenu, having run down to see the baby and to attend one of Emily's social functions. Lanny recalled that the diva was scheduled with one of the Paris symphony orchestras; she would have to be replaced, and Lanny asked Emily to get busy on the long distance telephone. She knew the conductor of this orchestra, and suggested Hansi Robin to replace the damaged singer; Mrs. Chattersworth being a well-known patron of the arts, it was natural that she should offer to contribute to the funds of the symphony society an amount equal to the fee which Hansi Robin would expect to receive.

The bargain was struck, and Lanny got to work on Hansi at some twenty francs per minute, to persuade him that German music ought to be promoted in France; that every such performance was a service to world culture, also to the Jewish race, now so much in need of international sympathy. After the Paris appearance, Emily would have a soirée at Sept Chênes, and other engagements would help to make the trip worth while.

"All right," replied the violinist, anxious to cut short the expenditure of francs. "I'm scheduled to give a concert at Cologne, and that is half way."

Lanny said: "For God's sake, keep off the streets at night, and don't go out alone!"

VI

Lanny missed his inside news about Germany, because the government forbade the publication of *Vorwärts* for three days, as a punishment for having published a campaign appeal of the Social-Democratic Party. Communist meetings were forbidden throughout the whole nation, and many Communist and Socialist papers were permanently suspended. "In ten years there will be no Marxism in Germany," proclaimed the Führer. All over Prussia Göring was replacing police chiefs with Nazis, and the Stormtroopers were now attending political meetings in force, stopping those in which the government was criticized. Next, all meetings of the Centrists, the Catholic party, were banned; the Catholic paper, *Germania*, of which Papen was the principal stockholder, was suppressed, and then *Rote Fahne*, the Communist paper of Berlin. These events were reported in *L'Humanité* under the biggest of headlines, and Uncle Jesse denounced them furiously in the Chamber of Deputies; but that didn't appear to have much effect upon Hitler.

What the Nazis were determined to do was to win those elections on the fifth of March. If they could get a majority in the Reichstag, they would be masters of the country; the Nationalists and aristocrats would be expelled from the cabinet and the revolution would be complete. Papen, Hugenberg, and their backers knew it well, and were in a state of distress, according to Johannes's reports. A curious state of affairs—the gentlemen of the Herren Klub defending the Reds, because they knew that Hitler was using the Red bogy to frighten the people into voting for him! Goebbels was demanding the head of the Berlin police chief because he wouldn't produce evidence of treasonable actions on the part of the Communists. "The history of Germany is becoming a melodrama," wrote the Jewish financier. "In times to come people will refuse to believe it."

He was now beginning to be worried about the possibility of attacks upon his boys; those gentle, idealistic boys who had been playing with fire without realizing how hot it could get. Being now twenty-eight and twenty-six respectively, they ought to have had some sense. Johannes didn't say it was Lanny's half-sister who led them into the worst extremes, but Lanny knew the father thought this, and not without reason. Anyhow, he had got a trusted bodyguard in the palace—a well-established and indubitable Aryan bodyguard. Freddi's school had been closed; such a simple operation—a group of Stormtroopers appeared one evening and ordered the people out. Nothing you could do, for they had arms and appeared eager to use them. Everybody went, not even being allowed to get their hats and coats in February. The building was closed, and all the papers had been carted away in a truck.

The Nazis wouldn't find any treason in those documents; only receipted bills, and examination papers in Marxist theory. But maybe that was treason now! Or maybe the Nazis would prepare other documents and put them into the files. Orders to the students to blow up Nazi headquarters, or perhaps the Chancellery? Such forgeries had been prepared more than once, and not alone in Germany. Hadn't an election been won in Britain on the basis of an alleged "Zinoviev letter"?

The headquarters of the Communist Party of Germany was in Karl Liebknecht Haus, and that was the place where treason was to be sought. The police had seized the documents, and two days later Herr Goebbels's press service gave details about "catacombs" and "underground vaults," a secret and illegal organization functioning in the basement of the building, and so on. Johannes reported an embittered conflict in the Cabinet over these too obvious forgeries; they were considered beneath the dignity of the German government—but perhaps the German government wasn't going to be so dignified from now on! The Jewish financier couldn't conceal his amusement over the discomfiture of the "gentleman jockey," the "silver fox," and the rest of the Junker crew. They had made this bed of roses, and discovered too late how full of thorns it was.

The thing that worried Lanny was the possibility that some Nazi agent might produce letters proving that Hansi Robin had been carrying dynamite in his violin case, or Freddi in his clarinet case. They must have had spies in the school, and known everything that both boys had been doing and saying. Lanny said: "Johannes, why don't you and the whole family come visit us for a while?"

"Maybe we'll all take a yachting trip," replied the man of money, with a chuckle. "When the weather gets a little better."

"The weather is going to get worse," insisted the Paris end of the line.

VII

Lanny talked this problem over with his wife. She couldn't very well refuse hospitality to Johannes, from whom she had accepted so much. But she didn't like the atmosphere which the young Robins brought with them, and she thought them a bad influence for her husband. She argued that the danger couldn't really be so great as Lanny feared. "If the Nazis are anxious to get votes, they won't do anything to important persons, especially those known abroad."

Lanny replied: "The party is full of criminals and degenerates, and they are drunk with the sense of power."

He couldn't stop worrying about it, and when the day for Hansi's coming drew near, he said to Irma: "How would you like to motor to Cologne and bring them out with us?"

"What could we do, Lanny?"

"There's safety in numbers; and then, too, Americans have a certain amount of prestige in Germany."

It wasn't a pleasant time for motoring, the end of February, but they had heat in their car, and with fur coats they would be all right unless there happened to be a heavy storm. Irma liked adventure; one of the reasons she and Lanny got along so well was that whenever one suggested hopping into a car the other always said: "O.K." No important engagement stood in the way of this trip, and they allowed themselves an extra day on chance of bad weather.

Old Boreas was kind, and they rolled down the valley of the Meuse, by which the Germans had made their entry into France some eighteen and a half years ago. Lanny told his wife the story of Sophie Timmons, Baroness de la Tourette, who had been caught in the rush of the armies and had got away in a peasant's cart pulled by a spavined old horse.

They reached Cologne late that evening, and spent the next day looking at a grand cathedral, and at paintings in a near-by Gothic museum. Hansi and Bess arrived on the afternoon train, and thereafter they stayed in their hotel suite, doing nothing to attract attention to a member of the accursed race. Among the music-lovers Hansi would be all right, for these were "good Europeans," who for a couple of centuries had been building up a tradition of internationalism. A large percentage of Europe's favorite musicians had been Jews, and there would have been gaps in concert programs if their works had been omitted.

Was the audience trying to say this by the storms of applause with which they greeted the performance of Mendelssohn's gracious concerto by a young Jewish virtuoso? Did Hansi have such a message in his mind when he played Bruch's *Kol Nidrei* as one of his encores? When the audience leaped to its feet and shouted, "Bravo!" were they really meaning to say: "We are not Nazis! We shall never be Nazis!" Lanny chose to believe this, and was heartened; he was sure that many of the adoring Rheinlanders had a purpose in waiting at the stage door and escorting the four young people to their car. But out in the dark street, with a cold rain falling, doubts began to assail him, and he wondered if the amiable Rhinelanders had guns for their protection.

However, no Nazi cars followed, and no Stormtroopers were waiting at the Hotel Monopol. Next morning they drove to the border, and nobody searched Hansi's two violin cases for dynamite. They went through the routine performance of declaring what money they were taking out of the country, and were then passed over to the Belgian customs men. Lanny remembered the day when he had been ordered out of Italy, and with what relief he had seen French uniforms and heard French voices. Eight years had passed, and Benito, the "Blessed Little Pouter Pigeon," was still haughtily declaring that his successor had not yet been born. Now his feat was being duplicated in another and far more powerful land, and rumors had it that he was giving advice. In how many more countries would Lanny Budd see that pattern followed? How many more transformations would it undergo? Would the Japanese conquerors of Manchuria adopt some new-colored shirts or kimonos? Or would it be the Croix de Feu in France? Or Mosley's group in England? And if so, to what part of the world would the lovers of freedom move?

VIII

The tall slender figure of Hansi Robin stood before the audience in the symphony hall; an audience of fastidious Parisians whose greeting was reserved. In the front row sat Lanny, Irma, and Bess, greatly excited. Hansi's appearance was grave and his bows dignified; he knew that this performance was an important one, but was not too nervous, having learned by now what he could do. The conductor was a Frenchman who had given a long life to the service of the art he loved; his hair had grown white, and what was left of it stood out as a fringe under his shiny bald pate. He tapped upon the edge of his stand and raised his baton; there came four beats of the kettledrum, followed by a few notes of a timid marching song; then four more beats, and more notes. It was Beethoven's violin concerto.

Hansi stood waiting, with his instrument in the crook of his arm and his bow at his side; the introduction is elaborate, and not even by a movement of his eyes would he distract anyone's attention from the sounds. Lanny Budd, in the front row with his wife and Bess, knew every note of this composition, and had played a piano transcription of the orchestral part for Hansi at Les Forêts, on that fateful day seven years ago when Bess had first met the shepherd boy out of ancient Judea and fallen under his spell. That was one reason why Hansi made a specialty of this concerto; love infused his rendition, as love has a way of doing with whatever it touches.

The march acquired the firm tread of Beethoven; the orchestra thundered, and Lanny wanted to say: "Careful, Maestro. He didn't have so many instruments!" But the conductor's expressive hands signed for gentleness as Hansi's bow touched the strings. The song floated forth, gay yet tender, gentle yet strong—those high qualities which the soul of Beethoven possessed and which the soul of Hansi honored. The fiddle sang and the orchestra made comments upon it; various instruments took up the melody, while Hansi wove embroidery about it, danced around it, over and under it, leaping, skipping, flying in feats of gay acrobatics. A concerto is a device to exhibit the possibilities of a musical instrument; but at its best it may also illustrate the possibilities of the human spirit, its joys and griefs, toils and triumphs, glories and grandeurs. Men and women plod through their daily routine, they become tired and insensitive, skeptical or worse; then comes a master spirit and flings open the gates of their being, and they realize how much they have been missing in their lives.

For more than twenty years this sensitive young Jew had consecrated himself to one special skill; he had made himself a slave to some pieces of wood, strips of pig's intestine, and hairs from a horse's tail. With such unlikely agencies Beethoven and Hansi contrived to express the richness, elegance, and variety of life. They took you into the workshop of the universe, where its miracles are planned and executed; the original mass-production process which turns out the myriad leaves of trees and the petals of flowers, the wings of insects and birds, the patterns of snow crystals and solar systems. Beethoven and Hansi revealed the operation of that machinery from which color and delicacy, power and splendor are poured forth in unceasing floods.

Lanny had made so many puns upon the name of his brother-in-law that he had ceased to think of them as such. There was nothing in the physical aspect of Hansi to suggest the robin, but when you listened to his music you remembered that the robin's wings are marvels of lightness and grace, and that every feather is a separate triumph. The robin's heart is strong, and he flies without stopping, on and on, to lands beyond the seas. He flies high into the upper registers, among the harmonic notes, where sensations are keener than any known upon earth. The swift runs of Hansi's violin were the swooping and darting of all the birds; the long trills were the fluttering of the humming-bird's wings, purple, green, and gold in the sunlight, hovering, seeming motionless; each moment you expect it to dart away, but there it remains, an enchantment.

IX

Hansi was playing the elaborate cadenza. No other sound in the auditorium; the men of the orchestra sat as if they were images, and the audience the same. Up and down the scale rushed the flying notes; up like the wind through the pine trees on a mountain-side, down like cascades of water, flashing rainbows in the sunshine. Beethoven had performed the feat of weaving his two themes in counterpoint, and Hansi performed the feat of playing trills with

two of his fingers and a melody with the other two. Only a musician could know how many years of labor it takes to train nerves
and muscles for such "double-stopping," but everyone could know
that it was beautiful and at the same time that it was wild.

The second movement is a prayer, and grief is mixed with its
longing; so Hansi could tell those things which burdened his spirit.
He could say that the world was a hard and cruel place, and that
his poor people were in agony. "Born to sorrow—born to sorrow,"
moaned the wood-winds, and Hansi's violin notes hovered over
them, murmuring pity. But one does not weep long with Beethoven;
he turns pain into beauty, and it would be hard to find in all his
treasury a single work in which he leaves you in despair. There
comes a rush of courage and determination, and the theme of grief
turns into a dance. The composer of this concerto, humiliated and
enraged because the soldiers of Napoleon had seized his beloved
Vienna, went out into the woods alone and reminded himself that
world conquerors come and go, but love and joy live on in the
hearts of men.

"Oh, come, be merry, oh, come be jolly, come one, come all and
dance with me!" Lanny amused himself by finding words for musical themes. This dance went over flower-strewn meadows; breezes
swept ahead of it, and the creatures of nature joined the gay
procession, birds fluttering in the air, rabbits and other delightful
things scampering on the ground. Hand in hand came young people
in flowing garments. "Oh, youths and maidens, oh, youths and
maidens, come laugh, and sing, and dance with me!" It was the
Isadora rout that Lanny would always carry in his memory. When
the storm of the orchestra drowned out Hansi's fiddle, the listener
was leaping to a mountain-top and from it to the next.

Others must have been having the same sort of adventure, for
when the last note sounded they started to their feet and tried to
tell the artist about it. Lanny saw that his brother-in-law had won
a triumph. Such a sweet, gentle fellow he was, flushed from his
exertions, but even thinner than usual, showing the strain under
which he was living. People seemed to realize that here was one
who was not going to be spoiled by adulation. He wasn't going to

enjoy himself and his own glory, he would never become blasé and bored; he would go on loving his art and serving it. Nobody in that hall failed to know that he was a Jew, and that this was a time of anguish for his people. Such anti-Semitism as there was in Paris was not among the art-lovers, and to shout "Bravo!" at this young virtuoso was to declare yourself for the cause of freedom and human decency.

Lanny thought about the great composer, friend of mankind and champion of the oppressed. His concerto had been played badly in his own lifetime, and what a revelation it would have been to him to hear it rendered by a soloist and a conductor, neither having a score. But then Lanny thought: "What would Beethoven think if he could see what is happening in the land of his birth?" So the dreams of art fled, and painful reality took their place. Lanny thought: "The German soul has been captured by Hitler! What can he give it but his own madness and distraction? What can he make of it but an image of his distorted self?"

X

Hansi always wanted to be taken straight home after a performance; he was exhausted, and didn't care for sitting around in cafés. He entered the palace and was about to go to his room, when the telephone rang; Berlin calling, and Hansi said: "That will be Papa, wanting to know how the concert went."

He was right, and told his father that everything had gone well. Johannes didn't ask for particulars; instead he had tidings to impart. "The Reichstag building is burning."

"*Herrgott!*" exclaimed the son, and turned and repeated the words to the others.

"The Nazis are saying that the Communists set fire to it."

"But, Papa, that is crazy!"

"I must not talk about it. You will find the news in the papers, and do your own guessing. The building has been burning for a couple of hours, and they say that men were seen running through it with torches."

"It is a plot!" exclaimed Hansi.

"I cannot say; but I am glad that you are not here. You must stay where you are for the present. It is a terrible thing."

So Hansi did not go to bed for a long while. They sat and talked, and Lanny, who had friends on *Le Populaire,* called up that paper to get further details. It was believed that the great building was gutted, and the government was charging that it had been deliberately fired by emissaries of the Red International.

All four of the young people were familiar with that elaborate specimen of the Bismarck style of architecture, and could picture the scenes, both there and elsewhere in the city. "It is a frame-up," said Bess. "Communists are not terrorists." Lanny agreed with her, and Irma, whatever she thought, kept it to herself. It was inevitable that every Communist would call it a plot, and every Nazi would be equally certain of the opposite.

"Really, it is too obvious!" argued Hansi. "The elections less than six days away, and those scoundrels desperate for some means of discrediting us!"

"The workers will not be fooled!" insisted Bess. "Our party is monolithic."

Lanny thought: "The old phonograph record!" But he said: "It's a terrible thing, as Papa says. They will be raiding Communist headquarters all over Germany tonight. Be glad that you have a good alibi."

But neither of the musicians smiled at this idea. In their souls they were taking the blows which they knew must be falling upon their party comrades.

XI

What happened in the Reichstag building on that night of February 27 would be a subject of controversy inside and outside of Germany for years to come; but there could be no doubt about what happened elsewhere. Even while the four young people were talking in Paris, the leader of the Berlin S.A., Count Helldorf, was giving orders for the arrest of prominent Communists and Socialists.

The list of victims had been prepared in advance, and warrants, each with a photograph of the victim in question. The Count knew that the Marxists were the criminals, he said; and Göring announced that the demented Dutchman who was found in the building with matches and fire-lighters had a Communist party membership card on him. The statement turned out to be untrue, but it served for the moment.

Next day Hitler persuaded Hindenburg to sign a decree "for the safeguarding of the state from the Communist menace," and after that the Nazis had everything their own way. The prisons were filled with suspects, and the setting up of concentration camps began with a rush. The Prussian government, of which Göring was the head, issued a statement concerning the documents found in the raid on Karl Liebknecht Haus three days before the fire. The Communists had been plotting to burn down public buildings throughout Germany, and to start civil war and revolution on the Russian model; looting had been planned to begin right after the fire and terrorist acts were to be committed against persons and property. The publication of these documents was promised, but no one ever saw them, and the story was dropped as soon as it had served its purpose—which was to justify the abolishing of civil liberties throughout what had been the German Republic.

XII

As the evidence began to filter into the newspapers of Britain and France, the young Reds and Pinks spent many an hour trying to make up their minds about one of the great "frame-ups" of history. What brain had conceived it? What hand had carried it out? For the former role their suspicions centered upon a German World War aviator who had fled to Sweden, where he had become a dope addict and had been in a psychopathic institution. Hermann Göring was a great hulk of a man, absurdly vain, with a fondness for gaudy uniforms which was to make him the butt of Berlin wits; he was also a man of immense energy, brutal and unscrupulous, the perfect type of those freebooters who had ravaged the borders of the German empire in medieval times, had given themselves titles, and now had huge white marble statues of themselves in the Siegesallée, known to the Berlin wits as "the Cemetery of Art."

Hermann Göring had got his titles: Minister without Portfolio, Federal Commissioner for Air Transport, Prussian Minister of the Interior. They carried the same grants of power as in the old free-booting days, but unfortunately they were subject to elections; on the following Sunday the proletariat might go to the polls and strip Hermann of his glories—and this would be extremely annoying to a man of aristocratic tastes, a friend of the former Crown Prince and of Thyssen. As it happened, the man of action was in position to act, for his official residence was connected with the Reichstag building by a long underground passage; also he had at his command a well-trained army, eager to execute any command he might give. What did a building amount to, in comparison with the future of the N.S.D.A.P.?

The man whom the Nazis were finally to convict of the crime was a feeble-minded Dutchman who had been expelled from the Communist party of that country and had been a tramp all over Europe. The police maintained that at his original examination he had told a detailed story of setting fire to the curtains of the restaurant with matches and fire-lighters. But the restaurant wasn't the only room that burned; there had been a heavy explosion in the session chamber, and that vast place had become a mass of flames and explosive gases. The head of the Berlin fire department had observed trains of gasoline on the floors of the building. Immediately after the fire he announced that the police had carted away a truck-load of unburned incendiary materials from the scene of the fire; and immediately after making this announcement he was dismissed from his post.

Such were the details which the young radicals abroad put together and published in their papers. But the papers which might have spread such news in Germany had all been suppressed; their editors were in prison and many were being subjected to cruel tortures. A sickening thing to know that your comrades, idealists whom you had trusted and followed, were being pounded with rubber hose, danced upon with spiked boots, having their kidneys kicked loose and their testicles crushed. Still more terrible to know that civil rights were being murdered in one of the world's most highly developed nations; that the homeland of Goethe and Bach was in the hands of men who were capable of planning and perpetrating such atrocities.

XIII

The fire had the intended effect of throwing all Germany into a panic of fear. Not merely the Nazis, but Papen and Hugenberg were denouncing the Red conspirators over the radio. All the new techniques of propaganda were set at work to convince the voters that the Fatherland stood in deadly peril of a Communist revolution. Friday was proclaimed the "Day of the Awakening Nation." The Nazis marched with torchlights, and on the mountain-tops and on high towers in the cities great bonfires burned—fires of liberation, they were called. "O Lord, make us free!" prayed Hitler over the radio, and loud-speakers spread his words in every market-square in every town.

On Sunday the people voted, and the Nazi vote increased from nearly twelve million to more than seventeen million. But the Communists lost only about a million, and the Socialists practically none. The Catholics actually gained, in spite of all the suppressions; so it appeared that the German people were not so easy to stampede after all. The Nazis still didn't have a majority of the Reichstag deputies, so they couldn't form a government without the support and approval of the aristocrats. What was going to come out of that?

The answer was that Adi Hitler was going to have his way. He was going right on, day after day, pushing to his goal, and nobody was going to stop him. Objections would be raised in the Cabinet, and he would do what he had done in party conferences—argue, storm, plead, denounce, and threaten. He would make it impossible for anyone else to be heard, raise such a disturbance as could not be withstood, prove that he could outlast any opposition, that his frenzy was uncontrollable, his will irrepressible. But behind this seeming madness would be a watchful eye and a shrewd, calculating brain. Adi would know exactly what he was doing and how far he could go; if the opposition became too strong, he would give way, he would make promises—and then next day it would be discovered that his followers were going right ahead doing what he wanted done, and he would be saying that he couldn't control them. If it was something serious, like the Reichstag fire, he would know nothing about it, he would be completely taken aback, astounded, horrified; but it would be too late—the building would be burned, the victim would be dead, the die would be cast.

For more than a decade he had been training his followers to these tactics. They must be a band of desperadoes, stopping at nothing to get their way. Nothing on earth or in heaven was sacred except their cause; nothing was wrong that helped their cause and nothing was right that delayed it for a single hour. Individually and collectively they must be the most energetic and capable of criminals, also the most shameless and determined liars. They must be able to say anything, with the most bland and innocent expression, and if they were caught they must admit nothing, but turn the charge against the other fellow; he was the liar, he was the crook, he alone was capable of every wrongdoing. Adolf Hitler had never admitted anything to anybody; he had never told a lie in his life, had never committed any improper action; he was a consecrated soul, who lived and was ready to die for one single cause, the triumph of National Socialism and the liberation of the German *Volk*.

For ten years he had been organizing two private armies of young men, several hundred thousand fanatics imbued with that spirit: the Sturm Abteilung, or Storm Division, and the Schutz Staffel, or Defense Formation. They were the men who were going to carry out his will, and by now they knew it so well that they could act while he was eating, resting, sleeping—even while he was telling the world that he didn't want them to do what they were doing. Even if he told them to stop they would go right ahead to crush the last foe of National Socialism inside the Fatherland, and make the streets free to the brown battalions—the promise of that *Horst Wessel Lied* which Hitler had taught them to sing.

XIV

A dreadful series of events to watch; and the fact that you were physically safe from them wasn't enough for persons with any sensitiveness of soul. Hansi and Bess couldn't eat, they couldn't sleep, they couldn't think about anything except what was happening to their friends and associates at home. The Stormtroopers came when they pleased and did what they pleased; the police had orders to co-operate with them. They came to people's homes at night and took them away, and nothing more was heard of them. But gradually, through secret channels, word began to leak out concerning the dreadful happenings in the cellars of the Nazi headquarters in the Hedemannstrasse, in the Columbus-Haus, and in the old military prison in the General-Papen-Strasse.

Papa wrote brief notes, carefully guarded; he said: "Don't worry about us, we have friends." But Hansi and Bess knew a hundred people to worry about, and they read all the papers they could get and tried to put this item of news together with that and guess about the fate of their "monolithic party." They wrote anxious letters and then worried because no replies came. What had become of this leader and of that? Surely some must have escaped, and it didn't take long to get from Berlin to Paris.

Very difficult to practice music under such circumstances. What did the turn of a phrase matter, when madmen were loose in one's homeland, when a great civilization was being strangled. But the young couple had made engagements and had to keep them. They had to let Lanny and Irma drive them to Juan, dress themselves properly, and go to Emily's villa and play a program, not too mournful. When an encore was called for, Hansi played one of his favorites, Achron's *Jewish Prayer*, and he put two thousand years of weeping and wailing into it; it was quite wonderful, and the fashionable audience was deeply moved. The tears ran down Hansi's own cheeks, and he would have liked to say: "It is my people, weeping now in Germany."

But no, he couldn't say anything, it wouldn't have been good form; art must remain inside its ivory tower, and not descend onto that darkling plain where ignorant armies clash by night. Elegantly gowned ladies with sensitive souls enjoy mournful tones from the G-string of a fiddle, but do not care to weep over a bunch of Jews being beaten and kicked in the underground dungeons of old castles and prisons on the other side of the eastern border.

15

Die Strasse Frei

I

HANSI and Bess didn't return to Germany. Papa and Mama forbade them to come, and Lanny forbade them to go; Robbie Budd cabled, forbidding Bess; and more important yet, Adolf Hitler forbade them both. He did it by hunting down and jailing all prominent Communists, and making it plain that they could no longer exert any influence or accomplish any purpose in Germany. The policy of *Schrecklichkeit*, made famous during the World War, hadn't worked on the outside world, but could surely be made to work inside the Fatherland.

There was the Lodge at Bienvenu, and the young couple settled down in it. Beauty felt exactly as Irma did, she didn't want Reds about her, or want her home to have such an atmosphere; but she, too, had been a guest on the *Bessie Budd* and at the Berlin home, and couldn't fail to make a return; nor could she fail in kindness to Robbie's daughter. A compromise was worked out without ever

a word being said about it; Hansi and Bess didn't invite their Red
friends to the estate, but met them in Juan or Cannes. That helped
a little, but not entirely, for the young couple couldn't help bringing their troubles home with them in their thoughts and aspect.

It was the same thing Lanny had witnessed ten years ago, when
Mussolini had seized power. Swarms of refugees fled from the terror, and naturally it wasn't long before they found out where Hansi
and Bess were staying. The young couple were supposed to be rich,
and, compared to the status of most Communists, they were. They
could hardly say no to anybody—for what did the word "comrade"
mean if not to open your heart and your purse in a time of agony
such as this? Papa would send money; they didn't tell him what it
was for—since it was to be assumed that letters both going and
coming were liable to be opened; but Papa could guess, and no
price was too high to keep his darlings from coming back into
danger.

But he couldn't send enough; not the purse of Fortunatus, not
the touch of Midas, would suffice for the needs of all the Hitler
victims, from this time on for years beyond any man's guessing.
Either you must have the hide of a rhinoceros, or you would have
heartache for your portion. Fate would devise new ways to make
you suffer—every day, every hour, if you would permit it. The
most pitiful victims, the most tragic stories: people who had been
tortured until they were physical and mental wrecks; people whose
husbands or wives, sweethearts, children, parents, or what not, were
being tortured, or might be tomorrow. People who had fled, leaving everything, and had not the price of a meal; people begging for
railroad fare to bring this or that imperiled person out of the
clutches of the fiends.

Hansi and Bess were having their own meals, with one of Leese's
relatives to work for them, and presently this girl began to report
that they weren't having enough to eat; they had given their last
franc to some hungry comrade, and were even taking out of the
house food which they had obtained on credit. Beauty would invite them over to a meal, and they would come; because, after all,

you can't play music if you don't eat, and it wouldn't do for Hansi to faint in the middle of concerts which they were giving for the benefit of refugees. Beauty broke down and wept, and Bess wept, and they had a grand emotional spree; but there wasn't a word they could say to each other, literally not a word, without getting into an argument.

Beauty wanted to say: "My God, girl, don't you know about Europe? I've lived here more years than I like to tell, and I can't remember the time when there weren't people fleeing from oppression somewhere. Even before the war, it was revolutionists from Russia, and Jews, and people from the Balkans, and from Spain, and from Armenia—I forget most of the places. Do you think you can solve all the problems of the world?"

Bess wanted to reply: "It is your bourgeois mind." But you can't say that to your hostess, so she would content herself with the statement: "These are my comrades and this is my cause."

I I

Lanny and Irma went back to Paris, and it was the same there. The refugees had Lanny's address—the first arrivals got it from Uncle Jesse, and the rest from one another. It was an extremely fashionable address, and it was incomprehensible to any comrade in distress that a person who lived, even temporarily, in the palace of the Duc de Belleaumont could fail to be rolling in wealth, and be in position to help him, and all his comrades, and his sisters and his cousins and his aunts back in the homeland, and bring them all to Paris and put them up in one of the guest suites of the palace— or at least pay for the rent of a garret. It was a situation trying to the tempers and to the moral sense of many unfortunate persons. Not all of them were saints, by any means, and hunger is a powerful force, driving people to all sorts of expedients. There were Reds who were not above exaggerating their distress; there were common beggars and cheats who would pretend to be Reds, or anything whatever in order to get a handout. As time went on such problems would grow worse, because parasites increase and multiply like all other creatures, and are automatically driven to perfect the arts by which they survive.

Lanny had been through this and had learned costly and painful lessons from the refugees of Fascism; but now it was worse, because Hitler was taking Mussolini's arts and applying them with German thoroughness. Also, Lanny's own position was worse because he had a rich wife, and no refugee could be made to understand how, if he lived with her, he couldn't get money from her. He must be getting it, because look at his car, and how he dressed, and the places he went to! Was he a genuine sympathizer, or just a playboy seeking thrills? If the latter, then surely he was a fair mark; you could figure that if you didn't get his money, the tailors and restaurateurs and what not would get it; so keep after him and don't be troubled by false modesty.

Irma, like Beauty, had a "bourgeois mind," and wanted to say the things which bourgeois ladies say. But she had discovered by now what hurt her husband's feelings and what, if persisted in, made him angry. They had so many ways of being happy together, and she did so desire to avoid quarreling, as so many other young couples were doing. She would repress her ideas on the subject of the class struggle, and try by various devices to keep her weak-minded partner out of the way of temptation. The servants were told that when dubious-looking strangers called, they were to say that Monsieur Budd was not at home, and that they didn't know when he would return. Irma would invent subtle schemes to keep him occupied and out of the company of Red deputies and Pink editors.

But Lanny wasn't altogether without understanding of subtleties. He had been brought up with bourgeois ladies, and knew their minds, and just when they were engaged in manipulating him, and what for. He tried to play fair about it, and not give too much of Irma's money to the refugees, and not so much of his own that he would be caught without funds. This meant that he, too, had to do a lot of dodging and making of excuses to the unfortunates; and then he would feel ashamed of himself, and more sick at heart than ever, because the world wasn't what he wanted it to be, nor was he the noble and generous soul he would have preferred to believe himself.

III

In spite of the best efforts in the world, Lanny found it impossible to keep out of arguments with the people he met. Political and economic affairs kept forcing themselves upon him. People who came to the house wanted to talk about what was happening in Germany, and to know what he thought—or perhaps they already knew, and were moved to challenge him. Nobody had been better trained in drawing-room manners than Beauty Budd's son, but in these times even French urbanity would fail; people couldn't listen to ideas which they considered outrageous without giving some signs of disapproval. Gone were the old days when it was a gossip tidbit that Mr. Irma Barnes was a Pink and that his wife was upset about it; now it was a serious matter, and quite insufferable.

"I thought you said you were not a Communist," remarked Madame de Cloisson, the banker's wife, with acid in her tone.

"I am not, Madame. I am only defending those fundamental liberties which have been the glory of the French Republic."

"Liberties which the Communists repudiate, I am told!"

"Even so, Madame, we do not wish to make ourselves like them, or to surrender what we hold dear."

"That sounds very well, but it means that you are doing exactly what they would wish to have done."

That was all, but it was enough. Madame de Cloisson was a *grande dame*, and her influence might mean success or failure to an American woman with social ambitions. Irma didn't hear this passage at arms, but some kind friend was at pains to tell her about it, and she knew that it might cancel the efforts she had been making during the past year. But still she didn't say anything; she wanted to be fair, and she knew that Lanny had been fair—he had told her about his eccentricities before he asked for her, and she had taken him on his own terms. It was her hard luck that she hadn't realized what it would mean to have a husband dyed a shade of Pink so deep that the bourgeois mind couldn't tell it from scarlet.

IV

The new Reichstag was summoned promptly. It met in Potsdam, home of the old glories of Prussia, and Hitler applied his genius to the invention of ceremonies to express his patriotic intentions and to arouse the hopes of the German *Volk*. All the land burst out with flags—the new *Hakenkreuz* flag, which the Cabinet had decreed should replace that of the dying Republic. Once more the beacons blazed on the hilltops, and there were torchlight parades of all the Nazi organizations, and of students and children. Hitler laid a wreath on the tomb of his dead comrades. Hindenburg opened the Reichstag, and the ceremonies were broadcast to all the schools. The "Bohemian corporal" delivered one of his inspired addresses, in which he told his former Field Marshal that by making him Chancellor he had "consummated the marriage between the symbols of ancient glory and of young might."

Hitler wanted two things: to get the mastery of Germany, and to be let alone by the outside world while he was doing it. When the Reichstag began its regular sessions, in the Kroll Opera House in Berlin, he delivered a carefully prepared address in which he declared that it was the Communists who had fired the Reichstag building, and that their treason was to be "blotted out with barbaric ruthlessness." He told the rich that "capital serves business, and business the people"; that there was to be "strongest support of private initiative and the recognition of property." The rich could have asked no more. To the German peasants he promised "rescue," and to the army of the unemployed "restoration to the productive process."

To enable him to carry out this program he asked for a grant of power in a trickily worded measure which he called a "law for the lifting of want from the people and empire." The purpose of the law was to permit the present Cabinet, and the present Cabinet alone, to make laws and spend money without consulting the Reichstag; but it didn't say that; it merely repealed by number those articles in the Constitution which reserved these crucial powers to the Reichstag. The new grant was to come to an end in four years, and sooner if any other Cabinet came into office. Nobody but Adolf was ever to be the Führer of Germany!

This device was in accord with the new Chancellor's "legality complex"; he would get the tools of power into his hands by what the great mass of the people would accept as due process of law. His speech in support of the measure was shrewdly contrived to meet the prejudices of all the different parties, except the Communists, who had been barred from their seats, and the Socialists, who were soon to share that fate. A mob of armed Nazis stood outside the building, shouting their demands that the act be passed, and it carried by a vote of 441 to 94, the dissenters being Socialists. Then Göring, President of the Reichstag, declared the session adjourned, and so a great people lost their liberties while rejoicing over gaining them.

V

During this period there were excitements in the United States as well as in Germany. Crises and failures became epidemic; in one state after another it was necessary for the governor to decree a closing of all the banks. Robbie Budd wrote that it was because the people of the country couldn't contemplate the prospect of having their affairs managed by a Democrat. When the new President was inaugurated—which fell upon the day before the Hitler elections—his first action was to order the closing of all the banks in the United States—which to Robbie was about the same thing as the ending of the world. His letter on the subject was so pessimistic that his son was moved to send him a cablegram: "Cheer up you will still eat."

Really it wasn't as bad as everybody had expected. People took it as a joke; the richest man in the country might happen to have only a few dimes in his pocket, and that was all he had, and his friends thought it was funny, and he had to laugh, too. But everybody trusted him, and took his checks, so he could have whatever he wanted, the same as before. Robbie didn't miss a meal, nor did any other Budd. Meanwhile they listened to a magnificent radio voice telling them with calm confidence that the new government was going to act, and act quickly, and that all the problems of the country were going to be solved. The New Deal was getting under way.

The first step was to join Britain and the other nations off the gold standard. To Robbie it meant inflation, and that his country was going to see what Germany had seen. The next thing was to sort out the banks, and decide which were sound and in position to open with government backing. The effect of that was to move Wall Street to Washington; the government became the center of power, and the bankers came hurrying with their lawyers and their brief-cases. A harum-scarum sort of affair, in which all sorts of blunders were made; America was going to be a land of absurdities for many years, and the Robbie Budds would have endless opportunities to ridicule and denounce. But business would begin to pick up and people would begin to eat again—and not just the Budds.

Lanny didn't have any trouble, for the French banks weren't closed, and he had money to spare for his refugees. If Irma's income stayed in hock they could go back to Bienvenu—the cyclone cellar, she called it. She had never had to earn any money in her life, so it was easy for her to take her husband's debonair attitude to it. If she lost hers, everybody else would lose theirs, and you wouldn't have any sense of inferiority. Really, it was rather exciting, and the younger generation took it as a sporting proposition. Irma would swing between that attitude and her dream of an august and distinguished salon; when Lanny pointed out to her the inconsistency of the two attitudes she was content to laugh.

VI

Rick came over to spend a few days with them; he was no longer so poor that he had to worry about a trip to Paris, and it was his business to meet all sorts of people and watch what was going on. A lame ex-aviator who would some day become a baronet, and who meanwhile had made a hit as a playwright, was a romantic figure, even though he was extreme in his talk. The ladies were pleased with him, and Irma discovered that she had what she might call a home-made lion; she would tell the smartest people how Lanny had been Rick's boyhood chum, had taken him to conferences all over Europe and helped to plan and even revise his plays; also how she, Irma, had helped to finance *The Dress-Suit Bribe*, and was not merely getting her money back but a considerable profit. It was the first investment that had been her very own, and she could be excused for being proud of it, and for boasting about it to her mother and her several uncles.

Irma decided more and more that she liked the English attitude to life. Englishmen felt intensely, as you soon found out, but they were content to state their position quietly, and even to understate it; they didn't raise their voices like so many Americans, or gesticulate like the French, or bluster like the Germans. They had been in the business of governing for a long time, and rather took it for granted; but at the same time they were willing to consider the other fellow's point of view, and to work out some sort of compromise. Especially did that seem to be the case with continental affairs, where they were trying so hard to mediate between the French and the Germans. Denis de Bruyne said: "*Vraiment*, how generous they can be when they are disposing of French interests!"

The Conference on Arms Limitation was still in session at Geneva, still wrangling, exposing the unwillingness of any nation to trust any other, or to concede what might be to a rival nation's advantage. Rick, the Socialist, said: "There isn't enough trade to go round, and they can't agree how to divide it." Jesse Blackless, the Communist, said: "They are castaways on a raft, and the food is giving out; they know that somebody has to be eaten, and who will consent to be the first?"

There was a lot of private conferring between the British and the French, and British officials were continually coming and going in Paris. Rick brought several of them to the palace for tea and for dancing, and this was the sort of thing for which Irma had wanted the palace; she felt that she was getting her money's worth—though of course she didn't use any such crude phrase. Among those who came was that Lord Wickthorpe whom she had met in Geneva last year. He had a post of some responsibility, and talked among insiders, as he counted Rick and the Budds. Irma listened attentively, because, as a hostess, she had to say something and wanted it to be right. Afterward she talked with Lanny, getting him to explain what she hadn't understood. Incidentally she remarked: "I wish you could take a balanced view of things, the way Wickthorpe does."

"Darling," he answered, "Wickthorpe is a member of the British aristocracy, and is here to fight for the Empire. He's got pretty much of everything he wants, so naturally he can take things easy."

"Haven't you got what you want, Lanny?"

"Not by a darn sight! I want a better life for masses of people who aren't in the British Empire, and for many in the Empire whom Wickthorpe leaves out of his calculations."

"But, Lanny, you heard him say: 'We're all Socialists now.' "

"I know, dear; it's a formula. But they write their definition of the word, and it means that Wickthorpe will do the governing, and decide what the workers are to get. The slum-dwellers in the East End will go on paying tribute to the landlords, and the ryots in India and the niggers in South Africa will be sweated to make luxury for British bondholders."

"Oh, dear!" exclaimed the would-be *salonnière*. "Who will want to come to see us if you talk like that?"

VII

Lanny was interested in the point of view of these official persons, and sat in the splendid library of his wife's rented home and listened to Rick discussing the Nazi movement with Wickthorpe and his secretary, Reggie Catledge, who was also his cousin. It was a point of view in no way novel to Lanny, his father having explained it when he was a very small boy. The governing classes of

Britain made it a fixed policy never to permit one nation to become strong enough to dominate the Continent; regardless of which nation it might be, they would set themselves the task of raising some rival as a counterweight.

Wickthorpe disliked the Nazis and what they were doing, but he didn't rave at them; he just said they were a set of bounders. He took it for granted that their fantastic promises had been made as a means of getting power. "Just politics," he said, and refused to be disturbed by the possibility that the bounders might mean what they said. The two Englishmen listened with interest to what Lanny had to tell about his meeting with Hitler, and asked him some questions, but at the end they were of the same opinion still.

"We've had so many wild men in our public life," said his lordship. "You and I are too young to remember how old John Burns used to rave in his speeches at Trafalgar Square, but my parents got up slumming parties to go and listen. Long afterward you could meet the old boy in the New Reform Club and hear him talk about it—in fact you could hardly get him to talk about anything else."

"He was a very strict teetotaler, but his face was as red as a turkeycock's wattles," added Catledge.

"Hitler doesn't drink, either," said Lanny; but the others didn't appear to attach any importance to that.

They went on to point out to Rick that the French imperialists were arrogant, and their diplomats had made a lot of trouble in Syria, Iraq, and other places. French bankers had a great store of gold, and made use of it in ways inconvenient to their rivals. Wickthorpe didn't say that Hitler would serve to keep the French occupied, but his arguments made plain the general idea that you couldn't entrust any one set of foreigners with too much power. It was even possible to guess that he wasn't too heartbroken over what had happened in Wall Street during the past four years; because a large part of Britain's prosperity depended upon her service as clearinghouse for international transactions, and it had been highly embarrassing to have the dollar prove more stable than the pound.

Wickthorpe and his cousin had it comfortably figured out what was to be Hitler's role in world affairs. Assuming that he was able to continue in power, he was going to fight Russia. He was the logical one to do this, because of his geographical position; for Britain this factor made it almost impossible. Lanny wanted to ask: "Why does anybody have to fight Russia?"—but he was afraid that would be an improper question.

Here sat this tall young lord, smooth-skinned, pink-cheeked, with his fair hair and little toy mustache; perfectly groomed, perfectly at ease; one couldn't say perfectly educated, for there were many important things about which he knew nothing—science, for example, and the economics of reality as opposed to those of classical theory. He knew ancient Greek and Roman civilization, and Hebrew theology made over by the Church of England; he had recent world affairs at his fingertips. He possessed perfect poise, charm of manner, and skill in keeping to himself those thoughts which particular persons had no right to share. He was sure that he was a gentleman and a Christian, yet he took it for granted that it was his duty to labor and plan to bring about one of the most cruel and bloody of wars.

"You know, you might do quite a spot of trade with the Soviet Union," suggested Lanny, mildly. "They have the raw materials and you have the machines."

"Yes, Budd, but one can't think merely about business; there are moral factors."

"But might not the Reds be toned down and acquire a sense of responsibility, just as well as the Nazis?"

"We can't trust the blighters."

"I'm told that they meet their bills regularly. The Chase National gets along with them quite well."

"I don't mean financially, I mean politically. They would start breaking into the Balkans, or India, or China; their agents are trying to stir up revolution all the time."

Lanny persisted. "Have you thought of the possibility that if you won't trade with them, the Nazis may? Their economies supplement each other."

"But their ideologies are at opposite poles!"

"They seem to be; but you yourself say how ideologies change when men get power. It seems to me that Stalin and Hitler are self-made men, and might be able to understand each other. Suppose one day Stalin should say to Hitler, or Hitler tc Stalin: 'See here, old top, the British have got it fixed up for us to ruin ourselves fighting. Why should we oblige them?' "

"I admit that would be a pretty bad day," said young Lord Wickthorpe. He said it with a smile, not taking it seriously. When Rick pinned him down to it, he gave yet another reason why it was impossible to consider a large-scale deal with the Soviet Union—the effect it would have upon politics at home. "It would set up the Reds, and it might bring labor back into power."

Said Rick to Lanny, when they were alone: "Class is more than country!"

VIII

The Nazi program of repression of the Jews was being carried out step by step, which was going to be the Nazi fashion. Civil servants of Jewish blood were being turned out of their jobs and good Aryans of the right party affiliations put in their place. Jewish lawyers were forbidden to practice in the courts. "Jew signs" were being pasted or painted on places of business which belonged to the despised race. Beatings and terrorism were being secretly encouraged, for the purpose of driving the Jews out and depriving them of jobs and property. When such incidents were mentioned in the press they would be blamed upon "persons unknown masquerading as Stormtroopers."

But refugees escaping to the outside world would report the truth, and there was a ferment of indignation among the Jews of all countries; they and their sympathizers held meetings of protest, and a movement was started to boycott trade with Germany. The reaction in the Fatherland was immediate, and Johannes wrote about it—very significantly he wrote only to Lanny, never to his son, and mailed the letters unsigned and with no mark to identify them. It had been made a prison offense to give information to foreigners, and in his letters Johannes addressed Lanny as a German, and warned him not to tell anyone in Paris!

The boycott was worrying the business men of the country, and at the same time enraging the party leaders, and it was a question which point of view would prevail. Jupp Goebbels was calling for a boycott of Jewish businesses in Germany, and the result was a panic on the stock exchange—for some of the principal enterprises of the Fatherland were Jewish-owned, including the big department stores of Berlin. These were the concerns which the original party program had promised to "socialize," and now the ardent young S.A.'s and S.S.'s were on tiptoe to go in and do the job.

The Cabinet was having one of its customary rows over the question, so Johannes explained. The business magnates who had financed Hitler's rise were coming down on him; how could they pay taxes, how could the government be financed, if rowdies were to be turned loose to wreck business both at home and abroad? The result of this tug-of-war was a curious and rather comical compromise; the boycott which the party fanatics had announced to begin on the first day of April was to be carried on, but it was to continue for only one business day of eight hours; then Germany would wait for three days, to see if there was a proper response from the foreign agents and Jewish vampires who had been so shamelessly lying about the Fatherland. If they showed repentance and abandoned their insolent threats, then Germany would in turn permit the Jewish businesses to continue in peace; otherwise they would be sternly punished, perhaps exterminated, and the blame would rest upon the Jewish vampires abroad.

This boycott was the idea of Dr. Goebbels—the Führer himself being busy with the reorganizing of the various state governments. On the evening before the event the crippled little dwarf with the huge wide mouth spoke to his party comrades at a meeting in a hall of the West End, and all over Germany the Stormtroopers listened over the radio. The orator called for a demonstration of "iron discipline"; there must be no violence, but all Jewish establishments would be picketed, and no German man or woman would enter such a place.

The day was made into a Nazi holiday. The Jews stayed at home, and the Brownshirts marched through all the cities and towns of the Fatherland, singing their song to the effect that Jewish blood must spurt from the knife. They posted "Jew signs" wherever there was a merchant who couldn't prove that he had four Aryan grandparents. They did the same for doctors and hospitals, using a poster consisting of a circular blob of yellow on a black background, the recognized sign of quarantine throughout Europe; thus they told the world that a Jewish doctor was as bad as the smallpox or scarlet fever, typhus or leprosy he attempted to cure.

These orders were followed pretty well in the fashionable districts, but in poorer neighborhoods and the smaller towns the ardent Stormtroopers pasted signs on the foreheads of shoppers in Jewish stores, and they stripped and beat a woman who insisted on entering. That evening there was a giant meeting in the Tempelhof Airdrome, and Goebbels exulted in the demonstration which had been given to the world. The insolent foreigners would be awed and brought to their knees, he declared; and since most of the newspapers had by now been confiscated, the people could either believe that or believe nothing. The foreigners, of course, laughed; they knew that they weren't awed, and the mass meetings and distribution of boycott leaflets went on. But the Nazi leaders chose to declare otherwise, and next day there was a washing of windows throughout Germany, and "business as usual" became the motto for both Aryans and non-Aryans.

IX

There were curious outgrowths of this anti-Semitic frenzy. An "Association of German National Jews" was formed, and issued a manifesto saying that the Jews were being fairly treated and there was no truth in the stories of atrocities; some leading Jews signed this, and the name of Johannes Robin was among them. Perhaps he really believed it, who could say? He had to read German newspapers, like everybody else; those foreign papers which reported the atrocities were banned. Perhaps he considered that the outside boycotts would really do more harm than good, and that the six hundred thousand native Jews in the Fatherland were not in position

to offer resistance to a hundred times as many Germans. The Jews
had survived through the centuries by bending like the willow instead of standing like the oak. Johannes didn't mention the subject
in his letters, either signed or unsigned. Was he a little ashamed of
what he did?

It seemed to an American that a man could hardly be happy
living under such conditions. Lanny wrote a carefully guarded
letter to the effect that Hansi was giving important concerts and
Irma various social events; they would be delighted to have the
family present. Johannes replied that some business matters kept
him from leaving just now; he bade them not to worry about the
new decrees forbidding anyone to leave Germany without special
passports, for he could get them for himself and family whenever
he wished. He added' that Germany was their home and they all
loved the German people. That was the right sort of letter for a
Jew, and maybe the statements were true, with a few qualifications.

The Nazis had learned a lesson from the boycott, even though
they would never admit it. The brass band stage of persecution was
at an end, and they set to work to achieve their purpose quietly.
The weeding out of Jews, and of those married to Jews, went on
rapidly. No Jew could teach in any school or university in Germany; no Jewish lawyer could practice; no Jew could hold any
official post, down to the smallest clerkship. This meant tens of
thousands of positions for the rank and file Nazis, and was a way
of keeping promises to them, much easier than socializing industry
or breaking up the great landed estates.

The unemployed intellectuals found work carrying on genealog-
ical researches for the millions of persons who desired to establish
their ancestry. An extraordinary development—there were persons
who had an Aryan mother and a Jewish father, or an Aryan grandmother and a Jewish grandfather, who instituted researches as to
the morals of their female ancestors, and established themselves as
Aryans by proving themselves to be bastards! Before long the Nazis
discovered that there were some Jews who were useful, so there
was officially established a caste of "honorary Aryans." Truly it
seemed that a great people had gone mad; but it is a fact well known

to alienists that you cannot convince a madman of his own condition, and only make him madder by trying.

By one means or another it was conveyed to leading Jews that they had better resign from directorships of corporations, and from executive positions which were desired by the nephews or cousins of some Nazi official. Frequently the methods used were such that the Jew committed suicide; and while these events were not reported in the press, word about them spread by underground channels. That was the way with the terror; people disappeared, and rumors started, and sometimes the rumors became worse than the reality. Old prisons and state institutions, old army barracks which had stood empty since the Versailles treaty, were turned into concentration camps and rapidly filled with men and women; motor trucks brought new loads daily, until the total came near to a hundred thousand.

Lanny wrote again to say what a mistake his friends were making not to come and witness Hansi's musical and Irma's social triumphs. This time Johannes's reply was that his business cares were beginning to wear on him, and that his physicians advised a sea trip. He was getting the *Bessie Budd* ready for another cruise, this time a real one; he wanted Hansi and Bess to meet him at one of the northern French ports, and he hoped that the Budds would come along— the whole family, Lanny and Irma, Mr. and Mrs. Dingle, Marceline and Baby Frances, with as many governesses and nurses as they pleased. As before, the cruise would be to whatever part of the world the Budd family preferred; Johannes suggested crossing the Atlantic again and visiting Newcastle and Long Island; then, in the autumn, they might go down to the West Indies, and perhaps through the Panama Canal to California, and if they wished, to Honolulu and Japan, Bali, Java, India, Persia—all the romantic and scenic and historic places they could think of. A university under Diesel power!

X

This made it necessary for Irma to come to a decision which she had postponed to the last moment. Was she going to take the palace for another year? She had got used to it, and had a competent staff well trained; also she was established as a hostess, and it seemed a shame to lose all this momentum. But, on the other hand, money was growing scarcer and scarcer. The dreadful depression—Lanny had shown her the calculations of an economist that it had cost the United States half a dozen times the cost of the World War. Thanks to the Reconstruction Finance Corporation, interest payments on industrial bonds were being met, but many of Irma's "blue chip" stocks were paying no dividends, and she was telling her friends that she was living on chocolate, biscuits, and Coca-Cola—meaning not that these were her diet, but her dividends.

She had Shore Acres on her hands with its enormous overhead; she had had to cut down on her mother, and the mother in turn had notified all the help that they might stay on and work for their keep, but there would be no more salaries. Even so, the food bill was large, and the taxes exorbitant—when were taxes not? Mrs. Barnes's letters conveyed to her daughter a sense of near destitution.

"You don't really care very much for this palace, do you, Lanny?" So asked the distressed one, lying in the pink satin splendor of the bed in which Madame de Maintenon was reputed to have entertained the Sun King.

"You know, dear, I don't undertake to tell you how to spend your money."

"But I'm asking you."

"You know without asking. If you spend more money than you have, you're poor, no matter what the amount is."

"Do you think if we come back to Paris after the depression, I'll be able to start as a hostess again?"

"It depends entirely upon how much of your money you have managed to hold on to."

"Oh, Lanny, you're horrid!" exclaimed the hostess.

"You asked for it," he chuckled.

Nearly a year had passed since the Queen Mother had seen her grandchild, and that was something to be taken into consideration. Her satisfaction would be boundless; and it would be a pleasure to meet all those New York friends and hear the gossip. Lanny could stand it if it wasn't for too long. And what a relief to Uncle Joseph Barnes, trustee and manager of the Barnes estate, to know that his charge wouldn't be drawing any checks for a year!

"Lanny, do you suppose that Johannes can really afford to take care of us all that time?"

"He could go alone if he preferred," replied the son of Budd's. "As a matter of fact, I suspect the rascal has more money now than ever before in his life. He makes it going and coming; whether times are good or bad; whether the market goes up or down."

"How does he manage it, Lanny?"

"He's watching all the time, and he keeps his money where he can shift it quickly. He's a bull in good times and a bear in bad."

"It's really quite wonderful," said Irma. "Do you suppose we could learn to do things that way?"

"Nothing would please him more than to teach us; but the trouble is you have to put your mind on it and keep it there."

"I suppose it *would* get to be a bore," admitted Irma, stretching her lovely arms and yawning in the pink satin couch of the Grand Monarque's official mistress.

XI

The young couple ran down to Juan, and Irma and Beauty held a sort of mothers' conference on the problems of their future. Beauty was keen on yachting trips; she found them a distinguished mode of travel; she had learned her geography and history that way, and Irma might do the same. But the important thing was the safety they afforded. Beauty didn't care how much Red and Pink talk her young people indulged in, provided that outside Reds and Pinks couldn't get at them, to borrow their money, get them to start schools or papers or what not, and involve them in fights with Fascists and police. Carry them off to sea and keep them—and perhaps find some lovely tropical island where they could settle down and live in peace and harmony until the cycle of revolutions and counter-revolutions had been completed! Let the yacht serve as a supply ship to bring the latest musical compositions and whatever else they had read of; but no Communist or Socialist agitators, no Fascists or Nazis marching, shouting, brandishing guns and daggers! "Do you suppose they have mosquitoes in the South Seas?" inquired the soft pink Beauty Budd.

She persuaded Irma that this was the way to keep her temperamental husband happy and safe. Paris was a frightfully dangerous place right now; look at the way Jesse was carrying on, rushing about from one meeting to another, making hysterical speeches, calling the Nazis all the bad names in the French language! A copy of *L'Humanité* came every day to Bienvenu, and Beauty would look into it sometimes, thinking that it was her duty to keep track of her brother's doings; it made her quail, for she knew what fury it would arouse in the Hitlerites, and she knew how many rich and important persons in France sympathized with them. The Croix de Feu, the Jeunesse Française and other groups were preparing to meet force with force; the great banks and other vested interests would surely not permit their power to be destroyed without a fight, and it would be far more bloody and terrible than what had happened in Germany. "Let's get away from it," pleaded Beauty. "Stay until the storm blows over, and we can judge whether it's safe to return."

Irma was persuaded, and they sat down and composed between them a letter to Nina, tactfully contrived to be read by Rick without giving him offense. There wasn't any danger in England—at least, none that Rick would admit—and the word "escapist" was one of his strongest terms of contempt. To Rick the cruise was presented as an ideal opportunity to concentrate upon the writing of a new play. On Nina's part it would be an act of friendship to come and make a fourth hand at bridge. To Alfy it would offer lessons in geography and history, plus a chance to fight out his temperamental differences with Marceline. If the parents didn't want to take the youngster from school so early, he could cross to New York by steamer and spend the summer with the party.

They read this letter to Lanny, who said it was all right, but he could do better as concerned his chum. Lanny was cooking up in his head a marvelous scheme. He was guessing the psychology of a Jewish money-master who had just witnessed the seizing of his country by a bunch of gangsters. It was bound to have made a dent in his mind, and dispose him to realize that he and the other capitalists were living and operating inside the crater of a volcano. Lanny was planning to lay a subtle and well-disguised siege to one of the wealthiest of Jews, to persuade him that some form of social change was inevitable, and to get his help to bring it about in orderly fashion. It was the plan which Lanny had already discussed with Rick, to start a weekly paper of free discussion, not pledged to any party or doctrine, but to the general tendency towards co-operative industry conducted under the democratic process.

"We can have him to ourselves for several months, maybe for a year; and if we can persuade him to back us, we can do the job on a big scale and make a real go of it. Won't you come and help? You can answer his questions so much better than I, and I believe you could put it through."

This was a greater temptation than any Utopian dreamer could resist. Rick said, "All right," and Lanny telegraphed the decision to Johannes. He was tempted to repeat the quotation from Tennyson's *Ulysses* which he had used a few years ago on a similar occasion—"My purpose holds to sail beyond the sunset and the baths of all the western stars, until I die." But he reminded himself that the Fatherland was now Hitlerland, and a sense of humor has never· been a prominent German characteristic. What might not a Nazi party censor make out of eight or ten lines of English blank verse telegraphed from the French Riviera!